PROMISES
BROKEN
PROMISES
KEPT

PROMISES BROKEN PROMISES KEPT

JANET Q. BEDLEY

LIFEJOURNEY
BOOKS

David C. Cook Publishing Co.
Elgin, Illinois • Weston, Ontario
Nova Distribution Ltd., Torquay, England

LifeJourney Books is an imprint of David C. Cook
Publishing Co.
David C. Cook Publishing Co., Elgin, Illinois 60120
David C. Cook Publishing Co., Weston, Ontario
Nova Distribution, LTD., Torquay, England

PROMISES BROKEN, PROMISES KEPT
©1991 by Janet Q. Bedley

Book design by Dawn Lauck
Cover illustration by Kathy Kulin Sandel

First printing, 1991
Printed in the United States of America
95 94 93 92 91 5 4 3 2 1

Bedley, Janet Q.
        Promises Broken, Promises Kept
I. Title
PS3552.E316P76   1991   813'.54--dc20   91-6306
ISBN 1-55513-609-5

*To the memory of all the gallant men and women
who have suffered and paid of their life's blood to give
us today's freedoms, I dedicate this book.*

ACKNOWLEDGMENTS

It is with humble gratitude that I express my thanks to all who have made this book possible. Because no one was more important than the other, I list them alphabetically:

Virginia Atwood, for her candor as a critic; Robert Bedley, Jr., for his patient demonstrating of old firearms; Lt. Stephen Bradbury of the Newburyport, Massachusetts Fire Department, for his extensive copying of the history of Newburyport's fire engines; Phil Baumgartner of Merrimac for the loan of his book on the history of Newburyport during the Civil War; Robert Jordan, Civil War historian, for the loan of the Haffner's book and maps; Dorothea Fulton, for her advice on music; Blue Jays Mountain librarians Jill Dessaux, Britt Gunden, Barbara Martinez, and Susan Galvin; Newburyport's accommodating librarian, Cecile Pimental; Tony Hoag, missionary to Japan but former Wisconsin dairy farmer; Professor Hall, history professor at Liberty University, Lynchburg, Virginia; Pastor Richard Link of the First Presbyterian Church of Newburyport, for his tour and historic account of the old edifice; Susan Plant and Kitty Thurlow, for their information on Newburyport schools; Betty Quibell and Alfred Sawyer, for their assistance on old firearms; Phyllis Shippee of Dover, Vermont, for facts on early bucolic life; and especially family and close friends who patiently encouraged me for all the years it took to get this story into print; and, far from least, Jennifer Hoos and David Hoos, Sr., for the hours put in on the computer and the laser printouts. God bless you all.

PART ONE

1

SIXTEEN-YEAR-OLD CAROLINE could not pinpoint the first time her father had spoken of the antagonism between the states. For years there had been talk of the unpopular Fugitive Slave Law, the Missouri Compromise, William Garrison's editorials, and Harriet Beecher's incendiary novel . . . none of these a subject that would interest a young girl. It was not until one morning in the early days of 1860, when the quarrel between the states had, like a sore boil, festered to a point of rupture, that she realized that the things Father continually discussed with Uncle Hank could have a bearing on her own life.

"If the Dred Scott decision stands, we shall certainly be at war," Clinton Haddon declared as he entered the kitchen after finishing the morning milking. He hung his coat on a wooden peg beside Hank's and came to the table.

His brother-in-law, Hank, picked up the previous day's newspaper and sat scowling, his slate-blue eyes sharp and piercing. "War is inevitable!" he stated in his gravel-coarse voice, as unemotionally as a Greek philosopher.

Nabby Haddon, who was rendering pork scraps at the stove, looked up at her husband. "Is that so, Clinton?" she asked.

Clinton, habitually slow to speak, seemed even slower this time. "We can't countenance soft tactics forever," he stated emphatically.

"Well, I wish Garrison had kept his thoughts to himself!"

Nabby snapped. If a war were to take her husband, she was most certainly not in favor of it.

Matthew straightened, suddenly interested in the conversation. At fourteen, he was an avid student of history, and was generally encouraged to express his views. He cleared his throat for attention. "I am glad he spoke out. He woke up the people!"

"And nearly got himself hung! Admit it, you just liked him because he was a native son," needled Caroline. She enjoyed the verbal sparring with her brother.

"No such thing. I've studied his papers, and I like his candor and his editorial skills. I could only wish his boldness had had more contagion!"

"But a little restraint, Matthew. Who would choose a conflict?" It was Nabby speaking again.

"A time to speak and a time to keep silent. . . ." mused Caroline.

"And who is to know those times?" asked her mother, her tone waxing impatient.

The sun had risen and the roosters were crowing. Clinton seemed engrossed in his own thoughts. Talk was already abroad in Massachusetts that the Southern states were planning secession. Nabby's question brought him back to the discussion.

"Men of God speak out when God moves them. That is, if they are obedient."

Having said this, his glance went to the wall to the yellowed portrait of Thomas Jefferson. It was flecked with stains and fly-specks and slightly frayed. It had hung here in Clinton's boyhood home for as long as he could remember. "He knew the day would come when we would have to deal with the situation."

"How do you know that, Father?" asked Caroline eagerly.

"Jefferson said, 'Commerce between master and slave is despotism. Nothing is more certainly written in the book of fate than that these people be free.' "

"You like Jefferson," observed Nabby.

"He was a friend to the farmer, the common man. My ancestors held him in high esteem, though he was misguided when he signed the Embargo Act. Nearly got our poor Newburyport off the map as a shipping port!"

By this time the conversation had arrested eleven-year-old Bethia's attention.

"You wouldn't go to war even if there were one, would you, Papa?"

Pragmatic Bethia. She would be the one to ask the question that was on the mind of everyone present. Clinton only studied the plate in front of him and didn't answer.

The protracted silence sent a wave of terror through the child. "Would you, Papa?" she asked again.

"He wouldn't have to. They conscript young men first." Matthew hoped he had saved his father the necessity of answering.

"I would do what I believed was right, Bethia, even if it were difficult."

Matthew glowered at Bethia. Girls were like that. Her persistence had forced an answer from their father, and Matthew was certain the remark would ultimately color his father's future decisions.

"If you go, I shall go with you," he said, jutting out a jaw as square and determined as his father's.

"And what could a boy your age do?"

"Blow a bugle—beat a drum!"

"Indeed, I believe you could." Clinton paused and then continued. "But I have better things in mind for you."

Matthew's expression changed. "What things?" he asked, the threat of war suddenly forgotten.

"I have talked to Hyram. He is looking for a printer's devil."

"Matthew isn't a devil!" exclaimed Joshua, who up to now had been content to listen. The youngest Haddon, eight years old, looked so dead in earnest that the entire family chuckled.

"A printer's devil is only a helper at the newspaper office," explained Nabby.

Matthew, meanwhile, had sucked in his breath and was sitting with a look of wonder on his face.

"He wants me?" he asked. "Did he say he wanted me?"

"He wants to talk to you. I arranged an interview."

"Oh, Father, that is everything I have ever hoped for!"

"It will mean hours after school and Saturdays, too—and through the summer."

"I would not care if I should live there!"

"—and no neglect of studies."

"Imagine! Access to all the news! That could do wonders for my grades!"

"Seven o'clock in the morning, and you will go alone."

That was Clinton's way. He would take his offspring to the portals, but the rest was up to them.

For a while Matthew sat quietly savoring the bright prospect of working on the newspaper staff. Printer's devil could be a stepping stone to typesetting, and typesetting to proofreading . . . and perhaps someday he'd even be an editor of the finest paper in Newburyport, Massachusetts! Then he'd be respected!

But what about the farm work? He ventured to speak. "Won't you need me here?"

"You will gain more with Hyram."

When they were alone that evening, Matthew brought up the subject again. The asking was not easy.

"Am I a disappointment to you, Father?"

"Because you have not taken to the farm?"

"Yes." Matthew's eyes were downcast.

Clinton forced his son's chin up with a gentle hand. "No, son. Some are born farmers and some are not, and the way this Union is growing, we shall need more than farmers."

"I could still do my share of milking."

"No, your hours will be long enough. I have Hank and your

brother, and the women whenever there is a bind. Now go to bed. You've got to be fresh and smart in the morning."

Matthew felt a rush of affection for his father, whose strong hand rested on his shoulder. He wanted to hug him, but resisted the impulse and bounded for the stairs.

Caroline came from the kitchen, pleased to catch her father alone and have his undivided attention.

"That is an answer to prayer, Father."

Clinton looked up. "You have been concerned for Matthew?"

"Yes. He doesn't seem to realize his own good qualities. All his friends are growing so tall—even the cousins are taller, and they are younger."

"But Matthew makes up for his smaller size with his larger intelligence!"

"It isn't enough. He wants to be like you, tall and strong."

"Then I would say we have an obligation to help him like himself just as God made him. He must learn that strength is not measured by the pound—and we must do it with no molly-coddling."

Caroline smiled, satisfied that they understood one another.

"Have I told you how much I count on you, Carrie?"

The abbreviated name was one of endearment, saying all the tender things a New England Yankee could not. It pleased her, although she had always known she was special to her father.

Clinton went on with the conversation almost as though Caroline were not there. "You are, well, the family watchdog. They will always need you."

"But they have you, Father."

"For now—but perhaps not always."

He was standing before the window, looking out but not seeing. Caroline shot a glance in his direction and shivered. There it was again, the cloud, the forecasting of something ominous, chilling. The possibility of war. Could it really happen?

2

THE MARVELS OF AUTUMN were already appearing on the New England landscape. Overnight frosts were nipping the countryside, and Newburyport's trees were wearing riotous colors. Tyrian purple asters were in late bloom along the country lanes, and extra hands were being hired to gather in the last of the harvest. It had been a bounteous year, and the cellar bins were bulging.

Clinton was hammering pens together for the hogs. The animals would root at first in the harvested potato fields and glean in the turnip patches, and then be pampered on barley feedings, peas, and brassica until it was time for butchering. By Christmas some would be sold and the remainder slaughtered, cut into flitches, carved into shanks with butts and bacon readied for the smokehouse. There would, of course, be lard enough for the winter.

Clinton had already planted winter cabbage where the corn had grown, and grain had been taken to the grist mill. Apples were in full crop, and Nabby had taken a load to the cider mill, reserving the best for shipment to the British market.

After the harvest there would be time to rest and days for recreation. With most of the fields empty, the men would head off for the hunting grounds, and the women would gather in sewing groups to plan for the coming holidays, sample the town gossip, and work on their Thanksgiving dresses.

Overhead could be heard the honking of Canada geese as they left for warmer climes, leaving behind the gloom of late October's low stratus, water surface fogs. It was a time to rekindle fires and family ties. Caroline would be busier than ever with the season's baking, for this year the Haddons, all of them, would be celebrating Thanksgiving at her father's house.

Matthew had been hired at the newspaper office and was proving an able assistant to the editor of the *Morning Bugle*. Joshua had joined himself to the woodcutters with their hooked pike-staffs, axes, and carts, and Bethia tramped after them, making herself useful by stacking next winter's supply of firewood, and at the same time keeping a sharp eye on the heavy underbrush in hope of dislodging an orphaned animal. To date she had raised a raccoon, a fox, and a Canada gosling.

CLOSE TO NOVEMBER an easterly wind swept in from the sea, driving before it a cold rain. In the early morning Caroline could hear the rain as it lashed her windows. Most folk complained, but for some reason, the sound was pleasant to her ears. As she watched the rivulets of water ease down to the sash corners, she thought of her cousin Allen, who lived just a stone's throw away and shared her interest in the things of nature. He had taught her not to fear the thunderstorms but, instead, to watch the fireballs as they fell to earth and to appreciate the marvels of the heavens.

She could hear her mother in the kitchen stirring up the fires. Off to the ell, Uncle Hank would already have set the logs ablaze in Grandma Adkinson's fireplace and left for the barn. Grandma had taken to her bed in early October. It was the season for the ever-lurking red horseman to descend upon the little city, and this year he had set his sights on the fragile white-haired matriarch.

Caroline arose and dressed. By seven o'clock the men would be in from the barn for breakfast, and it was her duty to have a hearty repast there to greet them. She stopped long enough to brush her long, dark hair and to tie a pink ribbon in it, thinking as she did it of Thad Paxton—for he was the one who always noticed such extra touches.

Today she would have to carry an umbrella to school and struggle with the impossible task of keeping the younger children dry. She awakened Bethia and Joshua and went on down the creaky, complaining stairs. The house had been in the family for many years and bore the marks of use.

Caroline prepared the tea tray and took it to her grandmother. She could not help noticing how gaunt the elderly lady had grown.

"You needn't read today, dear. I know how busy you will be with the children, and you will have to leave early."

"I always have time to read to you, Grandma. What will it be?"

Caroline went about fluffing the pillows and setting the tray on her grandmother's lap. Then she reached for the Bible. Its tattered and dog-eared cover attested to its age and use.

"The Psalms, dear. So much comfort."

Caroline read, the sound of her voice in the early dawn euphonious and sweet. The sweet oil of comfort blessed her own soul.

"Though I walk in the midst of trouble, Thou wilt revive me. . . . The Lord will perfect that which concerneth me."

Caroline lifted her head and savored the promise. Would God really perfect that which concerned her? Would He come against the threat of war? Oh, she did so earnestly hope there would be no war—and yet everything was pointing to a confrontation. But she must not trouble her grandmother, who had enough to bear. Caroline smiled and patted her hand.

"That should see us through the day, Grammy!"

WHEN THE CHILDREN left for school, Joshua and Bethia ran ahead, garnering from the saturated earth the decaying, waterlogged white ash seedpods and pinning them to their noses. They dashed about with their broken branches, enjoying mock swordplay. They dug through the leaves for horse chestnuts and filled their pockets with the mahogany treasures.

Caroline smiled. Keeping the children under the umbrella was out of the question. They were two gazelles in a meadow of pleasant discoveries, blissfully unmindful of the elements.

The rain had diminished to a mist, settling in Caroline's hair and beading her thick black eyelashes. The brisk wind had teased a healthy flush to her cheeks, and her complexion had taken on a vibrancy. Ahead she saw Thad Paxton waiting for her at his usual place. She could not remember when he had not been there at his fence, waiting to join her and Matthew. Self-consciously she touched the ribbon in her hair.

With the exception of Uncle Vaugn Haddon, the Paxtons were the nearest neighbors to Caroline's family. They had a pioneering ancestry much like her own. They, too, had known the hardships of the New England climate, the sultry humidity of August and the sub-zero temperatures of·January, and the labors of the soil. Mary Paxton had been there at the birth of Nabby's children. Her husband had helped to raise their barns. The men together garnered in the hay of the salt marshes and traveled to the Brighton cattle market to select good breeders. They had early introduced their progeny to Boston's historical old Faneuil Hall, once a meeting place for the Colonist Fathers but now the Quincy Produce Market, its degeneration from its first estate stoically tolerated by Boston's first families and appreciated by bargain-hunting commoners as well as the commissioned salesmen of the day. The men had gathered kelp and blackfish, gone clamming on the mud flats, followed the river regattas, pulled stumps, and been more than neighbors for as far back as Caroline could remember.

Surely Thad would always be in her life. He was as comfortable as an old hat. Her peers were certain they had been born for one another, and their parents, too, seemed to think positively about a marriage that would unite the two families. Caroline was not sure she wanted her future planned so simply for her, but she had found it difficult to dismiss the suggestion that had come, just once, from Thad himself last summer.

It had been a hot, sultry August day. Katydids sent forth a

forecast of torrid temperatures, long-haired dogs hid themselves under porches, and morning glories closed their faces before the dew was dry. The barley had been six-rowed and heavy, the oats clustered, and the cattle had hung together in sympathetic groups making vignettes of abject misery.

It had been the great family picnic day for the farmers who owned marshland. The men had previously cut and spread the hay to dry and it lay, a yellow carpet, ready for the wide, flat-bottomed gundalows to transport. The boys, still in clothes for decency's sake, jumped into a tidal bay. Caroline, barefoot, followed after the sounds of revelry, deploring the fact she had been born a female. Her faded red gingham clung to her perspiring body, dank and miserable, and her long, dark hair lay hot against her neck and back. She watched quietly, covetously as the boys laughed and splashed. Then Thad appeared, coming up out of the water like a playful dolphin and striking a sheet of water in her direction.

"Don't you swim?" he asked.

"Of course!"

"Then come on in!"

"Oh, no! Father'd thrash me!"

"Even if you fell in?" And he seized her ankle and yanked.

Into the icy waters she fell and then came to the surface gulping and sputtering. Two feet away Thad appeared laughing, and she swung her open hand across the water and giggled. The relief from the heat was sweet, and she was forced to admit that the "accident" had been a delight.

They crawled out, onto the prickly stubs of cut grass. Standing wet and disheveled, clothes dripping, Thad had planted a clumsy, wet kiss on her lips.

"Someday I will marry you, Carrie Haddon!" he had said.

And somehow she had never doubted his intentions, although she would have much preferred that he ask her.

Since that day they had never spoken of the incident.

As Caroline approached Thad now, she could see on his face

that confident, assured look that was peculiarly his. He accepted her invitation to share the umbrella.

Their conversation turned from the weather to the coming elections.

"This year the Wide Awakes are hosting the Republican Dinner. Father wouldn't miss."

"We shall be there, too," said Thad.

Bethia and Joshua turned in at Bromfield Street, where their school was located. Matthew hurried on ahead to join some friends, but Caroline walked more slowly with Thad.

"After graduation it won't be like this," Thad was saying. "Spring planting, plowing and all, and Father has enrolled me at Harvard. He has dreams of having a gentleman son. You know, Thaddeus B. Paxton, Esquire!"

Caroline did not like the sound of it. She would remain at the farm, and life would be colorless. Many of her friends had already sought employment at the mills, and now Thad with his bit of news! There seemed nothing in the days ahead but loss and gloom.

"I don't look forward to another year. I'm afraid there will be a war."

"Well, we can't cross that bridge yet."

"You will be old enough to go."

"Not so fast, Carrie. But if I did . . . would you wait?"

Was this his way of securing a commitment? She had dared to dream of something more romantic. She searched his eyes.

Thad flushed, swallowed hard, and went on. "Because you are the only girl I will ever want."

Caroline remained silent.

"Would you?" he persisted.

"We can't cross that bridge yet!" she mimicked.

Promises should be made with the utmost caution. Once made, they could become a cumbersome debt.

THE WEEKS MOVED ON, painfully slow for the young and extravagantly swift for the committee folk responsible for the big dinner. There was a chill in the air, and already the citizenry had retrieved their cold weather clothing from attic trunks. Caroline went early to the dinner with her mother, for Nabby was responsible for the table settings.

Buntings of red, white, and blue had already been hung and draped at the speaker's table, and flags with thirty-three stars hung from the balcony. The hall was buzzing with activity, the city so predominantly Republican that the attendance was already gathering in impressive numbers—a coterie of congenial political allies. The band had arrived and were setting up their stands and sending dissonant sounds through the cavernous building as they tuned their instruments.

Pictures of the Republican nominee were hung about the walls. There was something about the lanky, rawboned candidate in his rusty black frock coat, wrinkled and baggy trousers, and stovepipe hat that had touched many hearts. His star was rising rapidly. The man's ability to speak to the working class and at the same time impress the well-born was just short of miraculous. For all his simplicity, this Kentucky-born commoner was lacking neither in administrative ability nor pragmatism, as the nation would soon discover.

The young gathered in small groups to share gossip, while the older women busied themselves keeping the food hot. The men sat on the perimeter of the festivities and discussed the buildup of hostilities that were foisting hard decisions on the Union's leaders. Caroline was drawn toward their conversation, yet remained at a polite distance.

"The man was in no way insane," someone was avowing.

She looked in the direction of the voice and saw a man with a most interesting face. He was slight of build, and illness lay hidden in his fever-red eyes. Those eyes were circled with dark shadows, and their owner coughed intermittently, but he still had a nice face. His expression seemed to say that he was sampling the intellect of his companions, tasting to see if the conversation were worth his expenditure of energy; his healthy, alert mind belied his weakened frame. His clothes were definitely out of style, yet there was something about him that commanded respect. Caroline surmised he was from the backwoods, but very possibly a man of letters. His audience pressed in to hear him.

"I resent that!" he was saying with forthright indignation.

"You cannot think that he was in his right mind!"

"I most certainly do think so. He was a true patriot, and our dear editors are not only insensitive to his memory but are exploiting the general public in their effort to discredit the man's motives. He did what secretly we wish we had done. One would do well to boycott the miserable press!"

"But you do read the newspapers!" The sly rebuttal came from a man of obvious means.

"And that I do with my cuffs turned up! I hear the gurgling of the sewer through every column. I feel I'm handling a paper picked out of the public gutters, a leaf from the gospel of the gambling house, the groggery, and the brothel, harmonizing with the gospel of the merchants' exchange! Newspapers—bah! They have made a good man look like an ogre—a demented ogre at that!"

"But he crashed a military arsenal!"

"More power to him! Rest his soul. When trusted men choose to close their eyes to duty, it seems God will raise up a martyr. John Brown had more courage than any of us, and I, for one, will speak and write on his behalf!" And the pale, slightly built man took himself off for better company, coughing harshly as he went.

"Who is that man, Father?" asked Caroline, watching him depart.

"Thoreau's his name—a strange codger. He's ahead of his generation, I think. Controversial in many ways, yet sound in others. I can't always agree with him, but I do like him."

The Paxtons were just arriving, and Caroline lost interest in her father's remarks. Suddenly Thad stood beside her.

"You look very pretty, Carrie," he said, wanting to please her. "Come outside. I have something for you."

"It's cold outside," Caroline protested.

"Bring your wrap."

Out on the porch, Thad withdrew a small box from his pocket, and Caroline opened it expectantly. On a bed of white satin lay a porcelain pendant, a hand-painted bluebird with a flaming breast, all encased in filigreed gold.

"It must have cost a fortune!" she managed, catching her breath.

"I wanted you to have it—sort of like a promise—until my years of school are over."

"You will be gone for a long time, Thad."

"But not so far away that I won't get home."

"I really don't know." She closed the box, looking troubled. "Aren't we young for a promise . . . and so secret?"

The innocence of her question and the bright moonlight reflected in her eyes fired something inside of him, and he took her in his arms and kissed her hard on the mouth. It was not the kiss of an adolescent.

"Are we?" he asked.

Caroline pushed him away, feeling heady and frightened. "I . . . guess I love you, Thad." She was apologetic . . . embarrassed.

"Then it's settled."

Thad's manner was that of a businessman effecting a successful transaction, and a momentary uneasiness swept over Caroline.

"I'll feel guilty about keeping a secret, Thad. We have always had an openness in our family."

"It won't be for long, Carrie. Then we can tell the whole world."

Aah! It was the most romantic thing he had said since the day he had declared he would someday marry her.

When they returned to the hall, folk were already being seated.

Bethia was watching her elder sister with an amused expression on her face.

"I saw you leave, Carrie. Did Thad kiss you?"

Caroline's face felt hot. "Honestly, Bethia! Why do you ask such silly questions?"

" 'Cause your face is all pink!"

As ELECTION DAY drew nearer, the mood of the citizenry turned increasingly profligate. Taverns were overcrowded, and boisterous political arguments spilled over into the streets. Women remained indoors to avoid the gutter ribaldry, while speeches, bands, and barnstorming became the order of the day.

It was Matthew who came home waving the newspaper: Abraham Lincoln had been elected the sixteenth president of the United States. The general public was pleased; only the old and cautious seemed morose. They knew Lincoln's feelings about a divided nation.

"He is the man we shall need. We won't neglect to pray for him," commented Clinton.

"—And his election will fire the fuse!" added Hank, the habitual realist.

President Buchanan seemed relieved to turn the affairs of state over to another. The gulf had grown so wide between the states that it seemed unlikely a reconcilable solution could be found. The constant strife over state's versus federal rights had wearied the handsome Pennsylvania statesman, and he had aged perceptibly.

As Hank predicted, the election of Lincoln fired the fuse. Southern delegates met in Charleston and declared themselves a free and independent nation. In two months' time, Georgia, Florida, Alabama, Mississippi, Louisiana, and Texas had joined South Carolina—and Jefferson Davis, who over a decade before had met with Newburyport's Caleb Cushing to discuss Franklin Pierce's presidential candidacy, was chosen president of the new Confederacy.

Of course President Lincoln deplored the action and came out strongly avowing that "no state upon its own motion can lawfully get out of the Union." He went on to assure those states that he had no inclination to abolish slavery in the states already engaged in the practice, but explained that he had an oath to fulfill in keeping the entire country one nation under God.

"In your hands, my dissatisfied countrymen, and not in mine, is the momentous issue of civil war. The government will not assail you—you have no conflict without yourselves being the aggressors. You have no oath registered in heaven to destroy the government, while I have the most solemn one to preserve, protect, and defend it."

The speech was carried in the daily newspapers and had its impact. The North was delighted with the new president; the South incensed. Under Jefferson Davis, the former Secretary of War, the South went boldly on to implement their declaration of separation. One of their first acts was to claim all military installations within their own territory.

"Davis may have things well in hand now, but wait until he starts issuing orders from a central desk to fellow Southerners bent upon keeping their state's rights!" observed Clinton as he followed the swift course of events.

Fort Pickens off Pensacola and Fort Sumter in Charleston Harbor under Union control were a thorn in the flesh to the New Confederacy. Having failed to strike a bargain for transfer of the forts under the Buchanan administration, they now met to decide appropriate action. To them the moment had come when men must move from words to action—*averbis ad verberam*, and the cannon moved into place.

3

WHEN THE FIRING BEGAN at Fort Sumter in April, commander Major Robert Anderson of the Union army knew from the beginning of his vulnerability, and steadfastly hoped for reinforcements. They never did arrive. For days the uneven assault took its toll. Civilians in Charleston watched the cross-fire bombardment from rooftops and from the promenade. Some stood in awe of the open conflict while others cheered. The South had entered a war with the erroneous optimism that the struggle would be brief.

Matthew came in the door with a face like thunder. He threw a newspaper across the long sitting-room table, nearly knocking Hank's tobacco humidor over the edge, then stomped up the stairs to his room and angrily slammed the door.

The family, already assembled at the kitchen table, looked to one another with startled expressions.

"Isn't he going to eat?" asked Joshua innocently.

Clinton arose and retrieved the paper, then followed Matthew to his room. When he entered, Matthew hastily ran a sleeve over his eyes.

The boy's voice trembled. "President Lincoln is calling for seventy thousand volunteers."

"Is that the latest?"

"Yes! And you will go."

Clinton sank down into a cane-bottomed chair, the only chair in the sparsely furnished room.

"God help us," he said, staring vacantly.

"I know you will go!"

"Let me think, son."

Already Clinton's pragmatic mind was racing. Lincoln would need men and quickly if he were to avert another Sumter. How much time did he have?

"Father, I don't want you to go!"

Matthew's pleading broke through Clinton's thoughts.

"Men have to make their own decisions, Matthew, and they aren't always easy." He spoke slowly, deliberately. "You remember when I read you the life of Martin Luther?"

Matthew nodded.

"How on his way to the Diet, a knight encouraged him, saying that if he believed he was right, to go on and fight with all of his might?"

"Davey Crockett said that, too—and he died!"

"Yes, I know, but that was not the end. The cost of being right has ever been high, but God has made His laws and He has called men to defend them—to stand in the gap. Sometimes his men survive, and sometimes they do not. Some things are bigger than the lives of men.

"This is a good nation, Matthew, founded on God's laws, and it will prosper as long as we live by them. We have got to give this nation a chance, and I am certain we can never succeed if divided. Should I sit back and watch others do the job? Can I watch old world sectionalism rule this country, with constant border wars? Matthew, what would you do?"

The question had its sobering effect. Clinton watched his son's countenance change.

"I think—I would most likely go. May I?"

Clinton laughed out loud, relieved and pleased. He rose and hugged Matthew roughly.

"I need you here, son, but don't fret. Your time will come."

"Will the war go on for a long time?" Matthew asked.

"I wish I knew."

LINCOLN'S APPEAL for men had phenomenal results. Within forty-eight hours, volunteers had stormed the hastily set-up recruiting offices, and Newburyport's own Cushing Guard left to protect the nation's capital. Women were quick to set up sewing machines in the Whitefield church vestry and begin turning out uniforms. The Harris Street church distributed Bibles to the enlistees and sent them on their way in a downpour, but not without the fanfare of waving flags and martial bands.

The editorials read with impassioned zeal: "Let the guns of Sumter unite us all. Lay on! Let the cannons roar! Let the swords and bayonets gleam wherever the sun shall shine." And on it went, with fresh hysteria daily. Church services became sounding boards for the general feeling, and songs of liberty took precedence over the usual celestial hymns. Colt revolving rifles were purchased and issued to the first enlistees as news filtered in from Boston that daily drilling was taking place and men were forming hollow squares and attacking mock cavalry.

The littlest Yankee seaport had answered the call to arms in a most commendable way. Their regiments numbered at the top for speedy mustering, and already the sound of rifle practice could be heard from Davenport Hill.

Such were the days that followed the fall of Fort Sumter!

With the passing of weeks, Clinton grew increasingly thoughtful. Seldom one to follow the crowd, he would consider all that lay at stake and move only after weighing all options. To enlist and accept the one-dollar-a-week allotment for each of his dependents was unthinkable. Farmers had no need of charity as long as they possessed a sound mind and a strong body. He sounded out Hank as to his willingness to take over the farm, and found his brother-in-law delighted to be considered for such a responsibility.

To be useful and needed was sweet balm to the aging man.

And there was another problem for Clinton. Grandma Adkinson's health had taken a swift decline; her cheeks had grown hollow, her eyes were sunken, and she coughed incessantly. He stopped by her chamber frequently to encourage his mother-in-law.

On one occasion she complained that the blankets felt heavy. Inconceivable as that sounded to the robust Clinton, he knew she would not have mentioned it if she had been comfortable. That afternoon he came in from the late milking and found Bethia busy setting the table.

"Bethia," he began, with an expression his elder children had learned meant he was about to teach his progeny a profitable bit of philosophy, "I haven't seen your hoop lately."

Bethia looked puzzled. "It is hanging in the barn where it has always been," she answered.

"Grandma needs it," said her father.

Now Bethia was doubly perplexed. Papa would not joke about Grandma, especially in her weakened condition. Bethia gave him a look of incredulity.

"Grandma has a problem. Do you think we might help her?"

"Oh, yes, anything! She is really very ill."

"I was thinking that if we could cut the hoop in half—"

"Half a hoop?"

"—it could take the weight of the blankets from off her feet."

Clinton watched as Bethia turned the thought over in her young mind. No doubt she was counting the cost. After all, she was one of the few girls the boys allowed in their hoop wars.

Clinton motioned for her to sit beside him.

"You know, Bethia, love isn't just a feeling. It is really action—and quite often means giving, even sacrificing. It has its own special reward, something beyond description, but something worth having."

"The hoop is mine, Father."

"Yes, and so is the decision, child. I am only suggesting. I have found that when we neglect to help someone in need, we wish many times over that the opportunity would come again, but it seldom does."

The hoop had come down from generations past, and Bethia prized it highly. To give it away was one thing, but to desecrate it was another. . . . She jumped to her feet, her decision made.

"I will get the hoop. May I watch?"

Clinton was pleased—he had gained far more than a hoop. "Of course, little Beth."

He lost no time cutting the hoop and heading for Grandma's room, with Bethia and Nabby close behind. Grandma looked up, surprised at so large a delegation. Nabby went to work placing the half hoop under the heavy blankets, then stood back for her reaction.

"Mercy! What a difference!" the old woman exulted. "Who in the world thought of this?"

"Bethia wanted you to have it," Clinton answered hastily.

"What a dear child! Thank you so very much!"

Her words fell upon Bethia's ears like the oil of Aaron, and it was then that she understood her father's words. What a holy sweetness indeed there was in giving.

By June, Jefferson Davis had established the Confederate capital in Richmond. Robert E. Lee had struggled with his loyalties, even voiced his distaste for the slave trade, but had chosen to offer his services to the Confederate president. Like many others, he could not bring himself to fight against family and neighbor.

"This is a sad day for the Union," declared Clinton. "Lee is the best military man in the nation." He sat atop a pasture fence talking to his younger brother, Vaugn. At first the farm and the crops had dominated their conversation, then the real issue surfaced.

"When are you going?" asked Vaugn, knowing full well his brother's intentions.

"Not yet certain. We've got to finish the planting, Hank and I. There'll be work to lay out, maybe hands to hire come fall, and I'll have to feel good about Nabby's ability to keep the kids in tow."

Vaugn studied the ground. "I've debated going, but Phoebe isn't the manager your Nabby is. And the boys—Allen I can count on, but Timothy is different."

"Can't expect them all to be farmers, Vaugn. The world is changing. Matthew is already off to a journalist's career."

"Going after planting then?"

"I will wait until the bottleneck is over. They are still not ready for the men, and the governor and Wescott are having a battle of words over the length of enlistment and the men's preference to join the Cushing Guard."

Vaugn listened attentively for awhile, then his expression told Clinton that his mind had wandered off.

"Something troubling you?" he asked.

"I was wondering. . . ." said Vaugn with some embarrassment.

Clinton waved him on.

"Well, before you go—I've been thinking—though God forbid—but men do die in battle."

"You want the property you work to be in your own name."

"Yes."

"And you want Allen to be your heir."

"Yes."

"Then I shall see Lawyer Bancroft in the morning. You know I can't break the legacy about the eldest being sole heir, but I am sure he can write up something that will keep the trust and at the same time give you and your family some security."

Clinton had struggled for many years with the strange document the first Haddon had left, desiring to modify it and escape the family rifts it had engendered. Years before he had told his brother, "There is land enough for us both. Choose where you will and build. Plant and expect no quarrel with me." Consequently, Vaugn had situated on fifteen Haddon acres to the south, where he raised horses and the grains and produce necessary for a comfortable existence. The path between the two farms was well worn, and the brothers and their families seemed to enjoy a warm relationship.

"Thanks, Clint. I have hoped for that."

Then they were down and heading for the barn.

"Duchess foaled last night," said Vaugn. "Good-looking colt—come see him. Must get the older one's hoofs rasped and then off for Vermont. The army will be looking for horses, and I aim to beat 'em to it."

Vaugn's stable stretched from his house to the rolling hills beyond, connected by a row of poorly constructed sheds. Separate from the horse stable was a new building where Haverhill carriages were kept. The younger brother's interest was just beginning to encompass the sale of carriages, and with the tales of the devastating 1811 fire, Vaugn had chosen to keep the livery stable separate. The enterprise was booming.

Phoebe came to greet them. Not for the first time, Clinton wondered why his brother had elected to marry such an uncommonly plain woman. Awkwardly angular, pale faced and petulant, the woman gendered few friendships. Having never been able to crash the ostentatious upper crust of Newburyport, she had increased her efforts to gain attention by naming her twin sons in a rare manner. One was called Allen Timothy and the other Timothy Allen.

Still Clinton felt the responsibility of maintaining family unity, and a clannish relationship had miraculously flourished.

Phoebe spoke with embarrassment, giggling nervously.

"We've been thinking about going to Vermont for young breeders—taking Clara with us. The twins are old enough to care for themselves."

Clara was Vaugn's third child, born six years after the twins. As a result she was *l'enfant gate* and about as endearing as any thoroughly spoiled young one.

"Mighty long trip for a young one. Why don't you leave Clara with us?"

"You've enough of your own, Clinton," Phoebe replied.

"Always room for one more. Send her over."

Phoebe looked to Vaugn for his approval.

"Good idea, but ask Nabby first," he advised.

The twins, younger than Matthew but decidedly taller, came through the big end door. In appearance they were identical, and Clinton had to wait until they spoke before he could identify each one.

Timothy was ever of an ebullient nature, jovial, lighthearted, inquisitive, and friendly. His dark eyes were bright and alert, seeking the fun in every circumstance—but he was also volatile. Allen was the opposite: slow, deliberate, and thoughtful, more settled than his brother.

The two joined the adults just outside the straw-bedded stall. Timothy slapped his uncle on the back good-naturedly, grinning as he felt the muscular resistance.

"What do you think of him?" he asked.

Allen moved slowly toward the mare, touching her nose gently and then rubbing it. She bobbed her head and looked nervously toward her offspring, ears twitching slightly.

"Allen's the only one she accepts," said Vaugn.

Clinton could understand that. His nephew's hands were large, and he touched with a calming stroke. Vaugn's quiet son was as much like Clinton as any he had fathered, and he felt a strong affection for him.

"Got all your crops in?" he asked the boy.

"Not completely. Still at it—late spring this year."

"We're trying broomcorn. Predicting a good market this year, and Hank can grind the seed for the pigs and chickens."

"We've put in our own oats—same with potatoes and onions. The army should buy all we don't use."

As they spoke, eight-year-old Clara approached the group. Her flaxen curls hung below her shoulders, the loose strands apparently as unmanageable as her disposition. She had an abundance of freckles splashed over a pale skin, and she wore an impudent expression.

"That's my horse," she announced, pointing a bold finger in the direction of the new colt.

Timothy, quick to grasp an opportunity to tease, spoke up. "No, he's mine!"

Clara frowned and kicked him.

"Clara! That's not nice!" admonished Phoebe.

Clinton wondered if the child had ever been nice. Perhaps he'd been a little hasty with his kind invitation. He watched as she swung a small fist at Timothy, who caught it in midair and laughed.

"Those two!" exclaimed Phoebe, used to their quarrels and only feigning exasperation.

Vaugn was neither that patient nor reticent to exhibit his true feelings. He picked up his irascibly tempered daughter and deposited her hard upon a barrel.

IN THE EVENING, as was his habit, Matthew returned home with a newspaper tucked under his arm. It was his privilege to read aloud from the paper after family devotions; then followed the discussions so appreciated by the children.

"The cartoonists really do poke fun at President Lincoln," commented Matthew. "Such outlandish, elongated drawings!"

"I think it is disgraceful!" came Caroline's retort.

"You simply do not appreciate good journalism, Carrie." Matthew's new position had made him more sophomoric than ever.

"I think our president should receive more respect. Journalism doesn't have the right to ridicule the leaders of our nation. The people already passed judgment on him when they elected him!"

"You don't understand politics," Matthew replied in a superior manner.

"What's politics?" asked Joshua.

"Politics are what politicians do," answered Bethia.

"So? What's a politician?"

"Someone who doesn't dare say all that he thinks—'til he gets into office!" Uncle Hank had made a rare entry into the room, as well as into the conversation.

Joshua's curiosity was now aroused. "Why is that?"

"Because the wolves would tear him apart, that's why!" Caroline returned with disgust.

Clinton rested back in his chair, smiling, obviously enjoying the exchange. The children were maturing fast, and he was glad to see they were doing some serious thinking. Though the hours of planting were increasing, he managed to spend time with them. The psalmist was certainly right when he said that children were a heritage of the Lord, and happy the man who has his quiver full of them! They were a blessing and a treasure which a wise man did well to guard and appreciate. Soon he would be gone, and he wanted to leave knowing he had armed them with godly precepts to fight the battles of life.

"By the way," he interjected, "Phoebe and Vaugn are going to Vermont for horses. I offered to keep Clara until they return."

The statement fell into the party like a dud cannonball.

"And I suppose she will have to sleep with me," sighed Bethia.

"I'd put her in the barn with the rest of the animals!" declared Joshua.

Though Nabby understood her children's dislike for her niece, she came at once to the child's defense.

"She is not that bad, children. Aggressive, but smart, too. The two often go hand-in-hand."

"I think she is a featherbrain just like her mother!" said Caroline.

"Carrie! Don't encourage them!" scolded Nabby.

"Well, she really is, Mother. Nothing like the twins!"

"And I shall have to amuse her!" said Bethia in a despairing tone.

"She will be treated as a guest," said Nabby firmly.

"I'll amuse her," whispered Joshua to Bethia, mischief already sending a sparkle to the cerulean blue eyes.

Nabby turned a serious countenance toward her youngest. "You will behave, young man, or you will rue it," she warned.

Clinton watched his wife, glad to observe her strength and to know she could control their children.

"Clara is a little aggressive," he said apologetically, "but if that tendency could be turned in the right direction, it could be an asset."

While Caroline and Matthew went to the kitchen with their books, Joshua and Bethia climbed the stairs to their bedrooms.

"I hate sharing my bed with Clara," complained Bethia. "Wish I could think of something to make her as miserable as she makes me!"

Joshua grinned. "I can," he said.

"What do you have in mind?"

"Well, if we can get a tin container—maybe an old tea box—and a spool of thread—"

"What in the world could you do with a tin can and thread?"

"Just wait—you'll see."

The impending visit was looking more promising.

CLARA ARRIVED as planned and promptly displayed a small red valise to her cousins. "See?" she cried proudly, opening it. "My gown, my brush, my very own towel and face cloth, and my pink dress!" Then she asked where she was to sleep.

"Take her upstairs, Bethia, and show her," said Nabby.

Bethia struggled up the stairs with the valise and set it down with a thump in the room she normally shared with Caroline.

"Carrie will sleep on the daybed downstairs," she explained, anticipating her cousin's next question.

"I have my own bed," said Clara proudly.

"That must be very nice," conceded Bethia.

"Where are your kittens?" asked Clara, suddenly changing the subject.

"We don't handle newborns," explained Bethia.

"I do!" Clara retorted.

"But you shouldn't!"

Knowing where the kittens were likely to be, Clara made a beeline down the stairs and out to the barn. Bethia followed, a worried expression creasing her forehead.

Clara's quick hands delved into the box and pulled out a puff of yellow, complaining fur from the side of the mother cat. She held it high in the air, thoroughly enjoying the frustration of the animals and Bethia.

"Put her back!" demanded her cousin.

Clara only smiled.

Fortunately, Uncle Hank came upon the scene just then. "We wait until they are older!" he admonished Clara.

The child went petulantly back to the house. "You do have toys, don't you?" she asked her cousin, but it wasn't really a question. It was Clara's way of suggesting that the Clinton Haddons did a poor job of supplying their children with the luxuries of life.

The day seemed to move at a snail's pace, and by bedtime Bethia had reached the end of her patience. Her only encouragement was the knowledge that Joshua had already placed the tin box under her bed and run a thread unnoticed across the floor to his own bedroom.

She'll wish she had never been born, Bethia thought with satisfaction.

The children retired in an unusually cooperative mood. Caroline carried the lamp behind them, the flame causing great grotesque shadows to leap upon the walls. She tucked them in and left, taking the lamp and leaving the children in the black of night.

Lying there, the girls could see the stars shining brightly in the sky, moonlight having already clothed the fields with white magic. Budding forsythia bushes scraped the sides of the house, stirred by a gentle breeze.

"I miss my mama," said Clara in an uncertain voice.

"Do you get scared in the dark?" asked Bethia hopefully.

"All the time!"

"That's too bad. I don't ever get scared."

"You don't?"

"No. I try to be nice, the way the Lord Jesus wants me to be. Then I know He will take care of me."

A hollow scratching sound came from under the bed.

"What's that?" whispered Clara.

"What's what?"

"That scratching sound!"

"Oh, you must be hearing the bushes against the house."

"No . . . no. It's closer than that!"

They lay very quiet. The sound came again. Clara threw the blankets over her head, and Bethia stuffed them into her mouth. The grating sound continued.

"Someone must be under our bed!" said Bethia solemnly.

Clara gasped.

"Confess. You must have done something very mean, and the devil is after you, Clara."

But Clara was beyond speech.

"All right, have it your way. If you won't confess, the spooks will be here all night. They'll never go away!"

At this, the covers flew off, and Clara went flying down over the stairs, shrieking as she went and bringing out the entire family. Still screaming, she collapsed into Nabby's arms.

"Whatever is going on?" asked Nabby, glancing from the hysterical Clara to the cool Bethia.

"There's gremlins up there!" sobbed Clara, pointing toward the stairs.

"She's hearing things, Mama."

"You must have done something to frighten her."

"I haven't." Bethia felt secure in the pleasant thought that Joshua had planned and executed the entire episode.

"Go back to bed, Bethia. I will put Clara on the couch. She will feel safer there."

"Yes, ma'am!" said Bethia, and she climbed the stairs choking back laughter. She poked her head in at Joshua's door.

"Goodnight, Spook!" she said. She felt quite confident that the rest of Clara's stay would be more pleasant.

SPRING MOVED into summer and summer into fall. Already there was a hint of frost in the air. The harvest was nearly over, and it had been a good one. Hired hands could be dismissed. In other years, Clinton would be looking forward to days of recreation, but this autumn he knew the time had come to leave. He had spent six months preparing, and now he could go.

"Days are getting shorter," said Clinton to Hank, though his voice betrayed the fact that he was not altogether taken up with the length of days.

Hank was quiet for a while, not sure if he could put into words what he felt he must say. "I want you to know things will be cared for here."

Clinton could see that the effort was difficult for Hank—Hank the introvert, the little bachelor who had wed himself to the bucolic life, hugging the shame of a crippled body to his breast, unwilling to become a part of the growing community.

"That means a lot to me," he assured his brother-in-law.

Encouraged, Hank went on. "I'm not much, but I'll do things the way you would."

"I shall be counting on you, and thanking God for you!"

In the semi-darkness, Clinton could see Hank straighten.

"Our dead are already coming home," Clinton continued. "Charles Burbank's funeral was yesterday. I dare say his death has taken some of the whistle out of our patriotic tunes. It is only the beginning—and time for me to go. I shall enlist tomorrow."

4

T HE FOLLOWING DAY A COLD WIND swept in from the North.
Clinton took Joshua and Bethia with him to the recruiting office,
but there was such a crowd of men on the stairway that he sent the
children to the bakery to select a treat. Once the lengthy enlistment
procedure was completed, he joined arms with the children and
headed down through Market Square and on to the waterfront. The
harbor was crowded with ships, their naked masts stark against a
rare and brilliant October sky. The Marblehead would soon be
launched at Jackman's shipyard. Gunboats were in demand, and
Currier had launched several; some were destined for a fiery grave,
though most would survive the blockade battles.

Retiring and aged "Old Fuss and Feathers" Scott, though a
thorn in the side of anyone pushing artillery financing, was no
squirrel when it came to a knowledge of the necessity of naval
supremacy. He had already espoused the Anaconda Plan: to
surround and crush.

The Custom House patricians were finding the increase in war
merchandising more to their liking than the idle days of the past,
and were off their rocking chairs and away from their tales of
bygone years to do a more practical service for the government.

Under McClellan, the Northern troops had sparred with the
Confederates at Philippi, gaining a short-lived upper hand, and the
Confederates had proven their mettle at Big Bethel Church.

Neither had had time to get in the training necessary for full-scale warfare, and both were smugly certain that the entire fracas would come to an early conclusion.

Citizens of the small city stood on street corners and discussed the Battle of Bull Run and the scandalous Hall Carbine Affair, doubtless the first major arms scandal in the land. To the honest citizenry of the old Yankee town, it was difficult to believe that opportunists were already at work. Apathetically, though, they accepted the highly publicized scandal as part and parcel of war.

The day, though kaleidoscopically clear, was tinged with autumn's nip, challenging the three Haddons to continue their walk. Clinton purchased mackerel and backtracked over to Federal Street. There he stopped to look at his beloved meeting house; its towering steeple only a decade ago so magnificently rebuilt, its high federal windows, the facade and the broad front steps so impressive.

Bethia noticed her father's hesitancy to pass the old building. "What are you thinking, Papa?" she asked.

"I am thinking that I shall miss this place. I shall miss every sabbath when I will not be with you. But keep in mind, I shall be somewhere where the Lord is honored. That way we shall be together on God's day."

"I think Jesus would like that," said Bethia, savoring the pleasant thought.

Clinton felt good about Bethia. She had such a knowing and familiar way when she spoke of the Son of Creation. It was as though she spoke of an elder brother.

They continued on together, enjoying the close-knit fellowship, gathering to themselves all the little kernels of love to enjoy in the lean days to come, not unlike the busy gray squirrels that were already storing up acorns for the long winter. When they turned into the dusty road that led to the farm, a four-horse, brightly-colored Concord stage swept past them, sending a cloud of dust into the sky. Joshua threw a rock after it, wondering how close he could come to hitting it and marveling at the beautiful animals outdistancing them.

"When I am big, I'll have me a ride in one," he vowed.

"You will travel a lot, Papa, now that you are a soldier," said Bethia.

"Yes, child, I am sure of that!"

In the distant driveway, they caught sight of Doc Slater's weather-beaten, black-hooded carriage.

"Grandma must be sick again!" cried Joshua, breaking into a run.

Bethia joined him, and Clinton quickened his steps.

When they entered the kitchen, they found it empty and silent. Caroline caught the running children as they entered the hallway leading to Grandma Adkinson's room. Clinton brushed past them and, entering the room, found Nabby on her knees beside the bed, crying. Hank stood silently on the opposite side of the room, an anguished expression making the lines on his face deeper than usual. Doc Slater waited at the window, allowing Nabby and her brother their time of grief. When he saw Clinton, he crossed the room to meet him.

"Sorry, Clinton. She could go on no longer. We can be thankful her suffering is over."

Clinton lifted Nabby to her feet. She fell against him, dabbing at her tears and looking angry with herself for crying.

The children, still standing in the open doorway, turned frightened eyes toward Caroline. It was always that way. Their eyes were full of questions, and she knew she must say something—must reiterate all that she was supposed to know about death . . . while secretly she wondered just how much she did know.

"Grandma has gone home to heaven," she explained, her voice dull and lacking conviction.

"But Grandma is still here, Carrie!"

It would be Joshua putting her to the test. Well, she would meet the situation as best she could, for it was clear the child was frightened and needed assurance.

"What we see is just the house she lived in, Joshua. The real Grandma, the one who loved us and cared for us—she is up there with Jesus."

"And she isn't coughing anymore!" added Bethia.

"But how do we know that?" persisted Joshua.

"It takes something called faith. You believe what Jesus said: 'Because I live, you shall live also.' It's all in the Holy Scriptures."

Joshua left, looking somewhat relieved. Bethia remained to console her mother. Caroline walked out toward the barn to be alone. She had saved the moment for Joshua, but what about herself? She turned her words over carefully: "It takes something called faith." But did she really have it? She lacked certainty—and the loss of Grandma Adkinson weighed heavily upon her own heart. The debilitating illness, the lengthy decline of health, the many duties associated with her grandmother's illness were things she had become used to, so the future without her would have a loneliness, a bleakness—the days of grieving would demand more strength than the days of ministering.

Immediately following Grandma's funeral, Caroline found that the days had at least the emollient of healing, for there was much to keep her busy; the folding away of clothes, the distribution of treasures, the boiling of sheets and towels, the scrubbing of walls. Nevertheless she was aware of the harsh pulling out of the family tapestry threads, and the grief remained for a long time.

Hank's needs seemed to overshadow her own, for he was of a quiet disposition, and that gave Caroline relief from her own thoughts. She expressed her sympathy with a gentle touch, gave him extra attention with his food preferences, and then kindly stayed out of his way.

Matthew adjusted quickly; Bethia, too, for the wonders of childhood had a way of beguiling her curious nature. Joshua clung to the heels of his strong father, for already the red horseman had taken peace from his world, and he dreaded an encounter with that horseman's pale brother!

It was not altogether a time of waste, for the change brought by Grandma's loss was also an opportunity for Clinton to observe how his family would adjust to his absence. He was not surprised that Caroline was the one to whom each member of the family turned. She discussed with Nabby the physical needs of the family, with Matthew his day at the office, with Bethia her honest questions, and with Joshua his uncertainties. For all of her delicate exterior, Caroline seemed to bear up under life's blows. Yes, she was the one he could trust with the family's decisions. He would yet have to do some briefing. The opportunity presented itself on the day before his departure.

Together they were packing his haversack. Outwardly, at least, the women appeared calm. It was their way of saying they respected his decision to enlist; they trusted in his judgment. Into the sack went the woolen socks, the towels, and the toiletries he would need.

"I'm putting in a tin of cocoa and some broma," said Caroline.

Clinton crossed the room and added a number of well-sharpened pencils. His gold pen he would carry in his coat pocket.

"I will need these. I've arranged with Hyram to send communications."

"That will be pleasant for Matthew," said Nabby.

Clinton would reserve his last hours for Nabby, but now he had to speak to Caroline.

"Come, Carrie," he said. "I would like a few words with you."

Caroline reached for her shawl and followed her father into the yard. It was colder than she had expected, and she clung to his arm as he led her toward the hills. They reached the top of a rise that lay just beyond the barn, where together they could look down upon the Haddon acres. The fields were shorn of their crop and lay in the shadowy dimness of twilight; the buildings were already taking on the inky color of night. The great elms, sentinels over time itself, stretched long limbs toward the river.

"I wanted this time with you, Carrie. It is possible I may not have it again. You do understand?"

47

Not trusting her voice, Caroline nodded.

At first Clinton spoke reflectively, explaining his goals and the work of the past and how he had struggled to retain the land. Now he must trust the care to others.

"Nabby is a fighter. She would die using her strength to keep this land. You must watch that she sets limits. She is the best partner a man ever had, but she is not a Haddon. You are! And you are the nerve center, Carrie, the spark that ignites and encourages. Can you handle it?"

"I am seventeen, Father."

"I know. I have hesitated to put so much weight upon you, but I have no other child with your perception, strength, or fidelity. Matthew needs constant encouragement, Bethia is too idealistic, and Joshua too young. I believe I can count on you."

"You know I shall keep your trust, Father."

"Important papers—the ones that have to do with the farm—I have locked in the bureau. Nabby knows where the key is kept."

Clinton hurried on, seeming to feel a great urgency, and briefing more his own self than the young girl at his side.

"That is the legal side for you to consider, should I not—" He stopped and thought better of his words. "I am counting on you to keep the family unified, to help each one—to keep them Haddons of whom I can be proud."

"I most solemnly promise, Father."

"Then I can go with some feeling of peace."

And Clinton sealed the verbal contract with a warm embrace.

Walking back to the house, Caroline felt closer to her father than she had ever felt. It was sweet to be so trusted—so honored!

"I shall miss you more than you will ever know!" she said, daring to express the feeling of her heart.

Any night now the snow could fall. She hoped her father would not have to leave in a storm.

5

AT FIRST THE RAINS CAME and then the creeping cold, forecasting snow before dawn. Troops were moving out now at regular intervals, but the weather was so inclement that the city had dispensed with the flag-waving and the marching bands.

Clinton had often envisioned the departure and had steeled himself for the day. He believed he could do it as stolidly as any man, but when the massive doors of the train station swung wide and the bell announced the train's arrival, he was not that certain. He managed a slow, dry smile, one he did not feel but hoped would quell the fear he saw in his children's faces. Joshua howled noisily, and Bethia buried her face in a handkerchief. Then the steel monster was bearing down upon them, and steam swirled and hissed around the driving rods. All around good-byes and kisses, crying children and brave-faced adults, hands clasping as though never to let go.

Then someone handed Clinton his haversack, and he quickly boarded the train. It was not until he had settled into the hard seat and the train had lurched ahead that he felt the finalities of a man going to war.

Looking around the car, he noticed that most of his companions were younger than he, but he had expected that. Some he recognized; others had come from border towns. Some clustered and talked loudly; others sat quietly alone, their moment of loss showing in eyes that stared dazedly at the passing landscape—

familiar pastures, scenes from which they were loath to part, swale upon swale of prolific pine, oak, maple, and ash, procrastinating geese on cold pond surfaces, grazing devons in frost-nipped fields, farmers mending fences, naked elms marking hometown streets.

Clinton shook himself free from the hypnosis and psyched himself for the venture that lay ahead. He must reckon himself alone now, without a family, realize that in place of hunting autumnal game he would be seeking human quarry. What a declaration of depravity for the human race. What blind destruction to the prosperity of a country so blessed of God from its beginning

But there was no turning back. Was it not ever the lot of a man to make decisions and then to live with the results? Here was certainly the pivotal point in the nation's life where God would be the equalizer and would bring about His own purposes. Clinton could find rest in that knowledge, for he knew the events of the future would go as his God decreed. He could put his trust in a creator God who was neither surprised nor influenced by the whims of man.

From Boston they went to a transport waiting in the harbor. It was on the Fall River, New York, line. The men crowded aboard, the ship moved out into the channel, and Clinton moved on to his baptism of ocean travel with the common foot soldier.

Night fell, and the crowded conditions began to try the soul. Weariness showed on every face, and a contagious depression had moved in upon them. If a man were to get any sleep, he would either have to fight for it or trust that the man before him would get his quota and vacate space enough to lie down. Most leaned against walls, their faces expressionless, and it did little for their morale to know that the officers had claimed the better accommodations. They were now abandoned to the will and whim of the top brass and to that strange military psychology—"make life so miserable that combat will be welcome." What could a lowly private in the Twenty-third Massachusetts Infantry expect?

Clinton took stock of his immediate companions. A young lad, certainly no more than fifteen years of age, sat staring at his surroundings. There was a scrubbed look about him that reminded Clinton of his own rosy-faced Joshua. Near him sat two profligate novices who, with home restrictions behind them, were trying their new freedom. Watery eyes betrayed their inexperience with strong drink. They grew increasingly obnoxious, impressing fellow travelers only with their bad manners.

Clinton turned to an older man and struck up a conversation.

"Where from?" he asked in a whisper.

"Lowell. And you?"

"Newb'ryport."

They moved closer.

"Where d'you guess we're heading?" the man inquired.

"Heard said the Potomac, but I doubt that. The New York Regulars and the Massachusetts Eighth are there."

"Where to then?"

"I'm guessing Virginia or North Carolina." Clinton shrugged his shoulders with uncertainty.

It was three o'clock in the morning when they docked in New York. The rest of the night was spent at the Park barracks, and then they were on to Philadelphia. Clinton heard no more remarks about getting on with the war; the need for sleep blotted out all other considerations.

The hospitality of the Philadelphians would long be remembered, and it was with regret that the men took their leave from the city of brotherly love. Through Delaware and on into Maryland they traveled, and the mood changed abruptly.

Here the place was teeming with military action; men were drilling in the streets, and mule-drawn wagons were everywhere. The sight brought back memories of Clinton's gelding, Dandy. By afternoon the Twenty-third had boarded a steamer and sailed into the Chesapeake Bay. The warming sun cast late afternoon rays upon the ship and was reflected in the waters. Clinton settled on deck, enjoying the scent of brine. It was like being back on his beloved

Plum Island, where with his father he had explored the natural barrier that protected Newburyport's harbor. In memory he again listened to the cry of the gulls, walked over the wind-drifted dunes, and felt the sting of coarse sand on his legs.

Overhead a flock of geese flew, drawing men to the rail to watch them, stirring memories of home where the hunting season was still on, and raising some resentment that they had been robbed of their well-earned, postharvest pleasures. Clinton could still see Bethia and the gosling she had rescued—the one with the broken wing and endearing disposition. She'd received a blue ribbon at the Mall for raising him. He could see Hank digging potatoes, could almost smell the earthy odor of the root vegetables. He could see Nabby loading the wagon with all the good things of the harvest and taking off for the market with wheels squeaking and complaining. Nabby, at middle age with a richer beauty than when he had first seen her, hair streaked with taffy and sunshine . . . blue eyes tinged with green, mouth softly curving. But he would have to watch his thoughts. Like the ancient sirens they could call a man back from duty—back to all he had forfeited in order to satisfy his convictions.

Well had Odysseus bound himself to a mast, thought Clinton, and by an oath of allegiance he had bound himself to the Union's cause.

His musings were interrupted by his older companion.

"Up ahead—Annapolis!"

The man had only whispered, but the message shot through the ranks like a spray of flak. All eyes turned toward the Naval Academy. They themselves were now a part of history—the Union army! Pride spread over each face as they watched the Union flag flying in a strong breeze; pride and dedication and more—a holy oath to deliver the Union from division. These were no draftees, no bounty enlistees; these were men who had consecrated their lives to a cause for which they would willingly die.

THE TRAINING AT ANNAPOLIS was vigorous, lasting into early January and proving to be an eliminating process. Recruits from the soft life found themselves shelved or discarded. With the rain and exposure to nature's elements, many contracted influenza or pneumonia and became victims of the "hardening process." Having spent so many years wrestling with the outrages of the elements, Clinton took to the rigors of army life as naturally as a beaver to aspen. His skin was toughened and tanned from sun and exposure. Strong already, he grew even stronger and now, living closer to the earth without the luxury of bed and roof, he began to take on the appearance of a backwoodsman. Added to the dark complexion of his Norman ancestry and to his brown hair that was as thick as a beaver's pelt, he now sported a swarthy beard.

Orders came to put out, supposedly for Fort Monroe—and from there only God and the high command knew where.

Clinton's regiment was split into two wings. His wing went aboard the schooner *Highlander,* the left wing on the propeller *Hussar.* At first there were no restrictions to prevent the men from viewing their departure, so they crowded the rails to watch the magnificent Union fleet. One after another, the ships moved into formation, swelling the armada as far as the eye could see. Old Glory billowed in a sharp mackerel breeze, stirring again the fierce patriotism of Yankee hearts—rallying the confidence of marshaled numbers.

Shouting broke out, and in the distance they could see General Burnside boarding one of the ships. He was no small man, and his august bearing was easily recognized.

"I see we are not the only ones with a crop of whiskers!" said Clinton to his companion.

"They call him old Mutton Chops, but don't be fooled. He is a soldier!"

The cheering went on for a long time, relaying from ship to ship and wandering off into the ether, and then the men settled in for the voyage. Their mood was good, but it was not to last. When they went below the situation changed drastically, for the government had a way of taxing every ship with a capacity load. There was strong evidence in the air that their ship had been used previously to transport horses.

"Smells better in my hog pen," complained a New Hampshire farmer.

Mess, too, was poor—soggy potatoes dripped over with grease and pork scraps—none of the country creamy butter of the Haddon dairy. As time went on, even the water supply was rationed, each man limited to two ounces per meal. And sleep had once again become an elusive luxury. Herded like cattle for the night, with little room for stretching their weary limbs, the men began to scratch. The place was alive with lice! At least they could look forward to an early morning reveille that would bring the tortuous night to an end.

Time began to hang heavily on the men, eased only by an occasional game of checkers or euchre. Some had brought aboard a cribbage board, and a good number read their Bibles.

Then the weather began to change. On deck Clinton scanned the heavens with the practiced eye of the farmer. Clouds were coming in, rolling and jostling together, hanging ominously over the sea, turning the docile waves to an ugly, convulsive black that reflected the anger of the heavens.

"We're in for it!" he commented.

The ship's crew worked feverishly on the sails as the wind grew stronger and the sea more turbulent. Labored mutterings broke forth from the sailors as they struggled against the devil's bull-whips, and the rain began to fall. It came not as the light, refreshing rains of a New England spring. The heavens opened up, sending torrents over the decks. For the first time, many realized that they had an enemy other than the butternut-clad sons of the South. They would suffer as much from the elements as from the enemies' muskets—and this new enemy was far less predictable.

The ship continued to plow through the heavy seas. Off to the starboard, Clinton could see a steamer over on her beam ends. Up ahead, two were about to collide.

"They'll hit, sure as shooting!" he exclaimed.

"Can't we warn 'em?" someone yelled.

"How? Besides, I'm sure they know already."

The troops were drawn to the rail as moths to a flame, mouths agape and nerves steeled, waiting and watching for the impact. It was quick in coming. The ships struck and shuddered, and passengers spilled into the icy waters of the Atlantic. Heads bobbed and some sank, and several started swimming courageously to escape the tow they knew would follow. In spite of the storm, Clinton was able to spot several making for his ship and went immediately to the task of getting lines over the side.

"Give me a hand!" he ordered.

Others joined him, pulling hard as they felt weight on the rope. They hauled in a sea-ravaged creature that looked more like a drenched rat than anything human. The man lay on the rain-beleaguered deck gasping for breath. Clinton tore off his greatcoat and threw it over the choking figure, then was back at the rail. A commanding seaman came toward them, roaring orders for the men to go below. They left reluctantly, muttering in their beards, feeling that this was no time to engage in branch rivalries. Clinton lifted the waterlogged stranger from the deck and steered him down into the stinking hold. The place was strewn with disgruntled and seasick men, and the stench of vomit was everywhere.

What a place to put a man inches this side of death! thought Clinton, dropping his burden on a narrow space between two soldiers.

Straightening, he was confronted by a bleary-eyed, bearded choleric. He was a man of no mean stature, and he snarled defiance, reminding Clinton of an enraged wolf he had once shot point blank.

"Ya can't put 'em here!" he sputtered.

Clinton stepped over the rescued man and faced the garrulous brute.

"That so?" he asked quietly.

Two of the men who had helped Clinton with the rescue arose simultaneously and stood behind Clinton. The bully shot a glance at the three, blinked and then moved back.

"Have it your way . . . for now," he snarled.

Clinton went to work removing the man's clothing and dressing him in his own spare allotment, all the while wondering if the poor creature would survive. He was blue with cold and shivered uncontrollably.

"What the devil kind o' man is that?" asked a young recruit of his companion, gesturing toward Clinton. "He's soaked to the skin himself."

"I don't know," answered the soldier, "but he looks to me like Jesus Christ!"

The rescued man looked at Clinton. From his exhausted eyes, Clinton did indeed look like portraits of the Galilean carpenter. The man blinked and shook his head as though to escape what he was certain was an apparition.

Clinton squatted down beside him. "Haddon's the name," he said. He looked over his self-appointed charge with the scrutiny of a physician.

The eyes that stared back were nice eyes. Little laughter lines were pronounced at the outer corners. For a man, especially a Yankee, the nose was small, and his upper lip was short. From the corners of his nose deep lines ran to his mouth, giving him a pixie expression. For all his youthful appearance, there was something manly about him. There had to be, for him to have swum the distance from the sinking vessel to the *Highlander* in choppy seas.

"Drake. Drake Singleton." The name emerged from purple lips, and he offered his benefactor a livid hand.

"Don't lean against the walls; they're crawling with vermin!" cautioned Clinton.

"What do you make of this?" asked Drake, sweeping a hand around the miserable quarters.

"Guess you'd just have to say no one was ready for a war!"

"Where you from?" The younger man was already warming to Clinton's charitable kindness.

"Newb'ryport. And you?"

"I'm from Salem."

The conversation was severed by the arrival of three more strangers, each bearing evidence of having been rescued from the sea. They were issued blankets and soon were out of their dripping clothes. Their voices cut the silence with a shrillness spurred on from the hysteria of having been saved from certain death.

"We threw ever'thin' overboard. Steel. Tons of it!"

"Idiotic waste!" exclaimed an onlooker.

"Reckon we'll get used to that," offered another.

When the call came for mess, they filed up through the narrow passageway. Once again they were offered the poorest fare. Clinton gave his ration of coffee to the sea urchin and was rewarded by seeing normal skin tones return to the face of his new friend.

As quickly as the storm had come, it passed, and the sun was soon pouring through the spent squall clouds like water through a sieve. A sutler had come aboard with a pilot, bringing apples and cheese to sell, as well as whiskey. The latter was quickly disposed of at the officers' quarters, and the man left with his pockets bulging.

THE SHIP CONTINUED ON, seemingly bent on a scheduled course. It was nearing the sixth of February, and the wretched accommodations had bred sympathetic alliances that in normal circumstances would never have occurred. Clinton and Drake had formed a genuine friendship, finding they had much in common. They idled away many monotonous hours talking of home, delighting in their mutual interests.

The ship dropped anchor ten miles from Roanoke Island where the Confederates were well-entrenched. Retrospectively, Clinton thought about the colony Sir Walter Raleigh had established there and wondered why they had disappeared. Always there were mysteries in the recorded advancement of civilization. Following his briefing he wondered, too, how many men would survive the offensive against the island. The troops by now were ready to take out their frustrations on anyone. They were anxious to get into the fray.

Gunboats came alongside and started a bombardment of the Confederate installations. They moved along in a line, Stars and Stripes rippling atop each vessel. Despite class differences and petty quarrels, the men shared a unified devotion to the colors.

Out on the ocean and beyond the two Atlantic squadrons lay a feeble, scattered rebel fleet, firing but damaging nothing and proving more of a cursing barrage than a threat. The Union gunboats, on the other hand, were finding their targets and sending flames and smoke skyward. The bombardment went on all afternoon, and as nightfall approached the troops prepared to land. Steamers came up and towed landing boats over the water. Clinton and Drake crouched along with the others, ready to hit the beach. Rifles ready and eyes sharp, they came up onto a mist-enshrouded shore.

After establishing a beachhead, pickets were sent out. The skies were threatening once again. They opened up and in no time had sent forth a fresh deluge. At first an effort was made to stay dry, but the attempt proved futile, and they were soon marching, impervious to the disagreeable elements and soaked through to the skin.

"Well—on to Richmond!" called Drake over the cacophony of battle, stamping on vigorously through the muddy terrain.

Clinton nodded, finding encouragement in his friend's bravado.

The rebels were as thick as fleas on a mangy cat's back—and they would be reckoned with! Drake fell in close to Clinton. Skirmishers kicked up a volley of resistance, and the Twenty-third moved into the thick of it. It was their first encounter with the enemy, and there was not a man who did not realize that the hum and buzz of the flying minié-balls was for real! It was now kill or be killed. Clinton's thoughts became erratic. To go marching on when men were falling all around was completely foreign to his nature—but to keep on sloshing and killing through the noise and the blood—to fill the lines—that was what he had been trained to do—this was now his sacred duty. Sacred? He rolled the word around on his tongue. How ridiculous, and how mad!

The Confederates had reckoned the swamp on their right to be impenetrable, so had moved their numbers to the left. Orders came from the crafty Burnside to go into the swamp on the enemy's right.

"Last one in is a turkey egg!" quipped Drake.

They sank waist deep, holding their rifles and powder high. The mud was like quicksand, the water stinking, and the relentless rains were still lashing them. Even worse was the darkness. They learned quickly that it was murderous to reach for the straggling swamp vines. Those who unwittingly did so withdrew hands ripped and bloody. Even their clothes were shredded. A sniper's ball struck one of their number, and he fell beneath the water. With troops at their back and a mission before them, Clinton and Drake went on together, faces sober and jaws set like flint with the determination to flush out the enemy before a ball got to them.

On they moved with the strangest of thoughts assailing—the postman bringing news of one's death to the family, children crying, stunned. The preacher's last sermon—what was it? Something about the high cost of being right. Clinton had thought about that many times, thought about the Revolutionary soldiers who had dedicated their lives, honor, and fortunes to the cause of freedom, men who had brought the remarkable Union thus far and had passed the torch to a new generation. How many had fallen in those early days, how many had given their lives, he wondered, and then resorted to the comfort of Scripture: "A thousand shall fall at thy side and ten thousand at thy right hand, but it shall not come nigh unto thee."

The intermittent silences of men around him, so many now falling beneath the water, and the minié-balls grazing his ears. He must not think of death, but of life, and fight for it. One must not look at the blood. One must concentrate on human targets, fire and reload, fire and reload.

The flanks were moving in now, and soon were overrunning. The New York Suaves were charging the front, and the enemy, breaking ranks, beat a disorderly retreat. Clinton stepped over dead Confederates and entered upon the breastworks, then on to the fort that had by now become a ghostly Confederate charnel.

Dead were everywhere, staring into space with unseeing eyes. He reached down to check the pulse of a soldier. There was nothing. Another had caught a ball in the temple. He did not feel for a pulse there. When entering the fort he had seen a man dying beside a prostrate mule. When he turned back, he found that both had expired. Another, who had been stationed at a cannon, lay sprawled against the weapon. The cannons stood, silent and hot. One was a twenty-four pounder; others were twelve.

"This one is from the Mexican War!" yelled Drake, stepping up to the console.

"This one is marked U.S.A.," answered Clinton, thinking to himself how well-informed was the former Secretary of War when it came to arsenals. The desolation of the place began to seep in. "Is this really victory?" he asked.

"If it weren't, you would very well be one of these, my friend!" Drake came alongside him. He had a surface wound on his left arm, and it was bleeding. His clothes were soaked from the swamp and the rain, but his engaging grin was still in place.

"Scratches don't count," he said, noticing Clinton's concern.

Clinton wondered what it would take to bring forth a pessimistic word from the man.

By morning the forts had surrendered, and three thousand rebels had been taken prisoner. Horses as well as men lay in death's frozen grip, and over the earth a horrible stench hovered. Clinton was given orders to accompany a captive rebel commander back into the brush where the fighting had been the hardest. Some of his men were unaccounted for and, as an officer, he was allowed the privilege of looking for them.

The Confederate captain was the first to see the bloodstained uniform of his fallen sergeant. He walked with a rapid step toward the dead man and fell on his knees beside him. He had been the victim of several balls. One had struck a metal button on his uniform and bent it double. The captain ripped the button off angrily, then stood and walked to a debarked tree. He held the button in his grasp and stared off into space. As Clinton approached him, he saw the man bury his chin in his gray uniform. Then he was sobbing—great, wracking sobs that seemed to come all the way from his toes.

"He was my orderly . . . young . . . a good soldier." The words came haltingly.

The entire scene was disconcerting. The captain was a man like himself, an American, fighting for what he believed was right. He was a gentle person, mild mannered. Clinton could hear his small son's oft-repeated question: "Why would Americans fight Americans?"

He returned to his regiment, quietly brooding, and Drake joined him.

"Find any of his men?" asked Drake.

"His orderly. It wasn't very pretty. I felt for him."

Drake was instantly alert to the debilitating effect the first battle was having on Clinton.

"Don't go soft, man. You'll be sure quarry for the Rebs if you do."

"I'm not caving in. Just somehow feel different about it all."

"You have got to think, I'm not killing a man. I'm shooting down an ideology—one that wants to chain a man's soul. Soul killing is worse than body killing, Clint."

His friend was right. Clinton had gone into this for a principle . . . and he would see it through.

6

WHEN THE DAPPER commissioned Boston salesman, Lerner Brisson, first appeared at the Vaugn Haddon farm, he aroused neither suspicion nor distrust in Vaugn or his wife. He was congenial and friendly, asking only questions that pleased his listeners to answer. Vaugn and Phoebe seemed amused and impressed with his city manners, and the fact that he gave considerable time to Clara, the family darling, pleased them even more. They were clearly giving serious consideration to employing the man as their Boston produce agent.

Timothy, never one to become too engrossed with his father's business, reasoned in an abstract way that if his parents had accepted the man, he must be above reproach.

Allen, on the other hand, harbored a distinct distrust for Brisson from the beginning. He was not sure why he felt as he did, but under the affable exterior the man seemed unnatural. Secretly Allen hoped the relationship would soon burn itself out.

With the harvest over, Vaugn and his sons were able to follow more stimulating pursuits. They had already bagged a good supply of wild fowl and rid the place of night-prowling raccoons. Now they had time to see to the winter's supply of wood.

The twins were leaning against the stable door watching as their father approached, Lerner Brisson at his side.

"What do you make of him?" Allen asked his brother.

"Brisson?" Timothy shrugged his shoulders, then looked at

Allen. "You don't like him," he observed.

"Something about him just doesn't ring true."

Timothy appraised the distant figure. Brisson was definitely a classy man. His clothes were neat and well-fitting. True, he walked like a peacock aware of his fine feathers. Maybe that was what bothered the unaffected Allen. The man had an air of agreeable condescension, somewhat patronizing—of the very mien the Haddons had always disliked in the merchant class. He was short and robust, and his thick black hair had been plastered down with concentrated egoism over a high forehead. His head had a roundness to it and his eyebrows a stenciled look that made him appear more fit for a European court than for a New England produce market. His oily skin had olive tones, his nose was broad, and he had a straight upper lip and an overworked lower that revealed a set of poor teeth when he spoke.

"If he were older I would think him a Bonaparte," said Timothy.

"I don't like the way he fidgets. He looks all around when he should be looking at you," said Allen.

"I've a feeling he is talking Father into selling our produce at the Quincy market."

"Faneuil Hall?"

"Yes. I have heard them discussing it."

"Then Father had better hire someone to watch Brisson. I'd trust that man about as far as I could throw a pung!" Allen's voice was contemptuously crisp. "I'm going over to talk to Hank," he said and took off for his uncle's dairy.

Hank was just finishing with the work, and he smiled as Allen entered the barn. Vaugn's son was a true Haddon and much to Hank's liking.

"What brings you here, 'sides gettin' your milk?" asked Hank, quick to notice Allen's creased brow.

"Guess I just like being around Uncle Clint's place."

"Missin' your uncle, huh?"

"I liked talking to him. Heard from him yet?"

"Sends letters to your Aunt Nabby. She shares 'em."

"Wish he were here. I'd like to talk with him."

"Won't I do?" asked the little man.

Allen hesitated, studying Hank. He seemed such a fixture to the place. Hank had worked with his Uncle Clint for as long as Allen could remember, hobbling about with the crippled leg dragging behind. Handicapped early in life by a mysterious disease, he had proudly disdained sympathy and avoided pampering, setting about to prove he could match any man in his ability to work the soil. As a consequence, Hank's upper torso was overdeveloped, his shoulders and chest broad and muscular, and his spirit proud. He was a loner, a private person usually, but down-east honest to the core.

"It's that merchant man," ventured Allen.

"Brisson?"

"Ay-uh."

Hank turned away from Allen and made a pretense of untangling Dandy's spare trappings before hanging them back on the wall. Hank was not sure this was the time to discuss his own misgivings about the presumptuous jobber.

"What about him?" he asked, rubbing mutton fat into the leather underside of the reins.

"Can't honestly say. Tell me, do you think it unreasonable for us growers to dislike the agents?"

"We've got our reasons."

"Like?"

"Well, I guess we're still chewin' on the injustices of the past." Observing Allen's blank expression, Hank continued. "We don't forget quickly the way we were treated after the Revolution—courts ordering our farms to be sold 'cause we couldn't meet the int'rest rates, throwing good men into prison, shootin' at us like we were common crim'nals when we marched on Springfield for our rights—and merchants turning down our money. Even now, we are the ones who do the plantin', gamble on the crops, clear the land, sweat, pray, even pay the freight for the big city markets—and these charlatans gettin' a percentage. For what? Guess you'd say we don't appreciate their sharin' the harvest when they don't share the sweat!"

"When did all this happen, Hank?"

"Oh, way back after the Independence War. Folks were encouraged to borrow. Gaulderation, son. Don't you have it all in your history books?"

"Yes, I guess we do. I just hadn't paid too much attention. Didn't realize how that part of history could affect us today."

"History's good to look at, boy. We should learn from our mistakes."

"Why not go back to selling our own stuff? Enough in a family to do that."

"Yes, indeed. Now you're thinkin'!" A smile flashed across Hank's face.

Allen smiled, too, revealing strong, white teeth. His face still reflected the summer sun and the golds of autumn.

"Wish I were through school," the boy said wistfully. "Seems a waste. I could do so much more at home."

"You'll be through soon enough. Bide your time, Allen. Learn all you can learn. Your folks wouldn't feel they had done their job if they didn't give you a chance at an education."

"I suppose. But I'm ready for more action!"

The sound of wagon wheels interrupted their conversation. Nabby was driving Dandy to the barn. She waved to Allen, then drew in the reins and tossed them down to Hank.

"Come in and have some cocoa and doughnuts, Allen," she called, alighting from the wagon with the grace and ease of a young girl. Hard work had kept Nabby slim. She was wearing the usual morning garb—tight-bodiced, high-collared dress and woolen cape.

She's a pretty woman, thought Allen as he followed her into the kitchen, noticing the way the sun was reflected in her blonde, braided crown of thick hair.

"I've a letter from Clinton!" she called over her shoulder.

Having a batlike radar when it came to hearing Clinton's name, the children came running.

"Read it! Read it!" they chorused.

"Mercy! Let me get my wraps off!"

The weather was nippy, and the heat from the big wood stove felt good. Nabby held the letter to the light, straining to read the print.

"It looks like as though it came from Annapolis. Dated weeks ago!" Then, remembering her invitation to Allen, Nabby turned to Caroline.

"Caroline, make some cocoa and whip some cream for topping. Bethia, get out the doughnuts. This calls for a celebration!"

Her words fired the girls into action, and in no time the fragrance of chocolate was permeating the room. Bethia set a blue willow platter stacked with doughnuts in the center of the table. The smell of cinnamon sent an invitation of its own. After placing a bowl of whipped cream beside the doughnuts, Caroline sat down and folded her hands.

"Bless us all with Thy grace, dear Father, and receive our gratitude for our daily gifts—especially this letter!"

Nabby's hands trembled as she opened the envelope, and her voice quavered as she began to read.

My beloved wife,

Training at Annapolis is an experience one will not forget quickly. The order to form squares resounds through the compounds hourly and invades our dreams as well. We drill so constantly that I believe we could do it in our sleep. New recruits arrive daily and move systematically from barracks to cold-weather tents. You can single out the tenderfoots. Influenza plays no favorites. Hundreds are sick and ailing. Fortunately I remain well, for which I thank a merciful God.

I was issued a rusty gun. It was in the poorest condition, but I have cleaned it up considerably.

Tell Carrie and Matthew that I expect letters from them. Joshua and

Bethia may try their hand at one now and then. I would like to hear from Hank but will not insist. I know he is very busy. Perhaps you can tell me the prices you are getting.

Is it possible I have been away for two months? I am sending some money to you. Be sure to let me know when it arrives. I wish part of it to go to The Reverend Richardson's efforts to start a Y.M.C.A. Please see that he gets it, and keep me in your prayers. I sense action will be coming soon.

> *Your loving husband,*
> *Clinton Haddon*

Nabby looked up, her face radiant and as refreshed as a watered garden.

"Why did they give Papa a rusty gun, Mother?" asked Joshua.

"Oh, it's probably just a training weapon. No doubt they will issue him a good one when it is time to fight," Caroline answered.

Joshua was plainly disgruntled. "Do you know that for sure?"

"Come now, no more gun talk!" said Nabby.

Bethia waited until she and Caroline were alone.

"I don't like to think of Papa with any kind of gun," she said. "He never hurt anyone or anything, lest you call shooting the skunks out of the chicken coop something!"

Caroline felt her sister's distress keenly, but finding the right words to console her was difficult.

"Don't fuss, Bethia. Papa won't use it unless he has to."

Joining the family later, Hank was handed the letter. His face registered extreme satisfaction as he read.

"Must be excitin' to be at Annapolis!" he said.

"Our Capitol was there once," said Bethia, enjoying an opportunity to display her knowledge.

"Is that so?" asked Joshua.

"Yes, son," confirmed Nabby.

"I'd like living in a tent, like we do sometimes at Plum Island," Bethia remarked.

"Yes, but tenting here in the summertime is warm. Father says it is cold in Maryland," said Caroline.

"Can't we send him blankets?" asked the charitable Joshua.

"The Soldiers' Relief Society is already working on that, but that doesn't mean a family can't send their own box. A good idea, son," Nabby affirmed.

"And a good gun?"

"Where would we ever get a good gun, Joshua? The kind a soldier should have?" asked Bethia.

"Oh, girls wouldn't know about such things!" said Joshua impatiently. He moved away from the group, deeply engrossed in thought. He was angry about the rusty gun affair. How could his father engage an enemy with a weapon that might not fire?

By the time Matthew returned from work, Joshua had reached a highly agitated state. He quickly shared the news with his older brother.

"I think you are worrying needlessly, Joshua," Matthew replied kindly. "Father is smart enough to care for himself. He didn't get sick like the others, did he?"

Joshua had expected more from Matthew. He backed away from the rebuff, smoldering. He would have thought a man's own family would be concerned. He threw a coat over his shoulders and headed out into the early evening chill. Overhead a crow uttered a hoarse cry. Joshua let a stone fly in its direction, sending the frightened bird back to its rookery. He climbed over the hills, wanting to walk where he had so often walked with his father, wanting desperately to feel Clinton's hand on his shoulder, hear his voice. But the strong presence was not there.

For days the young boy struggled with the problem. If only he had the money to purchase a gun outright. He might earn it, but there again, his father had said that action was coming up—there was little time. At least he might look into the kinds of guns that were available. Hank would be going to town in a few days, and possibly Joshua could accompany him.

WHEN HANK STARTED to harness Dandy for his trip to town a few days later, Joshua made it a point to help.

"You can go," said Hank with a wink, knowing from the boy's expression what he wanted.

They rode along in silence, feeling the bitter edge of winter. Dandy's mane tossed rhythmically; the frosty air was to his liking. Hank reined him in at the market horse block and got down with no small labor to tie the horse. Then he lifted a box of butter from the back of the wagon and left Joshua to himself.

Joshua lost no time. He was off and around the corner to the gun shop. As he entered, the door closed behind him and set off a jangling bell.

Mr. Schmidt was at the back of the store with a customer. He looked up at the sound of the bell and, seeing that it was only a boy, went on about his business. That gave Joshua time to look over the assortment of firearms. One looked better than all the rest. It hung on the wall, a magnificent weapon—a percussion and an iron framed gun. It had a well-oiled and rounded butt stock of black walnut. A four-piece hickory cleaning rod fit snugly in the recess of the butt, and the barrel was well-blued. A printed sign under the gun explained that the magazine had a fifteen-round capacity. A repeater like that would be invincible! That was the gun his father must have!

The poky customer in back continued to monopolize the proprietor's time, while Joshua chafed at the delay. After all, he had only one question to ask. Still waiting on the customer, Mr. Schmidt finally spoke to him.

"What are you doin' here, young Joshua?"

Joshua went right to the point. "That gun," he said, pointing to the wall. "What's it called?"

"Why, that's a Henry, son. You planning to purchase a gun?"

"It's a repeater, isn't it?"

"Sure is. Uses forty-four rimfire cartridges. Shoots all week on one loadin'."

"How much are you asking?"

"Waal, now. . . ." Mr. Schmidt decided to be sporting. "For you I'd make it easy—say, forty-six dollars. Guns are gettin' scarce nowadays."

Joshua's eyes bugged out. Where in heaven's name would he ever get such a sum? He swallowed hard and withdrew from the counter, disappointed and embarrassed. He moved sheepishly toward the door.

"I-I'll have to think about it," he said lamely.

When he returned to the wagon, he could see that Hank was angry. Snow was falling, and Hank's clothes were already wet.

"Where the devil you been?" he asked, disgruntled and chilled.

Joshua did not answer. He swung up onto the seat, put his head down, and clasped his hands rigidly.

"Should have headed home ten minutes ago!" Hank was peevish at first, then wished he had not spoken so harshly, for Joshua looked pale and troubled. He sat like a lump of coal for the rest of the way home, silently brooding.

Whatever it is that's botherin' him, looks like he's of a mind to keep it to hisself, thought Hank. He understood. He reached for a rubber blanket in back and pulled it up over his young charge.

"Keep this over yer head!" he ordered.

Hank made two more deliveries and then turned Dandy's head toward home. Clinton's two dogs came to meet them. Joshua, who usually fondled them, brushed by them and hurried into the house.

Caroline, working in the kitchen, saw him get off the wagon, heard the door close, and heard his steps up over the stairs that led to his room. She decided to follow. When she entered his room, he was lying on his bed.

"Are you sick?" she asked.

"Nope."

She left and returned to the kitchen. When it came time for supper, Joshua still did not appear. Caroline sent Bethia for him, and he joined the family with unmistakable reluctance and picked abstractedly at his food.

Nabby gave Caroline a quizzical look and reached to feel Joshua's forehead.

"I am not sick!" he declared defensively.

"Well, I am sure you are not," answered Nabby. "You're as cool as a cucumber. Probably just a passing chill from the storm."

Bethia could scarcely wait for an opportunity to question Joshua privately. But sensing her intent, and not wanting her company, he ignored her. It was evident to him that no one else was really concerned. He alone had to solve the problem.

As was their usual way, the younger children retired soon after family devotions. Bethia endured the separation for less than an hour, then wrapped herself in a blanket and made her way to her brother's room. The door was closed; still she ventured to knock. No answer. She turned the knob and entered. Joshua pretended sleep. It was an old ruse, and it did not deceive Bethia.

"What is eating at you, Joshua?" she asked.

No answer.

"I know!" she continued. "It's that rusty gun, isn't it?"

"Little Miss Know-it-all!" Joshua clearly resented his sister's clairvoyance.

"Well, it is! I can tell!" She hesitated and then went on. "Well, what are we going to do about it?"

Joshua lifted his head. She had said "we." He swung his feet over the side of the bed.

"I am going to buy Father a good gun!" he declared.

"How much will a good gun cost?" asked Bethia.

The miserable question brought a groan from Joshua. His answer was almost inaudible. "Forty-six dollars."

"Forty-six dollars!" echoed Bethia. "Are you plum crazy? We've never even seen that much money!"

"Well, if we don't see it now, you needn't expect to see Papa again. Can't you just see some Reb aimin' at Papa, and him just standing there poking a ramrod down the muzzle of a rusty gun?"

Bethia's face blanched. "Oh, Josh, he'd be shot dead!"

"Exactly!" At last he had gotten through to someone. He sighed heavily. It was a relief that Bethia now understood, but the problem of acquiring a reliable weapon was still unsolved.

"I have my gold piece that rich Mr. Paine gave me when I won the pet contest," Bethia offered.

"Don't want your gold piece. You said you would never spend it, and you shouldn't. I'll think of ways to earn the money!"

Bethia started to cry. "He's my father, too, and he can have anything that is mine!"

"Don't cry, Beth. We'll work this out together, but we can't let the others know. They wouldn't understand."

WINTER WAS MOVING ON uneventfully, leaving Caroline in a state of despondency. Thad had gone to Harvard as he said, and he had neither written nor returned to visit. She could not help wondering why he had been so adamant about extracting a promise from her. Didn't he, too, share in that pledge?

March came in like a lion and went out like a lion, knocking the age-old prophecy into a cocked hat. The nastiest blizzards and the coldest of winter winds seemed unleashed during the entire month of April, obstinately refusing to yield to Dame Spring's overtures. Nevertheless, farmers prepared their cutters for storage and their cabbages for planting.

By the middle of April, Matthew had been named valedictorian of his class and suggested as a candidate for West Point. He took great pride now in presiding over the evening devotions and following up with the day's latest news releases, which his family received with fascination. First the train race from Georgia to Chattanooga, then the battles at sea. The confrontation of the *Monitor* and the *Merrimac* had convinced the Union that henceforth steel-hulled ships would be a necessity. Shipbuilding increased on the waterfront; Currier's and Jackman's building spurring others on. Navy officers were commissioned regularly, and the blockade was stretching further to the east.

The Haddon family seemed to be adjusting to Clinton's absence, but they were also bracing for news of a spring offensive. To combat the short-handedness plaguing the farmers, Nabby relinquished her household tasks to Caroline and joined Hank in the fields.

They were in the long barn working one evening when an echoing "haloo" broke in upon the splashing sounds of pre-twilight milking. There was little mistaking Vaugn's familiar voice. He walked in, Lerner Brisson at his side.

"Just checking in to see if all is going well," Vaugn said.

"Right on schedule here. How are things at your place?" answered Hank.

"Planning to take on an extra hand. Know any couple past army age and wanting work?"

"You planting that much?"

"Ay-uh. Lerner here says the government'll buy all we raise."

"That right?" said Hank, appraising Brisson. Hank rubbed his leathery cheek thoughtfully. So Brisson had talked Vaugn into it.

"We'll be shipping everything to Boston. Lerner has a government contract. Thought you might care to sell there, too."

"We don't grow that much," answered Hank quickly, "and the local stores buy our surplus."

"It's fairer to the locals," added Nabby, who had come to Hank's side carrying a brimming pail of milk.

It was a masked rebuff, and Lerner knew it. He flushed slightly, but retained his gentlemanly composure.

"Probably get a better price from the government. Leastwise that's what I'm hoping for," he said.

"Mebbe," countered Hank. Then in curiosity he asked, "What you need more hands for, Vaugn?"

"Oh," said Vaugn nonchalantly, "plans coming up."

He is planning to enlist, Nabby thought, knowing well how the younger brother was inclined to follow the older.

"What's the latest with Clint?" Vaugn asked.

"Says that things are warming up," said Nabby.

"Still in Maryland?"

"I can't say. Letters have stopped coming."

"Well, tell him hello for me—and maybe I'll be seeing him."

Nabby looked questioningly at her brother-in-law.

"Can't let Clint do it all," he said with a grin.

"You signing into the infantry?" asked Hank.

"No, I'd best be in the cavalry. Could take my own Peg with me." He was referring to his horse, Pegasus.

"Clinton will like hearing. I'll tell him as soon as I get his latest address. Things are changing fast now," Nabby said.

"When you going?" asked Hank.

"After the crops are in."

And with that the conversation ended and Vaugn took his leave, disappearing over the hill with Lerner. Hank and Nabby stood watching, each silently thinking. It was like the stripping of corn—one at a time, sometimes two, with the hand of destiny removing the men from their place in the home. They wondered when it would end . . . and who would return.

When the evening devotions were over, Nabby broke the news to the children. Joshua received it with hoopla, glad to feel that his father would have some backing. Matthew behaved as though he had known it all along. The girls were openly troubled, hating the depletion of the family numbers.

Caroline displayed no outward emotion, but the news set her to wondering if Thad, too, would be caught up in the fervor to enlist. With his continued absence, he seemed far away—removed from her life.

It was easy to imagine many things. Men at Harvard had their social events, and it was not uncommon to hear of them marrying into the first families of Boston. Thad's first year would be over in a matter of weeks, and then he would surely be back in Newburyport.

Would he be changed? Would he find Caroline dull after a year in the company of lively and attractive people?

7

JOSHUA AND BETHIA WORKED feverishly to earn money for their father's gun. Hank fashioned a cranberry rake from an old pitchfork and promised to take them to the bogs to pick if they did well with their farm chores. They had earned pennies clearing snow and gathering kindling during the winter months, and had often visited Mr. Schmidt's gun shop to make sure the coveted weapon was still on the wall. Their kitty grew slowly, helped along with a few small coins received from distant relatives at Christmas. Easter was late, and that meant that they could hunt wildflowers to sell to the wealthy burgesses on High Street. Ritualistically, they counted their savings.

"How much?" asked Bethia one late summer evening, watching Joshua go over the procedure for the hundredth time.

"Only eight dollars and forty cents—but that is really more than I thought we had!"

"Well, we can't quit, that's for sure. In fact, we have got to try harder. We should have sent it with Uncle Vaugn."

"Uncle Vaugn isn't likely to be sent where Papa is, silly! But we must tap some other place. We've got to get money somewhere."

Bethia thought about her brother's remark for a long while. She knew that Caroline had fallen heir not only to Grandma's old room, but to many of her grandmother's treasures. She decided it was time to speak to her sister.

"Didn't know if I would find you awake," she said, entering Caroline's room one night. It was pitch dark, and Caroline arose to light the lamp. The glow spread over the girls' faces with a benign warmth. Caroline thought that Bethia should look at least a little sleepy, but there she was, as wide awake as an Indian on a hunting party.

"You had best get under the covers," said Caroline, but Bethia seemed not to hear. She settled herself on the top blanket.

"I couldn't sleep," she stated simply.

"And is that what you came to tell me?"

Bethia's usual buoyancy was absent.

"Tell me," prompted Caroline, resting a comforting hand on her sister's shoulder.

"I need money—lots of money—and I can't tell you why." Bethia chewed her bottom lip, then clamped her mouth shut.

"But I don't have money, Bethia. How could I possibly earn any? I'm stuck in the house more than ever now, and soon I'll be putting in my share of time in the fields."

"You have something you could sell."

Caroline looked puzzled.

"You have some of Grandma's jewelry."

"Oh, Bethia—I couldn't!"

"If you knew why I wanted it, you would give it to me right away!"

"Then why don't you tell me?"

"I gave a promise."

"Then I shan't insist." Caroline rose and crossed the room to the walnut lowboy with the trumpet legs. She returned with a small velvet box, and together the girls bent their heads over the contents.

"Oooh . . . loot!" exclaimed Bethia hopefully.

It was a colorful collection: beads, pins, bracelets, and brooches—a tangled collection of cheap jewelry, but also boasting a few valuable pieces. One, a genuine pearl set in real gold, had for years been passed along to the eldest girl in the family. It had doubtless come in on one of the great clipper ships of a bygone trade with the West Indies.

"Remember this?" Caroline placed the pin against her neck. "Grandma always wore it on special occasions. She said it was an heirloom."

"I couldn't take that!" declared Bethia. "It would be scree-religious."

"You mean sacrilegious!"

"Mmm."

Caroline continued lifting pieces from the case, finally holding a red stone up before the lamplight.

"I believe this is a genuine ruby. You can have it. Are you of a mind to sell it?"

"I must!"

"But dear, someday you will want something that was Grandma's. If you sell it, some stranger will have Grandma's keepsake. Do you really need the money that badly?"

"Some things come before heirlooms—before anything." Bethia clamped her jaw tighter than ever.

"All right, all right, if it is that important. I'll tell you what—I'll keep this for you one week, to give you time to think."

Bethia was already thinking. "What do you s'pose I can get for it?"

"Maybe ten dollars, maybe more. I really don't know."

Bethia's eyes were shining like two stars. She hugged Caroline and, in so doing, felt the sharp outline of the secret pendant around her sister's neck.

Realizing that her own secret was about to be discovered, Caroline spoke hastily. "It's just a bluebird," she explained. But Bethia would have none of the deception. "May I see it? Where did you get it?"

"Yes, you may see it and no, you needn't know where it came from."

"It's not Grandma's—and why are you blushing?"

"I am not blushing!"

"Maybe it's a promise thing!"

"Of course not. Who would give me a promise thing!"

"I know who would give you a promise thing!"

Caroline snatched the pendant from Bethia's hands and tried to look stern.

"Back to bed with you, and remember—one week!"

Morning dawned bleak and dark—not the customary overhang of ocean clouds—and it continued to grow darker by the hour. Finished with the morning milking, Uncle Hank stood at the windows while Caroline prepared breakfast.

"I don't like the looks of this one," he was saying. "A real Nor'easter."

Caroline placed a platter on the table, the fried pork still sizzling, and went about scrambling eggs. Bethia was packing lunch pails, and Nabby was moving systematically from the stove to the table, supplying thick slices of toast and a bowl of steaming applesauce. Joshua came in from the barn with his usual healthy appetite. Matthew, who had been reluctant to vacate all of his dairy responsibilities, came in after storing the huge milk cans.

"Wear your rain clothes, children. If it's too wild, I'll send Hank for you when school is out. Can't be having sickness this time of year!"

It took all day for the clouds to pack in. By afternoon the sky had turned a strange yellow and the winds had increased. The children were able to return home before the rains descended.

Matthew arrived home wet and cold, but went immediately to the task of getting farm implements under cover. The cows grew restless as Hank hammered loose boards. By evening the winds were blowing hard enough to dislodge shingles and branches. Even the flames in the lamp chimneys were dancing, and the rains were pelting down in earnest.

"Come, we will have prayer," said Nabby. "We'll clean up later." She led the way to the sitting room.

"May I light a fire?" asked Bethia, already placing logs on the firedogs.

"Yes, do, and then sit down. I'm tired!" Nabby settled herself in one of the five-backed maples with the rolled arms and sighed heavily.

The children gathered in close, as though to bolster and absorb courage from their indomitable mother. A sudden blast of wind shook the house strongly enough to make them all wonder if the place would continue to stand. Bethia's eyes were wide with fright.

"Do you s'pose Papa is out in this?" she asked, and then as quickly wished she had kept her fears to herself, for the words brought a definite chill into their midst.

"Let's just pray that he isn't," suggested Caroline.

Both Nabby and Matthew were unusually somber. The work of the day had its merits, but it was also taxing, and then there were the long evenings with memories of better days . . . and their shared longing for their protector husband and father.

"I am not sure I can read tonight. Someone else will have to." It was not like Nabby to vacate her proxy role.

Matthew took the old saffron-colored Bible from its usual place and opened it to the bookmark left there by Nabby the evening before. Then he shook his head.

"This is what Father read the day he left. I don't want to read it."

"The Lord is my Shepherd!" said Joshua, remembering.

Hank, who was usually hugging the stove, suddenly appeared in the doorway, an unlighted pipe in his hand. This was his family, the one over which he had promised to watch. Would they think him presumptuous? He could read reasonably well, thanks to his mother's insistence and patient encouragement—but the Bible? He moved into the room somewhat sheepishly. He had never intruded before, but there had never been the need.

"If you'll have me, I'll read," he offered.

Matthew was more than willing to hand him the heavy volume. Hank could feel all eyes upon him as he sat down and began to turn the pages. It would not do to read the passage Clinton had last read, so he carefully selected another. Hesitatingly at first, and then with confidence, he read. The wonderful sound of the older man's voice swept over them, filling the room with a sweetness and calm that had not been there since Clinton's departure.

The matchless words took root in lonely hearts, magic fingers over musical strings, the warmth of healing oil on wounded spirits: "The voice of the Lord is powerful . . . full of majesty . . . [it] breaks the cedars . . . divides the flame . . . shakes the wilderness . . . brings forth the young." And finally, "The Lord will give strength unto his people, and bless them with peace!"

The unfathomable power of the Word! The moment was beyond anything the family could have hoped for. Here was their beloved Uncle Hank reading the Bible! Caroline's eyes met Nabby's, both so blessed and so full of wonder that for a moment, neither could speak. Could his dear mother possibly know?

"That was beautiful, Hank. Thank you."

That was all that Nabby could say, but Bethia and Joshua took no pains to conceal their enthusiasm. They grinned, openly pleased. Even the sober Matthew was smiling.

Embarrassed, Hank arose, surprised at his action, but not without a little pride.

"You'd best get to bed, all of you. I will watch out the storm."

He little guessed how prophetic were his words, for he would indeed be the "watchman on the wall" for many days to come.

"Will you wake us if you need us?" asked Matthew.

"Yes."

So they left him, now returned to his place in the kitchen, but with the comforting knowledge that he would no longer be a stranger to their warm and loving family circle.

As tired as Caroline was, she could not sleep. She lay listening to the banging of the shutters and the cracking of the branches as they separated from the trees. It must have been midnight when the rushing sound of wind brought her upright. It came as the roar of a locomotive, making the entire house shudder. The dogs in the barn howled, and the sound of boards ripping loose came to her ears. She threw a wrap over her nightgown and hastened to the kitchen.

Nabby was already there, trying to light both a lamp and a lantern. Her hair was disheveled, and her hands were trembling. Hank, who had not retired, was hastening on with his coat. Joshua and Matthew were pulling on heavy boots.

"And Jessie about to calf! Come, Joshua!" Hank left, the door banging after him.

Nabby stirred up the fire and put a kettle on to boil. "They'll come in soaking!" she said wearily.

Outside, Hank was leaning into the wind, holding his lantern high and peering through the driving rain to see how much damage had been done. Joshua struggled behind him, staring into the black heavens. Thunder was rolling, and he could see the slant of the rain in the lightning flashes. The storm by now was directly overhead, and the rumblings were changing to sharp, crackling sounds. The winds were of hurricane velocity, raving and ranting in blustering fury.

With the next clap of thunder, Joshua heard the sound of wagon wheels. What idiot would be out in such a storm—and at such an hour?

Any horse would be maddened, he reasoned.

Another brilliant flash erupted, enough to reflect on a piece of metal in the road. Joshua froze. Curious at first, he walked into the wind. Then he broke into a run. A second flash had shown that the metallic thing was still lying in a large puddle. Could he be dreaming? Was that really a rifle butt? He reached into the pool and yanked the weapon from the water—and then he shrieked to the wild winds and to the heavens!

"God Almighty! You've sent me a gun!" Running his hands over the length of it, he laughed aloud. "Excalibur . . . you are mine!"

He danced over the ground, this time toward the house. The women would still be in the kitchen. He'd have to secrete his find in his own room so no one could take it from him. Safely in his room, he ripped one of Nabby's finest towels from the rack on the washstand and hastily wiped the gun down. In the dark he could only feel it, but his imagination was already fired. Papa would no longer have to depend on a rusty gun!

He wrapped it in another towel and placed it carefully in the back of his closet. Then he patted the rain from his face and scurried back down the stairs and out once again into the storm. Hank was out of sight, no doubt in the barn by now. Joshua found him holding the lantern high and staring at a gaping hole in the side of the barn. As he drew closer, Joshua could see that a door had been ripped off.

One cow stood just outside in a dumb stupor. Her belly was swollen, but it wasn't Jessie. Hank was pushing the dumb animal back to shelter.

"Where's Jessie?" Joshua shouted.

"She's taken off! You can help me find her."

Joshua broke for the doorway and crashed into Matthew, who was carrying a hammer and box of nails. The collision spilled the entire supply over the wooden floor.

"You should look where you're going!" said Matthew angrily. "Nothing's afire, you know!"

"But it's dark!" the excited Joshua defended himself.

"Well, calm down, or there'll be fire in your britches!"

"I've got to help Hank find Jessie." And Joshua was off, leaving his brother sputtering as he crawled over the floor, feeling for the nails.

"Do y'think we'll find her?" he asked Hank when he finally caught up with his uncle.

"Ay-uh, we'll find her—but I can't promise how she'll be."

The rain began to slacken. Now and then a double flash of lightning revealed the condition of the orchard. Everywhere, trees were toppled.

Hank went on sloshing through the mud, listening and looking. A soft bleat met his ears, and he turned in the direction of the sound. Huddled against a fallen trunk lay the missing cow, and beside her stood not one, but two staggering calves.

Joshua had never heard such oaths coming from his uncle's mouth. And to think the man had been reading the Bible only hours before! Ah, well, his uncle was now in God's own training school, and He would perfect without Joshua's help! Hank lifted one of the calves and started toward the barn.

"Can I heft the other?" Joshua yelled.

"Try!" came the labored command. "Jessie will follow you if she knows what you're doin'." He said more, but his voice was lost in the wind.

Joshua struggled to lift the calf. Fortunately, Hank had taken the heavier of the two, but even so, the effort took all the strength young Joshua could muster. The calf bawled, and Jessie struggled to her feet. Once Joshua fell, but he gamely arose and lifted the bewildered calf again. If it were not so dark, and if the rain would quit, he might be able to see the dips. But he could not be angry with the storm. It had brought him the best gift he had ever received!

Up ahead, Uncle Hank called encouragement and direction. "You still with me?"

"Coming!" answered Joshua bravely.

Reaching the barn, they could see Matthew busy with a hammer. They joined him, drenched, muddy, and breathing hard.

"Get more rockweed down in the end stall," ordered Hank. "And, Matthew, get towels and blankets."

Jessie was not too enthused about returning to the treacherous barn, but after much pushing and shoving they were able to get her to the dry stall. The women arrived with towels and blankets, and Hank went to work wiping the animals dry and covering them. Jessie had collapsed on the litter and was looking poorly. Already her nose was hot.

"It'll be touch and go with her, I can tell. Just hope she doesn't get pneumonia." Hank spoke more to himself than to those around him.

Bethia crept close to the calves, her eyes as large and wondering as theirs. She touched the soft hides.

"Aren't they beautiful? Aren't they a miracle?" she asked.

"Wouldn't Father love to see them?" added Caroline.

Outside the rain had stopped, but no one wanted to leave. Joshua walked over to where Bethia was standing and whispered in her ear.

"If you think this is a miracle, just wait 'til you see what I found!"

8

B̲URNSIDE CONTINUED ON. With a victory behind him, he crossed to the mainland and proceeded to take Elizabeth City. The battle was much the same as at Roanoke Island, the worst of the encounter being with the miserable weather. By this time, few seemed to give heed to the drenching torrents. They had all begun to accept the weather's tirades, marching through mud in daylight and sleeping with rivers running under them at night. They muscled the limbers and the gun carriages through hub-deep quagmires and daily sought bark under the fallen trees for kindling. It was their only way to heat enough coffee to wash down the inevitable hardtack and enough to silence the grumblings of empty stomachs.

Big guns were being brought up constantly. Cavalry often passed the lowly foot soldiers; theirs was the line-breaking task. The riders were the elite of the army, by far the best dressed and equipped. At the onset of the war, the Union cavalry had played a poor second to the skilled Confederates, but with encounters increasing, they were beginning to hold their own. The Confederate Jeb Stuart would soon find his equal in the Sheridans and the Custers of the North.

One morning as Clinton and Drake watched a cavalry unit pass by, they observed a man using abusive language and kicking his horse. Unknown to the ingrate, a commanding officer was also watching, a silent, icy fury on his face. He moved upon the scene quickly and, after a volatile upbraiding, ordered the man's punishment. He was to be spread-eagled and bound to a gun carriage for the day, there to serve as a warning to any would-be miscreant with the audacity to harm a horse. The common horse would be recognized as no less a soldier than the man who rode him, and he would suffer no indignities!

As time went on, a certain pattern seemed to be developing. Because of the Union's superior numbers, they seemed always on the offensive—and the practice seemed always to swell their casualty numbers. New Bern, North Carolina, would now be Clinton's offensive. One could grow used to the repetitious fighting. Clinton and Drake had not only adapted, but had hardened considerably. Up ahead they could see the results of the artillery bombardment. Smoke was ascending from the city in massive, billowing clouds. What the ongoing Union forces had not set ablaze, the retreating Confederates finished up. The city was in flames from the orders of both commanders.

Clinton wondered what it would be like to be on the losing side, to taste the defeat that the men in the city had experienced. So far, it had all been victory for his regiment. Victory did have a sweet side—and one in which the victorious foot soldier could share, for after days of sleeping in the rain and subsisting on a frugal diet, the victors could move hastily upon the abandoned enemy quarters and fall heir to unlimited spoils: tents, blankets, and food. All these were appreciated, but the aftermath of a battle always had a debilitating effect on Clinton's gentle spirit. Not only was the gory sight of dead horses and men a test, but the sudden quiet, the drastic change of pace and purpose, drove many to erratic behavior. The captured city often became the scene of Mardi Gras revelry. Drunkenness, brawling, and looting were the order of the day, and the officers were as much a party to the insanity as the others.

Clinton's regiment proceeded to a campsite to set up tents, and then on to New Bern to view the destruction. They were staggered by the scene. Buildings lay in ruins, many with gaping holes; it was a ghost city in many sectors.

Except for the frequent dress parades in honor of visiting generals, army life settled down to a familiar routine, and when Clinton was assigned to city provost duty, he welcomed the diversion. Provost headquarters occupied two houses on Broad Street in a pleasant part of town with a clear view of the Neuse River. Few of the city's inhabitants had left when the artillery bombardment had started. Rather than abandon their ancestral homes, most had remained. A number of offices and stores had remained operable, one being a newspaper office which aroused Clinton's interest. He would investigate further when the opportunity arrived.

A group of prostitutes had come down from Baltimore under the guise of female nurses, a Union captain having arranged their passage to satisfy his own hedonistic appetite. He had settled them in a large, three-storied house, made well enough to endure through many generations. It had remained untouched from the bombardment, standing like a grim sentinel guarding the ramparts of a bastille and looking down upon the scattered and devastated remaining buildings of the peasantry.

Clinton's assignment took him past the place daily. His soldier companions were an agreeable lot, though not necessarily of his own choosing. There was Leonard, a surveyor, whose good humor was always a boost; Dudley, a middle-class tanner's son and something of a lady's man; and young Danny, an especially devout Catholic lad.

A well-respected orderly sergeant marched them regularly to their respective districts. It was always appreciated to have a well-posted military man handling the orders.

The four never looked more dapper, for the dress rules required that they wear no slouchy clothing. All uniforms were to fit well to the body, shoes black and shining, guns polished and in the best working order, and each man in possession of forty rounds of cartridges. Leonard and Danny were of average height, so the contrast with the other two was distinctly marked. Dudley was tall and lanky, shifty, but at least agreeable.

Their detail did not go unnoticed, for Emma Bailey came often onto the street at night, making it a habit to be at the curb when the four men passed.

Clinton had an opportunity to study her features and decided that she might well have been a beauty in her youth. Now she wore the hard expression of a coarse streetwalker. One night she approached them, a twisted smile on her lips.

"Nice evenin', soldiers," she drawled.

"Yes, ma'am," answered the eager Dudley.

"Out for a little recreation?" she queried.

"On duty, ma'am," answered Clinton, quick to discern the direction of the conversation.

She walked close to the group, brushing against Clinton. Her cheap perfume was almost nauseating.

"A man the likes of you shouldn't have no trouble finding entertainment."

"Entertainment isn't on our agenda, ma'am," said Clinton, still studying her and wondering if there were any of the real woman left—anything of the young girl she might have been before entering her present style of living.

Her expression changed. She was not in the habit of being repulsed.

"Mighty selective, ahn't we!" she said, bristling with resentment. Then she walked slowly, swaggeringly, toward the house, glancing over a bare shoulder and giving Clinton half a smile.

"Fireations!" exclaimed Daniel. "That one o' them women?"

"Afraid so, Danny boy! But you can blame that flatheaded captain for bringing them here."

"He ain't much of a leader," observed Danny. Then, still curious, he asked, "Don't they have no family?"

"Guess they've chosen not to, though word is around that Emma has three young ones," Clinton replied.

"Seems there's more respectable ways of feedin' the young," observed Leonard.

"I'm afraid she has chosen the easiest," mused Clinton, at the same time thinking of his own capable Nabby with renewed appreciation. He was certain that Dudley would succumb to Emma's persistent invitations, and he wished he could head him off. Dudley had been married for less than a year, but seemed to take his vows lightly.

DUDLEY, DANIEL, and Leonard had stopped at a bakery one April evening, while Clinton walked slowly on toward the river. The smell of the water brought back memories. At home, the plants would be stirring, pressing up toward a warming sun, thirsty for the New England spring rains. Pigeons and martins would be building nests, and geese would be flooding the marshes. Hank would be turning the soil and laying it in ridges, high and sharp and ready for early cabbages. The cows would be stirring and restless, many heavy with calf. Cowslips would be close to blooming, their firefly blossoms waving above oversized leaves and roots stretching toward the brooks. Clinton could almost see the white trillium orchid blooms and feel the damp wooded places.

"Thinkin' of home, ahn't you, soldier?"

The voice broke into his thoughts, sharp in the night's stillness. There was enough moonlight that he could make out Emma's powdered face. Clinton's first impulse was to move on, but something stopped him.

"Home is a good place," he answered thoughtfully.

"Foah some folk," came the aspersion, tinged with bitterness.

Without facing her, Clinton continued. "Can't help thinking, for most folk—mothers, fathers, sometimes sisters and brothers."

Emma looked out toward the river and waited.

"You must have a family wondering where you are," he said.

"They disowned me yeahs ago."

"They might disown, but the bloodlines never stop flowing!"

"That is simple to say."

"Life—real life—is simple. It's as simple as breathing, when the rules are kept."

"Ah've not found it so. Some backgrounds ah meanah than othas. Ah nevah liked mine."

"But sometimes you think about Baltimore, and your family?"

"How'd you know Ah come from Baltimore?"

"Common talk around camp!"

Emma smiled, touched her hair, and pressed her neckline lower. "That's encouragin'. Tell me moah."

"There are other ways to earn money."

"But not so easy—and not so pleasurable as takin' Yankee money!"

"Keep telling yourself that, and in a few more years you will think differently."

Danny and Leonard were approaching, and it seemed the conversation would come to an end, but Emma had more to say.

"The oldah one looks at me, but Ah'd settle foah the young one."

Clinton wished he had followed his first inclination to ignore the woman. He felt the anger rising under his stiff collar.

"I'd suggest you leave the young one alone," he said.

"And Ah would suggest you keep to yoah business, and Ah will keep to mine! The captain sees to it that Ah am protected."

"The captain is egotistical and utterly unscrupulous!"

"Granted. But he will make it hot foah anyone intafeahin' with mah style!"

By then Dudley had come upon them and recognized Emma.

"You are mighty well dressed up tonight," he said, eyeing the red dress and matching headdress of feathers.

"And itchin' to be walked about!"

Dudley drew her arm through his, and with a debonair gesture led Emma away from the others.

"When General Foster learns about this, there'll be

fireworks—mark my words," said Clinton. "Everyone knows the house is a front for spies."

The situation was explosive, and the three that were left knew that the evening's confrontation would not be the end.

Several nights later, after returning to provost headquarters, the men were sitting around trying to pass the time by playing cards and writing letters. Several had found partners for games of checkers; others sat with opened Bibles. Clinton had started a letter and was busy counting the money he would send to Nabby.

A strange silence fell upon the room. Clinton looked up to see two of his companions at the window, eyes focused on a disturbance in the street below.

"It's the general! What's he doing here?"

Clinton joined the men at the window. Down in the street, he could see his commander astride a smart-looking horse. He was leaning toward the horse's neck with arms folded and was talking to his sergeant. General Foster was a handsome man. You couldn't mistake him—fair, clean looking, an aristocrat, attractive, and personable. He was surrounded by a company of cavalry. There was the sound of orders being issued—sharp, like the crack of a rifle. The door to the room flew open suddenly and an officer walked in, bringing the men to attention.

"There has been a shooting," he stated brusquely. "We believe it came from the big house near the river. Report immediately to the adjutant below!"

Tables cleared instantly, and coats, caps, and belts were donned.

The stairs to the street groaned and creaked under the small army that descended. They poured out onto the street and formed lines. An adjutant stalked up and down before addressing them, then spoke curtly.

"There are things going on here that should not have been allowed. General Foster has given orders to tear that house down. Stack arms and get to it!"

They broke lines and swarmed toward the house.

"Who was shot?" asked Leonard, coming alongside Clinton.

"Don't know!"

As they moved toward the house, they could see that a crowd had gathered. Two soldiers in Union blue lay stretched out on the ground.

"Merciful God! It's the kid!"

Clinton broke into a run. One look at the fallen soldier was enough. He could see that Danny was dead. Who could have perpetrated such a crime?

Leonard was already questioning people.

"Shots came from up there!" said one of the crowd, an indignant citizen of the town. He pointed to an upstairs window.

"Clear the house! Everyone out!" came the command.

"Did one of the women do this?" asked Leonard.

"Women? No woman could shoot that good!"

Dudley had been shot in the leg and was grimacing with pain. The big front door swung open and crashed against the clapboards, calling attention to a number of women who were being roughly ushered out.

Clinton found the back stairs and climbed them two at a time. He could hear children crying, so he opened a door. Standing before him was Emma Bailey, her heavily powdered face streaked with tears. Three small children clung in terror to her black lace dress, while she hastily packed an enormous trunk.

"Where are you going?" demanded Clinton.

"Ah didn't do any shootin'! Ah really didn't!" she avowed.

"Who did?" he pressured.

"Some of the girls had Confederate guests, lots of 'em. They wanted to make a name foah themselves, Ah reckon. That's all Ah know!"

"I want their names!"

" 'Tweren't any of mah business. You'd have to question Lily."

"You are ordered out. Did you know that?"

"Yessuh, and Ah am packin'."

"Where will you go?"

"Don't know."

"Where are the others going?"

"They got families."

"So do you. In Baltimore."

"They'd nevah take us in."

"You don't know that!"

"Ah've told you befoah, they don't want me."

"Emma, look at me."

Emma turned to face him, a strange mixture of pride and misery on her face.

"They don't want me, and Ah'm not shooah Ah wants them!"

Clinton felt the letter against his heart—the money he was to send home to Nabby. Would she understand? Would she approve? Knowing Nabby as he did, he was certain she would. Once in a person's lifetime comes an opportunity to make a right decision, and all some people needed was a shove in the right direction. He reached into his coat and drew out the envelope, then pressed it into Emma's hands.

The woman looked surprised, and she struggled to speak.

"Don't say anything. Go home, Emma, and do something for your people. They'll be needing nurses, teachers, and mothers!"

"You a preacher?"

"Heavens, no. What makes you think God expects only preachers to be accountable?"

"Ah ain't nevah seen the likes of you!"

"Go quickly. It should be enough to get you to Baltimore. And may God go with you! Now, go! I'll get your trunk to the street."

Emma swept the smallest child into her arms and walked to the top of the stairs. She stood there looking at Clinton with eyes full of tears and with something new; then she descended to the lower floor.

Clinton hailed two soldiers and ordered them to carry the trunk down, then he followed. He met Leonard on the lawn.

"They have arrested the owner and are questioning her. They think they have the gunman—but the woman! She's as defiant as a cornered tiger. They found two rifles in the house!"

Someone began ripping off the front porch. Others were swarming over the place with axes and hammers and heavy rope wrapped around their shoulders. Clinton could see the carriages as one by one they began to take their leave. Emma leaned from the window of one and smiled, her lips clearly saying "thank you," and then she was gone. Somehow Clinton knew that she would go home.

With the building completely razed, he returned to the provost headquarters. Dudley came, too, but he remained the most unpopular of men. The kid had been the company favorite, and forgiveness would be a long time coming. Dudley would pay dearly for his lapse of responsibility.

Although both Clinton and the town's citizenry were glad that the house was gone, there was a shared, lingering sorrow that so fine an old house had come to such an ignominious end. It was weeks before the incident faded into a categorical history—best to be forgotten.

The city's printing office had been confiscated, but the former editor, a Mr. Levy, had been allowed to keep his position. On applying for work, Clinton found the little man a most considerate person. He offered Clinton employment until his regiment moved on.

Skirmishes continued, but action seemed reduced to sentinel and provost duty. Casualties were brought in sporadically, but most deaths were from disease and months of exposure. Fever and dysentery had spread through the ranks, and the sound of taps and rolling drums were heard as often in camp as on the battlefield. Clinton had withstood the sight of men dying from battle wounds, but now the sound of the bugle and the haunting rolling of drums had a miserable effect upon him. It seemed as though hundreds must be dying, and from such a worthless cause.

Further depressing was news of the Union's defeat at Shiloh. Frequently rumors of victory were followed by contradictory news releases, all evidences of poor communications and adding to the demoralizing of spirits. After weeks at provost headquarters, Clinton was glad to return to his old campground and his own tent.

9

S PRING MOVED ON, and still there was not the action the men had anticipated. They grew increasingly restless. Clinton had time—too much time—to think about Hank doing the work by himself. The desire to be there with him became a tortuous thing to live with. Though the absence of action was intolerable, still it had some merit, for he was fast becoming an expert marksman, toughening to the elements and learning to grow hard to the general miseries of war. He had been promoted to sergeant and was enjoying a healthy respect from his comrades in arms.

When orders came to strike tents, he was ready. Three months of inactivity were enough. An expedition would be going upriver to test Confederate strength at Kinston.

Even with Confederate guns contesting their advance, neither Clinton nor Drake was sorry to be boarding a small propeller. The lead ships suffered some casualties, but Stringham's bold tactic of firing while moving was serving the Union well. Clinton's ship moved along unscathed.

In the distance they could see their objective. Black smoke billowed heavenward, just as they had seen it at New Bern. With Confederate guns still resisting, they disembarked at the outskirts of Kinston. Union artillery moved up, and the duel intensified. The sight of big cannon always bolstered the men's morale; nevertheless, they moved ahead with caution.

It seemed that the Confederates were enjoying the advantages of woodland cover and pouring it on to the advancing Union troops, sometimes fighting Indian fashion, riding and firing into the Federals and then racing back to their own lines to mobilize repeatedly. Balls hummed and buzzed so close to Clinton's ears that he could feel the air split, and he knew this would not be an easy victory. Their wing was definitely getting the worst of it, and men were going down all around him. Still, the order was issued to advance! It was then that the thing Clinton feared most happened. Drake caught a barrage of fire and went down, still firing, unwilling to yield his place in the line. With eyes still focused ahead, Clinton reached for his friend.

"No—go on—go!" Drake gasped. "Don't stop." He swung an arm forward to give emphasis to his words.

"No chance, man! You are coming with me." Clinton dragged his friend to cover, but not before a flying ball had caught him in the arm. It was a numbing feeling at first, and then searing. He ground his teeth and groaned. For one agonizing moment, Clinton was forced to take account of his strength—something he had never before had to do.

General Foster had underestimated the Confederate numbers and their courage, and now the command came to fall back—the enemy was already bayoneting through the lines. Clinton stopped to stare helplessly as his own youthful bugler took a ball in the face. The painful decision—to go to his aid or stay with Drake—split his loyalties, but he had no time to ponder.

"You've got arms! Get me around the neck!" he ordered Drake. Drake did as he was told, and Clinton began to move from tree to tree, now obliged to use his Colt revolver. Drake was bleeding profusely, saturating Clinton's clothing. Clinton could feel Drake's grasp weakening until he was nearly carrying the man's dead weight.

A rumbling sound met his ears—the best sound he had ever heard in his life! Union artillery was moving up, and from the height of the muzzles when they stopped to fire, he knew the high trajectory meant the Rebs would soon be tasting cannonball. He was not so confused that he couldn't mumble a prayer of thanksgiving. The enemy began to retreat, and mule-drawn ambulance wagons began picking up the wounded and dead.

Two men, bleeding themselves, helped Clinton and Drake aboard a wagon. Once on the bouncing vehicle and away from the immediate scene of battle, Clinton took time to examine Drake's wounds. He was sure his friend had been hit in the leg, but blood had soaked his shirt as well. There had to be another wound. He discovered a bloody hole in Drake's side and pressed his own fist in to staunch the flow of blood. All the while, the wagon rattled over the rough terrain, coming close to spilling its human cargo.

Clinton began to pray, not as he was used to praying, with the slow, thoughtful placing of words, the selection of proper diction when approaching that great divine throne—but with the agony of a Peter about to drown! God, save my friend!

Drake's eyes were glassy, and he was as gray as the woodash Nabby used for making soap. Would they never get to a medical tent? After what seemed like hours, the sound of gun and cannon grew distant, like the storms at home as they moved off into limbo.

Abruptly the wagon stopped.

"Help him!" Clinton called to an orderly.

A doctor stood at the door of a large tent, overwhelmed with the number on the wagon ambulance. Someone opened Drake's shirt and then examined his leg.

"Got two here. Get him to surgery immediately!" he barked.

Clinton fell to the task, wincing noticeably as he lifted Drake.

"You wounded, too?" the doctor asked.

"My arm."

An assistant rolled up Clinton's sleeve and shook his head. "You can walk?"

"Yes, sir."

"Then get moving—hospital tent further down. We can only take the worst here."

Drake was already on the table, and Clinton stood looking after him. Should he leave? Could he? It wouldn't be the same without Drake—without him walking, talking, jesting beside him. He felt utterly abandoned, a man on an island—and worse, the miserable arm was growing more painful by the minute. An orderly came by and observed the blood down Clinton's arm.

"I'll put on a tourniquet."

Glad for the delay, Clinton kept his eyes riveted on the narrow gap of the operating tent door. He could see that the doctors were already at work.

"Soft lead! You are shattered!"

"Is my friend going to make it? Drake, in there . . . is he going to live?"

The bandage was on, and still Clinton had no answer. He refused to move.

"Soldier, if you don't get moving to where you can get this arm fixed, your friend Drake won't have you for a friend!"

Clinton stayed only long enough to answer the orderly. "I'll go, but take care of that man in there, you hear?"

"We'll do our best."

Clinton moved away reluctantly. It had only been minutes since he had entered the field hospital, but already the ground was littered with wounded. He was certain that many were beyond human help, and more were arriving. How could the general have so miscalculated? Poor communications had to be the answer, for Foster was one of the best.

He began to run, and meeting up with more wagons, boarded one as it headed toward the river. A propeller was waiting there, and men hobbled aboard and huddled together below deck. With rebel guns firing, the ship moved along. Soon they were beyond danger and listening to the rhythmic sonance of creaking timbers. In New Bern they were taken immediately to the hospital.

Doctors were working around the clock as each ship brought in new casualties. Clinton's surgery seemed long, but it was not so.

Coming out of the anesthesia, he felt as though a ton weight had been placed on his arm. It pulsed and burned through the day and on through the night. A day passed, and the pain and the heat intensified. Another day, and still no relief. The doctors were clearly concerned. Clinton's temperature was up, and he shivered with cold.

The hordes of wounded became so overwhelming that on the fourth day Clinton was moved to his own cramped tent to make room for the others. He lay there for what seemed an eternity, moving in and out of consciousness. He was thirsty and painfully cold, and no one heard his cries for water. He was certain he would die alone, and he prayed that someone would stop by long enough to take a message home to his family.

God in His mercy answered. A soldier stopped by and took the time to throw Clinton's greatcoat over him and lift a mug of water to his parched lips. Then the man was gone to minister to others.

Within an hour Clinton had slipped again into unconsciousness and then awakened to stare again at the pointed canvas roof. Some kind soul had exchanged the coat for a blanket. The feeling of the soft texture sped his thoughts toward home. The blanket must have been sent by a women's group. Kind, caring, devoted women. Then the roof was spinning again, and he was caught in the blurred maelstrom of relief. Where was Drake? He dreamed he saw his friend still on the table. He hovered there, asking the surgeons to hurry, to save Drake's life, but they seemed to work beyond hearing.

During the night, someone lifted him and carried him back to the hospital. When he regained consciousness, he was staring at a high wooden ceiling, and men were stretched out on either side as far as he could see. He was weak and he was hot, and the pain was still with him. Once his own voice brought him to reality. He had been calling Drake.

"Drake. Where is he?"

"Who you callin', soldier?" asked the stranger on his right.

"Drake. Where is he?"

"Don't know no Drake."

Then darkness, roaring sounds, voices buzzing around his head like the threatening sound of minié-balls, and fire and flames everywhere. More days and more hours, and someone was giving him quinine and he was able to swallow. This treatment went on for a long time, until the very smell of the bitter Peruvian bark made him vomit. Diarrhea took over and, though conscious, Clinton remained in a lethargic, weakened condition, barely able to recognize the doctors.

"Transfer this man to Readville when he is able to travel!" was the clipped order.

Readville! That was almost home. Was it possible he was going to live? See his loved ones before he died? No! He would not die! The very thought of home had a therapeutic influence on him, sparking new strength and the will to survive. Home . . . up the dirt road and under the elm, white fences and gray stone walls, clover fields and flying chickens, Dandy trotting and Nabby driving.

Clinton awoke to his own sobs. The man in the next bed was looking at him.

"Thought you'd never come full circle," he said.

"What's going on?" Misty webs began clearing.

"You've been in and out."

"Where are we?"

"New Bern."

Clinton heaved a sigh. He must have dreamed that he was to go to Readville.

"You're goin' home, soldier."

"Where'd you get that notion?"

"The doctors signed you out. They don't keep men whose shootin' arm is gone."

Alarmed, Clinton looked at his right arm. Thank God it was still there. He shivered, remembering the times he had seen amputated limbs piled high behind the surgical tents. Indeed he could thank God! Looking down the long corridor of men in beds, he could see that he was one of the favored. He grew quiet, wondering at it all.

"You still with us?" asked his companion.

"Ay-uh. Still here. What happened at Kinston?"

"Bad breakthrough. Cost us plenty. Foster closed the lines, though. Got the upper hand, took prisoners. Cannon, too, and the usual."

"What about other battles?"

"McClellan did all right at Fair Oaks. Chased the Rebs back to Richmond."

"Lee won't settle for that!"

"Got that right! Johnston's one thing; Lee is another. Right now all hell is breaking loose at Malvern Hill."

"How we ever going to beat that man Lee?"

The man laughed. "If I knew that, I wouldn't be a corporal!"

A week passed, and Clinton was able to leave his bed. The arm was still useless, the bone fragmented. The food was better than it had been on the field, but his appetite remained poor. He caught sight of himself in a mirror one day and shook his head. His clothes hung on him, giving him the appearance of a clown. He must have lost at least twenty pounds. He made no attempt to write, because he didn't want his family to know that he was in a hospital.

Truthfully, his thoughts were not with the family. He wanted only to find his friend. On the first opportunity to leave the hospital confines, he made his way into town and went directly to the records department. Surely there would be information there, but the answer was always the same. No record of Drake Singleton. It was not a new thing, for many were unaccounted for. Was Drake to remain one of them? The persistent thought robbed Clinton of the joy he should have felt at the prospect of going home. He had not dreamed he could miss anyone the way he missed his comrade. If only he could have some word to take to Drake's mother.

Time became interminable before he could get his papers, and the men in charge of the rosters seemed unwilling to set sail until there was a full quota. The days moved on through July and August. Clinton thought often of the farm. This would be a real test for Hank. He'd be harvesting by himself.

It was not until the end of the month that they finally weighed anchor. Just as they were leaving, news reached the ship that General Lee, growing indignant at the Union victories, was at work taking the war out of Virginia and the wind out of the Union sails. He had sent Longstreet to strike at Pope's left flank, and the rout proved disastrous for the proud Pope, ending in his replacement by the slow-moving McClellan. The possibility loomed stronger than ever that the war would be fought to the last man.

The bow turned north with its cargo of sick and wounded. Hatteras was in its usual ugly mood, the seas choppy and the men seasick, but under strong propellers they were soon beyond the laboring seas. The sun suddenly appeared with a fresh white brilliance. Wisps of cloud spread across the sky. Gulls and fishing boats joined them, and the gray of hospital walls and the cries of the dying faded away. The food was the best that the men had seen in months, and their appetites picked up.

The smell of the sea sent waves of nostalgia over Clinton. The prospect of returning to all that he held dear overwhelmed him, and thoughts crowded in of the wonderful days that awaited him, walking in his own fields, feeling the arms of his wife and children, gathering together to read the Bible and the great books of the masters. He thought of Scott and his inspired observation: "Lives there a man with soul so dead, who never to himself hath said, 'This is my own, my native land'? "

Where had the war gone? The scenes he had left so long ago now came into view again, to be wondered at and appreciated anew.

10

WITH THE CALVES SAFELY housed and the storm over, Hank and Nabby discussed plans for the night.

"I will stay here until it's light. The rest of you may as well go to bed," said Hank, stacking a pile of hay for a pillow. "There'll be plenty to do in the morning."

With unquestioning obedience, the family went back to the kitchen. The kettle Nabby had placed on the stove was whistling smartly, the sound sending forth a promise of a drink and drawing them together to share in the rare pleasure of hot coffee.

For some strange reason, Joshua was unusually anxious to get back to his room.

"What's bothering you, Josh?" asked Bethia.

"Nothing. Maybe I'm tired!"

Soon they were tripping up the stairway, leaving Caroline to prepare a tray for Hank and Nabby to hang clothes to dry.

Joshua quickly lit the lamp, then went immediately for the closet. He returned with a bundle and quickly removed the wrappings, a look of supreme delight on his face. It was his greatest moment!

Bethia's mouth dropped open. "That's not the Henry. What—? Where—?"

"I think it came right out of heaven!" exulted Joshua.

"Tell me the truth, Joshua!"

"It did!"

"Joshua William Haddon!"

"It fell off a wagon."

"Whose wagon?"

"I don't know. It was flying up the road, and the thunder and lightning were wild! I didn't see the driver. Must have been addle-brained to have a horse out in that kind of weather. But look at her, Bethia! Isn't she a beauty?"

They settled down together on the floor, the lamp dimming before the early sunrise. Bethia reached a timid hand to touch the black walnut stock.

"It says here C.S.L." Beneath the block she noticed more letters. "James Warner, Springfield, Mass. Warners. Patent. Do you s'pose that's the owner's name?"

" 'Course not! That's the man who made it!"

"Well, it isn't rusty, and it is beautiful!"

"And we'll keep it hidden until we can get it to Papa!"

"If someone has lost it, won't we hear soon?"

"Won't do 'em any good. I found it, and it's mine!"

Bethia wanted desperately to agree with her brother, but if someone were to look for the weapon . . . what would their father say?

"Papa'd rather have us honest, Josh."

Joshua grew angry. "Well, I'd rather have Papa alive," he asserted.

The sky was growing lighter, and Bethia left Joshua and returned to her own room. For a short time she dreamed of calves and storms and shiny guns and then awoke to the sound of voices in the kitchen. Quickly she dressed and went downstairs.

"If I could leave off with school today, I could really get some great copy for Hyram," Matthew was saying. "The town must be devastated."

"I think you may," answered Nabby, knowing how deeply he coveted peer status and appreciation.

Joshua, entering the kitchen, thought it an appropriate time to ask for the same privilege. "If I stayed home, I could help Uncle Hank," he said hopefully.

"No, indeed, young man. One truant is enough. You will go to school."

JESSIE DID CONTRACT PNEUMONIA. She lay on the litter breathing heavily while Hank kept a vigil, stealing short naps and chafing under the delay to work in the fields. Allen showed up with a crudely made derrick and offered to help in righting the fallen trees. That they would survive was questionable, but from experience in times past, Hank knew well how to go about replanting.

Bethia willingly spelled Hank, watching over the sick cow and brooding over the calves. Like Clinton, she was in the habit of resorting to her own ingenuity, so she brought a bucket of milk to them. At first they stood dumb to all of her entreaties; then, impulsively, Bethia dunked her fingers into the rich, warm milk and poked them into a calf's mouth. He sucked so vigorously that her fingers hurt. Slowly she lowered her hand to the milk. The calf sucked and reared back, but the nourishment awakened ravenous desire, and he pressed for more. Patiently Bethia repeated the procedure. In a short time she had both calves drinking greedily from the pail.

"Well—that is an accomplishment, Bethia," exclaimed Hank, pleased to have such an able assistant.

However, the optimism was short-lived. Jessie grew worse, struggled for a week, and finally died. Of course the failure spawned thoughts of defeat for most of the family. Secretly they thought that if Clinton had been there, Jessie might have lived.

They had little time, however, to dwell on their failures. The work in the fields demanded many hands, and each one had to do his part. Fortunately most of the apple crop had been picked, and it appeared that the trees would take root again. There was always the marketing, the grinding of grains, the fattening of hogs, and the steady demands of the dairy.

Though the workload was heavy upon Hank's shoulders, he never complained. Rising while it was still dark, he labored on, ever faithful, ever trustworthy.

Clinton had been gone a year now, and the days of flag-waving and spirited band music had turned into days of hardship, weeping, and mourning. Trains arrived often with their grim cargo, narrow caskets housing the dead. The town gentry were always honored and eulogized in the pulpit; the simple folk were left to walk in silence to the cemeteries, taking with them the comfort of God's assurance that at least to Him, the death of His saints was precious. Casualty lists were printed daily in the newspaper, giving Matthew the first opportunity to scrutinize the roster. He well knew that as the elder son, it would be he who would have to break the news if his father's name appeared on the list. The thought kept him in a morbid, expectant mood. He was also awaiting reply from his application to West Point. Caroline watched him closely, more as a mother than a sister, for she knew he could be easily discouraged. Her own life had become dull and uneventful, and for a girl beginning to blossom and to know it, the situation was demoralizing.

Thad Paxton had not come home for the summer, and she had learned from his mother that he had gone to the Adirondacks with a classmate. His neglect stung her deeply, and she placed the bluebird pendant back in the small jewelry case along with other things of the past. She had abandoned hope of seeing him now that a new semester had begun, but one day, just as she was emerging from the barn with her pails of milk, there he was. He walked toward her, smiling as he came. Gone was the boy she remembered. In his place stood a man much older, more sophisticated. He wore a short-clipped moustache and sideburns.

"Thad?" she said with uncertainty. Why had he not written? She waited, lips parted, ready to speak.

Then his arms were around her and his lips on her own. He held her back to look at her, pleased with what he saw.

"Don't ask me. I know what you are thinking. I know I didn't write—I've always been that way. And the work—you could never guess."

Caroline thought the excuses lame, but just to see him again, the maturity, the handsome face! He spoke with a light air—confidence bordering on arrogance. But even with that, the fact was that he had come to see her now. In spite of the loneliness of the past months, she was flattered that he had come.

"I've liked going to Harvard, but I'm having second thoughts about continuing. Friends leaving, and me staying with the books. . . ."

Caroline didn't hear what he was trying to say. "I was sure you had changed your mind . . . forgotten."

"Forgotten you?"

"But there must have been girls—pretty Boston debutantes. I read about them."

"I haven't met any. Boston women aren't pretty; they're as plain as sourdough!" Then they were laughing together, just as they always had.

"But you do socialize—dance, perhaps?"

"Of course. That is expected."

"Come. We'll get some tea." Caroline went toward the house.

Hank had emerged from the barn with a box of squash. "Waal, hello, young feller. Back to visit the homefolk?"

"And the neighbors. Where is everyone?"

"Out in the fields—'cept Carrie, but I see you have found her."

They talked of crops and war and weather, and then Hank left in the wagon.

Thad and Caroline entered the old kitchen together, the same kitchen where they had spent so many wonderful childhood days, festive and family days.

"I don't believe you are hearing me, Carrie." Thad's expression had changed.

"Hearing what?"

"When I asked you to wait, I had no idea how long I was asking."

"I've waited this long," she said.

"I've got to go with the rest of them. Can you understand that?"

Caroline could not answer. Somewhere in the dark recesses of her mind she was remembering the words of Job: "The thing which I greatly feared has come upon me." This was her hour. She turned away from him, but he would not have it. He turned her around masterfully, assuredly.

"You need not promise. I'd just like to believe you would want to."

"Oh, Thad. How can I say I won't? You could die!"

"Yes, but I would have a reason to live!"

Caroline studied the lines of Thad's face. He had always assumed that the world was made for him, and he had been an expert at acquiring all he ever wanted. She felt a hesitancy about so binding a promise—but what if he were to die? She would spend her life regretting. Her answer was slow and hesitant.

"I will wait," she said. Then she smiled, pretending a lightness she did not feel. "Will I see you in uniform? Uniforms are so elegant." But the pretense failed utterly, and she weakened. "I really don't know if I can stand waiting!"

Tears were stinging her eyes, but she would not cry. She could not do that and have any pride left. Haddons made their decisions with strength! Tears were for the weak.

Thad went back to Boston that evening, leaving Caroline in a bleak despair.

THE PURPLE LOOSESTRIFE, the jewelweed, the trefoil, and the cardinal flowers gave way to the autumn goldenrod, tall meadow rue, and pigeon berry. Soon the milk pods would burst and shed their silk to the winds. Fall would come early with its wild, rich colors, and summer would be over.

Caroline wondered if that were not like her life: the warm summers of love, and now the dying of everything—and only the cold winter to look forward to. She did not expect to hear again from Thad. He had already hardened her to his neglect. The children would be back in school, and the days would be the same.

Matthew worked on his valedictorian speech, for he had decided to present it in Latin. He would have to work on it early.

It was well into October, and the wasps were swarming thick in an effort to find a winter hideaway. Out on the ponds, the haunting cry of the loon was heard. Hank was busy boarding up the barn and piling manure against the north side to keep out the winter's cold.

It was a true Indian summer day when they heard a carriage in the driveway. It was Eva Tuttle, the one close acquaintance of Caroline's from the High Street aristocracy.

"I haven't seen you for months, Caroline. Whatever have you been doing?"

"Need you ask, Eva?"

Eva seemed not to hear Caroline's answer. A person generally absorbed in her own interests, she was rambling on about her indulgent father's plans for her birthday.

"—and I have missed you, really, I have! Papa has said I may plan on a real celebration, even if it is wartime! And of course you will come!"

Eva was not a pretty girl. Her face was long and narrow, but with her father's affluence she had hired an artful hairdresser who had turned her out to be rather attractive. To begin with, she did have ash-blonde hair, and the silks and fine satins of her wardrobe could find little competition among her peers.

Her father, Cornelius Tuttle, had inherited his wealth from an enterprising merchant father and had managed his inheritance with the cunning of a Burr. He had chosen his wife from the peon class and took delight in flaunting his common treasures. In spite of his ostentation and indulgence, his only child was a nice enough girl, and Caroline had a genuine feeling of friendliness for her.

When Caroline didn't answer, Eva pressed for assent. "Oh, Carrie, you will come! You must!"

"I'm really out of the social picture these days, Eva."

Eva, realizing she was losing the battle, turned to Nabby. "Tell her she must come, Mrs. Haddon."

Nabby did not respond immediately. She was squeezing the bellows, coaxing a reluctant flame from the logs in the cavernous fireplace.

"It was cold last night. I'd like to get the chill out of the house."

Caroline hoped her mother would not side with her friend, but Nabby had turned around and was looking at her.

"Why don't you go, Caroline? You have not gone anywhere for a long time."

Caroline was disappointed that Nabby had not supported her. Eva's crowd was not hers. If she wore the watered silk once more, she would be a spectacle! And worse still, Eva would be pairing her off with an escort, and that would be unthinkable after her promise to Thad.

"Come now, Carrie, say yes!" prodded Eva.

It was true, she had been living a life of isolation—a cloistered, uneventful life. If she could persuade Eva to refrain from pairing her off—

"I'd have to have an escort, and that would be a problem. I don't like being matched up with an unknown for an entire evening."

"Then you shan't be. I shall send a companion only to drive you there, and you need not feel obligated to spend the entire evening with him."

With the two women appealing to her, Caroline felt she could not refuse. "All right. I will go."

Having accomplished her mission, Eva left hastily, murmuring something about her dressmaker.

Caroline turned to her mother. "I should not have agreed. I honestly have nothing to wear, and everyone will be showing off her best."

Nabby smiled and left the room, returning with a cumbersome bolt of glistening blue satin.

" 'Tis an imbecilic mother who doesn't keep spare goods on hand when she has two daughters!" The look on Nabby's face bespoke keen satisfaction. It had been months since she had indulged herself in any frivolous womanly pursuit.

"You'd think the president was coming!" commented Bethia, as she watched Nabby cutting and sewing for the next few days. She herself would never get caught up in the trifles of the day. Besides, she and Joshua had much more important plans a-brewing.

The grand celebration was a week away, but the evenings began to take on a little glamour, a welcome diversion from the austerity of the times. Long after devotions, Bethia could hear Caroline and Nabby talking as they worked on the dress—and long after Bethia had retired, she found it difficult to sleep. It had been weeks since Joshua had found the gun, but the thought that its owner might still be trying to find it caused her great anxiety.

One evening when Carrie had gone to Nabby's room for a fitting, Bethia and Joshua sat before the fire playing checkers. They were disturbed by a low attention-getting chuckle from Matthew, who sat nearby reading the paper. Matthew was not in the habit of laughing. When he did give way to any form of mirth, it was usually of a sardonic nature. They looked up from their game expecting him to share the joke.

"Is something funny, Matthew?" asked Bethia.

"Hear this! If anyone has found a Warner Carbine, please contact Mr. Elias Paine at the following address." He read it out. "As if there were anyone who didn't know where the wealthy Mr. Paine lives. And how could anyone lose a gun?" Matthew left the room shaking his head in disbelief.

Joshua and Bethia sat looking at one another with faces as grim as death. As soon as Matthew left the room, they were at the discarded paper. There it was in black and white! Mr. Paine was advertising for his lost firearm!

"What do we do now?" asked Bethia, her face registering extreme disappointment.

"Nothing! Absolutely nothing!"

"Josh!"

"I mean it! Who could prove that we ever read the silly old newspaper?"

"But that isn't honest!"

"Haven't you already told Carrie that we probably won't need her ruby?"

"Yes."

"Then we'd be right back where we started!"

Bethia felt trapped. In exasperation she struck out verbally. "Oh, Josh! Why does everything go so wrong? If Papa were here, none of these things would be happening!"

Nabby entered the room in time to hear Bethia's outburst.

"Bethia, I don't ever want to hear you say that again!"

"It's true, Mother. It is true!" answered the emotional Bethia.

"We miss him, yes, but if your Uncle Hank heard you say that, he would be discouraged beyond words. He is doing his level best to keep things going here. If we didn't have your Uncle Hank, we'd just have to close up shop!"

Nabby wished immediately that she had not spoken of that possibility. She had forgotten that children could not see a catastrophe until upon one, and she did not want her problems shifted to her children. She tried to undo the damage.

"Things could be worse, Bethia. We must appreciate all that we have. Wars are hard on everyone, and we must be as brave as our fighting men."

Bethia hung her head, the turn of events and the scolding bringing on tears. She would never wittingly hurt her wonderful uncle and never, never disappoint her mother. Such thoughts were too much.

"I'm sorry. I'll watch my tongue—I really will. It's just that I miss Papa awfully sometimes!" She left the room to seek a solitary place where she might cry in private.

Joshua soon followed up the stairs and closed his door. He had some serious thinking to do. He lay staring into the darkness for hours. Surely the good God up above had seen his dire need and sent the gun—just to him! Now with a knowledge of the weapon's rightful owner, was he to be deprived of his miraculous find? The suggestion was unthinkable!

The two children slept poorly that night, and when they met in the morning, they did not speak. Not until they were busy filling the wood box was the silence broken.

"I've made up my mind!" declared Joshua.

"About the gun?"

"I am taking it back to Mr. Paine."

Bethia was relieved. "Maybe he will give you a reward, Joshua."

"I don't want a reward. I want the gun."

Bethia pressed on with renewed optimism. "You don't think he'd just say thank you, do you?"

But Joshua wanted no conversation. "We will go later today," he said.

It was an unusually golden day for October. Winds had swept the skies clear and kissed the slender elm fronds gently so that they rustled, as though a giant, invisible hand were sifting a pirate chest of coins.

The children were glad for the walk that led down the parched roads and patterned brick sidewalks. In the midst of their disappointment and fears, it was the familiar things that gave them a sense of stability. They could see the Paine mansion up ahead. It stood in the blinding sunlight, reflecting a brilliance almost metallic. The children were well acquainted with the history of the big square homes and of the impatient men who had built them, some so much in a hurry that they had fired the masons and rusticated the facades.

Why the accumulation of wealth should be such a class divider was beyond Joshua's comprehension. The more he thought about it, the angrier he became. Today he did not feel like dragging sticks across the vertical balustrades. He was bracing for the encounter with the imperious Mr. Paine.

They passed under a trellis still heavy with drying honeysuckle vines. Beyond a privet hedge they could see vestiges of a faded summer garden. Joshua reached for the high brass knocker. The door opened, and a black man stood facing them. His hair was white as wool, and he waited politely for them to speak. Bethia curtsied and shoved Joshua forward.

"Please, sir," he stammered. Then looking as though he would run, he took a deep breath and announced that he had come about Mr. Paine's gun.

"Waaal, sho nuff! Sho nuff! Come right in. The massuh be delighted to see yo' chilluns."

He motioned them inside and then was off down the long hall. The two children clung together looking at the umbrella stand and the beautifully carved canes that stood there.

"What's he doing with a slave?" asked Bethia.

"They're not called slaves here. He gets paid!"

"How do you know that?"

"Teacher says we don't need slaves in the North, and the few that had 'em got rid of 'em quick or kept them for wages."

The servant returned and led them down the hall. The ceilings seemed cathedral high, and bright-colored tapestries hung on the walls. Inside the parlor, there were window hangings of dark green velvet and Baroque furniture. They were ushered into a small reception room where Mr. Paine was seated in a large overstuffed chair. He seemed surprised when he saw Bethia, recognizing her as the child to whom he had once awarded a prize for raising a wild gosling.

"How do, children," he said. "Bless my soul, if it isn't the little goose girl!"

Mr. Paine was a widower who thoroughly enjoyed the

prestigious image of being the small city's most generous philanthropist, and the place was well salted with evidences of his affluence. The big man's eyes were a rheumy, faded blue, but none the less pleasant. Over each pink ear was a little puff of graying hair. He arose, making the floor groan under his weight, and extended a hand of welcome. He seemed friendly enough.

"Mr. Paine, sir—we found your rifle."

"My word, that is good news. I've had that gun for a quite a while. George! Get these children some chocolate."

"We found it in the mud!" continued Joshua.

"I had loaned it to Archibald Hanning. Guess the storm drove him off from his hunting. Did you bring it with you?"

"No, sir."

"Of course not." He rocked on his heels. " 'Twouldn't be proper for children to be walking about with a rifle.'"

"That's not why we didn't bring it, sir."

"Indeed!"

"No, sir. We didn't bring it 'cause we wanted to ask you—"

"Ask me what?" Mr. Paine's cordial manner was cooling.

"If you would let us buy it. We have eight dollars and forty cents, and we'll have more soon. We would work out the rest!"

There! It was said.

Now the affable Mr. Paine was puffing up like a bullfrog. "That isn't possible. The gun is worth far more than that."

"We'd curry horses, rake leaves—anything!" put in Bethia.

"Child, you don't understand. That's my Johnny's favorite hunting gun!"

The chasm between the generations broadened, and Bethia could almost feel the adrenalin flowing under Joshua's tense exterior.

"Sir," he started again, boldly jutting out his square Haddon jaw, "my father needs a gun. He needs one that isn't rusty. He's fighting the Rebs!"

"And his gun is rusty?"

"He said so in his letter."

"You must be mistaken. The government doesn't issue rusty guns, I'm sure."

"Well, they did, and it isn't fair. My father needs a shooting chance. We want him back alive!"

Mr. Paine looked over his spectacles, removed his glasses, cleaned them, and then put them back on again. These Haddon children were a plucky lot and not lacking in family loyalty.

"Come, come," he said impatiently. "I am sure we can settle this. I'll come by and get the rifle, and of course pay you a reward."

He was dismissing them in the patronizing manner Joshua hated, the way of all the High Street Hamiltonians!

"Then you won't let us buy it?" he asked.

"No, son. Sorry, but no."

George arrived with the hot chocolate.

If the obstinate man wanted things final, Joshua was prepared to accommodate him. "Then we will leave!"

"Not until you have had your drink."

"Sorry, but no!" echoed the young Haddon. Then, giving the big man a scathing look, he said, "Come, Bethia, we'd best be going."

George followed them to the door. "Deah, deah," he kept repeating as he shut the great door behind them.

Mr. Paine lost no time in going to the Haddon home. Nabby and Caroline were flabbergasted to learn that Joshua had a gun in his closet. He brought it down the stairs still wrapped in the towel.

"Here's your gun, sir. I have kept it very well. It might have been rusty if I hadn't!"

Mr. Paine reached into a jangling pocket and brought forth a handful of coins, proffering them to Joshua. He might have extended a handful of scorpions, the way the boy backed off.

"That's blood money, and I don't want it!" he said savagely.

Mr. Paine's face reddened. "Then let your ma have it."

"My mother won't have it, either!"

Nabby was speechless at her son's behavior. Never had he displayed such flagrant disrespect for an elder. In a state of bewilderment, she could only resort to the discipline she had always administered to a naughty child.

"Joshua," she scolded, "apologize to Mr. Paine."

Joshua had never been one to back down, and he was not about to do so now. His father's life was at stake. He looked helplessly at his mother and then at Caroline.

"I cannot," he said quietly, with the resolution of an adult, and having said so he stomped off toward the stairs and on to his room.

Nabby stood baffled, and Caroline came to the rescue.

"This is not at all like my brother, Mr. Paine. He has been upset for a long time, ever since Father wrote that he'd been given a rusty gun. Joshua is honestly afraid for him. Your boy, he's fighting, too. I'm sure you can understand."

"Then he was telling the truth?"

"Joshua is honest."

Mr. Paine looked puzzled and embarrassed. "Things are going on today that none of us understand."

He was apologetic and anxious to take his leave. Hugging the disputed weapon to his breast, he boarded the luxurious carriage, lifted the reins, and was on his way.

Upstairs Joshua sat on his bed with hands folded. He was still without a trusted gun, and his only hope of having one was gone. Worse still, he had disobeyed his mother.

Bethia, his staunch ally, followed him to his room. "I wouldn't touch his money, either!" she vowed.

"Go away, Beth!"

"Well, I wouldn't. He's a selfish old man—and I thought he was nice!"

Joshua looked away from his sister. "And I'll get a good thrashing," he said ruefully.

"I'll help explain."

"No use."

Nabby entered the room and stood looking at her son. He arose and faced her squarely, eyes as blue as her own and as direct as Clinton's. She felt unsure, seeing the budding maturity for the first time. It was like looking at Clinton, and she knew she could not destroy what she saw.

"I know you had a reason, Joshua. Do you want to tell me?"

"He wanted to help Papa!" said Bethia quickly.

"Well, I can't punish him for that! Only Joshua, son, it is not right to be rude. The Haddons have a reputation for being gentlemen as well as for being wise. I will expect to see that you have learned that." Crossing the room, she hugged him warmly.

"Don't know why he hasn't written," she said, looking beyond them, sadder than they had ever seen her.

11

T HE DRESS WAS FINISHED and placed carefully over the back of a chair. It was well done, ice blue trimmed with black lace and velvet ribbons. Nabby now turned her attention to Caroline's hair. What to do with the long raven tresses?

Full hairstyles were in vogue on the European continent, and the young country was quick to imitate. Nabby twisted and braided Caroline's hair into a crown; then, wielding the shears with an expertise born of necessity, she cut the front pieces short and curled them.

"There, Cinderella," she said, standing back to admire her work. "Now all you need is a handsome prince!"

Caroline opened the jewelry box and lifted the bluebird pendant. "A perfect match!" she said, closing the clasp.

It was the first time Nabby had seen the pendant. "Perfect indeed. Where did you get it?"

"A friend gave it to me."

Whether Nabby guessed who the friend was, Caroline did not know and had little time to think about. Already, Eva's carriage was coming up the driveway.

"Ooooeee!" exclaimed Joshua, running to the window. "Bet that didn't come from Amesbury!"

Hank stood behind Joshua, studying the lines of the vehicle. Light from the doorway shone on the carriage top. He could see the dark green of the interior, the black striped moldings, and the smart red trim.

"Looks like a Brett. Made in Albany," mused Hank.

A young man in a uniform of Union blue descended from the driver's seat and approached the door.

"I am Lieutenant Theodore White. I've come for Miss Caroline," he informed Nabby.

Caroline, wrapped in an ankle-length cape, allowed him to lead her to the carriage. The white horse started up, and the carriage rolled out of sight.

"That's the best part of the party!" declared Bethia. "Only I would like to be the driver!"

Caroline, meanwhile, had relaxed against the plush interior. She did indeed feel like Cinderella. Now if she could escape the bold eyes and questions of her peers, and keep her escort at a distance, she might get through the evening.

As they neared the Essex-Merrimac bridge, a number of carriages fell in behind them. Arriving at the hall, Theodore yielded the reins to a door attendant and helped her down. The two ascended a broad front stairway and entered together, where a young woman took their cloaks. Eva came toward them at once, her yellow brocaded silk complimenting her flaxen hair.

"Thank you, Teddy, for bringing Caroline. I'll be introducing her to people you already know, so why don't you circulate? I'll bring her back later."

Caroline moved through the throng, stopping now and then to greet Eva's friends. She could see a raised platform at the far end of the room and fireplaces ablaze with huge logs. They crackled and roared and sent sparks up the chimneys. Rush lights were hung along the walls, and candelabra with small candles were reflected in great wall mirrors. Caroline had forgotten that such luxury existed. Clearly, the Tuttles had spared no expense in celebrating their daughter's birthday.

While Caroline stood taking in the festive beauty, she was suddenly spun around to meet others and found herself looking into the darkest eyes she had ever seen. In their depths was blatant appreciation and a searching boldness, mingled with surprise.

"I want you to meet Jerome Cavell," Eva was saying. "This is Caroline Haddon, my very dear friend."

The man was tall and impeccably dressed. His loose tunic and velvet breeches bespoke another world, that of the arts. He wore a wide silk cravat and had decorative frogging on his coat. The hand that took hers was long, the nails well manicured. Unlike the majority of those present, he was clean shaven, his hair neatly coiffed and collar length.

Caroline flushed slightly, not knowing why.

"And wait until you hear him play!" Eva was exclaiming.

Mr. Cavell smiled, his white teeth striking in the dark complexion.

"And where have you been keeping your very dear friend?" he asked.

Caroline felt uneasy. The man was definitely appraising her, and his eyes were saucy. She hoped her gown met with his approval and then wondered why she should care. Eva's friends seldom crossed her path, and this was only an evening's acquaintance. Suddenly a bevy of young girls descended upon the fellow and whisked him off toward the platform, leaving Caroline feeling unsettled.

"Who is he?" she asked Eva.

"His people were immigrants from France. Something to do with the Huguenots. They settled in New Jersey first. He's a very gifted person."

Caroline watched as he moved away. He had a bemused expression on his face, evidently enjoying the attention. He turned and looked back at her.

"I think the man is conceited," she said simply.

"Yes, I dare say you are right, but he has reason to be. Comes from Boston to teach piano. Our parents don't leave us alone with him, at least not for long. French, you know!" Eva winked.

He must have a terrible reputation. Mercy! And all the giddy girls falling all over him! thought Caroline.

The music started, and her escort came toward her. How could she tell him that her family had always frowned on the dance? They had mellowed somewhat from outright condemnation to toleration, now generously placing the pastime in the "non-essentials" category.

"If you don't mind, I would like to watch," she managed.

"Then you won't mind if I ask another?"

"Not at all. Please do."

That dispensed with, Caroline felt free to wander off toward a well-laden refreshment table.

How could anyone dance a Rigadoon with their own men dying on battlefield? she wondered. *Let them keep their reveling in Provence, France!*

The table was spread with dainty cakes and cookies, many glazed with white frosting and decorated with red cherries and sugar-dipped mint. She reached for one and had just raised it to her lips when someone spoke behind her.

"Caroline Haddon. The name suits you."

She turned to meet the Frenchman.

"I'm glad you approve of my name, but I had little to do with choosing it."

"The French have a feeling about their Carolinian kings, you know!" he commented.

There followed an awkward silence, while Caroline wondered how a Huguenot could possibly have a fondness for kings who made alliances with popes.

"Didn't I see you dancing?" she ventured.

"Yes, but I was relieved of that."

Caroline offered him a cake which he politely refused. He was more interested in conversation.

"I don't recall seeing you at our parties," he said.

"My social life is limited."

"Are you invited?"

"Yes, but I seldom have time."

"Professionally employed?"

"Employed, yes, but not professionally. My father is in the South and our family is left with the farm."

"What a tragedy. So young to be missing the fun—and cheating the young men."

The man was an artist at more than the piano!

"I never looked at it quite that way. Most of the young men I know are in uniform and content to be serving their country. Women have an obligation, too, to keep things as they left them."

"And you are wondering why I am not in uniform?"

"The question had crossed my mind."

There was an abrupt change in his manner. He grew thoughtful, and his words had a tinge of bitterness when he spoke.

"Frankly, I am no champion of those who advocate fratricide . . . and I cannot approve the way Americans get themselves into wars. We can't always do the bailing out, you know."

The statement shocked and angered Caroline. With her father and her Uncle Vaugn already facing an enemy, and Thad on his way, how could she allow this foreigner to get away with such unpatriotic aspersions?

"But you would enjoy our liberties!"

"Since my forebears paid for them, why not?"

"I suppose you are referring to the Marquis."

"Ah, the Marquis. There was a man!"

"He was a boy, idealistic and impetuous . . . like most Frenchmen!"

Eva appeared, frowning when she found them together. The expression did little for her long face. She came on, fussing about Mr. Cavell's absence when he had promised to oblige her guests with a brief musical offering.

"We shall talk about this at another time," he said, with Eva tugging at his elbow.

"That is not likely," answered Caroline, still miffed at his affront.

I do believe Eva has some of her father's shallowness! Caroline thought, watching them leave. *The way she is making over the man!*

But Eva was not the only one. As Jerome Cavell began to play, the eyes of every girl in the room were fastened on him, and with more than a casual interest.

Caroline was no music critic. She could pump out the congregational hymns at church and play simple compositions, but her knowledge of the masters was definitely limited. Jerome played at first to impress his audience, then he moved from self-aggrandizement to self-indulgence. He seemed to leave his audience stranded while he floated off into his own world, enchanted and alone.

A woman sitting next to Caroline leaned toward her and whispered, "He will make his mark someday, just you wait!"

Caroline looked at him again. Yes, he looked the part. Unexpectedly he returned her gaze, and the encounter sent a shock between them for a fleeting second. It was as though they had lived all their lives for this strange moment. Caroline was shaken.

Jerome smiled down at his hands and spoke as though to himself. "My compliments to an unusually beautiful lady. This piece is for her. Beethoven wrote it for a friend named Elise, but it suits this lady."

A murmur went through his audience, eyes scanning the crowd for a giveaway smile but finding nothing. Then the delightful notes of "Fur Elise" floated out over the great room, haunting and delighting the ear, but particularly entrancing the artist, amusing him that so capricious a composition could have come from the heavy, ponderous hand of the great prince of composers. A secret was divulged in the mystery of the music—the fascination for a lady whose memory would not go away . . . lilting . . . constant . . . the melody would be heard! Then the music was over and there fell a moment of silence before the applause—a moment of reflection, of wonder before being harshly returned to the flesh-and-blood world.

Caroline clasped the bluebird pendant in a cold hand. *What have I to do with all this . . . this superficial society?* she wondered. *After tonight, I shall never see him again, nor shall I ever allow Eva to talk me into another party!*

The remainder of the evening passed uneventfully, with Caroline making it a point to avoid the Frenchman. As soon as the birthday supper was over, she would ask her escort to take her home. She was anxious to escape the frothy, no-account chatter—and the curious dark eyes that seemed to follow her everywhere she went. She excused herself early and breathed a sigh of relief as the coach carried her back through the old city streets to her home.

Nabby and Matthew had waited up for her—the one from a desire to hear the latest gossip, the other out of an assumed patriarchal duty. When Caroline entered the door, it was as though she were seeing her mother for the first time since Clinton's absence.

Nabby's dress was threadbare, her hair wispy and carelessly braided, her eyes tired. Her pretty mother, the quiet servant of the family. Mother with the ministering hands—the encourager of dreams, the teacher, the laundress, the seamstress, the one who churned the butter and took it to market, who planted flowers and harvested crops! Little wonder she had grown careless with her appearance.

And me in all my finery! thought Caroline, tossing her cape over a five-backed chair.

"It is late for you to be up, Mother."

"Do you think I would miss all the news?"

"Mother, you are the one who needed an evening out—not I."

Nabby didn't hear her, and Matthew just sat reading his paper.

"Isn't your sister beautiful?" asked Nabby, realizing he had not seen the finished product before this moment.

"I can't approve of parties in wartime—but I'm glad Carrie had a chance for a little recreation." Matthew returned to his reading.

"Is something wrong? Bad news, Matthew?" asked Caroline.

"There's a battle going on that could end the war . . . or take a dreadful toll of lives."

"In the Carolinas?" asked Nabby. Town gossip suddenly seemed trite.

"No, in Maryland. A place called Sharpsburg. Lee wants this victory badly. If he gets it, he has a chance that Europe will recognize the Confederacy. He will be throwing everything into it."

"Do you think Uncle Vaugn is there?" asked Caroline.

"I have reason to believe he very well could be." Seeing the fear on the women's faces, Matthew wished he had not spoken. "Don't mention this to Aunt Phoebe," he cautioned. "I'll know more tomorrow."

Caroline's thoughts were in a state of confusion. Thad gone, Vaugn possibly in the thick of it, no word from her father, and the strains of "Fur Elise" still ringing in her ears—mirrored candles, swirling gowns, dark eyes in a handsome face.

"What was it like, Carrie?"

Her mother's voice brought her back to the present.

"I'll sleep with you tonight and tell you."

The women retired to Nabby's chamber. The stars could be seen just beyond the billowing curtains, and the moon was brilliant. Caroline told of the pretty gowns and the dainty refreshments, of her escort and of the latest romances. She could see Nabby's profile in the moonlit room. Nabby was smiling, doubtless remembering her own youthful days.

"Did you like your escort?" she asked.

"Teddy is a very nice boy, but not the fairy prince." Knowing her mother wanted to hear more, she went on. "Eva had a pianist there—very talented."

"And?"

"He was very sure of himself!"

"And you did not like him."

"Not at all. But he won't lack for attention. The girls were all over him."

"Anyone I should know?"

"He is from Boston."

"Then you will never see him again."

"We didn't get along very well, and he is definitely out of my social circle."

Caroline fell silent after that, twisting the pendant on the gold chain. She wondered what news Matthew would bring home in the morning. She wondered why Thad didn't write, wondered if he were dancing at a senior officers' ball that night. Fighting men did have their moments of respite.

12

As Matthew had predicted, news broke on the following morning. Those with men in uniform gathered at the telegraph office waiting for a full report. Matthew and Hyram worked feverishly getting out the casualty list, which grew with each new dispatch.

"God help us!" exclaimed Hyram. "Turning out a list this long."

Matthew saw no reason to converse. He worked rapidly, scanning the list and getting it blocked. It was a sickening operation. He recognized many familiar names, many of the city's sons.

That evening Matthew read the account of the devastating Antietam battle: Union casualties 12,000 men and the Confederates over 10,000. It would go down in history as the bloodiest battle of the war. The Union might have finished Lee's resistance, but under the cautious McClellan and his fear of useless loss, the opportunity slipped through their hands, and the war would go on. Matthew read aloud, naming the families of the deceased, while Caroline and the others sighed heavily at the mention of those best known.

"And Mr. Paine's son!"

Joshua and Bethia looked up, startled. So, the war had come home to their adversary!

Within days trains began to arrive with the dead. Wagons, carriages, and horse-drawn hearses trafficked for several streets over, each driver somber with the task at hand.

Each day Joshua and Bethia passed the Paine mansion feeling the grief and depression through the very walls. They hurried past as though to escape the covetous eye of death.

"I feel kind of sorry for Mr. Paine," said the gentle Bethia.

"I'm trying to. If only he had cared about Papa."

"What do you think about stopping to tell him we are sorry about his son? He must feel dreadfully alone now, with all of his family gone."

Joshua looked annoyed, but Bethia pressed. "Well, we should! Jesus said to be good to those who hate you and pray for those who despitefully use you!"

"Then I'll pray for him," replied Joshua stubbornly.

"How can you do the one without the other?"

"But he was so selfish."

"I'd like to do what Jesus said. It wouldn't cost us anything except a little pride, and Papa says we can always spare a little of that."

Passing the mansion another day, they noticed more activity than they had seen for days.

"I expect the first blow is over," observed Bethia.

Joshua made a sharp turn into the walkway. "Come along!" he called to the astonished Bethia.

He dropped the knocker with a loud thud, and George opened the door.

"What you chillun want?" he asked.

They could see Mr. Paine standing just beyond.

"We came to see you, and to say we are truly sorry about your son," said Bethia solemnly.

"We really are, Mr. Paine. And we came to apologize. I wasn't very nice to you."

Mr. Paine swallowed hard. "Let them in, George, and get them some cider." He waved them inside. "Come visit awhile."

George brought steaming mugs of cider while Mr. Paine settled opposite them. His eyes were red, and his huge figure looked flaccid, as though he had been thrown into the chair carelessly like an armful of laundry.

"What do you hear from your father?" he asked.

"We haven't heard anything for a long time," answered Joshua.

"Then you had better thank Almighty God for that!" He pulled a large handkerchief from his pocket and blew his nose loudly. The gesture reminded Bethia that they had come to comfort.

"We are mighty sorry, Mr. Paine, but you can be very proud of your son. If we can help—do chores for you, or gather wood or shovel snow this winter—"

Mr. Paine looked over his glasses at the girl and her brother. Then he removed the glasses to wipe the tears from his eyes. These Haddon children were certainly well-trained and good. Their father could be proud of them. He rocked, waiting politely while they finished their drinks. Then he stood and headed for the coatrack. He put on a heavy coat and stood looking more imposing than ever. He was indeed a large man.

He called to George. "Get the carriage ready. We are going for a ride!"

George appeared from nowhere and left again as quickly as he had come. He was just finishing the harnessing when Mr. Paine and the children joined him in the stable.

"Get in," Mr. Paine ordered gruffly.

"We never get to ride in a carriage this nice!" said Joshua.

"He's taking us home. I knew he was nice!" whispered Bethia.

Mr. Paine crowded in beside them, rocking the carriage. The handsome bay seemed pleased as punch with the unexpected exercise, and they were soon traveling down High Street at a jaunty clip. They turned into State Street, and Mr. Paine reined in the horse and tied him to a block in front of Mr. Schmidt's gun shop.

Joshua stared.

"Come, come," the big man said impatiently.

Joshua followed close behind, glancing at once toward the wall where the coveted gun hung. To his dismay, the wall was bare.

"Give this boy a gun!" said Mr. Paine. "Any gun he wants!"

Joshua stood unbelieving.

Mr. Schmidt looked puzzled, and Mr. Paine repeated his instructions.

At last Joshua found his voice. "But . . . the Henry . . . it's gone!"

"No, son, it's in the back," Mr. Schmidt corrected.

"If it's the Henry he wants, give it to him, though I must say the boy has expensive tastes," said Mr. Paine. "He'll need cartridges, too. Got the rimfire?"

"Yes, sir."

Mr. Schmidt placed the gun in Joshua's hands, and Joshua ran his hands appreciatively over the barrel. It was even finer than he had remembered.

"He don't look big 'nuff to handle it," commented Mr. Schmidt.

"It's for my father!" explained Joshua, about to burst.

Bethia's eyes were spilling over with tears. She made an attempt to thank Mr. Paine but found she could not talk. She leaned close to her brother as they drove away in Mr. Paine's carriage.

"Jesus does things up in good style, huh, Joshua?"

Mr. Paine declined their invitation to go into the house when they arrived at the farm. The gift of the gun would speak for itself.

Caroline and Nabby watched with surprise as the children descended from the carriage.

"Joshua!" called Mr. Paine.

Joshua turned, beaming.

Mr. Paine was looking at him as though seeing another young boy. His upper lip was straight and the bottom lip curling.

"Joshua, tell your pa to use it well—and to make it count!"

13

CLINTON WAS TAKEN to a battery near Castle Garden, then on to the New Haven hospital. Evidences of the Sanitary Commissioner's expertise were everywhere. The top man was unquestionably a true friend to the soldier. Not only was the bedding fresh and clean, but every consideration was extended. For the first time in over a year, Clinton ate food that was not only nourishing, but enough!

For Clinton, there would be continued medical attention. Since receiving the arm wound and suffering chronic attacks of fever, he had been plagued with recurrences of diarrhea. His weight loss was a source of embarrassment and concern to him. If he were to return home in his present state, he was certain no one would recognize him. He pinned his hope for complete recovery upon the hospital's reputation for excellence.

The ague kept him at the New Haven Hospital for two months, then he was ordered to prepare for furlough. He would leave in twenty-four hours.

On the evening of the same day he received his traveling orders, a young woman made her rounds dispensing small gifts of jelly to those whose digestive system could tolerate solid food. In a large basket she carried dozens of fresh baked rolls. The fragrance of yeast bread was still on her clothing, and welcome it was indeed.

"Thank you, ma'am," said Clinton. Knowing full well that the anticipated journey had already started a squeamish churning in his stomach, he offered up a prayer that his volatile system would behave.

"That your name on the chart?" asked the woman, pointing to the card attached to Clinton's bed.

"Yes, ma'am. Clinton Haddon."

"That's odd," she remarked.

Clinton looked puzzled. "Just a good old Yankee name."

"No, not your name. It's just strange that there's another Haddon in Ward D."

Clinton put down the rolls and got to his feet. "Where's he from?"

"He couldn't talk—he's in bad condition. But I noticed the name on his card."

Clinton was already at the wide entrance of his room and heading down the hall.

The young woman followed him. "Down the hall and to the left. Most of the seriously wounded are there. Do you think you know him?"

"I aim to find out!" he called back, even as he hastened his steps. He peered into each ward as he continued to walk the corridor. Once a male nurse stopped him.

"Aren't you off your beat?" he asked pleasantly.

"Where'd all the wounded come from?" Clinton asked the nurse, appalled at the numbers overflowing the wards.

"Haven't you been reading?"

"Haven't been up to it."

"Worst battle yet at Antietam, Maryland. Stupid to think they could outmaneuver Lee and that fox Stuart. The place has been full of wounded for weeks, and not all of them are here. Overtaxed everywhere. Must have been a massacre!"

Clinton was already moving on. He turned left as the young woman had directed. The wards were quieter here, and the forms of men under the white sheets seemed deathly still. He entered a large room and moved silently from bed to bed reading each chart.

Then he was looking at his own name. Haddon. Vaugn Haddon! Fireations! If the young woman had not spoken, he might have left never knowing! He crept anxiously to the side of the bed. Vaugn looked old, and his color matched the gray of the walls.

"Vaugn," he whispered, the sound of his voice unnerving in the silence of the room.

There was no response. Clinton bent close to the bearded face. God in heaven, don't let him be dead!

"Vaugn," he whispered again.

This time Vaugn stirred and blinked his eyes, turning Clinton's shock to gentle concern.

"Where'd they get you, Vaugn?" he probed. He glanced down at his brother's outstretched form and saw that under the cover there was evidence of only one leg.

"Merciful God!"

The realization that Vaugn's leg had been amputated swept over Clinton, and he staggered against a chair, making it scrape across the floor. He had witnessed the same thing many times before, but this was different. This was his brother—fun-loving, active Vaugn!

"How long you been here?" he ventured.

Vaugn shook his head slightly. It was clear he did not know.

Clinton pulled the chair close to the bed and sank down into it. That was where the nurse found him.

"Aren't you shipping out today?" he asked. It was the same nurse he had met in the corridor.

"This is my brother," Clinton replied, gesturing toward the prostrate form in the bed.

When the surgeons made their rounds, Clinton was still there at Vaugn's bedside.

"You next of kin?" one asked.

"Yes, we are brothers."

"Then you should know. There's been infection since the amputation, and now he has pneumonia. When we got him, he was shot up all over. Don't know how he's made it this far."

The blow fell like a sledgehammer. The doctors noted Clinton's pale face and trembling hands.

"Have you have been here all night?"

"Yes."

"Get back to your bed and get some nourishment."

Vaugn was breathing hard, and it seemed he would slip away any moment.

The doctor read Clinton's thoughts. "He's alive, soldier, and will be . . . for a while."

Clinton knew he could do little by remaining. Besides, the wretched weakness was returning, and he knew he would have to rest and get some food, clear the cobwebs from his own mind, if he were to be of any use. He returned to his ward with laboring steps. Should he wire Phoebe and the twins? Phoebe would just cry, that he knew, and that wouldn't help Vaugn.

What a miserable decision! He was sick of decisions, sick of war, and sick in body. All he had, and he knew it, was a God who could strengthen him. Where could he turn but to the promises of God?

"Fear thou not, for I am with thee; I will strengthen thee." "My strength is made perfect in weakness." There had to be purpose in it all. Now was a time to trust.

Clinton fell exhausted upon his bed. Some kind person placed a mug of hot tea in his hands. It was like the waters of the brook Cherith, and he knew instinctively that there would be provision when he got to his Zarephath. He drank the tea and felt it permeate his entire body. Then he grew aware of a soldier standing at the foot of his bed. It was one of his fellow companions who would go with him to Massachusetts.

"You ready to go?" the man was asking.

"How do I request that I stay?"

"You don't want to go home?"

"My brother is down the hall. He is dying."

"Vaugn Haddon your brother?"

It seemed the Roxbury soldier knew Vaugn. Very likely they'd been at Sharpsburg together, but that wasn't important now. Clinton nodded and went back to his tea. He remained on his bed only long enough to eat breakfast, then he was up and washing. When he returned to Ward D, the sun was pouring in at Vaugn's window. It spread the first warmth to the gray and white of the room, and with it came a ray of hope. Clinton took up his vigil beside the sleeping Vaugn.

Close to noon, Vaugn stirred, causing Clinton to be instantly alert. In the brightness of day, Vaugn recognized his brother!

"Who else!" he managed in a long breath.

"Feeling better?"

Vaugn smiled weakly at the ludicrous question. "Now I must do the asking," he murmured. "Family. Take care." The effort was exhausting him, but he seemed determined to talk.

"Won't have to, Vaugn. You'll do that."

Vaugn shook his head, and Clinton moved closer. He stayed there for hours, till Vaugn fell again into an exhausted sleep. Yet weak as he was, he held to Clinton's big hand. The hours drew on. Weariness began to creep in upon Clinton, striking first between his shoulders, then moving to his arms and neck. The amoebic infection rallied and started his stomach churning. By now Clinton had lost all sense of time. He knew only that Vaugn needed him, and he would stay until the millennium if need be.

But he hadn't reckoned on his own weakness. Things suddenly began to spin, and he reached for the headboard, releasing Vaugn's hand. He heard the rush of feet and was vaguely aware of someone half-dragging him, half-leading him back to his bed.

"Lie down!" the someone commanded.

"No."

"You aren't strong enough to do him any good."

What a time to be weak!

"I'll get you some coffee." The attendant left, returning almost immediately with the promised stimulant.

Clinton drank and leaned back into the soft pillow. He was tired. Wretchedly tired.

"Please call me if he wakes."

He must have slept for a long time. When he awoke, someone was pulling at his sleeve.

"Your brother is asking for you!"

Clinton hurried down the hall. Lamps flickered on the shadowy walls. When he arrived at Vaugn's bedside, he could see that his brother was wide awake, his eyes unnaturally sharp.

"Clinton!"

"Right here."

"Take over the farm . . . the stable. The boys trust you, same as I do."

Clinton started to speak, but saw it was useless to try calming his brother's fears.

"Phoebe . . . tell her good-bye. Help her, Clint—and Clara, too."

By now Vaugn was holding Clinton's hand with the strength of madness, struggling to say what he must.

"I couldn't go on like this, anyway." He swept his free hand in the direction of his one leg. "Wouldn't want to." Then he fell silent and breathed a strange, long sigh.

A doctor came in and took his pulse. Clinton looked across the silent figure of his brother. The physician shook his head, and Clinton read the message. Vaugn had crossed the crystal sea and joined the thousands of others who had made the supreme sacrifice—and who would remember the cost?

The moment left Clinton in a well of despair, yet he could not give vent to his sorrow. It was all unreal . . . just not possible. He remained there until shafts of morning light pierced the miserable darkness. He was beyond feeling, beyond grief. Ahead lay the task of telling the family.

At long last, he arose and returned to his ward, his footsteps like lead on the wooden floor. Outside he could hear the scraping of wheels, wagons stirring on the dirt road. The morning nurses were arriving, talking and exchanging salutations. Someone laughed. He was outside of it all—everyone so busy with living, and he aware only that he felt numb and in a strange dream. On the floor beside his bed was his haversack and the few bundles he had packed for travel. He would carry more now—his and Vaugn's.

A man entered the wide door and informed Clinton that a carriage was waiting and would take him to a transport. Clinton followed him outside. Fortunately the air was pleasantly brisk, with a providential promise of good traveling. The sun looked good, melting away some of the ice in his heart. Clinton blinked. His world was still there. Supply wagons were driving up to the hospital entrance. Just beyond the activity was a park. The grass was still green. Somewhere bells were tolling. Was it Sunday, or just a time for bells to toll?

More wagons and more wounded. Some were carried; others were on crutches. They would appreciate the clean beds. Then he saw the death wagons. Those who had died in the night were being taken to the large charnel house, a gray, foreboding structure, cold and final. Vaugn would be on one of those wagons. Suddenly he wanted to run after him. He didn't want Vaugn to be among the dead—alone! He wanted him living, wanted things as they used to be, wanted to walk into the stable and find Vaugn oiling down the horse trappings, wanted to pick up their old guns and go hunting the woodchucks that robbed the bean fields.

Stiffly Clinton placed the haversacks on the carriage and thanked the soldier who had helped him. Then he looked again at the death wagon, brushed his eyes on a rough sleeve, and climbed aboard. He hated the weakness of his body, hated weakness of any kind. Tears began to blur his vision. He remembered the Confederate captain who had wept for his orderly, and the dam broke; Clinton Haddon wept without shame.

"Yankees cry, too," he muttered. "Yankees cry, too."

14

WHEN AUTUMN CAME, the President presented his
Emancipation Proclamation to his cabinet, garnering support from
his friends and making enemies of others. The man at the helm,
honestly pragmatic, knew he would have to establish a purpose
clear and defined before going on with the war. The focus on
freedom for the slaves, he obviously believed, would bring support
from Great Britain and France.

Political enemies now turned their venom on Mary Lincoln,
who found herself in the unenviable crossfire of politically social
jealousies, the ambitions of news columnists, and the task of trying
to help her busy husband. She was labeled everything from an
ambitious and meddling wife to a spy. But the wolves did not
reckon with the power that controlled the gentle giant. From the
log cabin beginnings to the turbulence of political victories and
defeats, adversity had done its good work. He had cut his teeth on
the gristle of poverty, chosen honesty to personal gain, risen from
the ashes of defeat and stood tall before his colleagues as a man to
be trusted. But Honest Abe had more, for when a man chooses to
follow the destiny he knows God has ordained for him, he is
invincible, and there was little question that Abraham Lincoln was
aware of his high calling, though he could not possibly have known
that he would be remembered as a man of the ages. He probably
saw no more than that he was the man for the hour, and he
purposed to make his hour count!

Buell's Federals had discouraged Bragg in Kentucky, the Atlantic blockade was succeeding in piling cotton on southern wharfs, and both sides were growing impatient with the length of the conflict.

The month of falling leaves and diving loons, roadside asters and angry wasps was over. November came on with her usual chilling winds and threatening snows. The cider mills were in full swing, and ponds were freezing over. Thanksgiving would be upon the Haddon families in a matter of days.

Caroline had finished with the chamber and kitchen work and had packed a supply of butter for the market. On her way back from the barn, she stopped at the flour shed to get the week's supply of the priceless meal. Hank swung the wide barn door open, and Caroline stepped into the frosty air. A family of chickadees quarreled in a leafless oak, and she stopped to watch them.

A carriage was coming up the road, clinging to the ruts at a rakish angle. She could see the top hat of an already tall man inside. To her surprise, the vehicle turned into her driveway.

"It's the Frenchman!" she exclaimed aloud, pulling her shawl tight to her shoulders. Could she escape? How could she face a gentleman of his stature in a blue gingham dress? But it was too late to run. He had caught sight of her and was already alighting from the carriage.

"I've found you, Miss Haddon!" he exclaimed, openly delighted.

Caroline had to admit that the intruder was devastatingly attractive, though she hated herself for the observation.

"Eva has given you my address."

"She has, though it took a bit of badgering. I have come to ask you to accompany me to a dinner she is planning."

He seemed not to notice her shabby attire.

"No, I couldn't."

"I promise not to be obnoxious."

There seemed to be an honest humility in his attitude, and his smile was stealing its way into her heart. At least she would hear him out.

"Do you believe you could keep that promise?"

"Give the beggar an opportunity," he challenged.

Caroline looked at his expensive coat and polished shoes and wondered why, with all the affluent ladies in his own social echelon, he should be seeking her out.

"You know, Mr. Cavell, it is best that we understand one another. I'm really not an unfriendly person, but we should be realistic. We don't live in the same world. We are miles apart, with nothing in common, and I have no business encouraging you."

"Then we could teach one another!"

"Teach one another what?"

"To know each other's world. I would like to know yours!"

"I don't believe you!"

He ignored her remark and walked to the door of the big barn. "The only time I see an animal up close is on a dinner plate!"

"Would you like a tour?" It seemed a reasonable request.

"Yes, I'd like a tour."

"Come, then. I'll show you." They entered the door and proceeded down the wide center of the barn floor.

Cows stood in separate stanchions, oblivious to the intrusion, chewing contentedly on their cud, eyes enormous and liquid. Caroline pointed out a young heifer.

"Twins were born during the storm. The mother died, but my Uncle Hank saved the calves. We kept this one and sold the other. But come along and meet Dandy." She walked to an adjoining building where Dandy peered curiously over his stall door.

Hesitantly Jerome reached a hand toward the horse.

"Don't come at him like that. Horses like to feel confidence in the people who handle them."

"How do you know so much?"

"Farmer's daughter, remember?"

Descending a flight of rough-hewn stairs, Caroline pointed out a pen of pigs so heavy they could scarcely waddle. "These will be butchered in a few weeks."

Jerome made a wry face. "How savage!" he exclaimed.

"No, just necessary!"

"But you don't have a part in that!"

"Only in the swaling."

"What the devil is swaling?"

"Would you like to come and see?"

"No."

"I thought not. Swaling is scraping off the hair. Someone has to do it, and help is impossible to find these days. Unskilled workers move as fast as pond water, so we do it ourselves."

"Don't you ever do women's work?"

"Oh, yes, the house and the children—"

"Children?"

"My little brother and sister."

Jerome looked relieved and Caroline amused.

"When may I meet them?"

"They're just farmer's children, like me!"

"Don't discourage me, Miss Haddon. I'm being honest—and nice!"

"Yes, you are. Perhaps sometime I shall arrange a meeting."

"But you won't go to the dinner?"

"No."

"Then where would you like to go?"

"I'm truly sorry, but I cannot accept any invitations now. The work is overwhelming, and I have neglected the children. I promised my father I wouldn't do that. They are expecting me to take them skating Saturday."

"That's it!" Jerome looked pleased.

"That's what?"

"I would like to go skating."

Caroline gave him a look of incredulity. "Come now!" Aspiring young virtuosos did not aspire to such plebeian pastimes!

"I can skate," he avowed. "A bit."

This man would not be put off, Caroline could see. She toyed with the possibility that a miserable evening on the ice might put an end to his persistence.

"All right. Come Saturday evening. Dress warm and expect to walk."

She saw him back to the barn door, and Jerome left.

"Why am I always getting into things I never intended?" she said aloud.

JEROME ARRIVED PROMPTLY at six o'clock that Saturday and, after proper introductions to the family, the four started for the pond. It was already dark, and stars were beginning to appear in the sky. The little company wound their way through the pines, treading on carpets of brittle needles and at times retrieving pig nuts from the buried store of mast. Bethia and Joshua ran ahead squealing and yelling, their voices echoing through the woods and stirring a response from other youngsters flocking in the same direction.

"You probably grew up here," said Jerome, making an attempt at light conversation.

He seemed a little self-conscious about being out of his element, but at least he could enjoy observing the young girl at his side. Hers was a beauty that required no ornamentation—fragile, delicate in appearance, even in the way she moved her hands. How could they be so articulately graceful when she had so many menial tasks to perform? She was so different from the frivolous women of his world.

When they arrived at the pond's edge, he could see that someone had started a fire on a patch of well-cleared land. It did look inviting, and he began to appreciate the magic of the winter evening.

Caroline and the children went right to work putting their

skates on their shoes, declining help from him—an independent lot, these Haddons. It was commendable, but left little opportunity for Jerome to display any gentlemanly chivalry.

"I have not been on skates for a long time," he confessed, as he watched the younger Haddons step off at a healthy clip.

"I'll hold you up!" Caroline smiled into her coat collar, knowing she had punctured his masculine esteem.

But he was more than glad to have her no further than his elbow. Even at that, he managed to stub a toe on a tussock of frozen grass and fall with a jarring thud. Bethia and Joshua came to his assistance, laughing outright. Caroline scolded, repressing her own impulse to laugh, but Jerome was soon back on his feet. Gradually he was taking the challenge in stride and soon he was beaming at his own dexterity.

"This is delightful!" he said.

"You like my world?"

He wasn't ready to go that far. "I'm learning," he condescended.

The evening passed all too quickly, and it was not long before the old town clocks could be heard in the distance, each one contending boisterously for preeminence. The moon had risen silvery bright—a real hunter's moon. Caroline's little group retraced their steps through the piney woods. The sound of exuberant voices echoed through the night and blended with the hoot of a startled owl.

Jerome was surprised to find that there was no loneliness in the dark. Everything in God's green earth had its peculiar beauty . . . even a cold night in mid-November!

"If you watch the skies long enough, you will see the meteors," said Caroline. "But you must be patient. Eyes do not adjust to night skies in a moment."

As Jerome watched Caroline, he thought that the lights in her eyes rivaled anything the heavens had to offer.

"Mother will have hot cider for us when we get to the house."

"How very Spartan!"

"I warned you—we are miles apart."

It was as Caroline had said; Nabby did have a tray of refreshments awaiting them. Later they moved on into the library, a small room off the sitting room where bookcases lined the walls.

Matthew was there, deeply engrossed in his books, though he stopped reading long enough to be cordial to the visitor.

Jerome was instantly interested.

"You must be a studious family," he commented, studying the authors. "The Bronte sisters, Cleghorn, Holmes, Rome's apologist, Hawthorne, Longfellow, and Whittier... Tennyson, Thackery, Scott ... Dickens. You do have a library. And fairy tales for the young. A good selection, though I observe an absence of Flaubert, Manzoni, DeBalzac, LeSage, and Stendhal."

"Father has no patience with the naughty European writers," said Caroline quickly.

"And have you read all these volumes?"

"Yes, and I dare say more than once. Father always said that anything worth reading is worth reading over again!"

"I should like to know your father. And which is your favorite?"

"I have many. Right now I am enjoying Thoreau's writings. God rest his soul!"

"You surprise me."

"Why? Because he was such a renegade?"

"Well, yes. He was certainly that, though in a civilized sort of way. I just find it hard to reconcile your puritan ways with his anti-church views."

"I appreciated the good in the man, his fervor for the creation. But you are right. He seemed to be badly influenced by Emerson, giving ear to the Kantian philosophy and ignoring his own root traditions."

"Oh?"

"Intellectualism is not the answer, and I fear it is already becoming an open enemy."

"But it is an evidence of a nation growing up."

Caroline could see that Jerome was openly opposing her. "Are you also one of the blind?"

Now the simple farmer's daughter had changed. Jerome was both intrigued and surprised. These farm folk were not the ignorant and earthbound folk he had thought them to be.

Matthew had taken a place beside the fire, watching the duel progress and looking for all the world like a Caesar presiding over the arena. He wondered how Jerome would counter.

"I see what the brainiest men in the country see," he offered.

"Then you have never read that the wisdom of this world is foolishness with God."

"Are you opposed to wisdom?"

"Yes, when human wisdom pits itself against godly wisdom. Is there any contest?"

"But Thoreau believed in increasing knowledge. He was a progressive, and we need progressives!"

"Not when progressives have no moral boundaries. How long can a civilization endure with a blind side toward evil—and substituting license for liberty?"

"But civilizations can reach perfection and solve such problems!"

"Perhaps you would care to name one. No, Mr. Cavell, those who become a law unto themselves and despise God's laws have always invited sorrow and ultimately annihilation. I hope our Union never becomes so satisfied with its own wisdom as to invite God's judgment!"

Nabby, watching at a distance, could see that the gulf between the two was widening and thought it best to intervene. Politely she suggested that Jerome come back another day.

Caroline walked with him to the door. "You are walking back to town?"

"Yes."

"I am sorry if I have offended you. I have strong feelings about some things."

"Remarkable!" he said, a quizzical expression on his face. "I had no idea your family was so strong—as pure a breed as—"

"As the pseudo-elite?"

He shook his head, not sure how to respond.

Caroline's face was marble white in the bright moonlight. It made her hair shine with blue lights and her eyes sparkle. Any other girl would be lifting her chin for a kiss, but Caroline was holding him off.

"Why do I want to know you, Caroline?" he asked.

She did not like the seriousness of the moment.

"I suppose it is the same reason we eat our first raw oyster—curiosity, daring!"

"But many folk find that they like raw oysters!"

"Good night, Mr. Cavell!"

"Good night, Caroline."

15

THE TRAIN MOVED on at a healthy clip, the rhythmic clicking of the rails lulling Clinton to sleep. They stopped at Hartford, Springfield, and Worcester. Each time the end doors were flung open, the car was swept by an icy blast of air, amalgamated with the odor of bituminous coal. Still in uniform and wrapped in his heavy greatcoat, Clinton welcomed the familiar scents and scenes.

It was dark when they entered the Boston yards, and his temperature had begun to climb. He knew he would have to resist the strong desire to continue on toward home at once; if he could find lodging for the night, his fever would subside.

A traveling soldier noticed that Clinton only had the use of one arm, and offered to carry his baggage. On the drafty platform, Clinton stood trying to decide in which direction to move. A stocky, middle-aged man with graying hair approached him and extended a hand of welcome. It puzzled Clinton; he was certain he had never laid eyes on the stranger. He would certainly have remembered the merry triangular eyes, the moustache, and the neat appearance.

"You must be Clinton Haddon!" the man exclaimed, looking at a paper he held and then back at Clinton. "I'm from Sanitary Commission headquarters. We have lodging for you, if you plan to stop over."

Relief must have registered on Clinton's face, for the man was already packing him off to a waiting carriage. The headquarters were only a short distance from the train terminal. Clinton labored up the entrance steps of the large, two-storied brick building. His genial host was by now opening doors and waiting for Clinton to catch his breath. Up another flight, and he was opening another door to a small room. Clinton could smell fresh paint. In a corner of the room, a potbellied stove was throwing off welcome heat. A bureau, a chair, and a small wall table beside the bed were the simple furnishings. Nothing elaborate, only functional, clean, and nothing short of beautiful to the weary Clinton. He reached into his pocket to offer the kind man a sum for the accommodation.

"No, soldier—you have paid enough!" he said kindly, nodding with clear-eyed candor.

"Well, then—thank you."

After the man left, Clinton walked to the stove and warmed his hands. This drastic swing from chills to fever was demoralizing. How could a strong man be so devastated by a simple fever? He removed some small kindling from a box on the floor and replenished the firebox. After the fire had burned for a short time, he checked the draughts and walked to the bed, where he touched the clean sheets and blankets with an air of wonder. They felt more like the coverings of home than anything he had touched since leaving. If only the fever and the weariness would leave, and he could put from his mind the agonizing memories of the past two days.

Exhausted, Clinton stretched out on the bed and closed his eyes, only to be awakened by someone tapping on his door. For one instant he was utterly disoriented, then the room came into focus and he remembered that he was far away from the sound of battle. He was back in civilian life, and a young boy was standing in the doorway holding a tray. Thanking him, Clinton took the tray and carried it to the small table. On a white crockery plate lay a generous slice of beef along with a baked potato. A separate dish held a large serving of winter squash. There was also a pot of tea with a thin wisp of steam rising from its spout, and a plate of bread and butter—real butter! When he saw the white linen napkin, he felt like weeping. The unexpected kindness, the wonder of being on his way home, and his physical weakness overwhelmed him. He fell beside the tray with a gratitude greater than any he had ever experienced. That any man could take for granted the wonders of a well-laden table without thanking a providential God was beyond understanding.

"Lord, receive my thanks, my gratitude for this evidence of Your eternal care—and forgive those who can not see Your faithfulness. Amen."

He ate with great relish, savoring each *bon bouche* as though he were loath to come to the end. Once again he lay down on the bed and soon fell into the deep sleep that satisfied hunger engenders.

By morning the fever had left. It was indeed a strange, nocturnal adversary, attacking at sundown and shuffling off by daylight. He wondered if he would have to suffer the unsolicited invasion for the rest of his life. In the predawn he dressed and went below to look for his host. Following the sound of clattering dishes, he found his guide seated with others at the breakfast table. He motioned for Clinton to join him.

"I'm up early enough to walk," said Clinton, depositing his baggage on the floor.

"No, my good man. You will have breakfast, and then you will ride. I have made the arrangements." He pulled up a chair beside himself.

True to his word, after breakfast the host settled Clinton and his baggage into a hack and drove the horse over the bumpy cobblestones to the train station. Clinton felt better than he had in months as he boarded the train for Newburyport. In less than an hour he would be home!

Familiar scenes whisked by, scenes he had seen so often in his dreams, scenes he had wondered if he would ever see again. The leafless trees, the evergreen swales, pine, cat spruce, larch and cedar, crews of Irishmen cutting ice and driving horses, grappling irons, block and tackle and rectangles of stacked ice. Best of all were the small villages and towns—children racing to school and dallying at points of interest, bustling traffic, horse-drawn milk wagons, horse-cars, carriages, and bundled-up pedestrians. In each small township the high white church steeples flagrantly declared that man still revered God.

A conductor moved through the car after each stop. He seemed intent upon engaging Clinton in conversation.

"You been in the worst of it, eh?"

"Guess you could say that."

"I'll get you a paper. News that McClellan is being relieved of his command and being replaced by General Burnside. Now, he's a good one!"

Clinton showed interest at the mention of his former commander, but harbored his doubts about Burnside taking on so large a force. He was sure Burnside had not coveted such responsibility, but that was how things seemed to go. A few victories, and the high command began to think a man invincible. It did not seem fair. "Old Mutton Chops" would have to outdo himself to maintain respect . . . and if he failed?

But right now Clinton did not wish to think about the war. They would pass under the trestle in a matter of minutes, and he listened expectantly for the engineer to herald the train's arrival. When he did, the sound sent a wave of nostalgia to Clinton's very toes. At long last, he was home!

He removed the haversacks and small bundles from the overhead rack and prepared to leave. On the platform he stood, trembling and emotional. He watched the steam curl around the big steel wheels and the driving rods, then the train moved on.

It was early, and the population would be stoking morning fires. Smoke rose from countless chimneys, perpendicular streams wafting into the gray and yellow skies. There they stood, just as he had left them, the simple dwellings that had been there for a century—the beloved roofs, gabled and gambreled, mansard and hipped, the little saltbox houses and the colonial mansions, each with the symmetrically designed fencing.

"I said I'd come home!" Clinton felt a sudden surge of optimism and joy.

He looked toward Washington Street. Around the corner was the bakery where the Widow Cheney lived with her three small children. It would not do to go home without sweet rolls for the children. He started toward it, but was overcome by a wave of nausea—not an unusual reaction when his emotions ran high. He decided against the long walk and returned to the station in time to engage the depot wagon, already crowded with early morning passengers. The driver covered the familiar route; apothecary shops, tobacconists, dry goods stores, ship chandlery, leather, watchmaker, tailor, crockery and glass shops. It all seemed a dream.

Folk departed the wagon one at a time until Clinton was the only passenger remaining. Then the horses took off at a lively trot toward the farm. The house stood in the cold yellow morning sunlight of the winter morn—just as he had left it. Somehow everything looked smaller—but never dearer! The lump in Clinton's throat swelled to walnut size, and he felt like a weepy old lady.

The orchard trees that nestled into the sheltered hills caught his eye, and he wondered at the wooden props supporting them. The maples over the eaves were bare. Tonight they would be scraping against the house, cold and brittle—and he would be resting in his own bed and listening to them. His dogs came barking at the sound of unfamiliar wheels, and as quickly shied and looked embarrassed when the familiar figure swung down to the ground. Hank emerged from the barn, pail in hand and dressed in his kersey trousers and bright smock. His eyes narrowed as though to see better, and then Nabby appeared behind him. Her hands moved characteristically to her breast when she caught sight of the unannounced visitor, then she was running and calling his name.

In the house, Caroline heard her mother's shrill cry and dropped the towel she was about to hang behind the stove. She hurried to the window in time to see the depot wagon lumbering away. For one stunned moment she studied the figure that the wagon had left behind. The loss of weight and the beard disarmed her, but then she saw Nabby flinging herself at the man. Could it possibly be? The need to laugh mingled with the need to cry, and she was running, too!

"Father! Father!"

Hank, meanwhile, had set his pail beside Nabby's and was hobbling toward Clinton. Together the four walked to the house, everyone talking at once. On the door stoop, Clinton turned to look at the beloved hills—his hills—everything so precious. He hugged Nabby again.

Inside the house, she removed his heavy coat and saw the bandaged arm.

"Why didn't you tell us?" she managed through a veil of happy tears.

"He's dreadfully thin," whispered Caroline to Hank.

"No need to worry you," Clinton was saying. "Just grazed in a little skirmish."

"They don't send you home for a winging, Clint," said Hank.

Nabby's hand brushed his, and she frowned. "You are feverish!"

"Of course—the excitement!"

"And you are tired. Come, we'll get a fire going."

The dark circles under her husband's eyes were cause for alarm—and his emaciated body! She could never have imagined the strong Clinton Haddon looking this poorly. Their bedroom had been closed off for the winter months, and when Nabby opened the door, cold air swept into the kitchen, causing Clinton to shiver.

Hank brought the milk pails in and set them on the drain board, then went at once to the task of gathering kindling for the bedroom fireplace. It was not long before the logs were blazing and sending a welcome warmth into the room.

Clinton stretched out on his old bed and folded his arms under his head. Nabby removed his boots and tucked a thick comforter under his chin. Strange . . . he had forgotten how everything smelled of pine!

Caroline came with hot tea, and Clinton looked long at his daughter's lovely face.

"Thought you would be married by now," he quipped. "Prettiest girl in town!"

Caroline kissed him on the cheek.

"I'm waiting for a man just like you!" she replied.

"And you will never find one," said Nabby, her eyes aglow.

"Then I shall die an old maid!"

"That I doubt, young lady!" said Clinton.

The room took on a festive, holiday atmosphere. Clinton looked at the pictures hanging on the walls—his mother's framed and glazed embroidery sampler, a daguerreotype of his father, and a strange bit of artistry done by a cousin using the cuttings of various shades of family hair and worth nothing outside the family pride. It was good to be home—so very, very good! But now thoughts of where he had been began to move in and rob him of the sweetness of the homecoming. The last days with Vaugn overshadowed his return. He would have to get himself together.

"Glad to be home?" asked Hank.

"You will never know!"

"Hank, take the wagon and get Doc Slater." Nabby was taking charge.

"Now, girl, don't fuss. I get these fevers every day."

"Then it is time something was done about it!"

Hank left immediately, but Caroline lingered at her father's side. That wonderful inner strength was still there, but she realized that he had not relinquished Nabby's hand since arriving. It was marvelous to see such constant love evidenced between the two—so much more than a physical attraction, it was something of God's love, enriching their relationship and spreading to those around them . . . sheltering, enduring. An elusive something she herself coveted.

She thought of Thad. Why was it that in all of Thad's ardor she had never seen what she could now see in her father? Why had he still not even written? How could he spend weeks away and not even scratch a note? Was she alone the one who had made a commitment? She felt again the old uneasiness about their secret promise.

"Finish your tea, Father," she said and then left for the kitchen, closing the door on the lovers.

Doc Slater came in the afternoon and prescribed bed rest, nourishing food, and niter. Clinton stubbornly refused quinine.

"What have they been feeding you, soldier?" asked the old doctor, peering over his spectacles and taking note of Clinton's weight loss.

"When we were lucky, salt pork, strong coffee, and hardtack."

"Hmmph! Not even an iron man could long survive that. You have no doubt damaged your liver!"

Nabby took Caroline aside and gave her orders to take Dandy to town and purchase the niter.

"It's time Clinton had some care. Get tea and sugar, too."

"Don't feed him too well, Mother. You know he'll be back fighting if you do."

Bethia and Joshua returned from school, racing up the wide driveway with their usual ebullience, kneeling to pat the dogs as they came. When they entered the kitchen, Bethia noticed that her mother's chamber door was open. Knowing this was not customary for the winter, she turned to Joshua.

"Close Mother's bedroom door, would you? I'll fix us some molasses bread."

Joshua walked to the threshold and stopped, staring at the bearded man in his mother's bed. Then he let out a whoop that brought Bethia running. Soon shrieks and squeals were echoing through the old timbers, and hugs and kisses were abounding!

"You've grown five inches, Joshua boy. You look great! And my girl—how is my little girl?"

"Oh, Papa, just wait till you see what we have for you! You won't believe your eyes!"

The moment afforded them all a release from the usual restraints. Then the children were off toward the stairway.

"Good glory, Mother! They'll wake the dead!" complained Caroline, who had returned from her errands.

The word brought Clinton back to the solemn duty yet before him. He allowed the children their time of satisfaction as he exclaimed over the wonderful Henry, then he arose and prepared to dress.

Matthew came in the side door shortly afterward and hung his coat on the kitchen peg. Joshua, Bethia, and Caroline stood looking at him, and he could see at once that something unusual was going on.

"Father must be coming home," he said knowingly.

"He's already here!" came the chorus.

Matthew's face flushed, and he hurried to his parents' room. For a long moment he stood facing his father, fighting every impulse to show more emotion. Then Clinton laughed and hugged him.

"You even look like a newspaperman!" he said, wanting to break down his son's reserve.

"And you look like you have seen a few battles! We must talk for days. I want to know all the details!"

"There are details all right, son." Then facing them all, Clinton grew very serious. "Come, we must sit down together. There is something I must tell you, and I find it very difficult."

The family gathered in the big sitting room. Hank came, too, sensing something ominous.

"After I was wounded, I was taken to the New Haven hospital."

No one spoke.

"The hospital is a sort of central receiving place. Vaugn was there."

They leaned closer, fear already in their faces.

"He was wounded, too—badly!" He must spare them the details.

"Why didn't he come home with you, Papa?" asked the trusting Joshua.

Clinton looked away from them and sighed. "Because, Joshua, Uncle Vaugn is dead."

The words fell like hail on spring lilacs.

Bethia let the tears come; the others sat bewildered.

"I shall have to tell Phoebe and the children, though God knows, I do not know how." Clinton's voice had dropped to a whisper.

Caroline seemed to recover first. "Did he know you, Father?" she asked.

"Yes, by God's grace."

"Did he suffer?" Nabby had found her voice. With womanly insight, her mind was already at work as to the best way they might break the terrible news. Somehow, somehow, she must soften the blow.

Clinton described his last hours with his brother. When he stopped speaking, there was silence and no more questions.

"I shall invite them to come for the evening," said Nabby. "You, Clinton, must take the boys. Carrie and I will take Phoebe and Clara. There will be tears, but at least there will be family to comfort. Clinton, are you certain they have not been notified?"

"No notification would go out that promptly."

"We can be glad of that."

In a short time the Vaugn Haddons were at the door. They entered with high expectations and great joy. Uncle Clinton had returned!

The questions began as soon as their coats were hung.

"I suppose Father will be dropping in on us soon, just like you, Uncle Clint," said Allen.

Clinton was quiet, and his silence disturbed his perceptive

nephew. And the way Bethia and Joshua kept their eyes on their father, as though awaiting a cue. . . . Suspicion began to stir inside the young Haddon. When Vaugn's haversack was brought in and placed on the floor, he knew things were not right.

"That is my father's," he said, growing tense.

"Yes, Allen. We were at the same hospital."

"He's all right, isn't he?" asked Phoebe in a tremulous voice.

"I guess you know the battles have been pretty hot."

"Tell us, Clinton!"

"I spent two days with him. He was very ill." Clinton turned helplessly to Nabby.

"And . . . he died," said Nabby hesitantly, sensing her husband's inability to go on.

Phoebe let out a shriek, which started Clara crying. Clinton moved toward the twins and placed a strong arm over each one. Nabby placed loving arms around Clara and Phoebe, and they wept together.

Allen was the first to regain his composure. "Tell us about it, Uncle Clint. We want to know."

"Yes, we want to know," put in Timothy, though he was clearly shaken.

Phoebe and Clara sat wilted, softly moaning as Clinton recounted the days he had spent with Vaugn. He closed with an expression of gratitude that God had allowed him to be at his brother's side in his final hours.

"We will go home," Phoebe announced, rising.

Allen helped his mother on with her cloak and turned to thank his uncle. "They will be needing more enlistees, with things going so badly."

"Word is out that there will be a draft by March."

"I expect I should be joining."

In spite of her sorrow, Phoebe reacted venomously. "You will do no such thing! This war has taken my husband—it won't get my sons!"

Timothy picked up his father's haversack as though it were contaminated. Allen swept Clara into his arms, letting her lie against him, where she continued to sob.

Caroline, Matthew, and Hank walked with them across the fields and then left them to their grief. The ultimate sorrow had come to the Haddons' door.

16

TOGETHER THE HADDON FAMILY went to the early train to claim Vaugn's body. It was a solemn, dreary experience in the cold of winter, but they were not alone. Others were there also, with the same heaviness of heart. To carry the narrow pine boxes to their conveyances, knowing that within lay their dearest and best, demanded a courage and a strength beyond their own. It was so in every hamlet, city, and town.

Slowly they walked to the burial grounds, listened absently to the obsequies, and returned home with thoughts of their own—a future without a life companion, children without the patriarchal overseer, families without a male heir.

BY THE END OF 1862, the entire nation had felt the agonies of war. Still the worst was yet to come, for the muscle of the armies had been developed and munition factories were in full production. On the home front, food and clothing had skyrocketed, and many sole supporters of families lay cold and still in an ancestral grave. The possibility of keeping the average family afloat was fast diminishing.

Thanksgiving came and went with an austerity few had hitherto experienced, and then it was Christmas. For the sake of the children, elders clothed themselves with a gaiety they did not feel. News of Burnside's painful defeat at Fredericksburg did little to relieve the depression. Tears and blood had indeed mingled with the waters of the Rappahannock, and the affable, rotund general felt, for the first time in his career, the scorn and reproach of his battered troops—as well as Lincoln's keen disappointment. He would soon be relieved of his command.

As is characteristic of humankind, and particularly of a press bent on blowing out of proportion their pet peccadillos, eyes searched for someone upon whom the blame could be fastened. Scurrilous titles emanated both from Lincoln's political foes and from the pens of many an editor, but the man at the helm remained as fixed as an oak in a high wind. He wrote some time later to James Hackett that he "received a great deal of kindness, not free from ridicule—I am used to it." And to Secretary of War Stanton, "Truth is generally the best vindication against slander." For Lincoln, there were always the love of Mary Todd and the sure purposes of God.

On the heels of Burnside's defeat came dispatches of mounting casualties at Vicksburg. The place was proving to be a literal bastille, and five miles to the north, Sherman had lost 1700 men.

IN NABBY'S CAPABLE HANDS, Clinton shook off the fevers and by March was at last adding flesh to his bones. His latest visit to the Readville hospital confirmed his belief that his arm had also fully recovered, and he was apprised that any day now he would be returned to his regiment.

Matthew had qualified scholastically for entrance to the military academy and expected his appointment any day. When the summons arrived for him to take his physical, he left on the early train.

That evening, the family gathered without him for devotions. Clinton chose carefully the Scripture he hoped would give strength to his loved ones in his absence. He read the ninety-first psalm and then closed the book.

"I expect to be leaving in a matter of days," he said quietly.

"Let us ask the Lord to watch over us and bring us all safely together again."

The announcement was received with silence, each one struggling to hide his fears lest he put upon Clinton more than he should have to bear.

Caroline was in the midst of her petition when they heard the front door close. Matthew came in and stood silently on the threshold. Clinton moved noiselessly to pull up a chair, and Matthew sat down with an audible sigh, his face pale and his expression grim. Now the eyes of everyone in the room were on him. He took a deep breath.

"I shall not be going to West Point!" he stated flatly.

They waited for more.

"They said I have bad tonsils!"

Clinton's eyebrows converged like waves in a high wind. "They said what?"

"Bad tonsils!"

"And that would keep you out of West Point?" Anger surfaced in the usually passive man.

"Let's face it! It's my size. They let me down in a gentlemanly fashion!"

Nabby was outraged. "Really, Matthew! There must be another explanation. Little Phil Sheridan wasn't turned down!"

Caroline could see that the decision had left her brother in a dejected state. He wanted so much to be approved, to display his ability to succeed, and her parents' anger was doing little to help. She flashed her father a look of caution, which he seized upon immediately.

"Well, frankly, I am relieved," he managed.

Matthew looked astonished.

"Well, I am! I have just told the family that I will be leaving in a matter of days, and it will be of some comfort to know you will be here to help Hank watch over things."

The voiced confidence from Clinton seemed to be helping, so

he continued. "A military career for you would be like putting Hank on a circus trapeze. Just not for you."

"I'd like that!" exclaimed Bethia, never guessing the seriousness of the situation. "Flying through the air—turning somersaults!"

"Me, too!" agreed Joshua.

Caroline hung back when the others were dismissed. She felt keenly her brother's disappointment and humiliation. More, she felt resentment smoldering for the favoritism extended politically active families.

"You wouldn't look good in plebeskin anyway!" she said.

Matthew warmed to the empathy.

"I had hoped it would make a difference," he said. "Give me some reputation with my peers."

"It does make a difference, Matthew. You are free now to get on with your career. All you need is confidence in your abilities—and you know you have abilities!"

"You really mean that?"

"Of course, Matthew."

Matthew left the room savoring his sister's words and obviously encouraged. Caroline was left alone. She extinguished the flame in the lamp and walked to the window.

The yard was aglow with moonlight, and all was still. The tranquil scene beckoned her on into a moment of introspection. Why was there always something ahead for the others? Why the impending separation from her father? Why wars and why grief and why was there no word from Thad?

Then Clinton was beside her.

"Bless you, Carrie. Matthew listens to you. This might have knocked the props out from under him—I think it had . . . until you spoke to him."

She could see the soft, dark eyes looking down at her, and she dreaded the day that would take him away.

"Father, am I really strong? I mean—I seem to have all the

answers . . . but I have questions, too."

"Like?"

"The grief, Father. Why all the grief? Sometimes I understand, but lately I think I shall never know, especially when I read that God's thoughts are so much higher than ours. How can we know His reasons or His purposes?"

"His purpose has always been to make us like His Son."

"How could we ever attain to that? It is difficult enough to try to be like you!"

"Not high enough, Caroline."

"Well, it is high enough for me!"

"I'd rather you saw enough of Jesus in me to want to follow Him!"

"No. I like being like you. I like being me. That is enough!"

Clinton studied his daughter. Yes, she was like him, but only genetically and by imitation. How should he proceed with her? How could he tell her that her courage and good character were not enough, would not stand the tests of life, nor open the gates of heaven at death? No, this was not the time, for she was not truly seeking, not yet ready. He was not in the habit of picking green fruit. He could, however, sow.

"Carrie, we can choose to be satisfied all our lives with *hors d'oeuvres*, but we cannot grow on them. There is so much more. In fact, there is a banquet table and enough provision there to last a lifetime. Someday you will want more. Of that I am certain."

Caroline leaned into her father's arms, into the marvelous shelter of love and patience she had known from birth. There was comfort in his strength, his gentleness, the very sound of his voice.

"What if you don't come back, Father? Whatever would we do?"

"I will come back."

"Tell me that again—promise me!"

"I will come back, Carrie."

"Write to me—my own letters."

"I will write."

Then with a kiss on her cheek, he left. It was their last private conversation before his departure.

There was now time to be spent with Nabby; Clinton must leave her with more than responsibilities. They chose to walk through the woods and down by the pond. At the edge of the forest he marked several trees.

"When I return, we shall cut these down and pull stumps, but no need for that this year. I don't want you or Hank spending your strength unnecessarily."

Nabby was quiet, content with his presence.

Caroline watched her parents at a distance, marveling that the years seemed never to diminish their love for one another. They walked where Hank had already hung buckets on the sumac spiles, had stacked oak to dry and had chosen gluts to season over the fire. Hank, always the woodsman, preferred to make his own tools, particularly his axes.

When Caroline was alone with her mother, she waxed bold enough to ask the question that had piqued her curiosity.

"I have been watching you and Father when you walk together. What do you talk about?"

Nabby looked beyond her daughter, and for a moment Caroline wondered if she had heard.

"Nothing," she finally answered.

Caroline was sure there had to be more of an answer than that. "Nothing?"

"Yes, dear—really. This is one of those times when we know what is in the other's heart. There is much to be said for silence. When you love for a long time, there are things you know, and words only get in the way."

"Will I ever have that, Mother?"

Nabby smiled. "Yes, Carrie—I am certain that someday you will."

Clinton reserved the day before his departure for the younger children. They walked into town, where Clinton recounted the historical events of the old city; the call to arms for independence, the melting of silver teaspoons for the cartridge molds, the evacuation when false rumors had the British at their doorsteps, the helter-skelter flight from solemn church services, the hasty madness of grabbing up cats and leaving sleeping babies in their cradles—and the plans to burn bridges!

The Revolutionary chronicles, told aloud, always evoked laughter. The children went into paroxysms as Clinton wove the oft-told tales. It was marvelous to hear the laughter of his children. When they passed the Tracy house, now the city's library, he continued with his tales of the notables whose presence had graced the building: LaFayette, Washington, Jefferson, John Quincy Adams, Benedict Arnold—Aaron Burr. He told of the time the first president had visited the city; that remarkable Virginian, so sensitive to the whims of the people that he had obligingly left his carriage at a village green, mounted a white horse, and entered the city streets, doffing his hat to the cheering crowds and singing children.

"What a sight that must have been!" exclaimed Clinton, standing on the top step.

Joshua listened spellbound. Yes, he could see it all. Then he frowned.

"George Washington was a Virginian?" he asked.

"Indeed he was, and an aristocrat at that!"

"Then why are we fighting Virginians?"

It was not the first time Joshua had pondered the paradoxical situation, and Clinton knew his son wanted a valid answer.

"Sometimes in a family there are disagreements, but that does not mean we are not a family. It's that way right now. We are all Americans, but we are disagreeing."

"But we are shooting one another!"

"That is the sad part, Joshua—that we have come to that. I suppose there had to be a confrontation to make certain every member of the human family has the same rights."

"I don't understand it, Father."

Clinton looked long at his son before he spoke. "Perhaps, son, there is more than we see on the surface. Perhaps this is a purging, a cutting out of something that could ultimately destroy our nation. Surgery is seldom without pain. Perhaps our omniscient God has His own way of preserving His creation. It has never been in men to direct world affairs, even though they may think so. Nebuchadnezzar learned that."

Joshua looked unhappy, but Bethia seemed to grasp what Clinton was saying.

"But couldn't God straighten people out without a war?" she asked.

"No doubt He could, but He has been dealing with disobedience from the beginning of time. Sometimes He has to take His stiff-necked people to the woodshed to get our attention—and our obedience."

Bethia brightened. "Then all we need are more Christians!" She was certain she was the first to stumble upon the solution!

"Yes, Bethia, that is why we are compelled to see that the Gospel is preached in all of the world. Without it, there can be little hope that man will survive."

Bethia walked on, clinging to Clinton's arm. Joshua satisfied himself by keeping in step with his wonderful soldier father, dressed so smartly in his Union blue!

LATER CLINTON TOOK MATTHEW with him to bid farewell to his nephews. He had promised Vaugn that much. He was surprised to find Lerner Brisson there visiting Phoebe. When they entered the familiar parlor, Lerner arose from Vaugn's easy chair and extended a hand, as though Clinton were the outsider.

"You are leaving already?" asked Lerner, not completely masking his pleasure at the thought.

"Yes, in the morning."

Timothy and Allen entered the room in time to hear the end of the conversation.

"That's mighty soon, Uncle Clint," said Allen.

"Well, we can hope to see it over this year," rejoined Clinton.

"That isn't apt to happen!" retorted Brisson.

"Why do you say that?" asked Matthew.

"Should be clear as daylight. Neither side can withdraw now, having already spent its best."

Timothy chafed at the man's impertinence and his lack of sensitivity. "That, sir, is only poor conjecture." His tone bristled with sarcasm. "It is good that informed men do not share your pessimism."

Clinton could feel the antagonism growing and, not wanting to leave with the pot boiling, thought it best to change the subject.

"You must have done well in the market," he said, addressing Lerner.

Lerner rocked on his heels, enjoying center stage. "Yes, indeed. Thought it best to drop in on the family and advise them on the crops, come summer, and of course offer my help to Mrs. Haddon over her days of adjustment."

"She must be grateful for that," said Clinton, noticing as he spoke that neither of his nephews appreciated the comment.

"The older couple you hired, the Lindquists—are they proving worthwhile?" he asked the twins.

"Yes! Excellent workers, and knowledgeable, too. They'll see us through both planting and harvesting."

The boys followed their uncle to the door and on into the yard.

"Watch that man!" cautioned Clinton.

CLINTON LEFT THE NEXT MORNING, traveling on the Providence Railroad for New Haven, where Dr. Lyman examined him and gave him clearance for duty.

Back to cramped quarters and a new breed of companions. Most of his companions were bounty enlistees, some of whom would desert before they fired a gun. Judging from appearances, many had never worked a day in their lives.

As the train moved on, drunken soldiers began tearing up the car seats and smashing windows. Two of the worst took it upon themselves to rip the small and only stove from its moorings and send it flying from the train. Soon after that, the petty thefts began.

They moved from the train to a ship, where the outrageous behavior continued. Clinton began to think seriously about seeking an ally for the rest of the journey. After asking questions of a few men who seemed respectable, he decided on a returning enlistee like himself.

The man seemed glad to be asked for his companionship, and at mess they both managed to arm themselves with table knives. They also made a pact to take turns sleeping. The agreement proved profitable for both. Even in the dark, Clinton could see that the robbers had plans of their own. Pretending sleep, he waited until they were almost upon his companion, then he leaped and caught an assailant by the throat. Rolling and kicking, the two grappled, waking the entire hold. Sleeping officers were summoned, and not knowing for certain who was responsible for the fracas, threatened them all with court-martial. That warning proved a decided deterrent, at least for a time.

Clinton bedded down near his new acquaintance and turned for succor to his memories of his brief furlough.

Stormy seas and angry skies broke forth as they neared Cape Hatteras, and a detachment of volunteer blacks became the new victims of the ruffians' treatment. The situation became so explosive that the officer in charge felt obliged to separate the blacks from their tormentors. But instead of putting the rascals on the unsheltered deck, he placed the blacks there, explaining loudly that he did so in order to preserve their lives.

The incompetency of some politically appointed officers was appalling! Why, by all that was just, should the innocent men be placed on the cold, windswept decks, while the perpetrators had shelter below?

"What a shame," Clinton confided to his friend. "They don't get any better treatment from the Union than they got from their slave masters."

"Their war will be longer than ours," prophesied his friend.

Clinton welcomed the day they disembarked, and he went joyfully to his old campground just outside New Bern. There the conversation of the troops centered around January's Stone River battles and the emergence of two great Federal commanders: "Pap" Thomas and "Little Phil" Sheridan. There was, however, little over which to gloat, for the battles were of a seesaw nature. Persistent attacks came in skirmishes on the outskirts of New Bern, and Clinton seemed to welcome them, as he did the frequent occasions of provost duty in the city. It gave him an added opportunity to inquire about Drake Singleton.

"Where do I inquire about a missing soldier?" he asked his new commander.

"What soldier?"

"I had a buddy—Drake Singleton."

"In your unit?"

"Yes, sir."

"When did he disappear?"

"Months ago. We were both wounded near Kinston. I had to leave him at the field hospital. I was wounded, and he was shot up too much for travel. Last I saw of him, he was on the operating table."

"Was this near Whitehall?"

"Yes, sir." Clinton felt encouraged. This man seemed to know something.

The lieutenant grew thoughtful. Then, shaking his head, he uttered an oath. "That was a battle!"

"You know about it?"

"The Rebs broke through the lines. Losses were bad—hundreds of prisoners taken! We brought up reinforcements, though, and got the lines closed. It was mayhem!"

"And the hospital station?"

"Not there! Cremated!"

Clinton blanched. Drake—what of him? Blown to bits—cremated, too? He clenched his fists, feeling anger as he had never felt it before. He had told Joshua that he did not hate the Rebs. Now he would have to believe it!

"But there should have been a body!"

"There were enough of those."

Thanking the officer, Clinton turned away. The answer simply was not good enough, and the shock of the news and the void left by Drake's absence kindled and burned like hot coals within his breast. Once again he vowed he would never give up the search. He walked through the familiar streets, taking out his frustration on the pavement. Then he came to his old newspaper office. He entered and was surprised to find several of his old companions still there. The welcome he received did somewhat to relieve the misery he was feeling.

"Tell your commanding officer that you worked here before. He may let you come back," suggested one.

Within days, Clinton was back working in the office. Now he could remain informed about the battles taking place. The weather was warming and so, too, was the fighting. A large battle was forming at Chancellorsville.

News broke on the fifth of May. The Union general was no match for Lee. The Federals suffered a devastating defeat with casualties numbering 17,000. Lee's losses were not as severe, if one were to count numbers, but greater than the loss of 13,000 men was the shocking and distressing news of the loss of his dearest comrade in arms, the courageous and godly Stonewall Jackson. He had taken six shots from his own men when returning from reconnaissance. In a heavy fog, they had mistaken him for the enemy. After an amputation, he had contracted pneumonia and died, leaving his general in a state of distress and grief from which he would never recover.

Nevertheless, the committed General Lee moved on with his men in the direction of Pennsylvania, where a Union general by the name of George C. Meade awaited him.

News broke over the wireless as Clinton sat poised with pen and paper. The battle all had braced for was under way. Ninety thousand Bluecoats faced seventy thousand of Dixie's stalwarts. It was July first, and the town was Gettysburg!

PART TWO

17

For the young nation, July Fourth seemed ever written in the annals of God. While Confederate General Pickett squandered his troops on Cemetery Ridge, Grant, after months of fighting at Vicksburg, finally gained his objective. Confederate General John Pemberton was victorious at the mighty Mississippi, and the "Father of Waters" was opened at last. The victory had not been an easy one.

On the same day, news of the two major victories flooded into New Bern, setting off the usual fanfare and joyful celebration.

The defeat of the Southern forces should have dampened the spirit of the Confederates, but it did nothing of the kind. The Sons of Dixie remained intransigent, having no intention of deserting their noble commander. They would rally again and strike again, as long as General Lee gave the command.

On the heels of fresh victories came news of the death of Grant's close friend Admiral Foote. His demise brought to an abrupt halt any thought of unrestrained reveling. Instead of the victory cannonade, the guns on the River Neuse began thundering out a hero's requiem.

Clinton listened all day to the salute, wondering at the strange ways of man. What the wretched sounds of war could possibly do for the departed was beyond understanding. The man was already over the crystal sea and at rest under the shade of Stonewall

Jackson's trees. Far removed were they both from the vain glory of martial victory.

Were they standing together on that other shore—with Vaugn—shaking their heads at the folly of man? Were they at peace in the presence of the Divine Commander—allies in a greater world? And was it possible that Drake was with them?

Days and weeks moved on at the newspaper office much the same, but the respite was not to last. It seemed that the antidote of Nabby's nourishing diet had run its course, and the starchy army diet had resumed its degenerative work. Clinton broke out with severe boils, making sleep impossible. In a fit of desperation he went to the hospital seeking relief. Quinine and hot compresses brought about a slight improvement. But in the midst of his suffering, the orders came to move out.

Battles were exploding in the direction of Richmond. Tents were struck early, and the packing of gear ensued with the usual questions. Would this be the real thing or just another stalling tactic?

From both sides of the river, men began to board transports. It was noon before they weighed anchor, and they formed no small armada. As they moved into the Atlantic, once again the sight of the swelling squadron stirred the adrenaline. The men were ordered to find sleeping space on the decks. They settled down with little intention of sleeping, and by three o'clock in the morning they were still eagle-eyed, anticipating the unknown. The sea was alive with vessels; six to eight monitors lined up with the gunboats. In another direction lay the transports and the barges.

At five o'clock the order came, and the monitors took the lead, slipping by a muddy peninsula and along a narrow river. On shore, slaves danced excitedly about, and occasionally a handsome old Southern plantation came into view. The house shutters were always closed, but there was evidence on the grounds of life within.

There was a certain austerity about the scenes they passed. It was no secret that the South was hurting. Their currency had fallen, leaving a dollar equivalent to a former five-cent piece. Flour was nearly unattainable, and other essentials had skyrocketed. Indeed, a Spartan diet had already found its way to many a Southern general's table, and the slaves were running away, leaving the fields to untrained hands and scorching suns. Men on deck could make out a band of runaways throwing up entrenchments for their Union liberators. Was it possible that the "grand finale" was being orchestrated?

When the order came to clear the decks, the men were alerted to the signal that danger lay ahead. Clinton could see a flag of truce flying from a Union steamer anchored at a wharf. The crafty Butler had sent it ahead loaded with rebel prisoners. So! There was to be a prisoner exchange, and Mulford was directing the operation! The white-flagged vessel would forestall any form of treachery.

On the wharf, Northern parolees huddled in small straggling groups. Even from a distance one could observe their tattered condition. Confederate prisoners were sent even further upstream, and Clinton was ordered to join a detachment of officers acting as escorts for their exchanged men. Still on deck, he was able to study the motley group of Union men. They must have come down from the Belle Isle Prison. They were herded toward the waiting transport, guns trained and ready.

As they drew close to the scene of exchange, Clinton could see that many were on litters, and others were struggling for balance with only one leg for support. The filthy bandages and ragged strips of cloth covering leg and head wounds made them look like Stevenson's street Arabs. Clinton went down the lowered plank to the wharf with the other escort officers. As he neared the group, one man seemed to stand out from the others. He was taller and had a way of standing more erect, even as he leaned on a roughly hewn crutch. Clinton walked up to him, and at close range saw the crinkles in the corners of the man's eyes. His head spun.

"Drake—is it possible?" he managed.

Drake, with a heavy beard and his flesh hanging on him like an old garment, could still smile—still display the old game and cocky spirit that so marked him! Yet he knew the moment was a tense one, and knew also that any display or emotional outburst would endanger them all. He smiled broadly. It would have to be enough!

"Take this man to medical headquarters immediately!" ordered Clinton.

The men shuffled onto a steamer and headed downriver, leaving Clinton with a strange mixture of feelings. The exultation of finding his friend at last, followed by the prompt wretched parting, ripped him in two. He cursed the water that was stretching between them, and when the ship turned in the bend of the river, he hastened to the rail. From there he could see Drake waving his crutch over his head—then he was beyond sight.

Clinton started to cry, and then his throat filled with laughter. The strange sounds that erupted from him drew the attention of his companions.

"Someone you know?" asked the man next to him.

"Yes—yes, indeed. Someone I know!"

For the rest of the journey Clinton remained in a state of joy. After the prisoner exchange he found himself sailing up the coast to Albemarle Sound and then into the Chowan River . . . and still no sign of action. They had all been so certain that Richmond was the target, but it was not to be, and no explanation was forthcoming. The expedition proved only to be a diversional ploy, and the food offered the men was enough to give a fellow a case of scurvy, as well as mutinous thoughts.

Spring rains brought on the influenza again. Many men died. No mail came aboard, and the troops sank into emptiness. Clinton's thoughts turned toward home. The crops would be reaching their fruitful crest, and the wasted time on board the steamer was aggravating.

CAROLINE STOOD IN THE EARLY DAWN, looking out at the tasseled corn. Before the sun set, the ears would be husked and packed, and muscles would be complaining. She wondered if the women of the South knew anything of aching muscles and weary bones. She had heard that they were the pampered darlings of the plantations, shielded from labors so far beneath them. It would be easy to envy them—but deep inside she knew, too, that she could never live with such preference. It would give her a feeling of being the man's plaything, his mantel trophy, and the thought was appalling. No, she could never be placed in that subservient position! To be robbed of the pleasure of working in the fields, watching the arrival of spring, the full growth of summer, the harvest of autumn—no, never would that be her lot.

Her glance swept the dear scenes; the axweed, the smartweed, and the toadflax, all tempting the small hands of children; the rosy-plumed hardhack like royal sentinels standing at attention, the yellow foxglove clinging to rocky, dried-out roadsides, bees exploring the cool, sweet depths of her mother's dahlias. This was her world!

But there was something about the stillness of this particular morning—a breathlessness, as though the world were awaiting a climactic event. Somehow it frightened her. It was different from the other days when she had had only a sleeping fear of evil news. This morning she felt the presence of something ominous, and she knew she must dismiss the dreadful feeling. One could not get on with the work under such a cloud. Battles seemed to be swinging in favor of the Union, and word was abroad that Sherman and Grant were already headed for a rendezvous. Could that be what her senses were anticipating?

She finished with the dairy work and retraced her steps to the house. The day passed much as the days before it, with meals to prepare and general household duties to perform.

Matthew, as usual, returned in the evening with the newspaper and the inevitable casualty list. This evening he seemed unusually reticent, and this should have alarmed her. The family had retired early, for they would be up long before sunrise. When Caroline noticed Matthew watching her, she gave him a quizzical look. Then he was approaching her, and the fears of the morning moved back in.

"What is it, Matthew?" She steeled herself for the worst.

"Something you would want to know," he answered.

"Father?" She hardly dared breathe his name.

"No."

"Thank God!"

He handed her the paper. Her heart refused to quiet, and she could feel the pulse beat in her neck. Down the dreaded column—till the name Paxton met her searching eyes. Dead? No. Missing! Unaccounted for!

It was useless to pretend to Matthew that Thad was only a neighbor. Caroline leaned against the sink for support—cold support indeed, but at least it would steady her.

"I'm sorry, Carrie. I really am."

She must get her composure, but it was not easy. She must not cry, that was unthinkable, but why—why had Thad enlisted? There had been time enough for that . . . and what could it all mean? Why couldn't the commanders keep records? Could he be among the dead whose remains would be forever lost? Oh, dear God—why these testing times? Why not straight facts—facts one could adjust to? Matthew stood there observing her, waiting to see just how strong she was. Well, he would not see her naked self, her wounded heart—her weakness! She must say something.

"I—I must go to his mother in the morning." She left the room hurriedly.

It was like old times turning in at the Virginia fence. It was early morning and Caroline could see Mr. Paxton in the fields. He seemed to be scouring a steel plow, probably getting ready for a late crop. He and Thad were much alike, always engrossed and completely sold out to the interest at hand, to the exclusion of all else. The thought stirred little buds of resentment, and she checked herself. If such a judgmental attitude were to surface, it would surely show when she faced Mrs. Paxton. She had come to comfort, not to condemn.

Mary Paxton came to the door wiping her hands on a clean white apron. She was a small woman with eyes like her son's. She had been crying, seemingly without restraint, for the red eyes and damp cheeks divulged her grief.

"Bless you, child, bless you. Do come in. I'll have tea in a few minutes." She went to work cutting far too many slices of nut bread, anxious to keep her hands busy. Once she stopped to wipe her eyes on a small, crushed handkerchief, then she set out the teacups.

The house was so familiar, stirring memories of the past when they had all been younger, and peace was the order of the day. Caroline looked at the great high kitchen hutch with the pewter mugs and porringers, and then at the maple hoosier so much like her own.

"You must know why I am here, Mrs. Paxton," she began.

"Yes, dear. I have been expecting you."

"Please tell me, what have you heard?"

Mrs. Paxton shuffled off toward the parlor and returned with several papers.

"You can see from these that Thad is missing. I was notified only yesterday." Her tears overflowed again, as though the painful thought were squeezing a sponge that would not run dry.

Caroline read the documents and gave them back to her. "He didn't write to me very often." How could she tell his mother that he had never written at all? "Where did he disappear?" she continued, hoping to learn more.

"Mr. Paxton seems to think it must have been at Cedar Creek."

"Oh, glory! Matthew read us about that battle!"

"Was it really bad?"

Mrs. Paxton seemed ignorant of the details. Of course, that was the kind of woman she was, engrossed in her role of mother and housekeeper—and she was proficient at that. Her house was always shining.

"Maybe he was up against Jeb Stuart's cavalry!"

Mrs. Paxton looked down at her hands sadly, the whistling teakettle forgotten. "He wanted to be in the Cavalry. I had no idea of the danger. It sounded safer than the infantry."

"You must not lose hope, Mrs. Paxton. Men have often turned up after they have been reported missing."

"I am trying to believe that, Caroline, I really am. But all night I could see him lying dead on a battlefield. Is God trying to tell me he is dead?"

Caroline put her arms around the sagging shoulders.

"Don't give up hope. You must pray and believe that he is alive, and that when this is over, he'll come home. We will both pray."

The visit remained in Caroline's mind for days, and Mary Paxton's depression began to settle into her own breast. She wanted to believe that Thad was alive, but the nagging fear that he wasn't persisted. If he were never to come home, what then? She drew off by herself, her attitude forbidding the family to mention his name. The field work now demanded all hands available, and she was glad for the diversion. It took the edge from her loneliness. She managed to get through the summer unaware that the very grief she was trying to hide was engraving a solemnity to her face and an impenetrable armor to her mien.

She was glad when her mother spoke of planning a family dinner to take the place of the usual marshland picnic.

"We must invite Phoebe and the children for Sunday dinner," Nabby said.

Bethia and Joshua approved the suggestion heartily, and set off to take the invitation to Phoebe at once. They soon returned with her answer. She could not attend, as Mr. Brisson would be visiting, but the children would be delighted to accept.

The family made their ritualistic observance of the sabbath and returned home punctually to prepare for their dinner guests. Matthew had bought his five-cent lobsters from Joppa, and the women had spread the table with an abundance of garden vegetables. A knock on the door brought the young ones squealing.

"Mother sent a blueberry pie, Aunt Nabby!" said the jovial Timothy, placing the rare treat on the sideboard. "But you don't get any!" he teased, yanking on Bethia's braids.

Allen wrestled Joshua to the floor and pinned him.

"I'll get you when I am bigger!" promised Joshua, delighted with the attention.

"And I would guess that time is not too far away!" rejoined Allen. Then he sought out Caroline. "Let me whip the potatoes!" he offered.

"You wouldn't know how," she teased.

"Yes, I would!" he insisted, and Caroline relented.

Seated finally at the table, he leaned close to his cousin. "I wish it were like this at our house."

Caroline was still not ready for the old camaraderie. He might ask questions, and she was not ready to talk.

"Come now, Allen. Aunt Phoebe is an excellent cook!"

"It's not that. It's the change with Father gone."

"It must be difficult for your mother, too."

"It was at first—but lately—"

Timothy caught the end of the conversation and joined in.

"Mr. Brisson seems to be helping Mother over the hard days. He pays on time and does a lot of the accounts for her. You know she never did take much to that sort of work."

"I think he likes our mother," observed Allen, clearly not enchanted with the thought. Then in order to lighten the mood, he turned to his younger cousin. "And you, Bethia—do you like Mr. Brisson?"

"I think I could like him better if he'd take a bath!"

Joshua giggled and the twins broke out laughing, much to Bethia's surprise. She had not meant to be funny.

Nabby looked embarrassed, but Allen confided to Caroline that he thought Bethia more perceptive than most folk.

"You don't like him?" she asked.

"Neither did your father!" came the response.

It surprised Caroline that Allen would divulge that much. He was usually cautious with words. Perhaps he would explain more if they had a chance to talk alone.

Allen successfully changed the subject, turning to Caroline again and trying to draw her out. "There'll be a band concert next Saturday at the Mall. Mother thinks I should take Clara."

"That would be nice," Caroline replied without emotion.

Though national elections were still a year away, the table talk turned to the candidates being suggested. Opposition to Lincoln's demand for an all-out offensive had bred hostility and brought into prominence a candidate with a conciliatory platform—the procrastinating General George B. McClellan.

Fatigue lines were engraving the President's rugged features. His usual smile had a down-at-the-corners droop, and patches of gray now flecked his dark hair. The recent loss of his beloved son Willie had added a sadness to his countenance, and why he would go on in a presidency beset with so many trials and disappointments was a mystery. Still—it only answered more clearly the fact that his was an indomitable spirit, one that would not be vanquished until righteousness and justice prevailed. He could not, would not leave a task half done.

18

THE MENTION OF A BAND CONCERT not only took the fancy of the young children, but was a bright prospect in a world grown heavy and ponderous. The elders deemed it a welcome diversion from the depressive days of war, so the Haddons made plans to attend the social event.

When Saturday arrived, they started off in a cheerful mood. Allen fell behind the group to walk with Caroline.

"My mother is really testing us," he confided.

"How is that?"

"I think she will marry Lerner Brisson!"

Caroline stared at Allen, obviously shocked. "You must be mistaken. She wouldn't think of such a thing so soon!"

"I am sure she would. She listens to every suggestion he makes."

Caroline waited for more.

"Now he brings his Bordeaux with him—and worse, he wants her to dismiss the Lindquists."

"Allen, that doesn't make sense! There is still the harvest!"

"All of which could mean that Timothy and I will have to forego our last year of school."

"But no mother wants to remove her children from school in their final year!"

"I am sure it isn't what she wants, but Mr. Brisson has

convinced her that the Lindquists are an unnecessary drain on our finances. He says they are not worth their salt!"

Caroline grew silent, wondering what evil news could possibly come next. They had reached the Mall grounds, and she saw Timothy waiting for them with the children hanging on his arms. But her mind was not on the children or the band concert. Perhaps her mother could speak to Phoebe, dissuade her somehow from going on with her plans. Caroline's thoughts were so engaged that she brushed clumsily past the people crowding into the grounds and abruptly crashed into a man wearing a tall, gray felt hat. Suddenly she found herself face-to-face with Jerome Cavell!

"Well! If it isn't Miss Haddon!" he exclaimed with frank pleasure.

A young woman was holding fast to his right arm as though she might lose him, and she studied Caroline with bold curiosity. In spite of the confusion, Caroline resorted to her early training and began to make introductions.

"Mr. Cavell, meet my cousins Timothy and Allen, and their little sister, Clara."

"You are looking well, Caroline," he said, seeing no one but the dark-eyed girl before him.

His companion bristled at the slight, and he remembered he had an obligation to introduce her. Caroline didn't hear her name. She was looking at Jerome and wondering against her will why he attracted her as he did. Then they were moving away from one another.

"He likes you, Caroline," observed Allen.

"He likes many women!"

Allen could see that his cousin was dismissing any form of intimate conversation. He wished she would talk.

"Are you still grieving for Thad?"

Caroline's eyes grew misty. "Thad was very dear to me."

Allen was sorry he had asked the question, but before he could apologize, the younger children were upon them, laughing exuberantly.

"We met Mr. Cavell. Did you know he was here?" they asked.

"We asked him to sit with us during the concert!" exclaimed Joshua.

Caroline's face colored. "He didn't accept!"

"Yes, he did. He's so nice!"

Caroline swallowed hard. What had her father taught her? Sort out your problems, decide the best action for each one, and be done with it! She thought she had solved the problem of Jerome Cavell, and for good! Now, it seemed, it was all right back in her lap, and she had neither patience nor time to do any more sorting. He was already approaching them with his lady, and smiling like a gladiator who has overcome an opponent!

"I accepted your sister's invitation. I trust that meets with your approval."

"Of course," answered Allen, not wishing to seem inhospitable. Then he led the way to a row of seats, and Caroline followed. Jerome seemed to be glowing with pleasure at having disturbed the haughty Miss Haddon.

"I hope you realize I did not plan this." He spoke softly, sheltering her from the curious, but she refused to look at him.

The band struck up with its usual gusto. Caroline could feel his eyes upon her, and struggled to look unperturbed.

"If I am spoiling your evening, I'll leave," he said.

"Let me assure you, I care little one way or the other."

"Then I shall stay."

"Suit yourself." Then, stealing a glance at him, she inquired, "Aren't you out of your element?"

"The company or the music?"

"Both!"

"I rather fancy both! Does that please you?"

Caroline sent a helpless glance in Allen's direction. She could not be certain that he had heard any of the conversation, as he was looking in the opposite direction and scowling.

"She wouldn't!" Allen exclaimed, though the words came forth in more of a hiss than a casual comment.

Caroline followed his gaze.

Phoebe had arrived, clinging hard to the arm of Mr. Brisson, which might have passed as acceptable had she not been walking with uncertainty and stumbling as she went. Her voice carried above the clashing cymbals and beating drums, shrill and giddy.

"She's been drinking!" came the muffled cry of Timothy. "They'll have the gossips' tongues wagging before sunup."

The musicians went on with unrestrained enthusiasm until the intermission. Then Allen was on his feet, every muscle taut.

"What are you going to do?" Caroline asked.

"I am going to tell him to take my mother home!" He broke away from the group.

Seeing the distress on Caroline's face, Jerome leaned toward her. "Something wrong?"

"It's a family thing." Caroline rose to her feet and ventured toward the scene.

"You are making a spectacle of yourself, Mother. Please leave." It was Allen speaking.

"But we have just begun to enjoy it. We don't want to leave!" Phoebe giggled obnoxiously.

"The public should get used to seeing us together, and the sooner the better," declared Lerner.

"Sir, my father has been dead for a matter of months only!"

"That is of little consequence to us. I suggest you return to your friends. We intend to stay."

Allen's face grew scarlet.

"Then I shall take her home myself," he declared and whirled Phoebe away from the deceitful little man. It was clear that Lerner had been drinking, too. His nostrils flared like those of an animal about to do battle. The impudence of the adolescent was more than he could endure, and he swung a fist in Allen's direction, widely missing him. Timothy then went after Lerner, and Caroline moved to stop the altercation. By the time she got to them, Timothy was on the ground holding his jaw.

"Don't fight him, Timothy. He's too cunning for you."

But the irascible Mr. Brisson would have no interruption. He was enjoying the moment and had pulled Timothy to his feet, preparing to send another blow in his direction. Suddenly a hand came down on his shoulder, and he was spun around to meet someone more his equal. Jerome Cavell had entered the fray, and his first blow sent Lerner sprawling, utterly surprised.

"Take this lady home," Jerome demanded.

Lerner arose, brushing his coat and looking at his assailant with fear and curiosity. Phoebe had sobered enough to realize they were creating a scene. She was frightened.

"Yes, Lerner. Take me home."

Reluctantly Brisson moved off while Allen and Timothy wrung Jerome's hand enthusiastically.

"I'll kill him yet!" Timothy swore.

"Now you know why we have been concerned," Allen said to Caroline.

Jerome moved defensively beside her, flexing one finger and then the other of his right hand.

"You are proving to be quite a *femme fatale*—now I shall be obliged to perform my concerts left-handed!"

Caroline grew instantly sympathetic, realizing she had not been very courteous. "Thank you, Jerome. I do appreciate your help. My cousins are not in the habit of picking quarrels. They are going through very bad times."

It was the first time all evening that she had looked at him directly.

"I don't like a poor match. The boys were too young for the

bully. Who is he, anyway?"

"He's an extroloper!" put in Joshua, anxious to express his views.

"Joshua means interloper, Mr. Cavell," corrected Bethia.

By this time Jerome's lady had taken herself away from the display of fisticuffs and was nowhere to be seen.

"He must have talked marriage to my mother, or she would never have come out in public with him," said Allen, still troubled.

"Well, if that pompous little weasel ever moves into my father's house, I shall move out!" vowed the volatile Timothy.

"Not so fast, Timothy," cautioned his quiet twin.

Jerome walked with them to the street entrance, attempting to piece together the background of the feud. Timothy and Allen walked ahead, the children dancing beside them.

"I would like to see you again, Caroline," said Jerome, searching her face for some evidence of friendliness.

"I don't know what to say. You have been kind."

"It seems the fates have brought us together again, doesn't it? I had no part in it."

"Perhaps I will see you, but not right away. I am deluged with problems and with work."

"I shall be in town in October. Will you see me then?"

"If we could be just friends."

"We could go to the island."

"In October, then—but an afternoon, please."

Then he was gone, and Caroline was left with her thoughts . . . and her fears.

IT WAS NEARING THE END of August when Caroline opened the door to Timothy, who came bursting in with a sullen expression on his face.

"Mercy, Tim! You look like the end of the world!"

"It's that man again. He has sent the Lindquists packing. Can you believe that?"

"And Phoebe let him do it?"

"Mother no longer has a mind of her own!"

Secretly Caroline wondered if Aunt Phoebe had ever had a mind of her own.

Nabby had entered the kitchen in time to hear of the dismissal. Her eyes met Caroline's.

"The Lindquists are good people. What a dreadful way to treat them!"

Timothy went on. "I know it is that Brisson. He knows nothing of growing crops!"

Hank, too, had come upon the scene and stood silently by, wondering how to correct the situation.

"You will have a heap of work cut out for you without the Lindquists," he said.

"We had hoped Mother would have sense enough to keep them at least for another year. We'll be through school then. Allen likes the farm, but I had hoped to go on and finish. Father understood that. If we pull out for a year, it isn't likely we shall ever go back."

"There must be a solution, Timothy—and if there is, we shall find it!" Nabby tried to soothe Timothy's frustrated spirit.

The incident passed, leaving Nabby struggling to find the best way to help her nephews. School would be starting soon, and she could put off a confrontation with her sister-in-law no longer. She decided to take advantage of the fact that their church pews were adjacent. Phoebe would have to be civil there.

When Sunday arrived, Nabby watched as Vaugn's family filed into their familiar place. It was worth a try. The sermon was not long, and with the benediction pronounced and the final hymn sung, the good parson strode to the foyer. The massive doors were flung open, and the congregation poured down over the broad stairs. The elite drove off in fine carriages, and the bourgeoisie left in their wagons. The few males in attendance swung up and on to their horses and fled the scene, expecting more of the day than a dissertation! Nabby purposefully confronted Phoebe.

"Phoebe, I should like some time with you," she said.

Phoebe pulled a scarlet hood over her pale blonde hair and busied herself with a black knit glove.

"I am really in a hurry, Nabby. Can't it wait?"

"No, I must talk with you."

"Well, not now. Lerner is coming to dinner!"

"Then please come for afternoon tea, and bring Mr. Brisson with you."

"I will see what Lerner wants."

"It is very important."

"All right, all right. We will come."

"Thank you, Phoebe. Will you come at two-thirty?"

"Let us make it three o'clock. I dislike hurrying." She dismissed Nabby by expressing concern for Clara, who had wandered off.

Promptly at three o'clock Phoebe and Lerner appeared at the door, Phoebe clinging possessively to the arm of the obnoxious man. He smiled slightly, hoping to convey to Nabby that he was a reasonable fellow.

Like my cat before eating her catch! thought Nabby.

Matthew took their light coats and led them to the pleasant sitting room, where Lerner chose to sit on the coarse horsehair sofa. Phoebe pulled a Boston rocker close beside him. With pleasantries over, Nabby brought gingersnaps and tea from the kitchen. Caroline, at Nabby's request, had taken the children for a walk.

"You have something to discuss?" asked Phoebe, already uncomfortable in Nabby's presence.

Nabby came right to the point. "I hear you have let the Lindquists go."

Phoebe's eyebrows rose, as did her suspicions. "Someone been talking out of school?"

"Timothy did mention it, although the news seems to be common knowledge. The Gilberts have already snapped them up. They have an excellent reputation, you know."

"I can't see that their dismissal concerns you, Nabby."

"You and the children will always concern me, Phoebe."

How like her to put me on the defensive, thought Nabby. This will not be easy.

Phoebe fidgeted nervously. "Yes, we did let them go. Lerner felt they were more of a drain than a help."

"But you will need them for harvest and planting."

"I have two strong, healthy sons!" exclaimed Phoebe, looking to Lerner for support.

"But they will be in school."

Lerner cleared his throat. "Really now, Mrs. Haddon. How much education does a farmer need? But if the boys are at all serious about school, they can finish another year. We won't be getting the prices we get now if the war should end. You can count on that."

"The boys want to finish with their classmates."

"I don't see how that is important!" Lerner retorted.

In desperation Nabby appealed to the maternal instinct of the woman facing her.

"Is this really fair to your children, Phoebe?" she asked.

Phoebe arose from her chair, looking like a pot about to boil over.

"I have to be the judge of that. It is my family!"

"But Vaugn would never have done things this way."

"Vaugn is dead. I am now the one making the decisions. Lerner and I shall be married in a few months. He has been a great help to me, and I value his wisdom and concern. If he thinks the boys can finish their education later, that is fine with me."

Until now Matthew had remained silent, quietly listening. "You surprise me, Mr. Brisson," he said. "I would have thought you would want the goodwill of Timothy and Allen."

"They are mere children, and I intend that they adjust to my ways." He stopped and studied the frail form of the elder Haddon family heir. "And since we are to be in the same family, it does not seem out of order to have me selling your produce."

"My father makes those decisions, sir. And since you are not in the family yet, and since my father is absent, I find you not only presumptuous, but quite offensive!"

The remark sent fire into Lerner's eyes, fire he could not control. He jumped to his feet and strode toward the coatrack.

"We shall see who is presumptuous, young man. We shall see!"

The two left in a huff.

"How can she tolerate him?" exclaimed the usually quiet Matthew. "If he is this officious in a green season, how could one expect anything better later?"

"The boys will have to assert their rights, I do believe," sighed Nabby, as she watched them cross the fields.

Allen came several days later.

"I am going to visit the headmaster, Aunt Nabby. Perhaps we can arrange something."

"Will Timothy go with you?"

"No. He says he doesn't care, but I think he's just angry."

"Do you want me to go with you? Sometimes an older person has some influence."

Allen seemed relieved. "I'd welcome that!"

THE HEADMASTER ENTERED the small reception room and greeted his visitors cordially. He was man enough to appreciate the appearance of the attractive Nabby. Her hair was braided and pinned in a neat crown, giving her a regal look. Her eyes, blue as a September sky, were as appealing as ever.

He seemed not even to have seen Allen.

"And what can I do for you, Mrs. Haddon?" he asked.

Nabby studied her son's former principal. His hair was salt-and-pepper and parted in the middle. He was tall, with his long legs seeming to grow from a little balloon belly, and a button was missing from his vest. His face was pale, and his silver spectacles pinched an already pinched long nose. He kept his lips pursed, believing it added to his scholarly appearance.

"We have come to ask about making allowances for the coming school year," said Allen, intent upon getting to the point.

"The boys are good students," said Nabby.

"And the war has forced changes," added Allen.

"Yes, boy, I know. We are aware of your loss. A fine man, Vaugn Haddon. Such a pity—so strong and young. It's the good Lord's mercy that his wife has two fine sons to help carry on. That's not the case with many."

"That is what we have come to discuss," said Allen.

"The boys want to know if they might be shown some leniency. They have only themselves to shoulder the work now, and they were hoping they might be allowed to do some of their schoolwork at home—perhaps attend three days a week."

Nabby made her request with such an endearing smile that Mr. Todd melted. This lovely lady shouldn't have to beg!

"I think I might arrange something. I will take it up with my superiors. I can recommend consideration."

"You would do that?"

"The Haddons are well-respected."

"You are an understanding man, Mr. Todd. God bless you!"

The compliment went straight to the tall man's heart and sealed his loyalties. He would do all in his power to deserve it.

Nabby and Allen left the school in high spirits. They could have some optimism now, and perhaps Phoebe would be a little more tractable. They went together to tell her of the schoolmaster's reasonable attitude.

But Phoebe flushed with embarrassment when she saw Nabby. After all, their last meeting had not been a friendly one. Allen broke the tension.

"We have been to see Mr. Todd. I believe he is going to allow Tim and me to do our lessons at home. That way we can finish with our class. Isn't that good news?"

"Shouldn't I have been the one to see Mr. Todd?" Phoebe demanded.

Nabby looked away from her contentious sister-in-law, praying silently. "I am afraid you are still angry with me, Phoebe. I only wanted to help. The boys are precious to me . . . like my own. I find it difficult to think of them otherwise."

It was the nearest Nabby could come to an apology.

"What is the difference, Mother? I've got to be the man of the house someday, and this seemed the time. You should have seen how obliging Mr. Todd was. He said the Haddons were respected. I thought that was very gracious."

Phoebe stood silent, cool but appreciative of her son's inclination to fight his own battles. She could not with any grace oppose him now, with the principal already cognizant of the situation. She must not appear unreasonable.

"Go and tell your brother. He will want to know."

Allen hurried from the room, and Phoebe's eyes narrowed.

"I cannot say that I appreciate what you have done. I should have been told of your intentions. If you insist on turning my sons against me, I shall sever all relationship with the Haddons and move away."

"Would you really?" Nabby's comment had more of a challenge in it than an inquiry.

"Yes! I have had enough of this farm and of the Haddons."

"Then I shall hope that you will change your mind. This is home for your children, and they will always be Haddons. I am sure Vaugn expected more of you—more wisdom than you are showing."

It was time to go before any more was said, so Nabby took her leave. She stopped at the barn to see Hank.

Thank God for Hank. Whoever would have thought that her crippled brother could have taken on so much? She was rich indeed—with Hank, with her children, and with the love and trust of her husband.

19

With the Lindquists gone, and the work of stable and field increasing, the twins found it no small task to keep up with their school assignments. The days were long, and the nights under a flickering kerosene lamp became a wearisome thing. Even the elements seemed aligned against them, for rain was slow in coming, and the ponds and wells were at a low.

Nevertheless, the boys had the assiduous nature of the New England Yankee in their genes. They would prove to the covetous Mr. Brisson that they were equal to any obstacle he might place in their way.

Timothy withdrew from his mother's company, but Allen went on, kindly and philosophically trusting that she had not recovered sufficiently from the shock of her husband's death to think straight. He would be patient and do his best to keep the atmosphere in the home as pleasant as possible. His father would have expected that.

Shortly after a visit from Mr. Brisson, Phoebe startled Allen and Timothy with a terse announcement.

"Men will be coming in a few days to put up a fence. I want you boys to help." She spoke as though putting up a fence were an everyday occurrence.

"A fence? Where?" Allen was stunned.

"Down our property line."

Timothy's face clouded. He looked first at his mother to see if he had heard straight, and then at Allen, expecting him to resist.

As usual, Allen was measuring the seriousness of her remark. "I was not aware that a property line existed," he said.

Phoebe chafed. "Of course a line exists!"

"But we have never had a fence—"

"Well, we shall have one now!"

Timothy could remain silent no longer. "If a fence goes up, I shall tear it down, every inch. Count on it!"

"Then you shall live elsewhere!" threatened Phoebe.

She had expected Timothy to explode. When he did not, she grew apprehensive. This was not her volatile son. He was facing her quietly, and on his countenance was an expression she had never seen before.

"You are correct, Mother. If the fence goes up, I shall no longer live here."

Allen stepped between them.

"I do not believe you can put up a fence, Mother. The land is Uncle Clint's. He's been generous enough to share it with us."

"You are wrong, Allen. Before your father left, the farm was put in your father's name. "

"I would like to see that contract."

The request fired the short fuse of Phoebe's temper, and she turned in a fit of rage upon the contemplative son.

"Why do you insist on treating me as though I hadn't an ounce of good sense, Allen? First you go over my head with the school-master, and now you question my decisions and my place as head of this house! I know what your father told me. He assured me we would always be cared for and that the contract protected us. Must I run and look up the papers to prove that? Your Aunt Nabby certainly gets more respect from her children!"

Allen could see that further discussion with his distraught mother would prove futile, yet he knew also that he must somehow learn the contents of the contract. Whether it was her obstinate nature or her impatience with legal language that held her back, he was not sure. She had always disliked "lawyer talk," and had quite willingly left all legal matters to her husband.

But for now he had to cool his brother's short temper. Something in this new Timothy disturbed him, and he followed his twin to their bedchamber.

"You didn't mean that, did you, Timothy? About not living here if the fence goes up?"

"I never meant anything more!" answered Timothy, still seething.

Allen crossed the room and put a restraining hand on his brother's shoulder. "I can't run the place without you. Don't you know that?"

Timothy wished that he could have the cool head and harnessed temper of his brother. He lowered his head as he spoke.

"I know what will happen. That poor excuse of a man will gradually take over, while we sit on our hands and let him! The farm . . . the stables . . . everything! You want the farm, Allen. I know you do. If we don't stop him now, it will only get worse!"

Allen knew that with all of Timothy's fiery spirit, he possessed genuine discernment, and it sobered him more than he wished to admit. This was indeed a hard place. How did he honor his parent and still hold the fort? Timothy was not wrong. Lerner Brisson was moving on a steady course, winning every joust and growing bolder with each successful encounter.

"Yes, I do want the farm. I want it for both of us, Timothy. That is why we must move with caution, get the full measure of this Brisson, find the chink in his armor."

Timothy was looking at Allen with a strange expression. Then he blurted out his words. "Allen, you should know by now that I am no farmer, nor ever could be! I do the work, but I hate it. I'd have left long ago if I had had a choice. I've stayed only because I have been afraid for Mother and Clara."

Allen had guessed as much, though he had hoped Timothy's dislike for the bucolic life would change—and that at least he would ride out the storm until the war was over.

"Perhaps someday, Tim, you can go, but don't be hasty."

Timothy grasped the hand on his shoulder. "I'll stay as long as it is possible," he assured his brother.

Allen left. There were hog pens to build and cabbages to plant in the harvested potato fields.

The days passed, and the young Haddons worked together, taking out their frustrations on the tractable soil. Considering the few days they attended school, they managed to make good grades, with the restless Timothy surprisingly in front. Hank continued at Allen's side, sharing muscle and knowledge, but the former peace of the farm was not there.

One morning Nabby burst in the kitchen door, her hair disheveled and her eyes shooting sparks.

"You won't believe it! Look—out there!"

Strangers were in the field erecting a barricade!

Hank wrenched his hat from the wall peg and hobbled past Nabby, nearly falling in his haste. Down into the field he struggled, with Nabby and Caroline right behind.

"What you think you're doing?" demanded Hank.

"We've orders to put up a fence."

"Whose orders?"

"A Mr. Brisson and the missus over there," explained the man, gesturing toward Vaugn's house.

Timothy was already at the scene, his face contorted with anger. "That settles it!" He tore away from the bewildered little group and headed back to his house, taking long, angry strides. He entered the house, slamming the door loudly enough for those in the field to hear.

Phoebe started up from her place at the window. "Where are you going?"

Timothy did not answer. He was up the stairs that led to his bedchamber and was pulling out drawers from the fine old bureau. He could hear his mother on the stairs as he stuffed a battered valise with a few belongings. He knew what he had to do.

Phoebe entered the room and stood, wide-eyed and frightened.

"Tim! Stop! Answer me!"

Closing the case, he faced her. "I told you before, and I tell you now. This house will never be big enough for that man Brisson and me. And it is clear that you have made your choice. I am leaving."

"Timothy! Wait!"

This was no childish tantrum; the look on Timothy's face told her that. She began to cry, but a woman's tears were no match for the surging manhood in the bosom of the explosive son.

He descended the stairs and strode toward the place where the Haddons had gathered. Allen was accosting the workmen with cool argument, but he stopped when he saw Timothy and his valise.

"I cannot stay. Don't try to make me!" said Timothy, still hot.

"But where will you go?" asked Caroline, her face drawn with anguish.

"I have a little money," he answered, hoping she would not press to know how little.

Allen stood frozen.

"I'm sorry, Allen. If I stayed, I know I'd kill him!"

Nabby, watching the drama unfolding before her, realized there was more at stake here than the fence. She touched Timothy's sleeve.

"Come back to the house with me. I will help you."

Timothy followed his aunt into the big kitchen and stood shifting his feet awkwardly while she went to her bedroom. He could hear her rummaging through bureau drawers; then she returned, holding out a brown envelope.

"Take this, Timothy. You will need it."

Timothy backed off. "If it's money, no!"

"It is money, and it is only a loan." Nabby's sweet concern softened him.

"Things have changed so," he said lamely.

"Life is full of changes, dear, with a test at every turn." Then, with a mother's concern, she asked, "Where will you go?"

"I will try Boston. If I can't find employment, I'll enlist."

Nabby pushed a damp curl from his forehead. Yes, he was impulsive, but courageous, too . . . and she loved him dearly.

"Write to me," she said, following him to the door.

Timothy walked out into the bright sunshine. There was enough sharpness in the air to brace him. He loved the autumn. Soon everything would change, and winter would settle upon the land. He would miss hunting with his brother, and he would miss the close fellowship of the Clinton Haddons, but he could stay no longer and watch the inevitable. Remaining would only deaden his spirit, and he was too young to die. Allen would have to come alive and do the fighting.

Timothy thought about Benjamin Franklin with his pocketed loaves of bread, and how he ventured out into a new world and a new life. The world hadn't hurt him! Freedom . . . how marvelous the sound of the word! He walked down the long lane with the expectation of youth. He felt like smiling—and he didn't look back.

Caroline watched him go, his slim figure fading into the shadows of the high elms. Soon he was out of sight. Somehow she wanted to follow, to leave all the heavy responsibilities and the sorrow, the evil news that came from the battlefront, the loneliness. But even as part of her heart went with Timothy, she knew she had given a promise. And besides all that, there was something in the soil . . . something in her very genes that held her, and would always hold her.

Nabby's voice broke into her thoughts.

"That young man will be all right. I just know it!"

There was comfort in her mother's words, but with Vaugn gone, and her father, and Thad—and now Timothy—who would be next? Her world was crumbling, and she was powerless to stop it!

Hank stood at Allen's side, feeling with him the shock of

Timothy's departure. He was wondering if he should go and tell Vaugn's wife what a fool she was, when Allen began to walk away. Hank hobbled after him.

"I'll help you. You know I'll help," he assured Allen.

Allen looked at the older man, looked beyond the steel gray hair, the weather-beaten face, the patched clothing. Why was it that some men could reach the golden years with so much dignity and others with none at all? Under the massive shoulders and within that broad chest was a real man, one who could be trusted.

He is like my father, and like Uncle Clint. God knows I shall need him now! he thought.

The strange irregular thump of Hank's labored steps beside him was a comfort to Allen. Somewhere he had read that a friend is one who dwells in the bosom of another. How true. Together they had shared the heavy work and responsibility of both farms. They had watched the heavens for rain, exploited together the benefits of the spring and autumnal equinox, uprooted the scabbed barley and destroyed it, searched out the springs, and plowed the fields. Yes, they were cut from the same cloth and dwelled within one another's bosom. There was consolation in that!

The older man broke the silence. "There's wheat to cut, and I can see you have thinking to do. I'll see you later." He was gone as unobtrusively as he lived.

Allen continued on toward the pond. The grass under his feet was dry, almost brittle. At the pond, the waterline had shrunk, and the low brushwillows were already withered. Birds hung close to the water's edge, seemingly bent upon guarding their diminishing supply. He knelt to measure the waterline and rose still gauging, still planning. Yet in a matter of days he could be stripped of it all, should that man Brisson realize his goals.

Without the steady direction of Vaugn, Allen wondered if he could even go on. Why had he not valued his father more when he was alive? How he wished with all his heart that he could spend even five minutes with him. But the torch had been thrown his way, not even giving him time to grieve!

He bent down and wrenched a dry, aromatic berry from a seared staghorn sumac. That was how he felt, dried out and withered—and he wasn't even twenty years old. How could he continue honoring his mother when she was so deceived? Where had it all begun? He had felt a waive of distrust from the beginning, but he had had no right to interfere. There had to be an answer somewhere.

Allen found a large boulder and sat down. White-bellied swallows dipped over the still water, chirping noisily, and little mud ducks swam leisurely on the water's surface. In the water's depths he could see the elusive shiners darting about among the heart-shaped leaves of the pond grass. There was a pervading peace about the entire scene, one that beckoned him from the frustrations of life. Surely the One who knew the sparrow knew also the problems he faced.

He must see his Aunt Nabby and ask to see a copy of the contract. That would be a beginning. He arose and started for Nabby's house. He could see Hank in the wheat field, cutting close to the ground with his reaphook. After the twenty-four-hour drying period, Joshua could bind the sheaves—that strong young cousin was already proving his worth—and the moons of autumn would make night harvesting possible.

Nabby was packing greenings and russets when Allen found her in the cellar. She looked up, pleased to see him, and offered him an apple.

"They are good this year!"

Allen settled on top of a barrel and bit into the fruit.

"God's world is good—it is men who corrupt it!"

"Ayuh." Nabby nodded, knowing full well to whom he made reference.

"I have come to ask if I might see your copy of the contract Uncle Clint made with my father."

"I've been expecting that," said Nabby, pressing the last round apple into the barrel. "Hank will hammer the top on. Come."

She led the way upstairs, disappeared into her bedchamber, and returned with papers in her hands. She gave one to Allen and stood watching as he read.

He looked up in surprise. "Do I understand that I am already owner of the property measured off on our side?"

Nabby looked pleased. "Yes. Fortunately, Lawyer Bancroft saw the oversight of the old will. It prohibited the sale of any land, but not the gift of land to one worthy. You and your father were made joint tenants, and the oldest Haddon, who at the moment is Clinton, is trustee until you are of age."

"Then Mother has no jurisdiction?"

"It would seem that she does not, where the property is concerned. It also seems clear that God would have you take your place as head of the household."

"And what if Mother marries?"

"Then her care would fall to the man she marries, though until that time your father has delegated that responsibility to you. Here—read it!"

Allen became thoughtful. It was as though God had read his innermost longing—to hear again his father's voice.

"He trusted me, Aunt Nabby. But it's the timing— When do I make a move?"

"Perhaps God wants your mother to see for herself the kind of a man Lerner Brisson is. Let's give God that opportunity. Surely Lerner will show his hand before many more days have passed. I would not be too hasty."

"But God has all eternity! I'm a limited human being."

Nabby wondered what she could say to clarify her nephew's role in the miserable situation. God must have put her there, packing apples, in order to minister to the young man's needs. She had better reach into God's storehouse and keep her own ideas to herself.

"Do you believe that Jesus died for your sins?"

The question surprised Allen. "But of course, Aunt Nabby!"

"Then, so do you have all eternity!"

Allen savored the thought. How true—it was so easy even for Christians to get bogged down in the "now," acting brashly without waiting.

"Then you think I should hold off in setting things straight?"

"I think we should be somewhat as patient as our heavenly Father. We are not to think lightly of the riches of His kindness, His forbearance, or His patience—for the kindness is what leads men to repentance."

"Aren't there times when a man of God must take a stand?"

"A man of God will know the time."

"Like Ignatius—Justin—Polycarp—Huss?"

"And King David, too. He was close to God's heart."

"How did he know what God wanted?"

"He asked Him!"

"But David was special."

"As is any man for whom Christ has shed His blood!"

Allen placed his large hands on Nabby's shoulders. "Aunt Nabby, where do you get your wisdom?"

"You shouldn't have to ask that, Allen. It isn't mine. It comes from what I have learned of the Holy Scriptures. I am certain there is an answer for every problem within those sacred pages, if only men would look and see. I suppose also that my parents were blessed to have Adoniram Judson for a teacher when he was pulpit supply from Andover Seminary. My folk were strict about studying the Word of God."

Allen planted a kiss on Nabby's cheek, causing a warm smile to spread over her face and reflect in his own. She had driven away the doubts and planted strength where only an hour ago there had been nothing but defeat. He walked braced and strong back to the fields and joined Hank.

"And David, too!" she had said, piquing more than Allen's casual interest in Jesse's son of old. David had been very young, too, when God had put His hand upon him. He'd sent him forth to slay a lion, a bear, and a giant! He would have to know more of this David.

The rest of the day passed faster than any day he had lived. As soon as he could excuse himself from the family, he went to his room and began to search the Old Testament to learn what he could of this "man after God's own heart." Far into the night he read, scarcely noticing that Timothy's bed was empty, for there was something rich and precious in Timothy's place—the presence of a comforting God!

He read of David's battles and on to the time David was crowned king of Israel. No sooner was he crowned than the ancient enemies came to wage war. Ah! Here was a time when David asked God when he should strike at that enemy! God gave him permission at first, but the second time he told David to wait for a sign—hmmm. And the sign? The sound of wind in the mulberry tree! Mulberry tree? What had mulberry trees to do with him, Allen? He didn't even own a mulberry tree.

He closed the book and sighed. He had almost made the mistake of thinking he was special to God! How could he have been so presumptuous? But he slept well that night, and even with his doubts he knew there had been given him something from God.

The days that followed were good. The measure of peace God had given him pervaded the home, emanating from his own satisfied soul. Even Phoebe, though petulant about Timothy's absence, seemed quieter and more receptive to the idea of an open gate in the fence that now divided the land.

Lerner Brisson was at the house more than ever, now that he had dispensed with the problem of Timothy. As usual, Phoebe showered him with her inordinate adulation, serving him the finest of food and pampering his every whim. One evening he seemed to be in a rare good humor.

"Phoebe, my dear," he began. His words sounded as though he had practiced the speech, but not to Phoebe's dull ear. "There is a possibility I might purchase a house on High Street!"

Phoebe looked up from her useless task of setting the chair tidies straight. A rapturous glow spread over her face, and her watery eyes took on an expression of wonder.

"Oh, Lerner!"

"Yes, my dear. I want to take you away from all of this—" He waved a hand toward Clinton's home. "And from past memories, too."

"Lerner, could we really live on High Street?"

"Well . . . I will need a little more than I have to close the deal."

"How much?" Phoebe's thoughts were leaping ahead, unrestrained. Wouldn't that set the aristocratic snobs on their ears! She did not even hear his answer. He went on talking.

"Of course you would sell this place."

"But you wouldn't have our crops."

"Phoebe, my dear, I am a successful agent! I would never miss the produce of this small farm. I have dozens of growers!"

"Then I could sell with little compunction!"

"You are certain that you are the owner and could do that?"

"Oh, yes! Allen manages, but it is all under my direction. Vaugn explained everything before he left."

"And his sons?"

"They aren't of age, Lerner, so certainly of no consequence. Timothy hates the place, and Allen is bowed down with the work. I am sure he would welcome a release from it all. He could get into more respectable work and better company. Perhaps even go to Harvard or Yale."

Phoebe's dreams were out and on display for the cunning Brisson to exploit. Still he was not sure.

"I hope you are certain about this, Phoebe."

"Why, Lerner! Why all the doubt? First Allen, and now you! I shall put the farm up for sale this week if you wish!"

"Well, er, no hurry. I've made my offer and can't seem too anxious."

Lerner still had his misgivings where Phoebe's quiet son was concerned. Timothy, with his emotions on his sleeve, had been easy enough to read, but Allen was not that transparent. He would not capitulate without a struggle, of that Lerner was certain. Perhaps he should make his move while Allen was still a minor. Perhaps the dry season would be an appropriate time.

ALLEN STOOD LOOKING at the withered grass in the fields. The October winds were making things drier than ever. With Hank, he had already run trenches in from the pond, but even the little stream beds that ran down from the pond had dried.

Lerner appeared and stood watching Allen as he surveyed the situation.

"Pretty dry out there," he commented, joining him at the window. "Rain is late coming."

"We have the pond, and we will be digging more trenches. Our horses and Clint's stock should have enough to get by until the November rains."

"Hadn't you better make sure of that?"

Allen looked directly at the man. Why the sudden interest in the fields and the animals? The man's audacity stirred a burning resentment, one he would have to squash if he were to remain under God's control.

"I am no miracle worker. We do with what we have."

Lerner twitched nervously, started for the door and then hesitated. "I suggest you consider our interests first," he badgered.

The word "our" sent flames of indignation through Allen's veins. He was glad that Lerner had closed the door behind him as he left. He might have been tempted to settle things with the man, and as yet he did not feel free to do so.

Phoebe had observed the sparring. "I wish you would be kinder to Lerner. He is only trying to help us."

"So far, Mother, he has only succeeded in driving us apart. First the Lindquists, and now Timothy. How can I be kind to the man?"

Clara, who had been standing in the background, moved closer to Allen. In spite of Lerner's overtures toward Clara, he had not succeeded in winning the child's affections. She, too, felt an uneasiness in his presence.

"Allen is right, Mama. If it weren't for that man, we'd all be together. Don't make Allen go, too!"

Phoebe grew crimson, anger rising within her too strong to ignore. She crossed the room and struck with fury at the bewildered Clara.

The child stood shocked, holding her stinging cheek.

Allen shook his head, anger writhing within like an enraged bull beating itself against caged restraint. Then he left the room and Clara, not knowing what to do, ran after him.

"Don't go, Allen! Oh, please, don't you go!"

Allen waited for her and swept her up into his arms. "Don't cry, Clara. I'm not going anywhere."

They headed out toward the gate, Allen expecting to meet there with Hank. They did not see Lerner following until they had almost reached it.

"Someone in the family has got to use his head!" fumed Lerner. Placing his hands upon the top railing of the gate, he began to swing it closed.

"Get your hands off that gate!" demanded Allen, putting Clara down.

Lerner ignored him and pulled on the gate.

For one brief moment Allen stood still, listening, as though he were suspended in time. Then he heard it—the wind in the orchard sweeping through the treetops at an unreasonable hurricane force, whipping the branches over his head. Something inside exploded. In seconds he had Lerner by the collar and had thrown him to the ground. Standing back, he watched Lerner get to his feet, then Allen sent a murderous blow toward his adversary's mouth. Blood oozed slowly down over his lips and onto his chin.

Lerner wiped it away and swung hard at Allen. He had not expected such dexterity of the slow-thinking youth, but there he stood without having received even a glancing blow—daring him, Lerner, to come at him again.

Allen was built more like his Uncle Clint than like his own father and had the square, stubborn jaw of the Haddons. He stepped in to deliver another blow, moving with such celerity that Lerner was once again sent sprawling. Something new and exhilarating moved Allen on. Lerner lay on the ground pulling his legs up to kick. Allen latched onto a foot and turned him over, then released him and stood back smiling.

"Get out of here, Brisson!" he ordered.

Brisson got to his feet. He had had enough of the young Haddon. He hurried toward his carriage and left in a cloud of dust, while Allen stood pressing his sore knuckles, enjoying the pain.

Clara ran to him. "You did it, Allen! You did it! I hate him!"

"It's not always the best way to settle an issue, but there are times when we have no alternative."

"Like Papa when he went to war!" exclaimed Clara.

From the mouths of babes, thought Allen, looking up at the limbs of the trees. He was surprised to see them motionless—and suddenly he was awed at what had happened.

"Who needs mulberry trees with an orchard of apples! The Lord—the same yesterday, today, and forever!" Whatever the future held, he was certain of one thing. He was special to the Lord!

But the cup of iniquity was not yet full. Phoebe exploded in her usual manner when she learned of the fight. What could Lerner possibly think of her now? Each son in his own way had turned a cold shoulder toward him. Could she ever make amends for that? And the house on High Street—what of that? For days she hopefully watched the lane. Surely he would return.

When he finally appeared, she unashamedly ran out of the house to meet him. Allen watched, surprised that the man would dare return. But then, the stakes were high and of such significance that no runagate could walk away without first trying to regain what he had nearly forfeited.

Phoebe and Lerner entered the house together, both smiling pleasantly.

"Lerner wishes to speak to you," said Phoebe, the words dripping like sweet honey from her lips.

Allen stiffened, a look of extreme diffidence on his countenance. "Lupus pilum mutat, non nentem!" he said to himself—words remembered from his Latin class. "The wolf changes his coat—not his disposition!"

What now? He waited for Lerner to speak.

"I realize you were only doing your duty, believing you were helping your mother and Clara. I was wrong to interfere, and I am asking that you be generous and accept my apology."

Allen glanced apprehensively at Phoebe.

"It's all right, son. Lerner realizes now that you are not a child and that you have the right to make decisions. Please, for my sake, do let bygones be bygones."

Allen listened, but not without qualms. It was the first time he had seen a softening of Phoebe toward himself or any hesitancy on her part toward the covetous Lerner. Perhaps this was the time—his time to tell them of the contract's provisions. He was certain there would be a stormy scene with his mother, and he needed time to think just how to approach the issue.

"We'll discuss this tonight after I make my evening rounds," he said and left the room with Clara at his heels, wishing Timothy were there for support.

"Is he waiting until after the wedding to be mean again?" his little sister asked.

"Don't fret, Clara. I do not plan to give him that opportunity. When I come in from the evening rounds, I shall confront them both, and I have a feeling Lerner will not be around after he hears what I have to say."

Dusk settled in and Allen, still in his room, could hear the muffled voices of Lerner and Phoebe in the room below. It was time to get to the stable and finish the day's work. He tried to shake off the heaviness Lerner seemed to bring with him.

He walked down the center of the stable floor, welcoming the dumb affection of his horses. They stood like children in a large family awaiting a patriarchal blessing; Duchess, Salty the gelding, Jenny the sorrel mare, Sir Walter, Reggie, Josephine, Cicero, Cinnamon, and Poppy. There was something about the massive heads and the strong nudging that ministered to Allen's loneliness. He caressed them and spoke in soft, clucking sounds, then picked up his lantern and walked to the lone window in the building.

He wished that instead of the twinkling stars he might see a mackerel sky. He wished many things—that the war would end, and that the heavy, oppressive thing that hung so ominously over the farm would go away. He moved toward the big end door and, turning a corner, saw the wavering shadow of a man upon a wall. Curious, he stepped toward the apparition, wondering if his imagination were playing tricks with his eyesight. Then something struck him a blinding blow on the head. Lights flashed, brilliant as fireworks, and he heard the lantern fall. That was all.

CLARA, ALONE AND RESTLESS, decided to join Allen in the twilight duties. He had been gone much too long. She walked confidently into the bright path of moonlight, familiar with every pebble in the path that led to the stable. Suddenly she saw a figure emerging from the stable door, but it wasn't Allen. Allen was taller and not so rotund. It was familiar, yet out of place somehow. The stranger was closing the door and pulling down the heavy metal bar that locked it. Why would he do that? The door was never closed this time of year.

Puzzled and a little frightened, Clara stood still and strained to recognize the intruder. Suddenly he turned toward her, and she sucked in her breath. It was Lerner Brisson!

"Mr. Brisson! We don't put the bar down yet!"

Her voice, so high-pitched and strident, brought Lerner up motionless, a look of terror on his face. He reached toward Clara and secured both her hands in a viselike grasp. Staring into her frightened eyes, he spoke in a rasping, guttural voice.

"You did not see me, Clara—you understand?"

Frightened beyond speech, Clara could only stare back. Lerner shook her so hard she bit her tongue and began to cry.

He repeated his threat. "If you tell, I promise to kill you!"

"Wh-where's Allen?" she managed.

Lerner looked at the stable door, dropped her hands, and ran toward the road. Clara raced toward the door and reached for the high bar, but she wasn't strong enough to lift it. It was then that she saw the smoke curling under and over the top of the door.

"Allen! Allen!" she screamed. "I know you're in there! Answer me!"

She turned and started for the house to fetch her mother, then stopped short. Even Clara knew that her mother's best effort in an emergency was to cry or wring her hands.

Over the fields she ran, stumbling, falling and rising again in her flight. She turned only once to see the flames reaching toward the roof. The town clocks were striking, but she didn't wait to count the hour. She reached her uncle's side door and pounded with small fists on the unyielding oak. Was no one awake?

"Aunt Nabby! Hank! Caroline! Come quickly!"

20

THE ISLAND STRETCHED long before the mouth of the Merrimac, while beyond the sun-bleached coastal sands lay the treacherous sandbars. Whipped by wind and waves, they were a veritable land guard, a natural deterrent to any would-be invader, and only a seasoned pilot dared take his craft through the channels.

It was high tide when Jerome drove the hired Spider Phaeton over the causeway and bridge and on to the long stretch of sandy road. The day itself was golden and the entire beach deserted. Cottages had been boarded up and their wealthy owners, all of whom might be numbered on one hand, had returned to the city for the winter. The bayberry had developed its fragrant winter-white leaves, and though it was after five o'clock, the skies were still cobalt clear and delicately laced with shredded clouds. The public pavilion stood silent and deserted, and offshore gulls circled, crying raucously as they swooped over the crashing surf.

The waves were high and sounded like thunder as they crashed and broke against the shore. These were sounds precious to Caroline, for she had slept to them many a night when her father had taken the family there for relief during the heat of August. She led Jerome to the top of a sandy dune and peered down at the surf. Sand plovers skirted the creeping suds, securing the day's final meal of sand crabs.

"Don't they ever stop to sing?" asked Jerome.

"If they do, I have never heard them. They are like people who never lift their heads from the pursuit of wealth."

She sat down and removed her shoes, revealing small sun-browned feet. With her burnished cheeks, raven hair, and white teeth, she might have been an Indian maiden from the past.

"Shoes and sand simply do not go together," she commented, pushing her feet into the still-warm sand.

Jerome stood watching her, enchanted, and then removed his own blucher boots. Together they walked to the edge of the froth, where Caroline stooped to pick up a starfish.

"We called them five fingers when I was very young, and collected them by the dozens. And still they come and charm the children. Once I wondered where all the driftwood came from, since there are only plum trees on the island. And Father sat us down and recited the history of the great shipwrecks off this very coast: the *Three Friends*, the *Neptune,* and others. And now, another war." Caroline sighed heavily. "Ships out there we can't see; the *Sagamon*, the *Delaware*, the *Minnesota*. Wars must be as inevitable as the tides. And someday another generation of children will be wondering as I did at the little chunks of wood along this strand."

Jerome only listened and watched the elfin girl as she sometimes walked, sometimes ran before him. This was her island; she knew every inch of it. He wondered if she had forgotten he was there; then suddenly she was back beside him, holding to his arm, drawing him into her own moment of pleasure, sharing a fragment of eternity in the vastness of sea and sky.

"Don't you love it here?" she asked. "Such peace . . . such an escape! I never see it but I am reminded of God's fourth day—the land, the sea, the stars, the sun and moon and wind. Not a living creature, only the pounding of the surf and the wind in the beach grass. No babbling, no quarreling, no cannon, no bugle, no crying orphans or sobbing widows, no political speeches. Just silence. And then the voice of God bringing man into the picture!"

Deeply impressed, Jerome searched her face. This was the

beauty he had suspected all along, hidden beneath the cool and unemotional veneer. It had taken the marvels of creation to tear away the deceptive hard shards.

"You do appreciate beauty!"

"I love what God has made."

"And music? Do you like music?" he asked hopefully.

"Oh, yes. God's handiwork, and men putting it to song. They go together."

"Funny, I see it quite the opposite. When I hear music, I see the vignettes."

"That is because a man and a woman see things differently." She paused and then spoke again. "You have never told me of your family. You do have a family?"

"No. My parents died when I was very young, and I have no brothers or sisters. My grandmother raised me. She was a little French lady—very stylish, you know, thrived on *le beau monde,* and a stickler for the social graces. She had a royal look, and I believe was descended from a countess, but her ancestors forsook their claim to royalty when they were forced into the wilderness."

"The Huguenots?"

"Yes."

"And your music?"

"She insisted on my studying, which was difficult at first. But a child with no siblings must have a way of amusing himself. That was when I began to like music. It became my life."

"And was that all you had?"

"Grandmere did not neglect me. She provided everything pleasant—and there were always the teachers to torment!"

"You paint a picture of loneliness, Jerome, yet every time I have observed you, you have always had an entourage about you."

"Who could resist such a handsome fellow?"

Caroline laughed and swept a hand toward him. He caught it and held it fast till she pulled away, embarrassed.

"Was your grandmother a pacifist, too?" she asked, hoping to discourage any amorous thoughts he might be entertaining.

"I see you do not understand. She believed in defending one's rights, but was never pleased with Frenchmen killing Frenchmen."

"And it rubbed off on you."

"*Bella! Horrida bella!* Who likes to see Americans killing Americans?" He looked very serious as he spoke.

Caroline rose and ran toward a rising dune. "Look! I want to show you something. See these little wild sweet peas? Their blossoms are white, soft, and fragile—but their stems are tough and sharp enough to cut!"

"Like you, Caroline Haddon?"

She looked away from the piercing dark eyes. "I don't mean to be like that. Really I don't."

"You are afraid to show your real self."

What could she answer to that? Perhaps he was right. Perhaps she was afraid of many things—being shallow, failing to keep promises, forgetting Thad, watching what was happening to Vaugn's family. And more startling than all, afraid of the feelings this man was capable of arousing in her own heart.

He seemed to sense that he had struck home, and he ventured further. "You should be thinking of marriage. I am sure you have had offers. You are a beautiful woman. You know that, don't you?"

Caroline moved quickly to change the direction of the conversation. She brushed aside the compliment.

"I cannot think of myself right now. Wars change so many things! Out there are battles going on as far as the blockade to Europe. Men are dying, families being destroyed. How could I possibly be thinking of marriage?"

"Because it is natural, even in wartime."

She turned back toward the carriage. Jerome caught up with her, sorry he had spoken of marriage. They walked vigorously in silence for a time.

Caroline gestured toward the lighthouse ahead. "That has

stood here for a long time," she ventured, hoping to heal the rift.

But Jerome was not interested. He was wondering if he would ever reach the person Caroline struggled so hard to hide. When they reached the carriage, Caroline removed a basket from its place against the cushion-fall.

"I brought some cake and fruit," she said, finding a place where the sand was still warm and settling down. "Father and Uncle Hank come here in the springtime to gather seaweed. Can you imagine this beautiful place covered with seaweed . . . and dead cattle?"

Jerome laughed at her attempt at light conversation. "Must we have dead cattle and seaweed when we are about to dine?"

"I thought you would appreciate a little history. Long ago the farmers put their stock out here for the winter to fend for themselves. It was disgraceful! The beasts died or became wild!"

"Mean people, these farmers!"

"Eat your cake!"

They were at ease again. The wind picked up as the sun began to set, leaving the sky a flaming rosy glow.

"It has been heavenly to get away, even for a little while, and see something besides the farm and the work. But I must be returning. There is always much to do."

Looking back toward the city, Caroline could see the buildings silhouetted against an ashen sky, the skeletal ship masts in the harbor, and smoke from the river steamers.

"I love that city."

"Probably because you have never known anything else."

"Perhaps. It's just that once one becomes a part of this city—it becomes a part of you."

Jerome, having never been so bonded to a geographical site, struggled to understand. "Maybe it's the people?"

"Yes, part of it. Americans all! The Hamiltonians, the Statesmen, the college professors, the lawyers, the inventors; the mothers, fathers, children; little people, big people. They all have something good in them, you know. They're a courageous lot, the way they face life and death. This nation can never fail as long as we have the kind of people who live there."

"Why would America fail?"

"Can't you see it? So many elements creeping in. Bad elements, Jerome. People are being taken up with new philosophies: Darwin, and Fortiens, Brook Farm and New Harmony communal settlements—so caught up in their own egocentricities, making the creature greater than the Creator. Why must there always be the spoilers?"

"Caroline, be more capacious!"

"The age-old cry for license!"

"Let's walk!" suggested Jerome, not liking the trend of the conversation. The wind had come up, and the temperature had grown cold along with the mood.

"We have been here long enough. I must be getting back, or the family will start to worry."

CLARA PICKED UP A ROCK and threw it with all her might at the nearest window.

The sound of shattering glass brought Nabby from deep sleep onto her feet! Confused, she hurried to the door and flung it open. Hank was right behind her.

"Come quick! The stable's all afire!"

"What is it, child? The stable?"

"Oh, hurry! Hurry! The horses will die! And Allen!"

Hank was pulling on his trousers. Then he had blankets in the sink and was pumping water over them. Matthew had appeared and flew headlong toward the barn, where he jerked a handful of neck ropes from the wall and joined the army of people converging on the fiery scene.

Hand engines were already being pulled into the yard and Mr. Paxton, who had seen the flames and summoned the fire engines, was sinking a hose into one of the wells. Hank ran to the other.

"Bethia! Joshua! Bring your buckets here!" He turned the windlass with an eye on the flames, which were already dancing along the ridgepole.

Nabby had not stopped to dress, but had thrown a coat over her nightdress and followed the others. Clara ran with her aunt, her face streaked with tears and fear growing in her with each step.

A wind had come up and was whipping the flames out of control.

"Give me the ropes!" ordered Hank.

"You aren't going in there!" exclaimed Matthew.

Hank ignored Matthew's dismay. "You go for Doc Slater, Matthew. If Allen is in there, we'll need him."

From Matthew's expression, Hank knew the boy was loath to go, but after a moment of indecision, he tore himself away and followed his uncle's instructions.

Hank moved toward the wide door and lifted the searing metal bar. Once inside, he struggled to see through the smoke and flames. It was oven hot, and he threw one of the wet blankets over his head, leaving enough aperture for vision. The horses were in a state of panic, battering the stalls with wildly flying hooves and whinnying loudly. Hank stumbled over something and went sprawling. Then he realized that he had fallen over a human being.

Turning him over, he looked into the face of Allen. Flames were already licking at Allen's clothing. Hank beat at them and threw his blanket over him. Somehow he must get Allen to the door. Knowing how heavy the young man was, Hank wondered if it were even possible. But this was no time to wonder! Coughing and choking, he pulled with his mighty arms until at last he got Allen through the door and out into the air.

"Get him breathing. I've got to get the horses!" And Hank was gone, his voice trailing after him.

Nabby moved to take command. "Allen is burned! Get some butter quickly." Phoebe obeyed without a question.

Hank had already taken another wet blanket and disappeared

into the great cavernous inferno. He could see Salty, eyes showing white. He slipped first the neck rope and then the blanket over Salty's head, and then yanked. Salty, in the habit of obeying, settled down to the leading of his benefactor and was soon outside. Hank went a third time, this time for Duchess. A burning rafter fell and grazed Hank's head, and Duchess, mad with terror, was swinging her hoofs in all directions. Still Hank managed to get a blanket over her head and lead her out.

With the help of neighbors, they soon had three more horses tethered at the big oak tree just outside the stable. Hank headed back again, glancing at the wind. It was growing stronger, and he hesitated. Even though his face was black with smoke and streaked with perspiration, and his hands blistered, he knew he could not quit while there was any possibility of saving the others. Smoke clouds masked the autumn moon, and he could see dark silhouettes of men running over the rooftops with buckets of water. The stable was a hopeless loss, but at least the wind was blowing away from the house. He would make one last attempt. There were still three horses trapped inside.

"No more rescue possible!" shouted the foreman. "It can go at any time!"

But Hank was already inside the door and straining to see the remaining horses. He heard the rafters falling overhead and knew he had only seconds. Reggie's stall was at the far end of the building, and he could hear hooves on the travis. He ran down the flaming corridor and managed to get a rope over the horse's head. Then the flaming beams fell, and Reggie broke loose. This was it!

Hank could do no more. He made a dash for the open door just as the entire building collapsed. He could see two men racing toward him, and then something struck and he fell beneath a beam.

The women shrieked as they saw the building come down in an explosion of sparks. A group of men were already at the door, emptying their buckets over the hissing wood. Once the flames had been extinguished, they dragged Hank to safety, but he lay motionless on the ground. Neighbors tore sheets for bandaging as Phoebe pressed sweet butter onto Hank's arms and legs.

Allen had regained consciousness and lay there dazed and disoriented.

"What happened, son?" Phoebe asked.

His hand moved toward his head and he winced. "Someone hit me," he answered.

"Who?"

"Don't know. I only saw a shadow."

Clara was standing near her mother. She knew. She knew who was responsible for all of this, and she knew, too, that if she were to speak she would be the next victim. She started toward the house, hoping to avoid questioning.

"No, Clara, don't go in the house," Nabby warned. "Not until we are certain the sparks won't be spreading!"

"Who could have done this?" whimpered Phoebe.

"Yes, who? Did you hear anything unusual?"

"I was in the house waiting for Clara to come back. She had gone for Allen. It was late and we had had company. Lerner had been there, but he had left."

"And you saw no strangers around?"

"No."

Clara was clinging to Phoebe's skirt.

"When did you see the fire, Clara?" asked Phoebe.

Clara did not answer.

"Did you see anyone?"

Phoebe shook her daughter.

"I . . . I didn't see anyone!" she stammered.

She is lying! thought Bethia. She stared dumbly at the ruins of the stable, smoldering sulkily and sending an acrid miasma into the night. Under the rubble lay three of Allen's prized and faithful animals. Bethia wept for them.

21

J EROME AND CAROLINE CLIMBED aboard the carriage and turned the horses toward the city. Darkness moved in upon them. On the river they could see the reflection of ship lanterns from the anchored crafts. In the distance they heard the muted whistle of a train.

"Someday I should like to take you to Boston. Would you go?"

"That would be delightful. Yes, I would like that. Father used to take us by turns when we were children, and we loved it!"

"Then it is a promise?"

"Yes . . . a promise." The word was more disturbing to Caroline than Jerome could have guessed.

Reaching the city limits, they passed a number of carriages with their side lanterns aglow. Turning toward the farms, they could see lamp-lit scenes framed within sparkling clean windows. Something about lights in the dark always gave Caroline a sense of peace and comfort. She leaned against Jerome's shoulder and shivered slightly. Instantly he removed his coat and placed it around her shoulders. No one had done that since she was a small child, and the gesture melted away the strange fear of the man that she had entertained since their first meeting. He reined in the horse and placed a soft kiss on her cheek, the touch of his lips sending a flame of fire to her heart—but at the same time, bringing back Thad and making her feel shoddy. She drew away from him.

"Please, I am not ready for this!"

"For what?"

"For anything new or serious! I've too much to sort out. I don't need any more!"

"Then why do you take such liberties with a man?"

"I do that?"

"You deliberately draw a man with your beauty . . . your lips . . . sweet and promising . . . and then hold him off with your confounded Yankee dignity!"

Caroline looked at him speechless. She had provoked him, and the Frenchman could explode! It surprised her. He had always been so cool, sophisticated.

"Oh, come now, don't look at me like that! I'm not some sort of Minotaur who eats little girls. You have charmed me, and I'm not sure I like it!"

He was frustrated and angry with himself. She had to say something—anything—to relieve his apparent embarrassment.

But before she had a chance to speak, they were interrupted by the clang of fire bells. Behind them they could see the shadows of the goosenecked engines and hear the labored voices of the men who pulled them. The foreman's orders rose above the tumult as he shouted into a trumpet held to his mouth. The oil torches carried by several youths sent flickering shadows against the high trees.

The captain ordered their carriage off the road, and Jerome lost no time obeying. He drove the horse and vehicle onto the shoulder as far as the brush would allow.

Up ahead the sky was flaming a brilliant yellow-orange, and the road was clogged with running people converging upon the fiery scene. By now both their faces registered the same thought. The flames came from the direction of Caroline's house!

Within moments, Jerome and Caroline had converged on the wretched scene at the stables, terror mingling with questions on their faces. Then Caroline saw her uncle and cousin and was instantly on the ground beside them. Hank was very still, but she could see that he was breathing.

"Oh, Mother, will he live?"

"He is burned badly."

"And Allen?"

"He is hurt, too, though miraculously not as badly as Hank."

Caroline turned toward Jerome, desperation in her face. "We'll have to get him to the house."

Jerome left and returned a short time later with several helpers, who had put together a makeshift litter.

"Can he stand being lifted?" he asked Nabby. He stood with his sleeves rolled up and perspiration running down his face. This was a side of Jerome Caroline had not seen.

"Be as gentle as possible," Nabby replied.

Hank winced when Jerome lifted him onto the litter. It was clear that he was in severe pain. They carried him across the field and put him to bed. Then Nabby went to care for her nephew's burns.

"They must all stay here for the night. The foreman has forbidden them to enter their house until morning. Bethia! Caroline! Take cider to the men, and see that Jerome is given clean things to wash with."

Bethia went to the cellar and drew out a large pitcher of cider while Caroline stacked towels and facecloths in her arms.

She found Jerome, dipped a facecloth in water, and washed the smudges from his face, not letting her eyes meet his.

Out on the road, the hand engines were leaving, and so were many of the curious. Then it was Jerome's turn. His silent departure troubled Caroline. After all, he had been kind and caring about Hank, and he had given her an afternoon of blessed release from the farm work. She had not expressed her gratitude. She hurried after him in the cold night air.

"I—I want you to know what this day has meant to me." She leaned toward him and kissed his cheek. It seemed the thing to do—his kindness had so touched her, and she would not have him leave without knowing how she felt. But the nearness of Caroline was more than he could resist, and she found herself in his strong arms, and he was kissing her as she had never been kissed. When he held her away from him, he was smiling, still saying nothing. Then he was gone, leaving her bewildered and trembling. She moved a hand to her lips and stood watching him go, wondering why she felt no anger!

In the aftermath of the catastrophe, the Paxtons and some more distant neighbors still stood at the scene of the fire, wanting their presence to somehow diminish the tragedy. Caroline and Bethia saw to their needs, thanked them, and then turned wearily back to their house. Doc Slater had been there and administered care to the suffering men, giving strict orders for the women to keep his patients meticulously clean and quiet.

Phoebe was in the pit of self-pity, and indignant at the prospect of spending the night under the roof of her adversary.

Caroline sent the younger children to bed and then looked for a place to sleep. Her own room she had relinquished to Allen. Still in her day clothes, she bedded down beside the kitchen stove where she could help Nabby as she worked through the night.

Hank, who had never been one to complain, groaned audibly. She wondered if a man of his age could possibly survive the severity of his burns.

The day had brought so many new things that she found it impossible to sleep. She lay staring at the ceiling and wondering, wondering about the promises she had given so quickly. It had been right to promise her father anything he wanted, but she had known from the beginning that the promise to Thad, without consulting her parents, had been wrong. Now she was caught in an ambivalent quandary, with Jerome's kiss still on her lips and Thad's memory disturbing her.

And the fire! What would Allen do now, and worse, what would the family do if Uncle Hank were to die? The fieldwork would never be done; there was hay to cock and winter cabbage to set out and the continual responsibility of the dairy. If Matthew had to leave the newspaper to take up the fieldwork, would he fall back into his depressive state? She had promised her father she would not let that happen.

Sleep came sporadically, and each time she awoke it was with a feeling of dread for the future. What would the morning bring?

Upstairs, Matthew bedded down on the floor of Joshua's small bedroom, while across the hall, Bethia generously allowed her obnoxious cousin a place in her bed. She observed that Clara was unusually quiet and subdued. Her usual frothy chatter was absent, and her face was pale.

"I don't feel very well," she explained when she caught Bethia looking at her.

"I don't either. I keep seeing the roof fall in!"

The girls lay in silence, with only the wind sighing.

"I don't like this room or this bed!" complained Clara, remembering her last encounter with the specters of darkness.

"Well, you cannot go crying to my mother tonight. Every bed in the house is taken, and Carrie and Matthew are sleeping on the floor!"

"Do you think Hank will die? He was awful quiet."

"We'd better pray about that. Do you want to?"

Clara was preoccupied with her own fears. "I'm afraid to die. Pray for me, too."

"Clara, that is silly. You will probably live to be eighty years old like most people!"

"But someone could kill me!"

"Clara, sometimes you talk like a crazy! How many times do you hear of a killing?"

A long silence ensued, and then Bethia was sure she could hear her cousin crying.

"Whatever is wrong, Clara?" she asked.

Between sobs, Clara tried to explain. "I don't want to die!

They'll put me in one of those dreadful boxes like the ones that come in on the trains, and then they'll put it down in the ground! Oh, Bethia . . . how awful!"

Bethia could only assume that the sight of the burning stable falling on the horses had triggered this unreasonable fear. "I don't believe Reggie and the others knew what happened," she said, to comfort her cousin. "It was all so quick."

Clara stopped crying long enough to study her cousin. "If I don't tell someone, I'll just burst!" she declared.

"Tell what?"

"Tell that I know who started the fire!"

Bethia's mouth flew open. "You what?"

"If you tell anyone else, I shall die. I know I shall die. He said he would kill me!"

Bethia stared at her cousin. This was not the Clara she had always known. This terror was real. And there had been that strange look on her face when Phoebe had asked if she had seen anyone.

"If you know anything about the fire, Clara, you had better say so. Your brother nearly died and three horses did, and now Uncle Hank could be next!"

Clara swallowed hard. "I saw Mr. Brisson pull the bar down! He didn't know I was watching. Then when he saw me, he shook me so hard I could hear my teeth rattle. And he said he would kill me if I told!" She began to sob again.

Bethia was already slipping a sweater over her nightgown. "This cannot wait until morning!" she said and left the room. She found Caroline asleep and shook her.

"Oh, Bethia, how could you? I've been hours trying to sleep. Do you have any idea of the work we'll have in the morning? Go back to bed!"

"We've got to talk!"

"Not now. And don't wake Mother. She's been up most of the night !" And Caroline turned over, hoping to dismiss her sister.

"Clara knows who started the fire!"

Caroline sat upright.

"Bethia! Are you telling the truth?"

"Yes, I am! And I think the police should know before Lerner Brisson gets out of town, if he hasn't already. He threatened to kill Clara when she saw him at the stables."

Clara, who had followed Bethia, stood shivering in the semi-darkness. She shook with fear. "Do you think he'd really kill me?" she asked between chattering teeth.

"Oh, my poor Clara! What shall we do? If he wouldn't stop at Allen—"

There was a shuffling of feet in the doorway, and the girls fell in a tumbling heap, terrified and hugging one another.

"What are you girls talking about? You'll have the whole house up!" It was Allen standing there, holding to his burned and bandaged arm.

"Oh, Allen. Am I glad it is you!" exclaimed Caroline with relief. Then she explained the whole story, with help from Bethia and Clara.

Allen listened quietly, nodding as though he had suspected Brisson all along. Then he ordered them back to bed.

"We will see about this in the morning." If Brisson wanted Vaugn Haddon's farm enough to murder for it, he would certainly return. Allen believed there was time enough to go to the police.

At four-thirty, Nabby awoke Bethia and Joshua and sent them out to do the milking while she looked after the patients. Phoebe could not wait to leave Nabby's home and was out over the fields at a very early hour, dragging a reluctant Clara with her. With his mother gone, Allen confided in Nabby the events of the night.

Neighbors came early to Vaugn Haddon's place to bury the dead horses and clean up the charred remains of the stable. Some had even hammered together a lean-to to house the remaining horses in the severe winter days to come.

When Joshua and Bethia were coming in from the barn, they

noticed a carriage in Vaugn's driveway and summoned the others. Had Lerner really dared to return, and this early? If news got out that he was the arsonist, the townspeople would show him no mercy. The memory of the 1811 fire was still fresh in their minds, and retribution would be administered swiftly. Yet there he was, descending from the carriage and making his way to the door of Phoebe's house.

Allen turned to Caroline. "Go for Marshall Farnsworth and tell him what we have learned," he said.

Caroline saddled up as fast as she could, while Bethia and Joshua stood bug-eyed with wonder. What would happen next?

They had not long to wait, for Caroline soon reappeared, riding her horse hard up the road with Farnsworth close behind.

"Tell me what you know," said the young officer bluntly. He was looking at Bethia from under beetle brows and was intent on getting on with the interrogation.

Bethia gave her mother a look of panic, wondering why he had singled her out. He was altogether an ugly looking man.

"It's all right, Bethia. Tell him," urged Nabby.

"Clara told me about it. Clara is my cousin. She saw Mr. Brisson at the stable door."

"He in the habit of being there?"

"He plans to marry my sister-in-law," explained Nabby.

"This Clara—is she reliable?"

Joshua opened his mouth to speak, but Nabby broke in. "I do not believe she is lying."

Farnsworth crossed the floor and accosted Bethia. He seemed to enjoy the reaction he was getting from the pretty young girl. "Were you there when the fire started?"

"I was here in bed! Clara woke us up throwing rocks at the window."

Farnsworth paced the floor and twisted the corners of his straw-colored moustache. "If he is an arsonist, the town will tar and feather him! They just sent a firebug to the gallows in Haverhill! It will be my duty to protect him until there is a trial."

"I think he is worse than an arsonist!"

They all looked up as Allen spoke.

"I have reason to believe that he tried to kill me."

The inquisitor's interest was really fired now. He crossed to where Allen was standing and quizzed him further, then asked if he would accompany him to his mother's home. He was already reaching for his hat.

PHOEBE OPENED THE DOOR and stood looking puzzled. "Why, Mr. Farnsworth, what brings you here?"

"Just wanted to ask a few questions about the fire. Regulations, you know."

"Oh, do come in." She ushered Farnsworth into the sitting room, where Lerner Brisson stood nervously turning the brim of his hat.

"I doubt if you have met Mr. Brisson," said Phoebe politely.

Farnsworth was careful not to stare. He did not plan to put Brisson on the defensive . . . yet. He removed paper and pencil from his pocket.

"When did you first discover the fire?"

"Could have been eight-thirty. Maybe nine. Lerner—er, Mr. Brisson had just left."

Phoebe was being much too cooperative, and Lerner began to feel uneasy. Then Farnsworth looked directly at Lerner.

"You were here last night?"

"Yes. Yes, indeed."

"And neither of you heard anything unusual?"

Brisson turned away from the penetrating eyes. "Can't say we did," he answered.

"And you, ma'am. Didn't see or hear anything unusual?"

"Nothing. And Allen is always so careful with the lantern. All that hay, you know. I can't imagine how this happened."

"Who was first to discover the fire?" persisted Farnsworth.

"My Clara. She went to see what was keeping Allen."

"May I talk to Clara?"

"She is in the kitchen. I will get her."

Clara was indeed in the kitchen, hiding behind the pantry door. Phoebe had to drag her into the room where Lerner was.

"It's all right, dear. Mr. Farnsworth just wants to ask you a few questions."

Clara turned her face away from the austere-looking man.

"You must have seen smoke, Clara. Where?"

Clara clammed up and stared at Lerner.

"Answer him, Clara," prodded Phoebe, who seemed to be enjoying being the center of attention.

"I didn't see anything!" avowed Clara. How could she talk with Lerner standing there glowering, his glance threatening.

"You must have seen something, or you would not have gone for help."

The statement was directed toward Clara, but Farnsworth was observing Lerner. The man was still nervously turning his hat.

Clara looked petrified. Her glance darted from Mr. Farnsworth to Lerner, and then she broke for the door. "He'll kill me!" she shrieked, tearing away from Phoebe's grasp.

"Sakes alive, child! Mr. Farnsworth is only asking questions!"

"Not him! It's Mr. Brisson. He said he would kill me!"

"Mercy! Whatever are you saying, Clara?"

"I am afraid the child has good reason to be frightened," said Farnsworth. "Mr. Brisson knows more about this than he is telling. The child saw him at the stable."

Brisson took a step toward the door, looking like a cornered animal.

"I wouldn't try that!" snapped Farnsworth, his right hand moving quickly toward the holster at his hip.

"That child is a liar!" snarled Lerner.

"I don't think so, Mr. Brisson." It was Allen barring Lerner's retreat.

242

Phoebe looked at Lerner with disbelief as Farnsworth placed restraints on him.

"I'm sorry, ma'am," the marshal said.

Lerner, now shackled, resorted to his wits.

"I admit I was there." He was talking fast. "I went out to give Allen a hand."

"You were bolting the door!" accused Clara, feeling more secure now that Lerner's hands were tied.

"You were bolting the door!" Brisson thundered back at the child.

Phoebe's face flushed. The veil was lifting slowly before her eyes. If what Clara was saying was true, then Brisson had tried to murder her son . . . and now he was trying to put the blame on her daughter!

"You tried to kill Allen!" she said in disbelief.

"Nonsense, Phoebe. All nonsense. Don't believe her!" Lerner was still professing his innocence.

"Lerner Brisson! That child could never lift the bar. That takes a man!" Phoebe's voice had grown cold and menacingly calm. "Take this man out of here!" she said dispassionately.

"We seem to have all the evidence we need," said Farnsworth, and left with his prisoner.

Allen remained, quietly facing his mother, remembering how Nabby had said it would be better for Phoebe to see her error than be told.

"I am sorry, Mother. I really am. I knew Lerner was an evil man, but I did not realize how evil. I should have told you both about Uncle Clint's contract, but truthfully I kept hoping you would see him as he really is. We might have been spared a lot of grief."

"The contract? What do you mean?"

"I asked Aunt Nabby to show it to me a week ago. The new contract has named me sole owner of the property, with Uncle Clint the trustee. Father stipulated that this was to be home for you as long as you were a widow. He wanted you and Clara always to be cared for—but the property and its responsibility were for me."

Phoebe looked at her son, shame covering her face, and as quickly looked away. She sank heavily into a rocking chair, seeing herself for the first time. When she spoke, it was without strength. Gone was the self-assurance, the demanding manner.

"You will never forgive me, son. Never! You and Timothy and Clara! I have been as much a fool as Lerner!"

Allen was generous. He could be no other way. True, Phoebe had acted the fool, but she was his mother and she had been through a year of intense loneliness and grief. He understood that she might have been attracted to anyone who would pay her attention.

"We all make mistakes, Mother," he comforted.

"But, Allen, how can I live with myself? I'm so ashamed."

"Let's just be glad it is over and that I shall soon be well enough to build again."

Phoebe looked hard at Allen, realizing how faithful and kind the quiet son had always been.

"And you have stayed with me . . . all the way. What can I say but thank you? You are a wise and precious son."

Allen was surprised and relieved that she did not cry. She had learned from her disappointment, and best of all she had reached a place of trust in his ability to run the farm. There would be no more conflict, he was sure.

22

THE PROLIFIC QUEEN ANNE'S LACE bloomed over the open fields, and purple Concord grapes hung in clusters over backyard fences. Matthew returned nightly with tales of naval battles on the high seas and wove magic into the long evenings for the family. The romance of the great sailing ships stirred the imagination of the young and heightened the interest of their elders.

The capture and burning of *Currier's Star of Peace*, the *Charles Hill*, and others made no small stir in the community, and the *George Griswold* held for ransom kept the appetite of the citizenry sharp. Even the evasive exploits of the pesky Confederate *Alabama* were taken into rivalrous account, and many a Union seaman breathed easier when news came that she had been sunk off Cherbourg, France, by the Union *Kearsage*. The Union's quarrel with the South was never easy or without cost. For every victory, there was a price!

Now the presidential elections were coming up, and there would be battles of a different nature. In order to ensure votes from the Democratic Southern states that had not seceded, the new Republicans went to political maneuvering and nominated North Carolina's Andrew Johnson for the vice presidency, little knowing how their skullduggery would backfire in the future.

"Little Mac" McClellan, still smarting from the disapproval of his commander in chief, was opposing Lincoln on a conciliatory platform. This stirred some optimism in Jefferson Davis's heart, giving him cause to believe that even in a defeat there could be leniency and compromise. He counted, too, upon the weariness of the North—but not on the fidelity of the general public toward the much-loved Lincoln. By this time, the lanky rail-splitter had a following greater than anyone could have anticipated.

The important thing now for the Republicans was to see that Lincoln was elected. Political rallies, parades, and speeches became the order of the day. Balls were held in patrician manors, torchlight parades were initiated, and business picked up in the local taverns. Cities were invaded by the usual hucksters, and women kept themselves from the streets.

The autumn colors still hung on, spot splashing the landscape, though the elms had already been shorn of their leafy beauty. Even the birch and the aspen had passed their season of yellow-gold, and the forecast was for an early winter.

The chill winter air had moved in prematurely, and the newspapers came out with vivid accounts of "Little Phil" Sheridan's courageous exploits in the Shenandoah and Sherman's conquest of Atlanta. Both were destined for a place in history as men who changed the tactics of war forever.

AT THE HADDON FARM, Hank's health improved, though not as rapidly as he would have had it. Doc Slater had made it clear that his patient should resist any inclination to return prematurely to the dusty fields, and Nabby was set as watchdog. Hank soon learned that he could not disobey without conflict.

He watched in agony as much of the harvest languished on the vine or rotted in the fields. The stock had to have first consideration, so the family banded together in order to share in the labor. Nabby hired apple pickers and paid them in shares. No farmer ever put out cash when he could substitute something else, and Nabby was determined not only to hold the land, but to manage the farm with wisdom until the return of her soldier-husband.

Hank could stand being idle no longer. He dispensed with the cumbersome bandages and ventured back to the fields.

"Do we go on with the farm?" It was Allen who spoke, standing with hands on hips and looking at the ash-strewn ground where the stable had stood.

"You can't quit. Too much at stake!" answered Hank.

"I may have to borrow. Will they turn me down because of my age?"

"Thunderation, man! Haven't I warned you against that?"

"Then where do we begin?"

"We'll get enough cows together to start your own dairy. Will take awhile, but you can do it."

"No, Hank, a dairy isn't for me."

"You could sell some of your pa's carriages."

"I can't do that, either. It would be like selling all that is left of him."

"Some sacrifices are tough, Allen. Sometimes there is no room for sentiment. You do with what's on hand, if you want to survive."

Allen turned his thoughts toward more immediate issues. "What's on the agenda today?"

Hank rubbed his beard with a scarred hand, and a gleam of humor spread over his wrinkled face. "Whaddaya say we start by pulling down that danged fence!"

Allen grinned, and the two started for the miserable barricade.

"Thank God that nonsense is over with! Mother doesn't talk much, which you know isn't natural for her. She's brooding and keeping her feelings inside her."

"Healing takes time," said Hank, remembering the long months it had taken for him to get over his mother's death.

"I can understand about grief," said Allen, reading his friend's thoughts, "but this is different."

"Perhaps Nabby could—"

"No, she can't face Aunt Nabby," Allen interrupted. "She's too ashamed."

"Maybe Timothy could come home now."

"I have thought about that."

BUT YOUNG TIMOTHY HADDON had no such thought in mind. He had signed on with an accounting firm and had his sights on much bigger game. The world of finance had utterly captivated his imagination, and he was determined to be master of it.

He left the office at noon and crossed Tremont Street to the Boston Common. In his pocket he carried a ham sandwich, and he stopped at a fruit stand to purchase an apple. The smell of the fruit stirred memories of the airy bins in the spacious Haddon cellars. What had Solomon said about the fragrance of apples?

Somewhere a band was playing, "God Save the Union," and a late meal had been set up on the dried grass. Young ladies were distributing rolls and doughnuts. Some also had bowls of hard-boiled eggs, along with hot tea and coffee. Timothy sat down on a bench and watched the activity with interest. It was growing cold now, and he would have to find a more accommodating lunchroom before winter.

Uniformed men milled about the bunting-draped tables, clearly more interested in the young ladies than in the food they served. The kettles of steaming coffee looked inviting, but Timothy was no soldier. He wished the wind would veer off in another direction so he wouldn't have to smell the coffee.

He buried his teeth in the apple and watched a young girl make her way through the crowded Common. It struck him as a fruitless task for her to accommodate all the eager hands. She returned repeatedly to the table to refill her pitcher at the coffee urns.

The young lady was unusually pretty, with her titian hair and accompanying olive complexion, but it was not her coloring that held his attention. It was her exuberance and the way she smiled. She seemed delighted with the privilege of serving. Everywhere she went, she left the soldiers laughing and lighthearted. God knew they needed that! Richmond was still in the hands of the Confederates, and would not be taken easily.

The girl looked up from her tray, caught Timothy's appraising eye, and came toward him. She was even more attractive at close range.

"Coffee?"

She settled herself on the bench beside him, soft pink lips drawn back over straight white teeth. Her eyes were a mahogany brown with tiny green flecks and lights dancing merrily in their depths.

"I am not a soldier—yet," said Timothy.

"But you are cold. Here!" She pressed a cup of the hot beverage into his hand. The cup was pleasantly warm, as was her smile. He thanked her for her kindness and gulped the stimulant with obvious relish. Then with some embarrassment, he spoke.

"I'm not certain this is right," he said.

She ignored his remark. "I have seen you here before," she said.

"Are you here every day?" asked Timothy.

"I am now. I had to wait for my birthday. My father is very protective."

"And which birthday was that?"

She looked amused. "I'll not tell you!"

"Yes. Birthdays can be a nuisance—the lack of them, I mean!"

"Lots of things are a nuisance!"

"Like?"

"Like wars. And older sisters!" She turned her inquisitive eyes on him. "Why aren't you a soldier?" she asked bluntly.

"I've another year before I can enlist. Right now I am working at something for the future." He pointed across the street. "Mallory and Brown."

She smiled. "My father is Harold Winston of the Winston Brokerage Firm!"

"Then we are competitors."

"I don't know about that. There is always room for both."

"That is nice of you to say, Miss—"

"Melinda Winston. My friends call me Lindy."

Timothy savored the name. "It's like the sound of a silver spoon on cut glass!"

Stars sparkled in the brown eyes, and a blush sprang to the girl's cheeks.

"I didn't mean to be forward," Timothy apologized. "It just came out."

Lindy had grown serious. "I hope you won't have to go to war."

"When the time comes, I shall go."

"All that's left are old men and little boys!"

"Old men aren't so bad, are they?"

"I think they are awful! My sister married one, and she never has any fun! Like Ruth marrying Boaz!"

Somewhere a clock began striking, and Timothy stood to leave.

"Will you come tomorrow?" she inquired.

"Yes. Good-bye for now." As he crossed the street, he heard her calling after him.

"What's your name?"

"Timothy!" he called back over the confusion of horses and carriages, then turned toward his building wondering whether he would spend the afternoon concentrating on accounting . . . or thinking about sparkling brown eyes.

NABBY FINISHED DELIVERIES EARLY and went to the post office. To her delight, she found a letter bearing a Boston stamp. It could only be from Timothy! She hurried home, anxious to share its contents with the family. Dinner could wait.

November 5, 1864

Dear Aunt Nabby,

I put off writing until I had something worth telling. I am now employed at the Mallory and Brown establishment. It is only a beginning, but they seem glad to have me, what with the man shortage. I like it more than I can say and hope to remain here at least until I am drafted.

I have a good bed in a fine home. The room is quite small, not like home, but it is shelter. If you had not given me the loan, I should have slept in the street. I am enclosing a small payment and shall send more later. Tell Allen of my good fortune.

How are things at home? What do you hear from Uncle Clint? Please do write all the news. Much must be happening in the situation I left. I especially want to hear how my mother is.

Your loving nephew,
Timothy Haddon

"Hooray for Timothy!" shouted Joshua.

"I'll write him a letter!" exclaimed Bethia, scurrying toward the kitchen in search of writing materials.

The letter was taken across the fields to Allen. He knew as he read that Timothy would not be returning. Phoebe, though proud of her son's ability to fend for himself, struggled to hold back the tears.

"He always did like numbers. I just wish I could see him long enough to tell him how sorry I am for all that happened."

"I shall write and ask him to come for Thanksgiving!" Allen promised.

The next week, Bethia seemed unusually eager to clear away the table after each meal. Once Nabby caught her pressing mashed potatoes into a cup and asked about her strange behavior.

Bethia's answer was vague.

"Are you feeding another stray?" her mother asked. "Because you had better not be! More mouths to feed right now are out of the question."

Added to her strange behavior were frequent trips to the barn . . . and Joshua seemed in on whatever it was she was doing. They took turns disappearing in that direction with a certain regularity.

"I am going to follow her," declared Caroline after three days of this activity. After all had retired that night, Caroline, with her mother's approval, listened for the telltale steps of her sister upon the stairs. Even Bethia's light step caused the old steps to creak and recoil.

Lying quietly, Caroline listened as the pantry door added its voice to the eerie chorus. When the back door closed, she rose and followed her sister. The hunting moon had never been brighter, coming in at the barn windows and showing brilliant and white on the floor. She watched Bethia climb the ladder to the hayloft, then retraced her steps and entered Nabby's room.

"Mother, wake up! I've tracked Bethia down. She has hidden something in the hayloft!"

"Must we tend to this tonight, Carrie?"

"By morning she could have moved it!" persisted Caroline.

Nabby rose slowly, complaining about the lack of sleep she was getting these days. They waited together in the dark till they heard the whine of the back door. Hurried footsteps and creaking stairs soon told them that the night prowler had returned to her bed.

They waited a short time and then proceeded to the barn.

"It can't be a wild animal, or it would run!" whispered Caroline.

Nabby raised a lantern and jumped when she heard a muffled sneeze followed by a thin cry like the sound of a prowling feline. Up the ladder they went and brushed aside a thin covering of hay. There, swathed in hay and dirty blankets, lay a tiny black baby with eyes larger and blacker than they had ever seen.

"It's a fugitive child, I'm certain!" exclaimed Caroline, reaching for the baby. "Wherever do you suppose she got it?"

They left the loft with their whimpering charge and returned to the kitchen, where Nabby set the lantern down and stared at the infant.

"Whatever will that child think of next? Now we have a real problem! We may be fighting for their freedom, but we still have jurists who can't decide who is and who isn't a fugitive slave."

Caroline listened with half interest. Already she had bathwater heating and was stripping the miserable rags from the baby's body.

"Poor thing. Must be itching terribly."

The women soon had the child bathed, powdered with corn starch, and dressed in Joshua's old baby clothes. In warm clothing and cuddled against Caroline's loving heart, the infant was soon blissfully asleep.

Nabby pulled a large crate from her closet and fashioned a small bed.

"We'll keep him here till morning. You may sleep with me. I wouldn't want you to miss the look on little Miss Nightingale's face when she learns that her secret has been discovered!"

Six hours later they were shocked into consciousness by the shrill voice of Bethia bursting through the door.

"He's gone! He's gone! Someone has stolen him, or something ate him! Oh, Mama! Carrie! Something dreadful has happened!"

"Quiet, Bethia. You'll have everyone awake! If that is what you are missing, you needn't fuss!" Nabby indicated the box bed.

Bethia ran to the box and looked in, sucking in her breath. "You found him!"

Nabby dragged herself from the bed. "Why didn't you tell me?" she asked her daughter.

" 'Cause you would have taken him away. I know you would!"

Caroline joined the conversation. "You can't keep a baby in a haystack, Bethia. You should know that!"

"I was caring for him. I really was. Besides, that's where I found him."

"In a haystack?"

Nabby and Caroline looked at Bethia as though she had lost her senses.

"Yes! In a haystack down by the smokehouse. I found him, so he's mine!"

"Honestly, Bethia, you talk as if he were a sack of potatoes!" Caroline said. "When will you realize that you can't mother every orphan in the world?"

At once Caroline was sorry she had spoken so sharply. Bethia's face was anguished, registering the pathos of a wounded animal. Bethia always would be the Good Samaritan in the family, and Caroline knew she could never be otherwise.

"I'm sorry, Bethia. I am sure you did what you thought was right. I can't blame you for that. He's content and healthy, too, and seems none the worse. But you should have brought him to Mother at once."

Nabby went to the kitchen to prepare milk for the baby. He gulped the food ravenously, and the morning soon took on a rare hilarity. Once up, everyone welcomed "Sir Moses," and it was not long before he had the Haddon clan wrapped around his chubby fingers.

Even the usually tacit Hank had to comment. "Cute little beggar!"

When Allen came to the door looking for Hank, he, too, was fascinated by the new arrival.

"You going to tell about him?" he asked, touching the small hand and looking at Nabby.

"I wouldn't dare! Folk would start accusing me of working with the Underground Railroad, and they'd send him off to an orphanage like the one they burned down in New York!"

Allen stood looking thoughtful. Clearly he had something of significance on his mind.

"Can't we adopt him, Mother?" asked Bethia.

Nabby, too, was engrossed in thought. No mother would just abandon her baby and forget about him. She was certain to come back for him. The fact that he was such a healthy child made it plain to Nabby that he had been blessed with a caring mother.

"Aunt Nabby, do you suppose Mother would take him?" asked Allen. "It could be the very thing she needs right now. She's closed herself off from everyone since the fire."

Nabby thought about it. "It's worth a try, Allen."

Bethia's countenance fell.

"It's all right, Bethia," Allen reassured her. "Mother may not even accept him, but if she does, you may visit him every day."

Matthew, who had been standing on the perimeter of the conversation, decided to speak.

"I know it would be good for Aunt Phoebe, but she should know the risks involved. The Emancipation Proclamation will not become law until it is amended, and our local courts are in limbo when it comes to making decisions. She could be harassed to death!"

Allen, who knew his mother's stubborn nature, said, "I'd be willing to take my chances on that. Want to come, Aunt Nabby?" His pragmatic mind was already planning a course of action. What his mother needed was a stirring up of the old dander!

Allen was already out the door with the child in his arms, Bethia at his heels, and the rest of the family bringing up the rear.

23

PHOEBE WAS SITTING in a Boston rocker in the kitchen, a letter from Timothy in her hands. She looked startled at the unexpected visit, then puzzled when she spied the small black baby in Allen's arms.

"Allen, what have we here?" she asked.

Allen placed the child in her arms, where he obligingly smiled. Phoebe's face softened and she smiled, too, oblivious to her audience.

Bethia spoke up, her face shining with pride. "I found him in the hay! Just like baby Jesus!"

"Probably left by a mother heading for Canada," suggested Allen.

"Who is caring for him?" Phoebe asked.

"No one!" answered Allen quickly.

By now, Clara had entered the room and was crowding in to view the foundling.

"You may keep him for a few days if you like," Nabby offered. "It would help me a great deal until we decide what to do with him."

Phoebe stiffened and sent a glance of sharp resentment toward her former antagonist. "I'd like him for more than a few days, if you don't mind."

"Keep him as long as you please. It is certainly better than an orphanage!" was Nabby's calculated response.

"Orphanage!" exclaimed Phoebe.

"Yes, when they discover we have him."

Phoebe bristled. "And who would have that say?" she asked.

"The courts," said Matthew.

"Well, we shall see about that!" And the old Phoebe was up and ordering Allen to retrieve the family cradle from the dust of the attic.

"Nabby, you have kept him nicely. Allen was chunky like this. Oh, and Nabby, Timothy is coming for Thanksgiving!"

The world seemed suddenly bathed in sunshine. The Haddons were once again a family. The little foundling must have been sent by heaven's angels. How unsearchable were the ways of God!

In spite of Clinton's silence, the days took on new meaning at the Haddon homesite. Hank, still noticeably weak, was back in the dairy where he was happiest. Phoebe joined Caroline and Nabby as they sewed their Thanksgiving finery, and the men took time off to go hunting. This Thanksgiving would be a day to remember!

The days moved on pleasantly, and Sir Moses became a part of Phoebe's heart and home. Each night after Clara had gone to bed, Phoebe returned to the sitting room and tucked the baby in, settling the wooden cradle close to her feet that she might rock it.

One evening she had settled herself in the usual manner. Allen went to the makeshift stable to check on his horses. It was twilight, and the gray of the sky was fast turning to black. The evening star was sending its benign light on a weary world. On the hearth, three stout logs blazed, sending comfort and warmth into the corners of the room. Except for the tick of the Simon Willard and the occasional explosion of the wood, a sweet peace and quiet enveloped the entire scene.

The day had been long, and Phoebe leaned her weary head against the high-backed rocker and sighed. A shadow flitted across the window. Had she imagined it? She remained quiet and waited. It passed the window again.

Could it possibly be Lerner? Had he escaped prison? Would he be seeking revenge? Phoebe arose and made a pretense of stirring the fire. The scratching of brush against the house convinced her that the prowler was still there. Then she heard the sound of running feet, and soon Allen entered the kitchen door. She hastened to meet him.

"What is it, Mother?" Allen asked, alarmed at her pale face.

"Prowlers! I've seen shadows and heard sounds!"

Allen walked to a back room and returned with a rifle. "Go to bed, Mother. I shall camp outside your door. If someone wants trouble, he'll get it!"

"I'd rather stay with you, son," she said.

"No need. I can handle things." He was already bedding down on the floor.

The night passed with no further disturbances. With the rising of the sun, fears were soon dispelled. Perhaps, after all, Phoebe had imagined the intrusion.

At ten o'clock, a knock at the kitchen door brought Phoebe to answer. Clara was at school, and Allen had taken two horses to the blacksmith's shed.

A heavyset man stood before Phoebe with an ostentatious air. He had a florid complexion and sandy brows and hair. His moustache was walrus-like and tobacco-stained. His eyes were a pale blue with flaccid circles so pronounced below them that he seemed to be wearing spectacles. He was dressed in a uniform of some sort unknown to Phoebe.

"I believe you are Mrs. Haddon," he said, rearing back and expanding his large chest, reminding Phoebe of a courting pigeon.

"Yes, sir."

"I believe you have a small child here. A Negro child."

How had their secret become known?

"And what is that to you?" she asked defiantly. It would never do to appear frightened or intimidated. Besides, Phoebe Haddon would not know much about that!

"Ma'am, I am with the state!" He produced credentials. "May I come in?"

Giving him a scorching look, but not daring to refuse, she indicated that he might enter the house.

"May I see the child?" he pressed.

Phoebe went to her room and picked the sleeping baby from his warm bed. She returned, hugging him to her breast.

"Where did you get him?"

"He was abandoned on our property—found in a haystack."

The officer looked him over and sighed. "You should not have taken him in."

"We should have left a child in a haystack?"

"Ma'am, if word gets around, we shall have a dozen black babies in our haystacks!"

"Mr. Lincoln declared the slaves free. You have no right—"

"Mr. Lincoln did indeed declare them free, but it is not yet the law."

"Well, it will be soon!"

"Perhaps. But until that time, we are required to return all fugitives to their owners."

Phoebe grew livid with anger. Was this to be the reward for giving her husband's life to a just cause?

"I thought a fugitive was a slave who had run away from his master."

"That is correct."

"But this baby can't even walk! How can he be a fugitive?"

"Well, he is obviously not your child, Mrs. Haddon."

"Fugitive, sir, is from the Latin *fugere* meaning 'to flee.' If this child could not have fled, and you insist on pursuing this further, you will have a legal case to contend with. A legal case that might cost you your job and brand you a northern Simon Legree!"

The man coughed and sputtered. Obviously he had met his match in this woman. Her story could inflame the public if it got out, and bring his superiors down on him. He backed away, somewhat bewildered.

"Well, uh . . . I was only sent to investigate. I shall take up the question with my colleagues." He left, muttering to himself.

When Allen returned, he was given an account of the visit.

"Mother! You were wonderful!" he exclaimed.

Phoebe looked doubtful at first, then her expression changed to surprise and delight. "I am? I am, aren't I!"

Allen was glad to see the old nature showing again in his mother's face.

"Of course. You gave the old hawk something to think about. I could never have fended him off like that! But now we must watch Moses constantly. Most anything could happen, now that they know we have him!"

The situation was a touchy one. News traveled fast, and now that the authorities knew, it was only a matter of time before there would be repercussions. When evening came, they drew together before the fire, Allen with his newspaper and Clara on the floor with the cradled Moses. Phoebe rocked the cradle with her foot and stopped abruptly when she heard again the rustling in the shrubbery outside the window. This time she was not alone. Allen had heard it, also.

"Don't act frightened. Just go on as though you had heard nothing."

He arose and walked casually to the kitchen door. Slipping noiselessly outside, he moved with stealth toward the shrubs. The leafless branches gave poor coverage to the crouching figure. Allen had fully expected to confront Lerner, but now he could see in the moonlight that the figure was much smaller than the portly Brisson. He waited until he was almost upon the crouching intruder, and then he spoke.

"Come out or I'll shoot!"

The prowler reeled in terror. "Oh, massuh! Don' shoot!"

With lightning speed, Allen grasped his captive by the scuff of the neck and threw him to the ground. Then he stood over him. The slouchy hat fell off, and long tangles of hair spilled down over the creature's shoulders.

"A woman?" exclaimed Allen, dumbfounded.

"Yassuh, yassuh. Ah comes to get mah Samson!"

"Samson?"

"Mah young'un. Ah seed him through da window! Tha's mah young'un'!"

Lifting the woman to her feet, Allen led her to the back door and into the kitchen, where Phoebe met them, staring in amazement.

"Here's your prowler!" said Allen.

"Ah'm sorry, ma'am. Ah only wants mah chil'!"

"Moses is your child?"

The woman laughed heartily. "What you call him? Moses? He ain't Moses. He be Samson!"

Phoebe watched her, spellbound—and relieved, too, that the prowler had not been Brisson.

"I thought you might come for him," she said. Then, gently, she took the woman by the hand and into the room where the baby lay. They stood together looking down at the small cherub.

"Where's his father?" asked Phoebe, already concerned that once returned to his mother, they would both need strong protection.

"Ain't seen him since he took off for Tennessee. Heard, though, that he be fightin' at Fort Pillow las' spring."

Allen gave Phoebe a knowing look. If that were true, doubtless the man was dead.

"Where will you take him?" asked Allen.

"Ah aims to go to Canada. Got a brother and sister there."

"You traveling alone?" The thought was preposterous.

"Ain't nobody else."

Phoebe placed the baby in his mother's arms and looked at her tattered clothing. Her rags were too thin to protect her from the cold of the North. Phoebe shook her head doubtfully.

"What is your name?" she asked.

"I be Delphi."

"Come close to the fire, Delphi." Leaving the woman there with her baby, she motioned Allen toward the kitchen.

"She can't go to Canada alone. They'll both die!"

"I am afraid that even if we oppose her, she'll try. It would be best to send her on her way equipped."

"What can we do?"

"River travel is the fastest—even if it freezes, they can take to the shore, and there are carries along the way. Get her dressed in warm clothing and pack a few supplies. The Indians in Maine will help for a price. I'll get Hank to find a pilot."

Allen left, and Phoebe moved rapidly, filling a waterproof supply bag and then bringing Delphi to the table for a warm meal.

"We will give you money to buy more when you run out—only, let the Indians get it for you. They are known and catered to. Now for some warm clothing!"

Delphi looked at Phoebe with grateful eyes. "Yo' a kind lady. Wouldn't a left him, ma'am, but he were cryin', miserable and hungry, and we was skeered o' stirrin' up the police. I had to do somethin' drastical! I did wait till I seed a little chil' pick him up."

"Don't fret. God sent him to us, I am sure—right when we needed him. He's a good baby, and we shall be praying for your safety."

Phoebe had not felt so appreciated in her life, and the satisfaction was already showing in her face.

Allen returned with Hank and, leaving Clara at Nabby's, went on with his mother and their guests to the Merrimack River. A man Phoebe did not know was waiting there in a dory. Delphi and little Samson climbed aboard and settled down in the rear of the boat where Hank wrapped them in buffalo rugs.

"Archie will take you as far as the carry. The Indians will have their batteaux there and will take you into Maine."

Allen pressed several bills into her hand and tipped his hat. The dory pulled away, with only the sound of the wind and the dipping of oars breaking the night's silence. They could hear Delphi singing softly. It was like the plaintive notes of a sonata stealing back to them on the shore, a coda, sweet and sad, until the dory moved into shadows and disappeared.

They started back to their wagon.

"Sometimes all a body has is a song!" eulogized Hank. A cold wind stirred as he lifted the reins. He shivered.

"You are cold," observed Allen, noticing that Hank was paler than usual. *He's determined to work the way he always has, and he isn't ready. I must be diplomatic about helping him to slow down*, he thought.

The following day, fog hung low over the rivers and ponds, and the November day held a severe chill. Hank insisted on cutting wood, and Nabby reluctantly allowed him to head out toward the woods. When he returned, he was coughing and blue from the cold.

"You are not to go for wood tomorrow, Hank," declared Nabby. "Enough has been dried for this entire winter."

But as usual, Hank rejected anything that smacked of maternal patronage. From habit he was up before dawn for milking and insisted that he had never felt better. When he did not appear for breakfast, Nabby grew uneasy, and when Allen came looking for him, the alarm bells in Nabby's heart were ringing.

"Wasn't he in the barn?" she asked Allen.

"I didn't see him. Would he go for wood before breakfast?"

"He never has." Nabby reached for her shawl.

When they didn't find Hank in the barn, they headed toward the woods.

"Do you have any idea where he was cutting?" asked Allen.

"Close to the pond."

They walked through the woods, listening for the sound of an ax. Except for the wind there was only silence. At the water's edge, they scanned the shore. Far away, Allen thought he saw the mulberry-colored frock Hank wore, but it was close to the ground. . . . Then he was running, leaving Nabby behind.

He found Hank lying facedown on the bank, his face almost the color of the smock. He lifted the older man in his arms and stood as Nabby approached.

"Looks like some kind of stroke, Aunt Nabby. Send Josh for Doc Slater—fast."

It was Election Day, and Doc Slater had been at the polls, but he came as soon as his wife apprised him of the summons. He entered the Haddon house, an expression on his face like a storm cloud about to burst!

"I knew he'd do something like this!" he sputtered. "Where did this happen?"

"He went to chop wood by the pond."

The silence was terrible while Doc Slater examined Hank. "He is alive, but I don't know why . . . nor for how long." His voice had dropped to a sullen whisper.

"I couldn't have kept him in if I had tied him!" said Nabby defensively.

Nabby herself looked ashen, and much thinner than the doctor was pleased to observe.

"You must all stop working so hard! This is rest season!" He turned back toward Hank's prostrate figure. "He has had a stroke, and I can't promise you anything. Send one of the boys if there is any change."

The good doctor was more brusque with the Haddon family than he had ever been. To him, the miseries of the war were taking their toll. Being the only doctor left in the city, he was as overworked as his patients. Nabby sympathized with him.

Gloom settled over the house, much as it had when Grandma Adkinson had been ill. Bethia and Caroline took up the vigil at

Hank's door, and Allen came to sit by Hank's bedside and would not be moved. He settled in with eyes large and troubled, watching the older man's shallow breathing.

Why couldn't the good man have realized his limitations? Didn't he know his age was against him? Allen watched for the rest of the day, stopping only to eat what Nabby brought to him. It was late when Nabby came with a lamp.

"I can stay now, Allen. Go home and get some sleep."

"If you don't mind, I will stay."

Nabby did not insist. She knew how much Allen loved her brother.

It was nine o'clock, and still Hank had not moved. The sound of a parade band disturbed their thoughts. Matthew had brought news of Lincoln's impending victory, and the confident populace was celebrating prematurely.

Nabby tucked the covers under Hank's chin and then went to the window. Parading civilians were marching up the road, preceded by two fire engines. She could see it all in the flicker of torchlight. She began to pray.

"Dear God, not now, with Hank so close to death!"

But still they came, and the band grew louder. She turned back in time to see Hank stiffen. Immediately, she went for a basin of water. When she returned, Allen was holding Hank, his young face wreathed in anguish.

"He's stopped breathing!"

Nabby stood frozen, devoid of any emotion. The basin of water fell from her hands and she reached toward Allen—and fainted.

24

THE WORK WENT ON, but the Haddon family members moved only by habit. The flux of tears ran its course till there remained no more than dull pain.

Away from prying eyes, Caroline gave vent to her grief and then took into account that there was now no one in charge. Matthew was despondent, having lost a man with whom he could fellowship. Bethia broke into tears at the most unexpected moments, and young Joshua placated his anger by wandering over the places he had shared with his beloved uncle.

Questions assailed Caroline. Why would God punish so devout a family? What were His purposes, and why did she feel so inadequate at keeping promises? She was caught in a raging storm and was as incapable of calming the adverse winds as she had been in stopping the tempest that had blown in off the ocean so brief a time ago. This bothered her more than anything. Haddons were strong people, masters of their own destinies, and she was most certainly being challenged by the powers that be. Well, she would deal with those powers! She would surmount any difficulty, and she would do it herself! The anger festered inside and made her take account of the situation in which the family now found itself.

When she came upon her mother and Matthew in conversation, she knew it was time for action.

"I belong here now," Matthew was saying. "I shall leave the

newspaper and do what my father would expect of me. There is no one else."

He sounded very noble and convincing, but Nabby was not so engulfed in her grief that she was unable to resist his brave rationale.

"I could not allow that," she replied. "There has got to be another way."

Common sense and years of living with the indomitable Clinton had taught Nabby much about dealing with adversity, but in all honesty, this was a new thing. Who could have guessed how harshly the "war gods" could deplete the numbers of a family? She must keep the farm at any cost, yet she must not allow Matthew to quit just as he was gaining a foothold in his chosen field.

There were no simple answers, only the vague hope that the war would cease and Clinton would return. The mental conflict had begun to rob Nabby of her usual strength, and Caroline knew she would have to act.

"Mother," she began one morning, "we must talk about the future."

"Yes, I expect we should."

Caroline went straight to the crux of the matter. "It is clear our numbers are not enough for us to carry on as we have in the past. Uncle Hank's death has taught us that much."

"What do you suggest?" Nabby asked.

"I see no reason why I could not work at the mill."

Nabby came up stiffly. "You would die in one of those sweatshops—and who would care for the dairy?"

"That would be the difficult part."

Nabby winced, sensing what would follow. She sank into a chair and grasped the rolled arms so hard that her knuckles turned white.

"Sell the cows?"

"Not all of them. We'd keep what we could handle, and the money from the others would keep us going. We might even put some money away to purchase others when Father returns."

Caroline was relieved to see that Nabby was listening, even though the suggestion was crushing her.

"I guess change is the most difficult thing we combat, but if we don't sacrifice principles it must be all right. We all know that when Father comes home, he will set things right again and I shan't have to continue working outside."

"And when would you go to work?"

"As soon as the stock is sold. I'd like to get on with it as soon as possible."

"I don't know, Carrie. I just don't know! I find it hard to even imagine you working at the mill."

"Well, we'll never know, will we, until I try? Many of my friends are working there, and the steady money coming in has seen them through the worst."

"Would you be working on those dreadful machines?"

"I'll ask first for a stenographer's work." Caroline knelt beside her stricken mother and patted her falling tears with her own handkerchief. "I'm sorry, Mother. You have done your best. We all have."

Caroline left for the barn, and Nabby remained seated. To sell the stock was demoralizing enough, but to have a daughter of the Haddons working in a mill! Yet it seemed the only alternative, if Matthew were to go on with his career and the family were to survive. Perhaps Caroline was right—perhaps it was all a state of mind. This was a time for the farmer to look beyond the war and see the many new fields being established for the young. Hadn't Shakespeare said something about the roles each man plays in a lifetime . . . changing roles . . . new sets of habits. . . And they as parents had established strength of character in all of their children, strength that could withstand criticism, hardship, anything! Even now Caroline was exhibiting wisdom beyond her years—and making it possible for Matthew to continue with his career. Clinton had wanted that.

The auctioneers came early one morning. Matthew remained at home to oversee. Bethia plunked herself down upon her grand-father's Hussey plow, covering it with her voluminous skirt. If no one saw it, no one would covet it, and she could shield her father from that loss. The old plow was to him a sacred treasure from the past.

Joshua hung close to the barn, watching as each animal was paraded before the buyers. He knew every cow by name, and losing them was not easy. If only he were older, he was certain this would never have happened.

Several buyers peered over the stall where Dandy stood.

"He's not for sale!" declared the youngest Haddon defiantly, hoping to discourage the bargain hunters.

Nabby, Caroline, and Matthew stood together away from the crowd. The very same buyers might well yet have their day of reckoning. No one was immune from the hardships of the times. For the most part, they were a good lot, willing to give a fair price.

As Caroline had pointed out, it would not hurt for some of the fields to lie fallow for a year. Nabby could plant a small garden, and Allen, with Joshua's help, could seed enough land to feed the remaining animals. Perhaps the two could cut ice. Another year and the hens would be too old to keep, and there were enough to sell. When things got better, they would purchase chicks.

Caroline arose early the morning after the auction. Even in the house, the emptiness of the barn seeped into her consciousness, and the absence of Uncle Hank still tugged at her heart. But this was no time to quail. It was her turn to pick up the reins and govern the course for the family. Her father had trusted her for just such an hour.

For her interview at the mill, Caroline chose to wear a striped wool with a princess waist, cut without seams and with bishop sleeves. At her narrow turned-down collar she tied a black cravat. Her crinoline was modified and her skirt looped up slightly, enough to keep the hem out of the dust. Feeling jittery, she had foregone breakfast and was standing before the full-length mirror in Nabby's room. After all, a good appearance was essential! Her hair had been brushed vigorously and secured in a neat chignon, the severity of the style detracting little from the fine features. She put on a red woolen cape and headed for the door.

"Wish me Godspeed, Mother!" she said, standing on the threshold.

Nabby gave her daughter an encouraging smile. "Who could turn you away!"

At the mill office, Caroline was ushered inside by Barney Tipton. Caroline knew his family only slightly. He had been raised by parsimonious parents, prudent enough to educate their children, though unable to erase the traces of peasantry from which they had sprung. Barney had grown into a brute of a man, and though still very young, he already showed signs of a creeping obesity. His jowls shook as he spoke, and he tried to hide his lack of chin with a scrubby beard.

"So, you want employment. Ever work in a mill?"

"No, sir. I had hoped for a stenographer's position."

"Good at numbers?"

"I kept my father's books."

"Sometimes the hours get long."

"My days have always begun before sunup. I would not find that a problem."

"We don't pay more than the usual. 'Course, stenographers get more than the mill hands . . . say two dollars and a half."

"That would be most appreciated."

"Are you prepared to start right away?"

"Yes, sir."

"You need not call me sir. I am Mr. Tipton, foreman and manager of floor one." He motioned her to follow him into a small room, where an older woman was seated at an oversized oaken desk.

"Maude, I have brought you some help. This is Miss Haddon. The two of you should be able to keep up with the invoices, eh? Show her what her duties will be, and she'll start after the holiday."

Caroline was both overwhelmed with the speed of the interview and relieved at its outcome. Now there remained only the work of proving herself worthy of Mr. Tipton's obvious confidence in her.

Mr. Tipton left, and Maude began her explanations. The work was not as complicated as Caroline had envisioned. When Maude was about to dismiss her, she spoke up.

"May I see the work section? I've never been inside a mill before today, and it would help to have a picture of the entire operation."

Maude studied her in surprise. "Mercy! Didn't expect anyone would care to see that, leastwise a young lady like you!"

But she obligingly left her desk and led Caroline through a narrow passageway that eventually opened into a cavernous building. It must have been three hundred feet in length and probably fifty feet wide, with hundreds of looms.

"This is floor one, the weaving room. Next one up's where the spinning jacks are, and over that floor are the carding machines. Do you want to see them, too?"

Caroline nodded, and they moved on. The girls working there were neatly attired and worked swiftly and adeptly at their assigned tasks.

Maude warmed to her subject as they walked. "We burn a thousand tons of coal a year, make a good number forty and sixty cloth, and ship it out."

The noise grew burdensome, and Caroline was glad when they returned to the small office. She had been spared work with the machines, and she was grateful. Her family would be glad to hear her good news.

When Caroline left, the wind had come up and the air was colder. She pulled the hood over her head and buttoned the cape tightly under her chin, then set out past the wooden shanties of Peanut Row.

Suddenly someone called to her from a moving carriage, and to her surprise and embarrassment she saw that it was Jerome Cavell. He was down immediately and holding the horse.

"Where are you going in such a hurry?" he asked, but his great dark eyes were saying much more—that he was glad to see her, and that he had not forgotten their last encounter.

Before she could find her voice, he was assisting her into the carriage. "Come. I'll take you wherever you are going."

"I have just been hired at the mill," she explained. "And now I am on my way home with the good news."

"Good news . . . you working at the mill?" He was perplexed.

"Oh, so much has happened since I last saw you. You can't imagine!"

He pulled a buffalo rug over her. "Tell me."

Caroline began to relate all that had happened since the fire. Jerome listened silently, a small frown creasing his forehead. At last she felt obliged to inquire about his progress.

"Tell me about yourself. I've wondered how your career has been getting on."

"Things are progressing. I've given several concerts, and the invitations keep coming, as well as new students. But, Caroline . . . this work at the mill. Are you certain you belong there? I mean—the company!"

"Come now, Jerome. Who can say where I belong? I've been in the company of cows and chickens all my life. Can mill workers be worse?"

"I'm talking about the kind of person you are. You are sensitive and fine, and not at all used to the rough element you will find there."

"Then I must adapt."

"Will you be working all week?"

"Not on Saturdays or Sundays."

He brightened and reached for her hand. "You made me a promise once."

Caroline gave him a blank look.

"You promised to go to Boston with me. Had you forgotten?"

"I remember now . . . but with things in such a state . . . I had hoped to see an end to the war before I got on with my own pleasures."

"But the war could go on for years!"

Caroline looked stricken. "Don't say that, please. I don't believe I could bear it!"

It was one of the rare times he had seen Caroline display any emotion.

The ride was a cold one. Caroline studied Jerome's sober, handsome profile as they rode along together. Always he remained the kind and gentle companion. Nothing impulsive about him . . . just steady and comforting. The way he looked at her, too. There was flattery in his attentions, and in any circumstances, a woman needed that.

When he took her to her door, she felt a strange reluctance to say good-bye. Why did he always have this effect on her?

MATTHEW WAS OBVIOUSLY PLEASED that he could remain at the newspaper. With his and Caroline's combined pay, the family would survive. With only a few cows left, he and Bethia and Joshua could handle the dairy work, and Nabby could handle the housework and even find time to join the city ladies preparing boxes for the soldiers.

The release from the heavy duties of the farm began to show in Nabby's face, to Caroline's great relief. The family could ill afford any more catastrophes, and Doc Slater had warned them about Nabby's failing health.

When Thanksgiving arrived, Nabby and her children made their way to Phoebe's. Caroline had offered up her largest turkey for Allen to butcher.

Timothy was due on the afternoon train, and the house buzzed with excitement. Tantalizing odors filled the house, blending with the sweet fragrance of pine logs that crackled on each hearth. The windows were fogged from the steaming kettles on the stove.

Joshua hung close to the kitchen, while Clara and Bethia set the table. Nabby and Phoebe chatted amiably together, the unhappy past seemingly forgotten.

Allen was the first to see the approaching depot wagon, and his whoop summoned the entire family to the windows. Timothy jumped down and then turned to help someone else.

"He's brought a girl!" exclaimed Clara.

"He's brought a lady!" declared Allen, noticing the fine clothes.

Timothy's companion wore a smart traveling porkpie hat of gray velvet with a saucy feather in the front, and a matching three-quarter length coat over a full-backed and gored skirt. On her hands were pink gloves, which she removed as she entered the house.

Allen reached them first and gave his brother a bear hug while Phoebe stood with tearful eyes. Then she, too, embraced her son, and all were talking animatedly.

The stranger stood staring at Allen in amazement. "He never told me there were two of him!" she exclaimed.

Timothy began the introductions. "This is Lindy. She has begged to meet the whole family, and I thought this a fine opportunity."

Caroline excused herself to get another place setting. How like the impetuous Timothy to have neglected to tell them he was bringing a guest!

"She's awful pretty!" said Bethia, moving close to Caroline.

"Indeed, she is . . . and knows something of fashion, too!"

Phoebe invited them all to the table, where Caroline's prize bird lay, looking festively golden brown and tempting. Laughter and light conversation took over, but when Allen returned thanks there was a moment of sorrow as the family felt the loss of those absent ones. A little more soberly, the plates were filled and conversation resumed.

Bethia had the privilege of sitting beside Timothy's guest.

"Your hair is pretty, Miss Lindy," she managed, looking at the tight shoulder-length auburn curls.

"Thank you, Bethia."

"You must tell us about yourself—where you live and how you met Timothy." Caroline was trying to put their guest at ease.

"Oh, she has been chasing me for weeks!" put in Timothy.

Melinda crimsoned.

"Don't mind him, Miss Lindy. We never believe him!" assured Allen.

"You will believe me when I tell you Lindy's father has offered me a position in his firm!" retorted his twin.

"But we shall be drafted in a few months," cautioned Allen.

"Don't let careless rumors concern you, brother. I expect a truce before that happens."

Matthew agreed with Timothy. "Sherman is already on his way to Savannah, and when he goes into the Carolinas, there'll be an Armageddon. Grant plans to stop Johnston there, and it will be over quickly."

"I'm not sure I could agree with the awful things Sherman is doing . . . the burning and all," said Nabby.

"Have you forgotten, Mother, how the Confederate Early burned four hundred Yankee homes?" Matthew was always one to set the record straight. "War has never been anything but cruel, and if our generals can bring it to a quick end, we shall all be better for it. You don't win wars with faint hearts!"

"And the Confederate prisons!" said Allen. "Parolees are back with incredible stories."

"What about the prisons?" Caroline asked.

"They are terrible, run by merciless men. The few parolees who have come from Anderson say there are at least 10,000 graves there."

Caroline shivered and fell silent. What if Thad were in such a place?

Allen, seeing her reaction, changed the subject abruptly. "We'll no doubt see some prosperity when this war is over," he said.

"Not until a few years of adjustment," cautioned Matthew.

"The national debt is horrendous, and still climbing."

"Well, I am optimistic!" declared Timothy. "If I had money, I'd invest. I see opportunities coming that could make a man rich."

"Is being rich important?" asked the inquisitive Joshua.

"Well, if I were rich, perhaps Miss Lindy would marry me," answered Timothy, enjoying Lindy's embarrassment.

"You will get used to him, Miss Winston. He likes to shock people." Again it was Allen coming to the girl's rescue.

"I'm not sure that I will," said Lindy, looking from one twin to the other. "I cannot get over how much alike you two look—but I can see that you are different."

It was Phoebe's turn to chime in. "You are perceptive! Now, tell us about your family . . . and eat!"

The afternoon passed all too quickly, and evening found the family basking in the warmth and repletion of full stomachs and reconciled relationships.

"I took the liberty of promising Lindy's parents that she would be properly chaperoned and permitted to stay at your house, Aunt Nabby. I hope I wasn't presuming too much."

"Not at all. We enjoy company. There's always room for one more."

A light sifting of snow had fallen throughout the afternoon, coating the dry grass in the fields between the two Haddon houses. Timothy and Allen fell behind as the little group crossed the fields.

Timothy's buoyant mood changed when he caught sight of the open ground where the stables had stood.

"If only I had money to invest. I see opportunities every day. Then you could build again."

"And we could open for business!" Allen enthused.

"You could open for business," corrected Timothy.

"And you?"

"I shall never return, except of course to see you and Mother. I like my new world and its opportunities. I think Father would be pleased with my choice."

"Yes. He would be very proud of you, Timothy. You left with nothing, and you have done well."

The two locked arms and walked together, while Lindy nearly bounced along ahead, asking questions of Bethia and Caroline all the while.

"I could love it here!" she exclaimed, catching her breath and looking around at the wide expanse of farmland.

"It's nice in the spring," said Caroline. "You must come back when it is pretty with flowers and birds, and we can go to the ocean."

"My mother would let me. It's Father who keeps the reins."

"Well, one of these days I shall visit Boston. Perhaps I could pay a call to your parents so they can see that we are quite respectable."

Allen watched the vivacious girl ahead of them. He could see why Timothy was attracted to her.

"Were you serious about marrying Miss Winston?"

"She is a catch, don't you think? And it could work out well. I would no doubt climb the ladder faster than if I chose to go it alone."

"Hmmm. I suppose that is the way things are done," said Allen, hiding his disappointment in the discovery that his brother had an opportunist's heart.

The visitors returned to Boston the following day, Timothy with a small gift of money Phoebe had salted away, and Lindy bubbling with promises to return.

25

December came on with limited days of sunshine, the skies almost always gray and threatening. One morning was darker than usual with a certain promise of snow before the day was over.

Bethia and Joshua hurried through the milking and prepared for school. Matthew was swinging an ax; they would need an ample supply of wood should the storm prove to be heavy. If Uncle Hank were there, the wood box would already be full.

Strange how it was always the little things about their uncle that remained in their thoughts. He had been a human weather vane as well as a trusted overseer. They saw him everywhere: in the barn, in the fields, harnessing Dandy, breaking off apple blossoms and presenting them to the girls, biting the barley to see if it had matured, and—in the loneliness of the long evenings—reading to them from the old family Bible. Truly, his home going had broken the family wheel, and life now bumped along unevenly without him.

For several weeks now, Caroline had walked to the mill and back. She had found Maude a most congenial coworker, and there were times when the work was actually pleasant.

News had broken about that bulldog "Pap Thomas" and how he had succeeded in demolishing Hood's troops—but there was also news of the Confederates' dogged determination to hold out in the West. Confederate General Johnston was striking out to do what he could to stop Grant from linking up with Sherman. If he failed, the newspaper editorials said, the war was certain to come to an end.

Matthew followed the trend of events with avid interest and, along with the rest of the family, felt the burden of consternation that their father would inevitably be in the very center of the coming conflict.

Even now as Caroline passed the Paxton farm, she prayed for her father and for Thad. Snow was coming down in earnest when she reached the river. Little flakes frosted the tendrils of her hair and set up stars in her eyelashes.

One could do a lot of thinking in the silence of falling snow. She lingered in memory over Timothy's recent visit. Were there really financial evidences of the war ending? And how would life ever go on again for so many folk? Surely even an armistice could mean little to the orphaned, the widowed, and the maimed.

What would her father say when he learned of Hank's death? His letters had fallen off, and Caroline was certain they would stop altogether with lines being formed near and around the Neuse River. Even if she wrote to him, once the guns began to fire, the mail would be held in reserve. And even if that were not so, she could not bring herself to write of Uncle Hank's death. That would hardly be inspirational for a man going into battle.

She passed a group of children on their way to school. They called to her from the opposite side of the street, and their laughter took her back to her own childhood. It seemed so long ago. There was something magic about the world of little children. They were so singularly alive to the present. They drank fully of sun and snow, wind and rain, friendships and play. She felt a pang of longing for those days, and wondered why she was so early removed from them. Had it really been so long ago? Why did she feel so old?

She crossed the street and walked close to the fences there. It was damp there near the water. Several workers fell into step with her, exchanging pleasantries as they walked.

Once inside the mill, they stamped the snow from their

galoshes and blew their noses. Caroline entered the office, shook her cloak, and hung it on a peg to dry. Her boots she placed near the heat in a long row of soggy footwear, watching as they shed little rivulets of water.

The office was always warm, and for that she was grateful. She ran her fingers through her tangled hair and then sat down at her desk. Maude was late, which was most unusual.

Barney Tipton came in and approached her desk.

Caroline looked up, expecting orders, and found him staring at her with an expression that sent a chill through her entire body.

"A woman like you shouldn't have to work in a mill," he said, eyeing her figure.

Caroline shrank from the bold eyes. She picked up an invoice and gave it more attention than it required, but he was not to be ignored. A hand came down over her own.

"A man would be glad to take care of a pretty woman like yourself."

Now she was openly irritated and took no pains to conceal it. "Mr. Tipton, I came here to work!"

He merely raised one eyebrow and took his leave.

The day wore on. Maude arrived, and Barney Tipton did not return. The storm passed over, and the sun broke through the clouds. The temperature, however, dropped to fifteen degrees.

The office clock sounded out the closing hour, and the factory bells began their harsh ringing. People flooded down over the wooden steps, sounding like a herd of stampeding elephants. Maude, who was always ahead with her work, donned her coat and left. She had barely closed the door behind her when Barney came into the office with a handful of papers.

"Can you rush these out? They are very important."

Caroline looked dismayed. It was already growing dark, and the walk home was long, but she knew she could not refuse. He had warned her of long hours when she took the job.

Sighing, she took the papers and sat back down at her desk. She could see that the work would take at least another forty-five minutes. By the time she finished, it was dark and the night fireman had come on. She was tired when she finally slipped into her boots, wrapped her cloak around her shoulders, and locked the office door.

She stepped out into the fresh, clean air, refreshing after the stale air of the office, and breathed deeply. She made her way down the path that was white with snow, a five-foot bank on either side. Except for the moon that had risen silvery white, there were no lights. She quickened her steps.

A shadow arose behind her, and she realized she was not alone. Hurrying, she felt the shadow move faster, too. Suddenly a hand touched her shoulder, and another went around her neck. She screamed and struggled to free herself. Instantly, a rough hand clamped down over her mouth, pressing so hard that she could taste her own blood. Then she smelled the tobacco on her assailant's hands and clothing and knew it was Barney Tipton.

"Let me go!" she managed, tearing loose.

"Too good for me, eh?"

The pig-jawed face was close to her own, sending waves of nausea through her entire being. Swinging with all of her might, she struck a stinging blow across the ugly face. It was hard enough to start blood flowing, and also hard enough to fire the man's anger. He swung back with a powerful blow, knocking her to the ground. A second blow sent the world spinning.

"God, don't let me faint," she prayed. "He'll kill me!" But that was all she could say, for another blow landed and everything went blank. The stars, the buildings, the snow, and the night all spun together and went off into a thick, black cloud.

WHEN CAROLINE REGAINED CONSCIOUSNESS, there was another face before her, and it was not Barney Tipton's, it was Jerome Cavell's!

Overhead the stars were brilliant, and an icy wind assailed her face. She touched the interior of the cutter as it sped over the snow and recognized her own sleigh, with Dandy prancing sprightly along through the fresh snow! She frowned and lifted a hand to her face. The pain was excruciating—but she was alive!

"You're all right, darling. All right. Hold this snow on your face, and I'll have you home shortly."

"Where is Barney . . . Barney Tipton?"

"I hit the bloke—though I could not have done it without the help of the night fireman. Tipton's in custody, and I daresay he won't be on the loose again."

"Your face is bleeding, Jerome."

"It is nothing. Be quiet."

She made an effort to sit up, but the pounding in her head was too much. She leaned back against Jerome, weak and trembling.

"My mother will die!" she managed.

"Your mother isn't one to die, Caroline. She'll be glad I arrived in time."

"How did you know?"

"Just rest. I'll tell you later." He pulled the warm rug close to her chin. When they drove into the yard, Joshua was there waiting to take Dandy. Jerome lifted Caroline and carried her to the door where Nabby stood, alarmed at the sight of her daughter lying limp in his arms.

"She was attacked by a man at the mill," explained Jerome.

Bethia was already going for bandages, while Nabby knelt to inspect the cuts.

"I shall kill him!" threatened Matthew, reaching for his coat.

"No, Matthew, wait. He's already in custody. Let the law take its course."

"Shall I get a doctor?" asked Matthew.

"No, please don't," protested Caroline. "I couldn't abide having this bruited about. Just get me some more snow."

She was touching the bruise on Jerome's cheek. "Whatever sent you? How did you know?"

Nabby quickly filled her in. "He had come to see you. When it got so late, we were worried, so we harnessed Dandy and sent Jerome to get you."

"I might have died!" Caroline said. Then she looked away, ashamed. "Oh, Mother, how shall I ever go back there again?"

"You should never have gone in the first place," said Jerome, anger sending a deep flush to his face.

Caroline knew there was truth in his outburst, but how could he know the situation the family faced? With the stock sold, no letters from Clinton, and Matthew's future threatened, there had been no alternative—but she would die before she would tell Jerome that. Tears of frustration clouded her eyes.

"I'll find something, Mother. Don't you worry."

"Shhh, child. Right now you belong in bed." Then Nabby turned to Jerome. "Thank you isn't enough," she said.

Sensing that the family wanted to be alone, Jerome moved toward the door. "I'll come back tomorrow," he said and left.

Jerome did return the following day and for several days thereafter. Caroline found herself listening for the sound of his rented cutter and was disappointed when he announced that he had appointments in Boston that he must keep.

He was gone for several days, and then one evening he appeared again. Caroline was up and around and openly pleased to see him. Matthew was engrossed in the evening paper, and the rest of the family had retired.

"Where may we talk alone?" he asked.

"You needn't be concerned about Matthew. He never hears anything when he is reading. But come . . . we can talk in the sitting room."

They sat together on the rough horsehair davenport. Caroline had never seen Jerome so serious. He was precise and to the point.

"I did not come for small talk, Caroline. I want to marry you."

Caroline stared at him and then at her hands, trying to mask the shock she was feeling. She could not speak.

"Carrie?"

"Because you feel sorry for me?"

"Don't be naive!"

She turned further away.

"Look at me, blast it!" he demanded.

Thoughts of Thad and that miserable promise flooded Caroline's mind.

"I love you, Caroline, and I want you."

"We aren't at all alike, Jerome. Don't you know that? Can't you see how that could affect a marriage?"

"So sensible, Caroline. So puritanical and practical!"

"But it's true!"

"If we were alike, I doubt if I would have looked at you twice!"

"Marriage is a forever thing, Jerome. And besides, there's Mother. She needs me. How can I think of marriage?"

How was it that he always put her in a defensive posture?

"She'd be my mother, too, and she would never want for anything. I'd see to that. Carrie, give me a chance. Good Glory! I never thought I'd be begging!"

"Let me think about it, Jerome."

That was a concession, and Jerome pressed the advantage. "You promised to go to Boston with me. If I come for you tomorrow morning, will you . . . would you come?"

"My face. It's still discolored."

He took her face in his hands and planted a soft kiss on her lips. "There is no cause for concern there," he said. "You are as beautiful as ever."

Caroline was up before five, the early breakfast being a thing established forever in the Haddon kitchen. She fried large slices of bacon, creamed potatoes, scrambled eggs, and toasted her mother's thick bread. In the absence of Hank and Clinton, she had still not learned how to plan for fewer people. She cleared away the dishes and sent the children off to school, then went to her room. She wished she had a suitable traveling costume, but she would have to stop wishing and get into her watered silk.

She pulled her hair back in the severe morning style and wound it in a plaited knot. Then on with the silk bonnet. Tying the wide green silk streamers in a neat bow under her chin, she looked in the long mirror. The ruched tulle on the underside of the brim and the dwarf roses softened the severe hairstyle considerably. Grandma Adkinson's stocking purse and short gloves finished her ensemble. With the hooded cape over her arm, she walked to the door and met Nabby coming from the barn.

She looked at Caroline, puzzled, but said nothing.

"Jerome is taking me to Boston today. I promised him . . . but I should have asked you first."

Nabby smiled. "I think you can make your own decisions. You are no longer a child."

"I wish I were more sure of my decisions. I sometimes wish I didn't have so many to make!"

"Is it Jerome you are not sure about?"

"No. It is Thad!" There! It was out!

Nabby placed her hands on Caroline's slim shoulders. "But Thad is dead."

"Is he, Mother?"

"Even if he were to come back, Caroline, he would not be the same."

"Father came back unchanged."

"Your father isn't just an ordinary man."

Caroline regretted having brought her father's name into the conversation, as Nabby's face had taken on that sad, wistful expression she wore more and more lately.

The sound of Jerome's carriage broke into their conversation, and Caroline quickly placed a kiss on Nabby's cheek.

"He will come home soon, I just know he will," she said. "And life will go back to being the way it used to be."

As Jerome and Caroline left for the train station, Caroline could see her mother at the window waving good-bye, a quiet, almost timid, expression on her face. This was not the strong, assertive, capable mother she had always known.

When they reached Boston, Jerome led her to the horsecars. It was of great interest to Caroline to take note of the many changes in the big city as they drove along. She had somehow never pictured the district where they traveled to be where Jerome lived. She had imagined him living alone in a dingy garret, as did all aspiring young artists! But then, she really knew very little about his personal affairs.

The streets were wider than those of Newburyport, and the car was going straight down a well-paved road. A string of odd-shaped houses came into view, looking for all the world as though they had been pressed together by a giant hand until they rose sky-high. Yet they were not uniform, nor at all alike. Each one had its own personality and all lacked anything green, not even so much as a shrub in place. It was all brick and iron grates and each portal with its own design.

The stairs leading to the doors were steep, and there were deep architraves around each window—six lights and double-hung sash. The bricks were a terra-cotta shade with brownstone trim, and the basements were of granite and brownstone.

To her surprise the roofs, in spite of their height, were not steeply pitched, and along the wide avenue opposite the houses where the horses were traveling was a broad sidewalk, one on which anyone would enjoy walking. Near the curb stood a row of young, bare elms. Skirting the lovely sidewalk, a great fence had been erected, leading to a row of livery stables.

Jerome leaned close to her and explained that his own carriage and horse were housed there, though many of the stables were rentals. He watched her closely as her eyes filled with wonder. This was a child, an adorable child, and it was his pleasure to place at her disposal all the delights he could possibly give her. They left the cars and climbed the stairs together, and standing expectantly, Caroline watched Jerome turn the key in the lock.

"Welcome to the Cavell abode!" he said, beaming.

They entered a wide vestibule where sat a Chippendale settee with ball and claw feet. To Caroline it was much too elegant a piece of furniture to be placed in an entry. While he removed her boots, she ran her hands over the acanthus carvings, remembering a painting she had once seen of King David on a throne.

An inner door was suddenly flung open, revealing a middle-aged woman standing stiffly at attention. She was dressed in a striped uniform with a starched white apron—and her hair was the brightest red Caroline had ever seen.

"This is my housekeeper, Kathleen. Kathleen, this is Miss Haddon."

Behind the woman stood a man, slightly younger but with many of the same features.

"And this is Galvin, Kathleen's brother."

Kathleen curtsied politely and Galvin bowed. Then, first taking their cloaks, Kathleen led them down a long corridor. Pine and gold-leafed mirrors hung the length of the hall, and most had ornate cups for candles. There were oil paintings, too. One in particular caught Caroline's attention. It had to be a Cavell, for the eyes were those of Jerome. She wondered if the portrait were a Copley.

A wave of uncertainty washed over her, and she reached for Jerome's hand and smiled timidly, and his arm went swiftly around her. This was luxury of which she had never dreamed.

Still leading, Kathleen entered the parlor, then curtsied again and left them. It was a magnificent room, heavily carpeted and tastefully furnished. The dadoes were painted white, and above them to the ceiling were painted vignettes, no doubt done by the famous duo of Dufour and Leroy. The main attraction of the room was an enormous fireplace, very ornate, made of different-colored woods with a white marble, heavy projecting mantel. Over the mantel, an enormous mirror reflected the entire room.

A fire burned hot on the double firedogs, while two winged chairs were placed a comfortable distance from the flames. Close to one side of the fireplace was a screen, also Chippendale with the ball and claw feet, and holding a beautifully needled tapestry of birds and flowers.

The red mahogany tables in the room had a high polish, reflecting the lamplight. The extravagance of day lamps burning disturbed Caroline. Such waste was unheard of in the Haddon home!

Chairs with crewel-worked seats stood against the wall, and by a window stood a French-style piano. She recognized it from its fragile lines; it was like the one she had seen in Eva's home. A richly embroidered shawl was draped artistically over the top. In another part of the room, two card tables with leaves folded over the top were placed precisely before an inviting large window.

"This is where you work," she said, somewhat bemused. He had succeeded in surprising her, and he was enjoying every minute.

"You do like it! I hoped you would!"

"I am overwhelmed, Jerome. You have been careful to keep your secret."

"I am more than a little fond of privacy. This home was my grandmother's, you know. She liked privacy, too."

Then he whispered to her. "You may change anything you like!"

Caroline drew back, eyes like those of a startled deer. "Oh, Jerome, how could I ever fit into all of this?" She walked toward the door, and he followed.

"I thought this would help you to decide."

"It frightens me out of my wits."

"I would help you to get used to it."

"You don't need me. You need a wealthy Boston socialite, someone with influence, who could open homes for your concerts. Surely there are dozens of young women who would love the opportunity."

"If I had wanted a socialite, I would have had one by now. I love you! I want you. How can I make you understand? I can only think of one reason why you would put me off. You must be in love with someone else. If that is so, tell me, and I'll give up."

Caroline did not feel it was a time for confidences. Jerome's ardor was too close to the surface and, selfishly, she wanted his friendship. She had grown used to his sustaining presence.

"Don't be angry, Jerome. I have such a fear of not being accepted. In my own city I could care less. There we understand one another. But in Boston! You know I would be resented for stealing their idol from under their noses. I'm not sure I could handle that."

"Caroline Haddon could handle anything!" he said, and then, "Come, I must show you the rest of the house." Through double French doors and off a spacious dining room, Caroline could see a patch of earth. It was unexpected so close to the house.

"Do you plant a little garden in the spring?" she asked, her face coming alive.

"No, but you could."

"What is the soil like?"

"Honestly!" He planted a kiss on her nose.

"A garden just outside the window would give this room what it lacks—and there would be flowers for the house."

"I want you to set a date."

"You won't wait until my father returns?"

He read her thoughts instantly. "I would open an account for your mother."

"It doesn't seem right."

"Why?"

"It's like . . . buying me!"

"What nonsense!"

"I'm afraid, Jerome, I—I can't give you an answer now. Give me time."

"How much time?"

"At least a week."

"Granted! And now let's see what Kathleen has for lunch!"

The kitchen was not at all like the wide sunny kitchen at home. It was windowless and dark. Caroline thought about that dark kitchen as they caught the return train for Newburyport.

"HE WANTS TO MARRY ME," Caroline announced to her mother the next day.

"Why would you put him off?"

Caroline could see the Paxton farm in the distance as she looked out the window. "Oh . . . I suppose . . . because I've always been taught to be careful about quick decisions."

"With all you have told me, I cannot see why you would hesitate."

"I just don't feel certain."

"My dear child, you have done everything possible for us here. And Jerome's generous offer to help me until Clinton returns tells me that he is a kind and caring person. I could relinquish my daughter to a man like that."

Looking at her mother, Caroline could see that the security of having her married would take a heavy load from Nabby's shoulders.

"Then I shall tell Jerome I will marry him whenever he wishes!"

PART THREE

26

T HE WHITE TULLE AND LACE of the wedding gown should have flattered Caroline's dark hair and eyes. Instead it only accentuated her pallor. Her eyes should have been bright and merry, shining with excitement. Instead they were dull, lusterless, and as moody as the gray January skies.

Beyond the windows she could see the hills lying half-mantled in the melting snows of a midwinter thaw. The roads were watery, half slush and half mud. Brittle, bare limbs scraped across the rough clapboards of the house—a sound she had always loved. Now it only served to deepen her depression.

Nabby entered the room and stood appraising her daughter. "You will be the prettiest bride Parson Richardson has seen in a long while."

Then, with a mother's natural bent for perfection, she went on. "A little more powder under your eyes. Gracious, you must be cold! I should have made a fire in here. I debated it, you know, what with our being gone for several hours. The risk and all."

It was a rare situation that could move the stable Nabby into a flustered state, but Caroline's wedding was doing just that. Her mind raced over last-minute details; the modest reception that would be held at the old house after the ceremony for a select few, the cider to be pushed to the back of the stove, the flues checked, and the dozens of pink cakes marked into reasonable slices and set out for Phoebe to cut. Now and then she peered anxiously toward the driveway, fearful lest Allen's Germantown rockaway be late.

Caroline did not hear her mother. She was thinking about her wedding dress. It wasn't the gown she had always dreamed about. And she had never planned to marry in winter! Winters in Newburyport were Siberian! But it had been Jerome's choice—impatient, ardent Jerome! She wished he might have waited until spring, when the weather would be more merciful and new life would be stirring under the sun's returning rays. A girl might wear short sleeves then, and a decollete neckline, but Jerome's timetable had not allowed her such luxury.

Caroline reached for an artificial rose and attached it to the high lace collar. That should help! The dress did fit well, the tight bodice, the pointed waist, and the lace flounces. Nabby had spent hours copying the popular princess pattern, and Caroline must not seem ungrateful. She had worked far into the nights under flickering lamplight, patiently making tucks and hems and attaching tiers of gathered lace over the full-backed crinoline, every stitch a labor of love.

Nabby lifted the veil from the bed, her thoughts far away, remembering the day she herself had worn it.

"I wish he were here, too!" said Caroline. She spoke casually, but inside the longing for her father had an agony beyond expression.

"If only he would write. Such a long silence is not like him."

"He will write, Mother. You will see."

Nabby appreciated her daughter's attempted comfort, but inside both women knew that the long silence could be followed by the dreaded official notice. They had lived under that Damoclean sword for over three years now. They could best hope the silence meant that the Union troops were being moved to a more strategic and advantageous position. Today they must think with optimism, forget the morbid alternatives, the frightening possibility that Clinton might never return.

Nabby handed Caroline a glaumina pin and watched as her daughter secured the veil.

"Your hair is prettier than I have ever seen it," she said.

It did look lovely. Caroline had dared to depart from the severity of everyday wear. She had enough thick hair to build a soft pile of curls on the crown and still have much left to arrange in romantic clusters in the back, a suitable backdrop for the delicate features. That should please her stylish bridegroom!

Impulsively she caught her mother's hand and kissed it. "I haven't said thank you, Mother, and you have done so much in so little time. I know I shall miss you terribly."

It was a rare and treasured moment, one that was not displayed often in the Haddon home, where the assumption was that one should know when one was loved or appreciated.

"I will miss you, too, Carrie, but I truly believe this is right for you."

Caroline wished she felt that sure. She had done her best to point out to her betrothed that they had certain differences, both in personality and social background, but he had waved aside her fears, declaring that opposites were good for one another.

A brougham turned into the driveway, drawn by two high-stepping steeds. Their coats were shiny black and eyes flashing nervous white. The carriage wheels splashed in the cold mud.

"It's Allen, bless him! He has come for the children."

Nabby hastened to open the door. Allen entered looking unusually handsome, though a little stiff in his Sunday suit.

"Everyone ready?" he called.

Joshua, in his usual clumsy eagerness, ran to greet his cousin and sent the hall carpet flying. Allen righted the carpet and stopped to set his young cousin's tie straight. Then he slapped him on the shoulder.

"You look right smart, Josh. Now get your jacket and come along. Can't have you late for your sister's wedding!"

Bethia needed no prodding. She had waited for weeks to see the event over and done with. She bounded out into the yard and climbed aboard the carriage with little dignity, scrambling onto the seat next to Clara.

Allen paused at the door and spoke to Caroline. "Tell Matthew the rockaway is all harnessed. And tell Aunt Nabby my mother will leave the church early to cut the cakes and fire the logs if you aren't back early enough."

"Thank her!" said Caroline, looking at her cousin. His eyes were full of questions, but there had been no opportunity for the two of them to talk since Caroline had announced her betrothal to Jerome.

"God be with you, Carrie," he said softly as he left.

The house grew silent, except for the long-throated David Wood clock ticking noisily in the sitting room. Nabby checked the kitchen stove and went looking for her gloves. Caroline flung a brown woolen burnoose over her shoulders and walked to the parlor. Matthew checked the reserve stacks of pine and oak beside each fireplace. It was time to leave.

When they returned it would all be different. There would be chatter and giddy conversation and noise. Like Clinton, Caroline hated the idle chatter associated with social events. Better by far were the quiet solitudes, the wonderful long winter evenings, the treks in the woods, the night sleigh rides.

Leaving as she was, she could not help but dwell on the springs of her life; turning the cows and Dandy out to pasture after the cold winter; leading the stock to their stanchions at the close of day, watching each go instinctively to its own place; watching the clumsy stammels resort to coltish antics, kicking up their heavy heels and yanking at the first green tussocks pushing through the earth. Later there was plenty of grazing; meadow sweet, cotton grass, and clover. She thought of the early soft spring rains, the tapping drops on the bud-encrusted maple, the morning song of the robin, the quarreling sparrows, the peepers, the sound of martins, the wood peewee, and the cheriwink. For one sweet moment she entered the wonderful past; roamed again the woods with Clinton; climbed over the fallen, lichen-covered trees, the mikania hidden oak logs; searched out the shaded glens, the carpeted places of purple violets, ladyslippers, and lilies of the valley.

We grow up and we grow away, leaving the best of our lives behind. I wish it were not so. I wish Father were here, and I could know I have his approval.

Matthew had brought the rockaway to the door, and Caroline and Nabby stepped out into the cold, damp air and climbed inside.

The drive to the meetinghouse was not long. Down a lane scarcely wide enough for two carriages to pass one another, the vehicle traveled. Branchy poplars and denuded elms starkly lined High Street. Caroline thought about Thoreau, sorry to realize that he had passed away and would not see the end of the war. She recalled his observation that the elms' one purpose was to grow. Even in their winter nakedness they seemed to be doing that. She wished Thoreau had lived to continue with his marvelous observations . . . but that was futile wishing. He had said something about a man's country being in the heart of its inhabitants. He was right about that! The city of Newburyport, with all of its faults and foibles, had entrenched itself well within her own breast, and that could never change.

As they turned into Federal Street, she could see wagons and carriages lined up for blocks, and latecomers hurrying toward the church entrance. The carriage came to an abrupt halt, as did her rambling thoughts, and Caroline climbed down to the wet pavement. Nabby held her long skirt with one hand and her mother's purse in the other. In the broad vestibule she arranged Caroline's veil, patted and tucked at her skirt, and then left to join the rest of the family in the Haddon pews.

The organ had begun to play the processional. Caroline drew a deep breath, reached a trembling hand through Matthew's extended elbow, and began to walk the aisle. She could see Jerome standing at the altar.

She had known he would be impeccably dressed. He had conspicuously forsaken his artist's apparel and donned the very latest in formal attire; trousers fawn colored and peg topped, waistcoat straight-bottomed, long-tailed coat with the M notches on the lapels, collar standing and silk cravat tied neatly at his throat. Not a wrinkle nor a thread out of place.

Walking forward, she searched his face, wanting something of the confidence she always felt from him. His was a handsome face, with only a hint of the foreign royal blood. His features were sharp and aristocratic, his eyes roguish, his mouth sensual, sculptured and, at this moment, smiling approval. He winked at her, embarrassing her before the curious. Always the performer, he knew what to do to draw attention. He was boldly himself, saucy, mischievous, and altogether attractive.

Caroline was not surprised at the large attendance. No one had declined her invitation, for though Clinton Haddon had the respect of the congregation, Caroline knew that most of those attending were the city's curious, come to view the wedding of the most sought-after bachelor of the day.

Candlelight reflected off the black and white marble of the cenotaph. Overhead the quasi-frescoed ceiling of Philip Guelpa's *trompe l'oeil* stretched like a banner over the solemn scene. Somewhere in the recesses of Caroline's mind, the words of Scripture stirred. "His banner over me is love." Strange the way Scripture, once learned, would leap to mind unbidden.

Neighbors peered over the balustrade of the whispering gallery, stretching their necks like curious birds.

Caroline stole a glance at the man beside her. He returned an admiring look, one that bespoke genuine approval and adoration and sent a sudden flush to her face. In a day of beards, mustaches, sideburns, and mutton-chop tufts, Jerome was singularly attractive with his clean-shaven face and neat collar-length hair.

The pastor droned on with his allegorical homily, likening the marriage to that of Jesus Christ to His bride, the Church. If Caroline had not been so tense, she might have enjoyed it. Then, at long last, he was bestowing the blessing. The organist had pulled out all of the stops and was pounding vigorously at the organ keyboard while her anxious husband, who was in charge of the bells, began to pull on the ropes with vigor. Caroline hoped his enthusiasm would not be mistaken for the frequent military tocsins.

Caroline walked with her husband back up the aisle and out into the vestibule. The faces before her were a blur, but somehow she managed to acknowledge the well wishers and join her family on the broad steps.

It was a subdued affair. Not only was levity forbidden in the sanctuary, but any reveling during the days of war was frowned upon. The guests made off hastily toward their wagons and carriages. Jerome turned their horses homeward, and the invited guests followed.

Caroline entered the front door with Jerome still holding her hand. She could smell the spiced cider. Aunt Phoebe had done as she had promised and was already passing the hot drink around.

Time passed swiftly until Jerome whispered that their train would be leaving in a half hour. Caroline slipped away to her mother's room, where her traveling clothes were already spread out on the bed. She closed the door and changed rapidly into the plain green traveling ensemble. The skirt dropped down over the full-backed crinoline and was topped with a matching, loose-fitting jacket, the kind she had always admired on the ladies she had seen at the train station.

The door opened, and Caroline could see in the mirror that Bethia had entered the room. Her little sister was beginning to blossom, taking on the high-cheekboned beauty of the Adkinson women. Her complexion was flawless, her cheeks softly pink, like the reflection of roses in alabaster, and her eyes even more blue than their mother's. She watched without speaking as Caroline straightened her skirt. In her eyes was a look of reproach.

Caroline pressed the round porkpie down onto her thick curls and fastened it with a long pin.

"Don't look so sad, dear. I am sure to come back for a visit, and you shall come to Boston. I will see to that."

The promise did little to change Bethia's countenance. As a conciliatory gesture, Caroline reached for her jewelry case, the one Grandma Adkinson had bequeathed to her, and placed it in Bethia's hands.

"Choose anything you like. I want you to have a special gift. And, Bethia, do remember to wrap the gown in paper. Wrap it well, for you will doubtless be the next to wear it. Only do have the sense to plan a summer wedding!"

Bethia pulled away from the proffered gift.

"Please, Bethia. I want you to have a memento."

Reluctantly Bethia complied. Jewelry, feathers, and geegaws were of little consequence to the earthborn Bethia. She was happiest in her comfortable plaids and aprons, bare feet, and loosely hanging braids.

Within the velvet-lined box lay a tangle of beads and chains. Bethia was familiar with the contents. She reached for the porcelain bluebird pendant.

"No, not that one! I don't want to give that away . . . yet!"

Bethia dropped the piece back into the box. "I don't believe you will ever give it away," she stated flatly. "And I think you will always love Thad Paxton. And someday he will come back."

The outburst could not have had a more chilling impact, nor given Caroline a more shocking jolt. These were not words she wished to hear. But it was a child speaking. What did Bethia know of loyalties and hard decisions? Bethia was one of the sheltered ones—someone always there for her, making decisions, holding the umbrella over her head.

Nonetheless, her outburst cut Caroline to the quick, stirring a desire to strike back, say something at least as cutting. Instead she turned her back to Bethia and bit her lip. She had promised her father she would keep the unity of the family and serve their best interests, and that was one promise she intended to keep. She made a pretense of packing last-minute articles.

Scarlet with remorse, Bethia closed the lid of the jewelry box and pressed it into a corner of Caroline's trunk.

"I'm sorry, Carrie. I really am. I don't want anything. You know how I am, just rough and unrefined, not at all like you."

Caroline did not answer. She knew that if she did, she would cry, and that would never do. Bethia moved toward the door and then she was gone.

Nabby appeared, looking for Caroline. "Your husband is waiting for you. I think he is getting impatient." Caroline closed the trunk with a muffled thud and stepped aside to let Joshua and Matthew carry it to the waiting carriage.

On cue, the newlyweds made a dash for the vehicle. Amidst tears, laughter, and fond farewells, the carriage rumbled down the driveway and out onto the road.

Caroline turned for a last look at the house. Nabby was in the doorway waving a small, white handkerchief. Bethia, at her side, looked miserable. But the house, even in the somber light of a January afternoon, stood splendid in all of its Puritan charm. Suddenly she was seeing her father and her Uncle Hank, clothed in their bright smocks and slouch hats, emerging from the barn. She was hearing the lowing of cattle and the contented clucking of barnyard fowl, interspersed with the sporadic jollop of the turkeys they always raised for the winter's big holidays. She was seeing the crops full grown and waving with a sheen-like beauty in a late summer breeze. How wonderful those days when they had all been together—Hank, her father, Grandma Adkinson, Uncle Vaugn. If only the war years had never come. If only peace would return. . . .

The slush was freezing again, and she could hear the frozen ice resisting the carriage wheels. Into High Street they passed the big square houses, all belonging to a society she had never liked . . . and now she had married into it. Would she . . . could she ever really adjust?

Matthew reined in the horse at the big brick station. The huge doors were already open, and the bell was announcing the arrival of the four o'clock train. The horse's sensitive ears twitched nervously, picking up the sound of the approaching iron monster. Matthew threw the reins down to Joshua, who in turn tied them at the block and then turned his attention to the heavy trunk. They scrambled clumsily with the trunk toward the baggage car and, leaving it in good hands, returned to Caroline and Jerome on the platform.

Matthew, suddenly realizing that his sister was saying a final good-bye, dropped his reserve and reached to embrace her. Joshua followed his lead and then politely shook Jerome's hand. A brakeman stood waving the passengers on, shouting "All aboard!"

Then the train lurched ahead. Caroline watched with misty eyes as the familiar landscape faded into the late afternoon. She leaned heavily into Jerome's arms and relaxed as his lips brushed her cheek.

"We'll come back often to visit," he promised.

Galvin McMahon met them at the terminal, a welcome face in the chill of the winter night. The glory of the emerald isles shone in the cobalt blue of his Irish eyes, so merry and roguish in appearance. His florid complexion was enhanced by a crop of burnished red-gold hair. Galvin was short and muscular and found it no challenge to lift Caroline's trunk into the carriage.

Soon they were off and over the Belgian blocks at a somewhat laborious pace, the horse noticeably straining at the added weight. The city did not look the same as it had before, and even though the hub city was south of Newburyport, the marsh-built metropolis held a dampness that chilled to the bone. The snow had a blue tinge to it and lay in watery patches, unpleasantly polluted by man and beast. Leafless trees stretched bare arms toward the sky, making the prospect of a warm house desirable.

Galvin helped them down when they arrived at the tall brownstone, then took the horse and carriage to the stable across the street.

Jerome lifted Caroline into his arms and carried her over the threshold.

"I have heard that in every part of the world, they do some such ridiculous thing as this!" he commented.

"Like coming home with a sack of apples!" said his bride.

They walked down the long hall together where the mirrors reflected their images and the portrait of Grandmere Cavell looked down upon them.

"Her eyes are following us!" said Caroline.

"But I am sure with her blessing," said Jerome with a smile.

He led her to the wide staircase with the exquisitely curving bannister, and on to the second floor. Opening a door, he ushered her into a spacious chamber.

"I have redone my grandmother's room for you. I thought neutral shades of green and white would be appropriate. The complimentary colors I have left to you."

Though the room was as large as the entire second floor of the Haddon home, the bedroom was furnished with experienced taste and, surprisingly, with none of the eighteenth-century accents Caroline would have associated with the Grandmere. Clearly, Jerome had personally selected the furnishings of a later period, with only a few old colony pieces.

Little painted chairs, black and gold with rosy fruit and flowers, gave a youthful brightness to the room. He had remembered her taste for gardening. Fiddleback and gooseneck rockers, mahogany dressers, and a canopied bed were reflected in the great wall mirrors. Jerome's sensitive, artistic nature had been at the root of each selection. His taste for Hepplewhite, so obvious in the rest of the house, he had foregone, or at least done with restraint, but she did have to admire the slant-front desk and delightful stationery he had chosen for her personal use. Everything in the room spoke of his love, and all she could do was look at him with wonder and a new appreciation.

He led her to a marble-topped commode, where a pitcher with warm water stood in a large bowl. He poured the water for her.

"You will want to freshen up. I can see that the day and the travel have wearied you. I'll be in the parlor."

She removed her short jacket and washed her face. Leisurely she inspected again the beautiful room. She could hear faint strains of music emanating from the parlor and opened her door to hear better. Jerome was at the piano filling the house with melody sweeter than Caroline had ever heard. She walked down the wide staircase to the door of the parlor, drawn by something eternal, something magnetic; the light touch of fingers and an undertone of sorrow. She could almost see little boys in sailor suits floating toy sailboats in a Versailles fountain, countesses and kings in an elaborate parlor, Grecian statues adorned with flowered garlands.

Leaning against the door frame, she found herself being drawn into Jerome's world, a world of unequaled beauty. The music stopped, and he stood beside her.

"Beautiful, Jerome. Utterly beautiful. And sad, too. What is it?"

"Chopin's Prelude in D flat."

"It's as though he were putting his grief to music . . . like knowing he was dying and not wanting to leave something . . . or someone."

"One could understand that . . . if he loved deeply."

The dark eyes met her own, and she knew he was speaking of himself. His lips found hers, and in spite of herself—in spite of her promise to Thad—in spite of everything—she knew she had waited all of her life for this moment.

27

In the days that followed, Jerome was the epitome of kindness, gently and patiently introducing Caroline to the general routine of the house, trying his best to make her transition from the farm to the cosmopolitan scene as easy as possible. He dispensed with all outside meetings in order to make her feel at ease.

Caroline was not used to such pampering, but she had to admit that his kindness was comforting, and she appreciated it. From a lifetime of rising at sunrise, she found she could not sleep after that hour. After days of struggle, she decided to investigate the life that went on in the house before the "master" was up. Dressing early, she found the narrow back stairway that led from the servants' quarters to the kitchen. Kathleen was standing over the stove, stirring a large doubleboiler full of farina. On the drain board sat two dozen yeast rolls in the process of rising. Little soft, round mounds they were, taking Caroline back to her own kitchen.

"Oooh, Kathleen! Might we have some tea?" she asked.

Kathleen studied the young girl, recalling her brother's description of her. "She's as fair a colleen as 'twas ever spawned by a blasted limey!"

Indeed, she was that! And it was pleasant to feel the change in the austere old house since she had come.

"And sit down with me, please," Caroline added. "I want to get acquainted." Her eyes wandered about the dark corners of the room. "My mother's kitchen has windows on both sides. The sun comes in when morning comes and shines in again at evening. It is always bright and cheerful, with Mother's begonias all along the sills. I wish you could see them."

" 'Twould be nice," answered Kathleen, a little perturbed that the "marm" should be in her kitchen at such an hour.

With water boiled and tea brewing, Kathleen was soon removing the rolls from the oven. They were golden brown and sent a heavenly fragrance through the room. Caroline sat down at a table no larger than would serve two and indicated that Kathleen should join her.

"Now, Kathleen, tell me about your family and your home. You must be the oldest sister."

"I was the eldest of twelve, marm. Galvin is my baby brother."

"You were a second mother, then," said Caroline knowingly.

"That I was."

"And Ireland—is it truly as green as they say?"

Kathleen's eyes brightened at the mention of her homeland— as though little candles were glowing in the green eyes.

"We had so very little, but oh, 'twas good!"

"And green?"

"Yes, lamb, every shade of green there is on God's earth! And fields abloom with potato blossoms!"

"I know. I have come from a farm, too."

"Have y'now! The master didn't tell us."

"Oh, yes, and I miss it already."

"Come, child, drink yer tea, and have some honey on yer biscuit."

Thus they sat for a long time, exchanging tales of home, until Kathleen, hearing the sound of her master's step on the front stairs, arose and excused herself.

Caroline finished her tea and joined Jerome in the dining room.

"Good morning, darling. Are you feeling at home?"

"I had tea with Kathleen."

"Ah, well . . . don't do that too often. The Irish do not bridle easily, and I don't want you undoing my work."

"We have much in common. I shall get along well with Kathleen."

Jerome smiled and pressed her hand to his lips. "You would get along with anyone," he said.

But Jerome's schedule soon disrupted the honeymoon days, and Caroline discovered that the house with all of its beauty could not compensate for the long absences of her husband. The entire mornings he spent closed off from her, alone with his music, practicing over and over what to her seemed already perfect. She grew accustomed to the light, flexible touch of the Chopin compositions—the arpeggios and the chromatic passages—the sonatas of Mozart, the symphonies of Haydn and Beethoven, and the concertos of Mendelssohn . . . but never to her husband's long absences. She was obliged to console herself with the small pleasure of hearing a master playing the music of the ages. When he was through, he would play that one special composition from Beethoven that he had chosen for her when they first met—the sweet, tantalizing notes of "Fur Elise"—and she would know that his thoughts were back with her.

The afternoons he was gone, having arranged lessons with his most promising students, but the evenings, except for an occasional concert, belonged to them. Kathleen would start the fires in his bedchamber and serve dinner on a small harvest table, then leave the young lovers to one another's company. Jerome brought home flowers and gifts, and together he and Caroline would read and share the wonders of the day and the wonders of being together until the burning wood became graying embers.

Several times they attended the Park Street church, each time feeling the curious eyes of the congregation turned in their direction. Once a Reverend Stone, who had returned recently from the war zone in North Carolina, spoke of the courage of the men stationed there. The news was heartening to Caroline, for she could envision a little of her father's hardship and courage. It was one of the few times since her marriage that she was overcome with a nostalgic emotion. She knew she must shake off the melancholia and consider her blessings. Had that not been one of Clinton's teachings?

This went on for several days, and the inactivity and the empty hours didn't help. She wanted to be content with such things as she had, but she realized that she could only do it if she had more responsibility in the home. Her first interest was, of course, the garden she would plant in the spring. The ground would have to be prepared.

She approached Galvin one day with a question. "Galvin, what do you do with the horse manure?"

He looked a bit startled. It was not a question one would expect from a genteel woman.

"Eh? We cart it off, Marm."

"Well, don't! Put it along the garden wall . . . out there." She pointed to the small, narrow plot just outside the dining room window.

"But, Marm, 'twill stink!" he exclaimed.

"Not for long—and we shall get used to it. I want it there before the spring rains come, and later you and I can turn it over."

"You will do that, Marm?"

"And why not, Galvin? I must do something!"

"More stuff to her than meets the eye!" he told Kathleen later. "I'm guessin' the little missus will add some life to these old bachelor quarters yet!"

Once Caroline insisted on crossing the street to visit the stable. On orders from Jerome, Galvin accompanied her.

"And this is Jerome's horse?" she asked, delighted to be in familiar surroundings.

"Yes, Marm, and yours."

"What do you call him?" she asked, glancing around at the

cramped quarters and the draughty shelter.

"When he came to us, he was called Jasper. That was a year ago. Master Jerome rescued him from a nasty foreigner who had overworked him and underfed him. We've improved his weight, but I daresay we won't be doin' much for his disposition. Master Jerome changed his name to Monsieur Javert after reading a new book he got from Canada."

Caroline reached out her hand to stroke the animal's nose, but he reared back and snorted.

"My, you are a mean little beast, Javert." Turning to Galvin, she said, "See that Javert gets more oats and a little corn. He's hungry!"

"Yes'm."

"And get a blanket on him. It must have been close to zero this morning. We'd be a little peevish, too, if we were cold and hungry!"

Galvin nodded, appreciating the new "missus" more as he came to know her.

"Who does the washing?" she asked Kathleen one day.

"The women who come on Mondays," answered Kathleen.

"And where do they wash? I have never seen any women or sinks of any size."

Kathleen took her to the basement where she examined the strange rooms below the street level. There she inspected the large tubs and ceiling-high racks for drying. Would she ever get used to having strangers do her washing? And what was she to do with her time? With a cook, a laundress, and a general housekeeper, what was left? She wanted to be more than Jerome's pampered poodle.

"Why can't I do the shopping?" she asked him one evening.

"Why go out in the cold when Kathleen has a delivery service?" he responded.

"Really, Jerome! I'd like to do more than sit on a pillow and sew a fine seam!"

"Then I shall find something suitable for you," he promised.

He returned home the following evening with an announcement. "There will be a concert on Washington's birthday at the Cunningham estate, and you will make your debut. Tomorrow you shall meet Monsieur Deschanel."

"And who is Monsieur Deschanel?"

Already the roster of names Jerome was laying on her was expanding, and it was becoming impossible to remember them all, let alone render each his due respect.

"He is the most sought-after stylist in the city. The wealthiest women go to him. When you are introduced to Boston society, I intend to knock out their eyeteeth!"

"Do you ever cease to enjoy being naughty, Jerome?"

He seemed not to hear. "I want to see you in black velvet . . . and wearing diamonds." He placed a small rectangular box in her hands.

Caroline looked confused.

"Open it," he persisted.

"Did you say black velvet?"

"Open the box, sweetheart."

"Jerome . . . black velvet! I have never worn black. That is an old lady's color!"

"No, no, my sweet. Not the dress I have in mind for you."

Her protests were useless; Jerome had made up his mind.

"Monsieur Deschanel will work out the details. Contrast, of course. White tulle and black velvet—white complexion and dark hair. A camellia perhaps . . . and these!"

He opened the box for her. There, on a bed of white satin, lay a diamond necklace with contrasting onyx stones. Caroline lifted the necklace up to the firelight where the diamonds returned the flame and sent out rainbow colors from their depths.

"I shall see that Mrs. Cavell is appreciated," declared Jerome with a light kiss on her flushed cheek.

Monsieur Deschanel did his work well. After many long hours of fittings, the evening finally arrived. The great ballroom was swarming with guests. Jerome felt Caroline trembling as she took his arm to descend the stairs to a recessed room, but it was his moment of triumph, and he would enjoy it.

"Smile," he whispered, knowing the charm her smile could work.

The black velvet rippled as she moved, picking up light and shadow as only velvet can do. Her arms and shoulders, smooth as ivory, were draped with white muslin into an *en coeur* neckline, accenting her own coloring. Excitement had sent a rosy blush to her cheeks, and her hair, dressed in the latest fashion, finished the breathtaking vision.

While men looked at Caroline with the boldness and admiration Jerome had anticipated, she could see that the women were whispering to one another behind opened fans. Caroline was certain their appraisal was not as charitable as that of the men. She continued to smile, however, as Jerome had coached her.

Introductions and music blended with the sound of tinkling glass. It was all very intimidating, but with Jerome at her side she found she could relax. Once, after he had introduced her to a fine-looking man who held her hand a moment longer than necessary, she noticed that Jerome cut the conversation short. Turning Caroline aside, he assured her that she need not go out of her way to be too chivalrous to the man, who had a questionable reputation where other men's wives were concerned. There was something in Jerome's eyes she had not seen before, and for the first time she realized that her lover husband could be jealous. She quickly put the thought away.

A light supper was served, and then Jerome was introduced and escorted to the piano. Caroline was alone. She watched as he bowed to his audience. She could not help but feel proud of him, standing there in his tight-fitting trousers, cutaway coat, and wide cravat.

He quickly had his audience mesmerized. He was a man keeping alive the riches of the past, something worth preserving . . . the beauty of another man's soul, the music of genius. This she could not despise. Had it not been the same with her father? Had he not been willing to give his life to keep the principles laid down by the country's fathers?

In his own way, and with his own loyalties and persuasions, Jerome was no different from her father. And he was not unlike his idol, Chopin.

Caroline thought about the Polish-born artist, his recorded history, his love for beauty, and his melancholy moods. Wondered just what it was that made a person a notable in his generation. Wondered why, so often, the talented ones lived so short a time—and wondered if her own down-to-earth nature could ever supply the man she had married with the backing and support he needed. She must . . . she really must fill that need . . . and by everything within her power, she would try.

There was a brief intermission, and she could see that Jerome's public had cornered him. He walked through the throng like a meteor drawing a fiery tail . . . and she was alone. It was clear that life with Jerome could be like this. He would draw the crowd, and she would watch.

She moved toward a dressing room, hoping to be unobtrusive, and it was not difficult. She sat down behind a teakwood screen at an ornate dressing table. There was a rustling of taffeta on the other side, then high-pitched laughter and the excited voices of young women.

"She seems at a loss," someone was saying.

"She'll get used to that!"

Caroline knew instinctively that she was the object of the conversation and should leave, but something held her there.

"He'd have done better to choose one of his own kind. I hear she is right off the farm—a dairyman's daughter!"

"Poor man. He doesn't need a such a commonplace marriage! But then—"

The music started again, and they left.

Jerome finished the concert and rejoined her. Now she was favored with affected attention. So, that was it. The fawning over her was only to impress Jerome.

Caroline drew a deep breath. This hypocrisy must be endured

by every woman married to a celebrity. Well, she had weathered impossible situations before and, looking at Jerome, she knew she would continue. Failure was not in her vocabulary.

They returned home late, Jerome bubbling with the promise of new students and more scheduled concerts.

There followed many such evenings after that, as well as the tedious fittings. It seemed that Monsieur Deschanel had found himself the perfect model, and his enthusiasm was unbounded. Caroline would bring clients to him now, in droves!

It was all part of the new life, with new challenges—and Clinton Haddon's daughter would meet them head-on.

28

GENERAL SHERMAN CAME on into North Carolina flushed with victory and murderously resolute about putting an end to the detested war. Confederate General Joe Johnston was sent to prevent Grant from linking up with the hated Sherman, and though it was all up to the Southern general, he himself knew he could do no more than delay the impending Union victory. Lee could not get out and past Fort Stedman at Richmond to help, and Sherman's army numbered ninety thousand. The odds against the Confederates were enough to discourage a St. George!

It began the first week of March. News came downriver that battle lines were forming near Kinston. The plucky Johnston prepared for the confrontation, his unenviable lot that of facing a now consistently successful Union army.

The Twenty-third was sent up to Kinston, where Clinton and his men set up camp. Clinton could see for at least twenty miles in all directions. White tents dotted the fields, and neat lines of Conestoga wagons stretched out on the roads by the hundreds. Some were already backed against tent depots. A multitude of circling fires sent smoke signals to the enemy, saying that the time of reckoning was at hand. Union soldiers squatted on slight rises above the scene, awaiting battle orders.

The men seemed in a strange limbo, knowing they had survived thus far and wondering how much longer their luck would hold out. Supplies of food, clothing, and military hardware were better now than at any time during the entire war, even glutting supply depots, but the will of the Confederacy remained strong. The obstinate Confederate president seemed to wax indifferent to Lee's appraisal of his starving men, and the trusted Lee remained obedient and subservient to his commander in chief.

News came of the fall of Fort Fisher, which meant that the blockade runners now would have no place to hide. The news was a dire blow to the South, but not enough to cause the leaders to extend a retreat.

Clinton had stopped writing letters, but knowing Matthew as he did, he was sure his clever son would know where the lines were being drawn. He had no desire to alarm the rest of the family. As the night drew on, the campfires flared. Like subtle rumors they started up, at first scattered and feeble, then growing and glowing brightly over the stubbled cornfields, becoming fiery altars . . . altars that stirred memories of home, hearth, and family. Frequently, Clinton could see enemy cavalry on the outskirts of the camp, but when the sun went down, only the fires, the shadows, and the apprehension remained. Newspapers had arrived that day, heralding the return of Fort Sumter to Union hands and containing Lincoln's second inaugural address. As always, the man in Washington was eloquently charitable in his quest for one union under God, with malice toward none.

It was one of these nights when the men were in the ambivalence of desire; longing for peace and wanting to get on with the fighting. A Union lackey whipped a flute from his haversack and began to play. The enemy lines had drawn closer, close enough to hear the plaintive sounds. From their numbers a voice boomed out.

"Play Dixie!"

The Union flutist obliged, and the notes took wing, carrying across the barren fields and into the lonely hearts of his listening audience—taking them beyond the miseries of war, blotting out ideological differences and making them one in the strangest of intermezzos known to the human race. When the music stopped, they poured out onto the fields, bringing with them an exchange of life's small necessities, even a few luxuries like tobacco, coffee, sugar, and soap. Of course, the Union men had the best to offer, but more, they had enough compassion to see that their enemy was running out of supplies, and many gave what they knew would succor the suffering Confederates. The incongruity of it all— depleting their own supplies and handing survival rations to the enemy! War did certainly have its madness, for they were soon back to their trenches and ready for a final overture—before they cocked their guns!

"Tenting Tonight on the Old Campground!"

The sweet tenor voice of a Confederate man joined with the Union flute, rising on the night air. The men listened.

"We're tenting tonight on the old camp ground. Give us a song to cheer our weary hearts, a song of home and friends we love so dear. Many are the hearts that are weary tonight, wishing for the war to cease. Many are the hearts that are looking for the right, to see the dawn of peace. Tenting tonight, tenting tonight, tenting on the old campground."

Men's voices joined in, some who could sing well and others who could not, filling the night and fading again, until all was silent and the men quiet with their thoughts.

Strangely, after that the Confederates seemed to disappear. Days went by, and still battle orders did not come, nor did an attack from the enemy. New regiments began to arrive from New Bern, and with them came three thousand Western recruits. Many had been with Sherman in earlier times. They came in, a likable lot, burly, rugged, and skilled sharpshooters, bringing a welcome diversion from the stalemate hours. Most carried 1841 short-rifled muskets, and could fell game with astounding accuracy.

Clinton found them amusing when rations were doled out. They looked with disgust upon the paltry offerings and complained loudly. It was like feeding sunflower seeds to a pack of wolves! When the complaints reached the commander's ears, he allowed them the privilege of hunting in the woods nearby. They returned with enough game to feed a large regiment.

When the rains descended, which was often, the Tennessee marksmen knew how to adapt. Summoning their survival inclination and ingenuity, they dug cellars beneath their tents and lived in improvised dryness, while the rest of the men looked on with candid respect. Clinton was glad to have them on the Union side.

When rumors of Johnston's approach would not die down, the men began to clean their guns and grow uneasy. The weather and the waiting became unbearable, depleting morale and producing restlessness. Someone brought a keg of whiskey down from New Bern. It was a pitiful offering for so large an army of thirsty, bored men. Quarreling broke out, and a surly lot, mostly bounty enlistees, began to brawl, each with a determination to garner for himself a fair portion. In the black of night, the uproar brought Clinton running from his tent. A young lieutenant joined him.

"I'd put them all in chains if it weren't for orders!" said the officer, spewing out blasphemies for emphasis.

"What orders, sir?" asked Clinton.

"We strike tents at two a.m. and move out!"

The lieutenant ordered the brawl to come to an end. When he was ignored, he whipped out a pistol and shot two of the brawlers in their feet. This resulted in a worse scuffle, sending a few more down, where they sloshed about drunkenly in the cold mud. When the lieutenant barked out orders to strike tents, the renegades ceased their struggle and looked up from the fracas with muddy, leering faces. Could they have heard straight? They blinked through mud-encrusted eyes, and Clinton found it hard to suppress a laugh.

Realizing that it was the order they had awaited for weeks, the men grinned, linked arms, and went tramping off through the night singing "John Brown's Mudsketeers all!"

With the tents down, they started their march toward the

waiting forces of General Joe Johnston. The Twenty-ninth, along with a New Jersey unit, joined the Massachusetts Twenty-third and headed for the city. This would be a decisive battle, and both the blue and the gray were marching toward the vortex. They hiked through sucking mud, using brawn and brain and not a few imprecations to get the caissons through the quagmires. Then they were in the midst of it!

For two long days they fought with no rest. On the third, they were able to stop and make camp—but not the Confederates. They were not about to quit, even though Union artillery was already booming out a threat to their commanders.

The men were bone-weary. Clinton, too, stood still as he watched the long rows of dead being laid out. Orders were issued for him and his comrades to tear down surrounding barns to make coffins. The fighting intensified hourly, and the losses continued to climb until an order came to fall back. Once again he was in the nightmare of war, shells bursting overhead, the whiz and the buzz of minié-balls so close to his ears he could feel the wind as they split the air.

Then a searing, numbing sensation struck him in the face. The pain was excruciating, stopping his breath. He staggered and fell, made an effort to rise, and fell again. He knew he had taken a barrage in the face, and wondered how many shots. It had to be more than one to rob him of his ability to stand. A river of blood was coursing down over his mouth and onto his chin. Even in the darkness his shirt was taking on a crimson hue.

Would he die now, after coming this far? No! No! Not Clinton Haddon. He had promised Caroline he would return, and he had every intention of keeping that promise. He got to his feet, wobbly at first, uncertain and dizzy. He staggered against an officer, who pointed toward the rear and shoved him roughly in that direction. That could mean only one thing. The battle was going against them. That was difficult to believe, after all the publicity of General Sherman's invincibility.

At any rate, there was little time for thought, and less for delay. He could lose no more blood and remain on his feet. He ran on blindly, choking on his own blood and still not certain of its source. He recognized a railroad route where they had previously camped, and just beyond he could make out a company of rebels. He turned in another direction and stumbled on to part of his own unit. They were throwing up breastworks at breakneck speed. Someone said they were a mile from the front lines. Had he really run a mile? Another man took a moment to steer him toward a medical tent, where the surgeon made a quick examination and motioned for him to sit on the ground with other wounded. Clinton was sure that many would not come out of it whole.

It seemed an eternity before he was taken inside for attention. Meanwhile, the wounded continued to arrive. An orderly approached.

"Sorry, soldier, they're coming in too fast. Go down the road to the regimental hospital. We can only take the worst here!"

There was something encouraging in his words. He, Clinton, was not "one of the worst"! He got to his feet and continued on down the road. When he reached a makeshift hospital, he noticed a steward cleaning wounds. The man ordered Clinton to lie down, which he did with no complaint. By this time he was so tired and weak that he could scarcely drag one foot after the other.

The division surgeon came to examine him.

"Your head clear?" he asked.

"Yes, sir," he replied, though he was honestly not sure. He knew only that he was conscious enough to be in extreme pain.

"Then you will have to keep on!"

The statement was preposterous! Clinton looked around at the group of men he was to join. They weren't complaining. If they could do it, he could, too. Head swimming, he arose and joined them, and they moved out together. Despite the groaning and suffering, they made it to the designated medical station, looking more like a roving colony of lepers than victorious Union soldiers.

At long last, Clinton was ushered into the operating tent. Someone washed the blood from his face and prepared him for surgery.

"There's shell in there," the surgeon was saying.

"I don't believe it is more than a minié-ball!" answered Clinton.

Then the surgeon was probing with his forceps. To Clinton, it felt like a dagger cutting through his nostrils, and he could feel the perspiration running down his neck. He wondered if it were possible to go mad with pain.

"Great God, Doctor! Club me over the head! Anything!"

"Ether!" commanded the surgeon.

A box came down over Clinton's face, and he breathed deeply. The ceiling spun crazily, and he was borne mercifully out of the pain, yet even in his anesthetized state he could hear the instrument slipping off metal. Once . . . twice . . . and then a great pressure.

He drifted off into a sea of meadows, places he recognized as his own. Nabby was running to meet him, her sun-streaked hair golden and flowing, then cool arms were lifting him. A woman's arms, like a Norse Valkyrie. She was lifting him and then placing him down on the ground . . . down . . . down in the row of dead soldiers. Was he really dead? Would he know it when they threw dirt on his face?

"Tell me, God! Tell me if this is death! Why don't You answer me? Hear me! Hear me!"

A dark figure began to take shape before his eyes. "We hear you!"

"Am I alive?"

The man placed a metal ball in his hand. "A souvenir for you." The voice was pleasant, comforting.

One in my hand, and another on my face! Clinton thought, picturing the ugly scar, but he could also breathe a prayer of gratitude. He was alive!

He was moved just outside the tent, where he could see the others as they came from the surgeon's scalpel. There seemed to be twenty or more, and he was surprised to see the lieutenant who had shot the brawling drunks. He had had his thumb shot off. That would cool his nasty temper for a while!

As soon as heads were clear and wounds of minor consequence cauterized, the group of men were brought to their feet and ordered to the railroad tracks. There they waited for three hours, intermittently harassed by Confederate sharpshooters. With the welcome sound of a train whistle, they prepared to board. The rebels moved off, fearing that reinforcements were arriving. Men stretched out on the wooden floors of the cars, and the train moved toward New Bern. Clinton lay staring at the walls of the moving car.

Poor comfort, he thought, but not unlike the "day of the Lord" for which all Christians hope.

The train was scarcely a heavenly chariot, but in a way, it had its own rapturous relief, removing battle-scarred and weary men from the scenes of battle to a better place of peace and comfort.

29

JEROME'S POPULARITY was mushrooming. It was evident from the invitations rolling in that to have the Cavells as guests was a social feather in one's society cap. Evening concerts became part of their lives, easing the sting of idleness from Caroline's day.

Returning one evening from a gala event, they handed their cloaks to Kathleen and went into the great parlor. As usual, Jerome drew Caroline close and kissed her, letting her know how pleased he was with the way she was playing her role.

"Now you must learn to dance," he said.

"I should trip you up miserably."

"No . . . come."

He whirled her over the floor with the expertise of a danseur. The moment was one of exhilaration as they spun around the tables and chairs.

"Oh, Jerome! You have filled my life with so much."

Collapsing on a chair, they laughed together until Caroline caught sight of an envelope on the table.

"Oh? I wonder when this came," she said, reaching for it. "It's from Bethia! Mercy, I should be writing home more often!" In her heart Caroline well knew the reason for her reluctance to write—it was the possibility that she might drop some hint of her insecurity in playing the role of Jerome's wife and, by so doing, cause her loved ones to worry.

She opened the letter and read.

March 1, 1865

Dear Carrie,

 Mother thought it best to put off writing so as not to interrupt your first days of married life, but I simply can wait no longer.

 I miss you terribly, and hope you have found it in your heart to forgive me for my bad judgment and mean words the day you left. I am sure it all came because I dreaded so to see you leave us.

 We are managing as well as can be expected, but the first days after you left were awful. I don't like to alarm you, but Mother does not seem herself. She is tired all the time. I shall send for Doc Slater if she doesn't improve.

 Joshua is proving quite a blessing. He works well with Allen. I can see he will take over Uncle Hank's share of the work come spring.

 We still have no news from Father, but we keep hoping. Please do write to me soon.

Your loving sister,

Bethia

Caroline wilted as she let the letter fall to her lap. "How could I have neglected them so, Jerome? I've been dreadfully selfish!"

"No, Carrie—"

"Yes, I really have. I must write and encourage my little sister. She is very young for all that she is taking over."

And though Jerome tried to persuade her otherwise, she took on again the concern she had always had for the family. Often she found herself staring at Jerome, wondering what black magic he had employed to have removed her so completely from her responsibilities where her family was concerned. And what of Nabby? Were Bethia's fears well founded?

A longing for home swept in upon Caroline with a ferocity she had never thought possible. Just to walk through the old barn, to smell the hay, to touch Dandy's nose and hear him whinny, to walk down Thread-Needle Alley or over the Mall, to see again the big square Federal houses and hear the elms complaining of the winter's cold.

She wandered aimlessly about the house, lonely and resentful. It was on one of these solitary wanderings that she let her eyes linger on a long Hepplewhite wall table. She knew its value, but thought little of its usefulness. It was something to be admired and kept polished, but to her Spartan mind, it was absolutely useless.

"Is it ever used for anything?" she asked Galvin.

"Well, now, 'tis holdin' a lamp, it is," he answered.

That was the end of the conversation, but not the end of the temptation.

The next day Galvin heard the sound of a saw coming from the basement. He hurried down the stairs with Kathleen on his heels.

There stood the "missus" with one foot on the leg of the long table, sawing away with the gusto of a Maine lumberjack.

"Saints alive! What are yer doin', Marm?" cried Galvin, scratching his mop of gold-red hair.

"Jerome said I might change anything I pleased!" explained Caroline.

Galvin took a look at the butchered table. Then, wanting to preserve both his master's trust and a repairable part of the furniture, he tried a bit of Gaelic psychology.

"Do y'need help, Marm?" he managed.

"Thank you, Galvin, but I like to saw!"

From the looks of things, she did indeed!

"I cannot see any need to leave this long table against the wall, when with a little carpentering, I can make it useful!" She went back to work.

Galvin and Kathleen retraced their steps to the kitchen.

"Praise be to God she turned me down, eh, Kathleen? The master might have thought we were in cahoots!"

"He'll kill her!" exclaimed Kathleen.

"Not without a battle," Galvin replied with a grin.

The servants awaited the return of their master, one with terror and the other with mischievous expectancy.

The inevitable question came only moments after Jerome's evening arrival.

"Where's the wall table?" he asked.

"I moved it. Come see!" And Caroline led the way to where she had deposited the ravaged antique.

Seeing that lightning was about to strike, Galvin and Kathleen made a hurried exit. In all their years of service, they had never heard Jerome so much as raise his voice. The sound they heard now was like that of a wounded lion.

"Whatever have you done, Caroline?"

"It was too tall and useless!"

"Stretchers and all!" exlaimed Jerome, seeing the roughly hacked nobby wood where the leg braces had been.

It was clear that he was not favorably impressed.

Caroline grew defensive. "Do you know how many times Kathleen must come for teacups? It is absolute nonsense, when all we needed was a nice, low table! I was careful to choose the one you would miss the least . . . and you did say I might change things!"

"I could have bought you a table, Carrie, if you had only asked. This was my grandmother's and worth a great deal to me!"

Caroline's eyes registered something between disappointment and white-hot rage.

"Jerome, if you don't give me more to do, I shall cut the legs off every piece of furniture in this house!"

Jerome stood stunned, his mouth agape. "I do believe you would!" he managed. Jerome had never seen the intrepid side of this creature before, and he was baffled. He had lived so many years in reasonable tranquillity—how could he now be bound to the angry creature before him? One moment she was a child, hurting from a rebuff, and in another five minutes she could be arguing the philosophies of Forier or Comte. And all the while daring Jerome to love her . . . which with all of his heart he did.

"Oh, Jerome, let's face it! I shall never be your Countess

Potocka! How are we ever to close this dreadful chasm?"

Then she was in his arms, not knowing whether to laugh or cry.

"Carrie, if you wanted a whole wagon full of Hepplewhite tables, you know I'd bring them to you."

She laughed and looked up at him, tears in her eyes. The situation was so ludicrous. "And I could remodel them all by myself?"

"Yes, my darling!"

"Then you must know I would never again destroy anything you valued. Only . . . Jerome, please, I must be more than a complement to the illustrious Mr. Cavell! I must have more to do!"

"I'm sorry. I did not realize. There is a great deal you can do, and I shall see to it tomorrow."

Caroline sighed with relief. The world was suddenly back on its axis. But loving Jerome and living with him, she knew, would be a lifelong challenge!

GALVIN APPEARED the following morning to inform Caroline that she was to accompany him to the Quincy Market. It was a cold March day, but mercifully lacking the usual winds. She dressed hastily, eagerly anticipating a change from the boredom of her usual morning schedule. Jerome had kept his word, and that made the day brighter!

Snow was still on the roads from the last storm, but the sun was shining and there was a faint whisper of the spring to come. Caroline settled into the plush silken seat of the Portland cutter, and Monsieur Javert stepped off at a brisk pace. It was like being home again, and Caroline buried her chin in the warm buffalo robe. Memories flooded in, giving her a grip on her threatened identity. Once again she felt like Clinton Haddon's daughter.

Galvin handled the rascal Javert expertly. She had thought to ask if she might have the reins, but she could see that Galvin was sporting a certain pride in driving the impossible horse, and she would not spoil his moment.

The market was alive with well-clad, frost-breathing merchants and folks storing up on bargains. It was an exhilarating morning, the best in many days!

After making their purchases, they took off and followed the horse traffic down several narrow streets unfamiliar to Caroline.

"Where are we going?" Caroline asked.

"The master has sent me to deliver a box."

They moved along through the crowded streets until Galvin pulled on the reins and they stopped at a large and many-gabled house.

"You are to accompany me, Marm," he said, getting down and extending his hands to help her.

"Do you think it proper, Galvin? I mean . . . it is early!"

"Shouldn't be no one more welcome than you, Mrs. Cavell."

His answer puzzled her. Looking at the place, Caroline could see that there was unusual activity here, and she wondered why she should be at all welcome. But she followed Galvin up the path to the big door. It flew open, and a jolly, rosy-faced woman greeted them. Her voice boomed a welcome, and her laughter made Caroline feel glad to have come.

"Come in! Come in! Ah, you've brought the new missus! Welcome, Mrs. Cavell. We've heard so much about you and, my, you must be frozen stiff! Not spring yet. Into the kitchen with you!"

Her cheery greeting was enough to warm any soul, but the busy scenes in the kitchen were even more exciting. A number of industrious, clean-looking women were there, dressed in starched aprons and looking the picture of efficiency. Breakfast trays were lined up, and the chatter was amiable and friendly. Just beyond the kitchen door, Caroline could see a number of beds and some men sitting in chairs—most of them in Union blue!

"Why, my goodness! It's a hospital!" she exclaimed.

"Y'didn't know?" asked Galvin.

"Know? Know what?"

Galvin was quick to see that he must shield his young charge from embarrassment and, while their hostess was busy with the milling helpers, he spoke quietly to Caroline.

"Just make out like you knew all along, and let me do the talking. I'll explain later." He cut open his parcel and lifted out an armful of cotton sheets.

"Oh!" exclaimed the gregarious woman. "Bless the dear, dear man. We were all out and wondering where the next ones would come from. Thank him!"

Who was "the dear man," Caroline wondered. Could it possibly be Jerome? But why had he never told her?

She was escorted through the many rooms and introduced to the patients. After a while they said good-bye and returned to the cutter.

"I am baffled, Galvin. What was that all about?"

"I took it for granted, Marm, that the master would have told you. The place is a hospital annex. Soldiers who improve get care there."

"But what has that to do with us?"

"The house, marm. It's Mr. Cavell's. He insisted the Sanitary Commission have the use of it."

"And he sends bed linens?"

"Oh, yes, Marm, and much more!"

Caroline grew quiet, turning the information over in her mind. There was so much to learn about her husband . . . more than she had dreamed. And his reticence!

"He never ceases to amaze me," she said out loud, and Galvin nodded.

After that, the days were better. She went often with Galvin to the annex and was able to bring some luxuries as well as necessities to the wounded. And in the evenings she could tell Jerome of her visits. Now the duty of accompanying him to concerts did not chafe, and knowing how much he loved her compensated for her loneliness . . . until the second letter from Bethia arrived. Caroline read it with a lump in her throat.

Nabby was losing weight and vitality. Could Carrie please come, if only for a visit? And they had at last received a letter from Clinton! He had been wounded but would be coming home soon! Matthew and Joshua sent their love, too, with a plea that she not delay!

The old longing for home took over and would not be denied. She kept busy, but always the picture of her mother failing robbed her of any peace.

"I must go home, Jerome, I really must, even if only for a day."

"I need you here, my love, at least until the benefit concert is over. After that you may plan to go."

It was the best he could offer, and Caroline accepted it, but the delay worked havoc with her fears. What if her mother should die? How would Bethia cope?

And when her father returned, what would he think of her marriage? Would he understand . . . would he approve? Such thoughts plagued her continually, keeping her agitated by day and awake at night.

Her natural rosy bloom faded, causing Jerome to worry secretly. He continued to shower her with gifts. To take her mind from worry, he took her to a new opera, performed by an out-of-state traveling troupe.

But the story only reminded Caroline of her broken promise to Thad, as the heroine displayed her faithfulness to her childhood sweetheart. The aria haunted Caroline for days: "In my lap rest thy weary head." Where could she rest her weary head? To whom could she go?

"Only another week, sweetheart," comforted Jerome.

Another week, thought Caroline, and another evening of enduring the pleasure-seeking socialites, their soirees, and their seeming indifference to the suffering of their men on the battlefields.

The week dragged by, and the hour for the benefit concert finally arrived. Jerome's promise seemed to revive Caroline's spirit, and she dressed with optimism. Tonight she would wear the royal blue, a color the soldiers would like, and wrap a white lace shawl around her shoulders. A mousquetaire hat adorned with white ostrich plumes finished the ensemble.

The streets were now devoid of snow, and the carriages rumbled over the pavement with their occupants in a festive mood. Dignitaries were out in full force, as the event would benefit a new soldiers' hospital and thus presented an opportunity to display political patriotism and concern before the electorate.

The hostess in charge was a large bosomy woman by the name of Chase. When the Cavells entered, she came immediately to greet them.

"I have everything arranged, Jerome, but you will want to check." She motioned him toward the platform at the far end of the hall. Jerome was off immediately, leaving Caroline with the nervous hostess.

The hall began to flood with people and the seats to fill. Caroline was escorted to a front-row seat and apprised that she would be introduced before the concert began. She had grown accustomed to the honor and thought little of it.

As the lights dimmed, she became aware of a disturbance at the hall entrance. Mrs. Chase was pointing to a block of seats to the right of the platform, and some wounded men in Union blue were ushered in. Then the introductions and acknowledgments proceeded.

"Mrs. Jerome Cavell."

Caroline rose and bowed slightly, looking over the crowd and acknowledging the polite applause. Suddenly she saw him—thin, pale, and dressed in an ill-fitting uniform. His eyes were still as blue as a bluebird's wing, his thick hair well-brushed, his moustache neatly trimmed, and his face frozen in shock and dismay.

They seemed the only two people in the room, both looking as though they had been struck by lightning. Blood crept up from Caroline's neckline and spread to her face, and she could feel a wild beating in her throat and temples. She sank back into her seat, feeling sick and wanting to die.

Jerome played several classical selections and then swung into the patriotic music: "Strike the Cymbal," "America," "Who When Darkness Gathered O'er Us," and "God Save the Union," but Caroline didn't hear a note.

Thad alive! Alive and watching her. She wanted to run, escape the oppressive situation, close her eyes to the whole scene. Finally the music stopped, and applause swept over the audience. Jerome took his bows and came to her side, noticing at once her lack of color.

"What is it, dear?" he asked, alarmed.

"I don't feel well!"

"You look dreadful. Get your cloak and wait at the door. I am obliged to see a student before I leave."

Caroline got her shawl and made for the exit. Soldiers filed past her, some under their own power and others with the help of a nurse. Suddenly Thad was there, within speaking distance, but he refused to face her. He kept his eyes on the floor. What was there to say? Then he opened his mouth, but Caroline could scarcely hear him.

"Why, Caroline?" He looked at her expensive dress, and contempt and anger swept over his face.

"Wherever have you been, Thad?" she asked, her voice trembling.

"Does it matter?"

"Oh, yes, it does matter!"

Thad shook his head and brushed past her, meaning to be rude.

A soldier behind him spoke up, sensing that something was not right.

"He don't talk much, ma'am. He was at Cedar Creek, in the worst of it, then taken to Andersonville. A miracle he came out alive. Most of 'em didn't."

Then Jerome appeared. "Do you know those soldiers?" he asked, his eyes clouding with something Caroline could not define.

"I . . . I went to school with him," she managed, nodding in Thad's direction. Tears welled up in her eyes.

"Then we must help him." Jerome moved to follow Thad.

"No. Wait!" Her voice was sharp, stopping Jerome in his tracks. He looked at her curiously with his black piercing eyes.

The talkative soldier hung back long enough to finish the conversation.

"He's a loner. He'll be discharged soon though, and he'll go home. He says there is a girl waiting for him. That should help!"

Caroline did not wait to hear more. She pushed her way to the porch and to the curb, the confusion in her mind beyond endurance. What had she ever done to deserve this? How could she have guessed that Thad was alive? Dear Thad. So hurt, so angry. And Jerome, searching her face for an explanation. Would she ever get away, now, from the guilt and condemnation of her own conscience?

They traveled home without speaking, then Jerome saw her to her room and left. Had he guessed?

Caroline sat down before her dressing table, hating the woman whose reflection looked back at her. Then she arose, crossed the room, and flung herself across the bed, sobbing.

Her own words, spoken so glibly and proudly to Jerome at their first meeting, returned to haunt her. Women have an obligation, too, to keep things as they left them! Now the words had a hollow ring, a hypocritical sting, branding her a cheat and a fraud.

How long she lay there she did not know. The moon was flooding her room when she became aware of someone standing by her bed.

"Jerome?"

He moved nearer.

"Why did you never tell me?" he asked.

"Tell you what?"

"That he has been between us from the start."

She looked at Jerome blankly. "Has he been between us?"

"Carrie!" His hands were pressing hard into her shoulders, sending pain through her arms.

"I thought he was dead. I really did!"

"But you married me without ever telling me!"

"I wasn't the one who pressed for marriage, Jerome. I wanted to wait—I wanted to do what was right. I thought I did what was right. Oh, Jerome, let me go. Let me go back home where I can gather my wits. I've been in a foreign country too long. I've never been so confused in my life!"

He released her roughly and stalked out of the room, leaving her convinced that nothing now could stop her from leaving at the earliest possible moment. She wept and struggled with her thoughts for hours and finally fell into an exhausted sleep.

She dreamed of marshes and water, breaking waves and war, her father with a gun that would not fire, and off in the distance, cannon firing and sending smoke into a night sky. Then the sound of running feet and rifles cracking and a city under siege.

She awoke, terrified. The gunfire was real and just outside her window. The running feet and voices were rising in a deafening crescendo. She had heard of the rebel yell, and she waited for the house to come under attack. Creeping to the window, she looked down upon wavering torchlights and mobs of people. Was it possible Lee was staging a last-ditch assault? But why on the Hub City? It made no sense.

She ran into the hall in time to see Jerome descending the stairs and holding one of a pair of Colt revolvers. Caroline reached him first, with Kathleen and Galvin close behind. Gently now, Jerome moved her behind him and went to the door, opening it just the slightest crack. Outside, they could see that there were as many children in the street as adults—and most were still in their nightclothes!

"Over! Over! The war is over!" The cry was everywhere!

Jerome's hands dropped, and he stood gazing at the frenzied crowd. Caroline crept to his side.

"Do they mean it? Is it really over?" she asked, between chattering teeth.

"Yes, my girl. The miserable war is over!"

"Oh, Jerome! Thank God! Thank God!"

Jerome led her to the parlor where Kathleen was lighting a lamp.

"Praise be to the Almighty! Now folk can get on with livin'!" Her face was wreathed in smiles.

Jerome didn't hear her. He knew only that when there had been danger, his wife had come to him. He cradled her in his arms until she stopped sobbing.

"It will not do to travel this day," he said, with all the tenderness he had always shown her. "The celebrations won't settle down for a long time. But afterward, I will take you to the train myself."

Within days, Jerome made true his promise, his consideration touching her deeply.

"I will not stay long, Jerome, but this is something I must do. Please understand."

She meant what she was saying. She would think out the problems as she had always done, and in the place where she had always lived. Right now it was what she wanted most—back to the warmth and comfort of the old sitting room, back to the days of hard work and the evenings when the family would gather around the old Bible and share each other's needs and pray.

On a cool April afternoon, she said good-bye to Jerome at the train station and left him standing there with his heart in his eyes. The train began to pull away, and soon all she could see was a solitary man fading into the distance.

30

WITH THE FALL OF PETERSBURG and the imminent collapse of Richmond's defenses, the Confederate command at General Grant's invitation began serious discussions, and President Davis made his flight toward Irwinville. On April 9, the white flags were hoisted, rebel arms were stacked, and the two generals met at the home of Wilmer McClean in a little town called Appomatox Court House. The terms of surrender were discussed and signed, and the War between the States came to an end.

At first the news came with small credence. Once before, in February, there had been a flash of hope, but Davis remained unyielding in his quest for two separate countries within the continent. This the man at the helm could never countenance, so the war had gone on. It now became more than a rumor, and the reality of peace began gradually to sink in much as did the spring rains that begin gradually, gain strength, and ultimately saturate a parched earth. The weary land lifted its seared and war-scarred face to the downpour of God's grace.

Suddenly, the belfry tocsins changed their tune, and the welcome sound of rejoicing broke forth and joined with the salute and thunder of a hundred cannons.

Clinton awoke to the barrage. In the eerie glow of flickering hospital wall candles, he watched his ward companions reach for guns that were not there. Thoughts spun crazily in his tired brain. Then came the realization of what the commotion was about. A

Union—a Union under one flag! Praise God, the Union had been preserved. Those who could left their beds and crowded to the windows. They could see the skies ablaze with fireworks and hear the cheering crowds in the streets, and—miracle of miracles—they were alive! There would be no more battles, no more of burying comrades. Clinton thought how only those who have lived through the agonies of war could fully understand what the sounds of peace could mean. Families reunited and the normal pursuits of life resumed . . . the turning of swords into plowshares!

Nurses came with candles and placed them in the windows, their amiable light reflecting fulfilled hope. Clinton donned his coat and walked outside. The display was thrilling! If only Vaugn were there to share it all. Soldiers in blue set up cannon on the hospital lawn and began their two-hundred-gun salute. Praise God, the roar and fire would no longer spell death for those who heard it.

For several days afterward, newspapers poured in, covering the surrender at the Wilmer McClean home. Much was said of the stately General Lee, his dignity and proud bearing, and the tribute paid him by his men. Much, too, was said of the magnanimity of the Union general, his disdain for the rumors that had him taking Lee's sword, the compassion of the rough, uncouth Grant who seemed always to be given the toughest assignments, his generosity when it came to giving rations and farm horses to his defeated foes, his dedication to his commander in chief's admonition to put into shoe leather the high principles of charity for all and malice toward none.

Now the mustering out would follow. Trains everywhere would be returning men to their hometowns. The thought brought a decided upturn in the recovery of many a patient, and a jubilant spirit invaded the former atmosphere of the wards.

In Newburyport, as in every village and town, the news broke with the same unrestrained joy. Church bells, fireworks, and dancing in the street became the order of the day. Folks left their warm beds to welcome the news! The celebration was for everyone, man, woman, and child!

Matthew and Joshua went into town with Allen and Clara. The women followed behind. By dawn, a parade had assembled and, with the usual display of civic pride and purpose, the city fathers did themselves proud in forming the procession. City Cadets, Steam Fire Engine No. 1, Young American Hook and Ladder Company Steamer No. 2, Eagle No. 5, Agile No. 6, and Neptune No. 8 paraded to the martial music and to the cheers of a small city gone mad with rejoicing! Firemen in their flat dress hats and white belts stepped along smartly in the midst of furling flags, banners, and badges.

Bethia helped Nabby into warm clothing and together with Phoebe, they ventured into the street. Oldsters, veterans of the war with Mexico, stood with bowed heads and hats pressed against thankful hearts. It went on for hours, until many left for home and for enough sleep and food to sustain a second round of celebration. The Haddons returned home with the expectancy of Clinton's safe return.

Nabby started a fire in the kitchen stove and then went to the sink to fill a kettle. Bethia was placing dishes on the table and turned in time to see her mother stagger and slide gracefully to the floor. Bethia ran to kneel beside her mother, rubbing her hands.

"She should never have gone out into the damp air! Whatever was I thinking!" Bethia moaned. With Matthew's help, she managed to get her to bed where Nabby lay, looking wasted and pale.

"Guess I just overdid!" she said apologetically.

THE DEPOT WAGON TURNED into the long lane that led to the farm. Caroline noticed the little bold crocuses already pushing their stout, persistent heads up through the damp earth. It had seemed to take hours for the train to get to Newburyport, and already the sun was going down and lamps were being lighted and set in clean windows. It was good to see one at the Paxtons' window. Praise be to God, those dear neighbors would by now have received news of their son's safe return. How gracious the Lord had been!

The horse's hooves struck clods of soil into the air, and the wagon tilted crazily in the ruts. Joshua sat on the stoop, his chin cupped in his hands, watching the approaching wagon with boyish interest. Then suddenly he was racing with wild acclaim to greet its occupant, dancing and shrieking Caroline's name.

Bethia heard him and ran to the door, with Matthew close behind her.

How sweet the loving arms, how precious the beloved faces! Home! Home! The sweetest word in any language . . . it meant all the things that satisfied the heart . . . and Caroline's heart was about to burst with the joy of returning. Matthew was the first to embrace her, with unpretentious affection.

"Joshua!" She held the youngest of the children, feeling all the tender love she had had for him when she had tended him in his infancy.

There was Bethia, standing back, shy now, tall and slim and with eyes filled with tears of relief. Carrie was home, and all would be well! Caroline held her for a long time, erasing the bitter memory of their last encounter, the hugs and kisses melting away every vestige of misunderstanding.

"Has it been hard, Bethia?" she asked, walking with her sister into the house. "Yes, I know it has. I know what it is like to have the weight of the family on your shoulders. You have been very brave!"

They entered the kitchen with all the wonderful windows. There was the table where she and Matthew had worked at their school assignments, there the same lamp burning, the old kettle steaming, the rocker by the window, the flyspecked painting of Jefferson. Caroline's tears overflowed.

"Now take me to Mother! How is she? You said she is tired and weak. Do you think she has consumption?"

"Doc Slater says no. She has damaged her heart."

"We might have guessed. She worked much too hard."

"And I let her go out for the peace celebration. I should have used more sense, but she wanted so badly to be part of it. We all went. It was so grand, Carrie! I wish you had been here. I wish Father could have been here, too. I've heard, though, that all the hospitals celebrated, too."

Caroline made her way to her mother's room, the same room where she had stood in her wedding dress and looked up at the eagle on the mirror just three months earlier.

Nabby's face was wreathed in smiles when she saw her daughter, and then they were in each other's arms.

"Mother, you are just too thin!" declared Caroline.

"You are a little underweight, too, daughter!" answered the observant invalid, and looking over Caroline's shoulder she asked, "Didn't Jerome come, too?"

It was the question Caroline had feared.

"He had concerts, but I am sure he will come later." It was the best she could manage.

"I hope you will stay a long time," Bethia said with apprehension.

"Oh, I will, I will. You have no idea how I have missed you . . . all of you!"

She told her family of the chance meeting with Thad, carefully leaving out the sordid details of his reaction, and listened to them exclaim with delight at how thrilled his parents would be to learn this news.

It was late when they retired. Caroline slept in her old spool bed, listening to the branches against the house, hearing the wind and the old town clocks, watching the stars appear in the sky just beyond the billowing curtains, and smiling as the train whistle sounded in the distance—everything pouring into her soul the oil of gladness, closing out the bitter moment with Thad and the gulf that was widening between Jerome and herself.

She settled easily into the old familiar routine, cooking, cleaning, caring and loving, finding again the sweet pleasure of being needed. Her days took on a sense of worth.

IT WAS THE MORNING of April 14, 1865. There was an ethereal tranquility to the day, a holy solemnity, for it was Good Friday, and the disciplined Yankee had a healthy respect for its place in the Christian calendar. Matthew had spent a short time at the newspaper office and returned with a bulletin telling of the Union flag-raising ceremonies at Fort Sumter. Evening prayers were said in Nabby's room, and the day was over.

Peace descended on the little city, and one by one the lamps were extinguished and the citizenry went to their beds. Who among them could have dreamed what the following hours would bring?

They were awakened by Allen pounding on the door sometime between ten o'clock and midnight.

"The news is terrible!" He stepped inside the door, his face a solemn death mask. "They have shot the president, and he could die!"

Only silence met his announcement. It could not be—it simply could not be true. Such things could not happen.

"Where did you hear?" asked Matthew, quickly dressing.

"Came in on the telegraph, and it's all over town. Details not too clear—only that he was watching a play at Ford's Theatre."

"Who would do such a thing?" whispered Caroline.

"Great men have their enemies," said Matthew on his way to the door.

Bethia burst into tears and fled the room. They found her on the sitting-room floor. Caroline was glad she had come home, if for no other reason than to help her sister. It was difficult for the young to understand the harsh things of life, the sorrows of an imperfect world. She held Bethia in her arms for a long time, smoothing the golden hair and kissing her softly.

By morning, more details had come in, and the news all had braced for came over the wires. The great heart of the nation's sixteenth president had stopped beating. He now belonged to the ages, a man whose spirit would inspire generations to come, whose dedication to duty would seldom be equaled and whose memory would never die. Abraham Lincoln had gone to meet the One he most endeavored to please.

Solemn-faced selectmen and town dignitaries conferred in the Merchant's Reading Room to plan memorial services that would synchronize with those held in the Capitol. Vows of support were wired to Andrew Johnson. Speeches, eulogies, sermons, and gun salutes would continue for thirty days. Sorrow spread itself over the nation like a shroud. Even the buildings took on the dolorous mood as storefronts, public buildings, homes, and churches were draped in black.

On the designated Wednesday, the Haddons' pastor was to speak first to his own flock and then at the Pleasant Street church. The sound of cannon mingled with the ringing of church bells.

An arthritic neighbor came to stay with Nabby while the rest of the family joined the mourners. Caroline raised a small, black-gloved hand to her throat as Dandy pulled the wagon into Federal Street. The high steeple and the tall Federal windows looked the same as always. The cenotaph with its Egyptian veined marble was hung with a black shroud, making the shadows deeper than ever. Families gathered silently in their own pews and sat with bowed heads.

Handkerchiefs came out as the good minister began to speak. The old New England laity was not ashamed of tears at this unexpected tragedy. Caroline looked around at the sober faces, people she had known all her life, people who knew how to deal with life and death, joy and sorrow. They knew what it was to bury grandmothers and little children and soldier sons, to strive against difficulty, to give themselves to honest pursuits, and to pass on to their children principles that would impart health to their families, their communities, and their nation.

They show so little on the outside, she thought, yet they truly are a people of great depth . . . and they are my people. How imbecilic to make class distinctions. Together we stand or apart we fall.

The thought began to soften her heart toward Jerome.

Differences could be—must be—overcome by understanding and love and definitely by patient persevering.

A Wesley hymn was being sung, and she listened to the words, her heart too full for utterance. How could that great man have known what solace his gift would bring to generations yet unborn when he wrote:

> Thou hidden source of calm repose
> Thou all sufficient love divine,
> Thou help and refuge from my foes,
> Secure I am while Thou art mine;
> And lo, from sin and grief and shame;
> I hide me, Jesus, in Thy name.
> Jesus, my all in all Thou art,
> My rest in toil, my ease in pain
> The healing of my broken heart,
> In war my peace, in loss my gain,
> My smile beneath the tyrant's frown;
> In shame my glory and my crown.

Then followed the benediction, and the congregation moved quietly to the exit. Matthew, Bethia, and Joshua went to their wagon and sat waiting for Caroline. They had no way of knowing that she was being confronted by the Paxton family with their soldier son. Eyes met and as quickly turned away, but that could not continue. Thad followed her to the top step.

"I want to ask your forgiveness for the way I behaved," he began.

"What can I say?" Her spirit was too saddened for smart conversation.

"If only you had kept your promise. . . . If only. . . ." He shook his head, still not understanding. He noticed Matthew waiting in the wagon.

"May we talk?"

"Yes. But let me tell Matthew to go on home."

This done, the two walked toward the river. Though it was

mid-April, there was still the sting of winter in the wind coming off the sea. It was good, though, to be walking together, something they had not done for a long time.

"Will we ever be able to remove this place from our hearts?" Caroline asked.

"We would have to die first."

"You must know that I thought you were dead, Thad."

"But couldn't you have waited? I would have died a thousand times, but I fought to live . . . believing you were waiting."

"Your mother thought you were dead, too. It wasn't easy to accept. It's very painful. You die a little yourself, and after a while you come back to life and pick up the pieces . . . struggle for purpose."

"I just know that I love you, and I always will."

"Thad, don't! You have got to make another life for yourself. We cannot undo what has happened. I, myself, must do what is right."

"Was it right to make me believe and hope?"

"There were many circumstances that forced my decisions. I don't believe you could understand."

It was true. Thad had been denied so little all his life. The only son of doting parents, he was used to having things his way.

"I can't let you go, Carrie. I won't! I'll be going back to Cambridge. We could see one another. No one would know!"

She looked at the boy before her. Yes, he had suffered greatly and was without doubt a casualty of a bitter war, but he was also still the young, impulsive boy who had waited at the Paxton fence . . . and she loved him, just as she had always loved him—like part of her own family, as she loved the walls of her parents' home, the orchards, the roads and the rivers, the island sands and the crying sea gulls, the very city. All had been woven into the very warp and woof of her life . . . but had Thad really been the love of her life?

She touched his sleeve and looked into his eyes, her own registering the maturity the war years had bred—a maturity that had not been there when the promise had been made, when patriotism had been fired high and women were kissing swords and making poetic speeches. With such a request as he was making, did he know anything of love?

"Thad, I don't want to hurt you. Come, let's walk."

They did so, silently.

"We have been through dreadful times, you in prison and I at home, and we've been drawn into situations neither of us would have chosen. Life has changed for us both, but somehow we have managed to survive, to adjust as the times demanded. Now we find ourselves on separate paths. Should we be something less than we really are? Do something wrong and expect something right to come of it? We would hate ourselves if we even considered such a thing."

Thad knew she was speaking the truth, even though he didn't want to hear it. He sighed and squared his shoulders.

"But I couldn't stay here, knowing you were here, too."

"Where would you go?"

"I believe . . . the western plains. Recruits are needed to put down the Indian uprisings."

"Then go! Go with my prayers, Thad."

His silence told her there was a struggle going on, a greater battle, perhaps, than he had ever known.

"Let's go home," he said.

Caroline shivered as they retraced their steps to the church. His parents had gone home with friends and left his wagon at the block. They got in and drove to the home road.

"Please don't see me to the door," said Caroline when they arrived at the farm.

She got down from the wagon and walked a few steps, then turned and faced him. Bitterness marked his face, and there were tears in her own eyes. To smile when they were choking her was not easy, but she managed.

"Good-bye, Thad. God be with you."

She walked to the big oaken door and entered, closing it with resolute firmness and with the knowledge that the door would be forever closed on their youthful relationship. His memory must fade into the past, into the years before the war, when life was simple and uncomplicated.

31

T HE WEEKS PASSED SWIFTLY after Caroline's encounter with Thad, and even though the black-draped buildings continued to remind the citizenry of their tragic loss, the need to get on with life, to rebuild, and to set the wheels of government rolling again began to pique the inherently industrious nature of the people.

With the release of guilt and the love of her family, Caroline began to live again. She knew that she had done what was right for herself and for Thad. He must learn to live again, too, and to live as a man. In a few days, she would write to Jerome and make plans to return to Boston.

One Sunday just before sunset, Allen came to ask if Caroline would walk with him to the pond. She was eager to go. She would let Bethia manage the Sunday evening repast: toast dipped in cream sauce.

Spring rains had softened the rich soil, pigeons and martins had returned and staked out their territory, and robins were nesting carelessly on extended branches, daring anything to invade their leafy nurseries. Even the peep frogs could be heard, and the dogs were running ahead and sneezing in the arnica.

"I shall have a little garden when I return to Boston—a very little garden!"

"In a window box?" asked Allen facetiously.

"No. It is better than that . . . though not much."

They were deep in the woods, passing the highly stacked logs that Hank had set to dry.

"I miss him, too," said Allen, knowing his cousin's thoughts.

"Wasn't life wonderful when we were all together . . . and young?"

Allen smiled. "You are still young, Carrie."

"I don't feel young. Is it because we've lived through so much, had so many decisions to make?"

"Yes, the times have tested us—I suppose to prove what it is we are made of."

Caroline turned a questioning face toward her cousin. "Allen, tell me truthfully. Do I seem hard . . . cruel? I mean, the way I have made decisions, cutting people off—Thad, Jerome, sometimes even avoiding you, my dear friend?"

"War breeds hardness, Carrie. We'd never survive it being soft."

"But sometimes I feel dreadful, and I don't like who I am. The testing has done so little for me. And I don't believe it has made me a better person. I seem to be lacking something."

"I think the testing shows us where our strength lies . . . in ourselves or in our faith." He meant to comfort her, but his words were troubling. He continued, "I have decisions, too."

"Tell me."

"It is complicated." He looked beyond the trees, not seeing them. "It's Timothy and Melinda."

"Will they marry soon?" Caroline asked.

"That is what puzzles me. They set a date and then change it."

"Well, she is young and still a little flighty."

Allen's brows knit together. "No, I don't think so."

"You seem to know a great deal about her."

"Unfortunately—more than Timothy does. You know Tim. Fun-loving, adventurous Tim."

"What are you trying to say?"

"I'm not sure. Perhaps, only that I hope he doesn't hurt her."

Caroline stole a glance at Allen. He had never before talked about a girl this way. Did she detect more than a casual interest? That could cause problems.

He seemed to sense the probing of her mind and changed the subject. "You will be going back to Boston soon?"

"Yes, but I have a bad feeling about leaving my mother."

"She should never have worked as she did. But God knows, we all were pushing beyond our strength."

"But Father will come home and find her this way. That troubles me."

"Well, don't blame yourself, Carrie. I know what you have given to them all."

Allen—always the gentle, caring person.

"I am so grateful for you, Allen. Thank you for saying that."

They walked further, and Caroline broke the silence again. "Before I leave, I'd like to take flowers to the cemetery, to put on your father's grave and Hank's. When I think what they gave, everything we have suffered seems trite. I often wonder how long they will be remembered. Only as long as we live? And all the others who died, will they leave something of themselves for the coming generations? Their courage—their high and holy principles—their dedication to God's ways for a nation?"

She was interrupted by the sound of heavy wings overhead. A flock of wood ducks came circling and dipped gracefully down upon the pond's surface. They foraged curiously among the protective reeds and spring sallows. Even the staghorn sumac was budding, the bud edges yellow and alkanet, and the sedge with their curled heads were springing up, speaking of new life.

Allen cut a birch withe for a fishing pole, moved as always by his inbred survival instinct. Shad were already at the river's mouth, and he would have his share.

"Always there is spring, and somehow the earth is replenished," he mused.

The sun was dipping into the west and turning the water to

liquid rose and lavender as they turned their steps homeward, both refreshed by the time spent together.

That night the family gathered to read from the Book of Ephesians about the family of God and the peace that rested on those who were related through faith in the Savior, Jesus Christ. Caroline wondered about that peace, wondered if it would ever be hers. Somehow she knew she had never quite attained that high place, and as she listened, she felt a deep longing to truly experience it.

"Jerome must be very rich!" said Bethia, as they climbed the stairs together.

"Why do you say that?"

"The clothes you brought home. They are so elegant!"

Caroline threw her dress carelessly over a chair. "You don't know how much I would welcome the opportunity to go back to my simple frocks, the ginghams and the striped wools. I hate these peacock feathers and all they represent."

"But it would be nice—just once—to dress like a lady. Not that I'd know where to start!" Bethia giggled.

"Don't even think that way, Bethia. Be content with all you have—please."

When they were in bed, Bethia spoke again. "What did Thad say to you, Carrie?"

Caroline had begun to doze off, and the question brought her back with a shock. Why did Bethia always have to ask questions? Was it an honest desire to know more of life, or was she just inquisitive? Caroline did not wish to think of Thad again.

"I don't know if I can tell you, Beth."

"He loved you so much!"

"Yes, but we were children . . . and there was a war."

"But what did he say to you? It must have been terrible. I saw his face when he drove you home."

"He wanted me to do something I could never do."

"What?"

"He wanted me to meet him secretly."

Bethia clapped her hand over her mouth in dismay.

"I think it was the first time I ever saw Thad as he truly is," Caroline continued, "and I felt sorry for him. I realized that he could neither think nor live beyond his own needs."

"I was a little guilty of that myself, Carrie, when I saw you falling in love with Jerome. I panicked. I couldn't imagine life here without you. I didn't mean to be selfish, but I was."

But Caroline wasn't hearing Bethia's confession. The mention of Jerome had stirred feelings she'd been trying to repress. She groped back through the events of the times and the things that had happened so fast. Falling in love with Jerome. Accepting his unselfish affection, his love, his courage when protecting her.

Suddenly she realized how blind she had been, how foolishly married to an ill-gotten promise. How she had resented Jerome's life-style, been intolerant of his friends . . . but it had never been Jerome himself she resented! She closed her eyes and felt his kiss and his loving arms . . . heard the music he played just for her. And she had left him there, standing alone in the cold Boston train station. She, too, had been selfish.

She arose and lighted the lamp.

"What are you doing?" Bethia was up on one elbow.

"I'm writing a letter to my husband."

WARM WEATHER BEGAN TO SETTLE IN, and the family hung a hammock for Nabby in a sheltered corner of the porch where the afternoon sun might strike.

"I had forgotten how beautiful everything is," she exclaimed, listening to the birds and enjoying the warmth.

Joshua waved to her from the barn, and the dogs came close to be fondled.

Allen had taken on hands and was already planning to get the bush beans in. From the distant woods came the song of the cheriwink and toward sunset the mournful voice of the whippoorwill. On the road an occasional wagon stirred the dust, and from town could be heard the chorus of the great church clocks.

It was not customary for a carriage to be on the road at this time of day, at least not on the country boreens. Yet one was approaching the Haddon farm, stirring the dust and disquieting the mottled grouse.

Each member of the family shared the same thought as the carriage drew nearer. Instinctively, they knew its occupant. Caroline, who had been sitting on a small wicker rocker, arose expectantly. Nabby's hands moved to her breast in her characteristic way. Bethia and Joshua stared with their hearts in their eyes and mouths agape.

When the carriage stopped, the figure of a man swung down with some effort. His clothes hung loosely, marked more as he reached a scrawny hand toward the baggage rack. Then he was walking toward them. In spite of the heavy growth of beard, they could see that he was smiling. The children ran, leaping and calling his name.

"Papa! Papa!" The name was sweet upon their lips.

Nabby, unable to join them, just let the tears fall.

"And they call us cold and reserved!" laughed Clinton, embracing his children. With his great arms still around the children, he hurried to Nabby and then lifted her into his arms. She did not mind the rough wool of his shirt as she leaned against him. He repeated her name over and over, and each time it fell on her ears as the oil of gladness, soothing, blessing. It was all she could ask for.

Practical Bethia danced on ahead and turned down the covers on her mother's bed. Joshua came with his father's trunk, swinging it about with ease and hoping to gain his father's attention. The carriage rolled away, grinding wheels on the gravel, and for one brief moment Clinton heard again the limbers and the cannon. Then the illusion was gone, and he sighed heavily.

"Is your gun in here, Father?" Joshua sat on the floor beside the trunk, eyes sparkling like ocean water under an August sun.

"Yes, son."

"You came on the afternoon train?"

"Yes, Carrie."

"Are you wounded, Papa?" asked Bethia.

"See if you can tell!"

"There's a scar on your nose. Does it hurt?" But before he could answer, she disappeared into the pantry to cut bread and prepare a quick meal. Soon the kettle was steaming on the stove, and Clinton's favorite tea was brewing.

He sank into a chair beside Nabby.

I know how he is feeling, thought Caroline. *The rooms look smaller than he remembered, and the furniture old and worn, but he is loving the sight of everything, and he'll go to sleep tonight fearing he'll awake and find it all a dream.*

Clinton kissed his wife's forehead, then looked around the room. He walked to the kitchen and pumped water in the long sink, then back to the sitting room where he touched the worn cover of the old Bible. The sculptured face on Hank's old green pippin grinned at him from the table; a leafy houseplant was now at home in the former tobacco humidor.

"Hank?" he asked, puzzled.

"We could not tell you."

Clinton had sensed his brother-in-law's absence from the moment he had alighted, and now, with the sober faces confronting him, the truth hit him like a dash of cold water in the face.

He walked to the window that looked out toward the barn. Surely the little man would come around the corner and greet him any minute—the faithful brother with the strange limp.

Clinton mustered strength to speak, his voice hoarse and breaking. "Then I can never thank him," he said wearily.

At that moment Matthew came running up the driveway and burst in the door. "I met the carriage! I knew it had to be you!" He was breathless, reserve fallen off like an old garment, and he was close to tears as he hugged his father.

Clinton took a long look at his eldest son. "Matthew, you have grown!"

"Yes, a little," Matthew replied with some embarrassment.

"And at work?"

"Just proofreading."

"I'm proud of you, son. I knew you would find your place."

"Come, Papa. You and Mother enjoy a tray together. I made the bread myself," said Bethia.

Clinton held high the slice of bread dripping with fruit jam. "I haven't seen the likes of this for months!" he exclaimed. "And I can see I'll not be looking at 'little Bethia' again, either."

Joshua pressed in close to his father, wanting his attention. "Did you know Carrie got married?" he asked innocently.

Clinton looked at Caroline in astonishment. So much news, all at once.

"I did send letters, Father," Caroline explained, "but we never seemed to catch up with you. I assume most were lost." Then, in an effort to ease his confusion, she added, "I'll tell you more later. Right now I must unpack your things."

When it had grown completely dark, they moved together to the old sitting room. The day had been long for Nabby, but she would have it no other way. Clinton's voice rose with all of its old strength and comfort, pouring into their midst the healing emollient that had been absent for so long.

"We sorrow not as those who have no hope," he said, and then he talked of the men who had been his comrades and the men who would carry in their bodies the marks of their sacrifice. He talked of Hank and Vaugn and President Lincoln and the brave women who had struggled at home, and he closed with a benediction of praise and gratitude for the return to his old place as head of his family.

"Now, off to bed. We'll be up early for milking. Right now, I am very tired."

"There are only three cows, Father," said Joshua apologetically.

"I know, son. Your mother has told me. But we shall have more."

Caroline and Bethia climbed the stairs with faces radiant, hearts rapturous, and life replete.

"The world seems right again, doesn't it, Carrie?"

Caroline smiled but said nothing.

"Stay another day, Carrie. Just one more day."

"Jerome has not written."

"But he will understand when you tell him that Papa has come home."

The temptation for Caroline to delay her return to Boston was too much, even though the desire to see Jerome was burning deep within. Yes, she would wait another day.

Before daylight, Clinton went to the barn, with Joshua holding the lantern just as before. Joshua watched his father's face, wondering how he would react to the sight of the empty stanchions. He need not have been concerned. Clinton was used to unsavory sights and knew how to bridle emotions with soldierly stoicism.

"We've still got Dandy!" said Joshua, stroking the inquisitive nose.

Clinton reached for the horse and was nuzzled with genuine recognition.

"To think that you are still here," he said, remembering the acres of dead horseflesh he had seen upon the fields. He looked into the loft at the thinly strewn hay.

"What you planning to feed the stock?" he asked. "It will be months before harvest."

"Allen is getting some oat-straw and hay for us."

"That had better be soon!" commented Clinton dryly. "We'll see Allen after breakfast."

CLARA WAS THE FIRST to see Clinton as he came over the fields. She let out a whoop and broke from the door. Allen went to investigate, a slow grin spreading over his face when he recognized the oncoming figure.

"When did you get in?" he asked, not trying to contain his genuine delight.

"Yesterday on the afternoon train." Clinton waved a hand toward the place where the stables had stood. "All gone, eh? When are you building again?"

"Waiting for you, Uncle Clint! But first we'll have to get the crops in."

"Should have bumper crops! It did the ground good to lie fallow."

"The bankers are talking loans."

"Not to us, they aren't!" asserted Clinton.

"Timothy has sent us some money. He's doing remarkably well."

"I'd rather have his muscle!" said Clinton, knowing the work that lay ahead.

"Ayuh, but he won't be back. Come. Mother will be glad to see you."

Phoebe flushed when Clinton entered the kitchen. With his pronounced loss of weight, he might have been her late husband.

"Mercy, Clint, you are a bag of bones!"

"But already beating the hogs to the trough!"

Clara pulled on his sleeve. "You missed seeing Moses, Uncle Clint."

"Who the devil is Moses?" asked Clinton blankly.

"A baby we found in the hay. But he's gone to Canada."

Clinton turned a puzzled look in Phoebe's direction.

"It's true, Clinton. We fell heir to a slave child when his mother left him in a haystack. But they both got away safely. We have heard from them."

"Guess I have got a lot of catching up to do," mused Clinton, rubbing his beard.

He stayed long enough to make plans with Allen for the

following day, then retraced his steps toward home.

"I have kept a little money for you, Clinton," said Nabby as they talked together on the porch. "Enough to get started again. We have managed on the allotments that got through and on Caroline's checks."

"Caroline's checks?"

"Her husband has been generous."

The fragments of news with which Clinton was being deluged was mind-boggling. He would find a quiet moment with his daughter and hear her story.

The leaves on the rock maples came on fast in the first few days after Clinton's return. They were already a tender bright green.

Clinton was feeling the strain of weak muscles as he tried to keep up with Allen and Joshua, and he stopped for a rest on the side-door stoop, the old fever stirring again.

"Matthew was right," he confessed. "I'd better take it easy until I get my land legs!"

Caroline settled at his feet, glad to be able to rest her head against his knees.

He brushed a hand over her hair as he spoke.

"I should not have let you do it, Carrie. I apologize for putting so much on your shoulders."

"I have done what anyone would have done, Father. No need for apologies."

"No, Carrie. I never planned for you to marry to keep us afloat."

"That was a part of it, but I do love Jerome . . . I just didn't know how much at the time. You must meet him, Father. I know you will like him. He's a lot like you—but different, too. I wanted to wait until you came home, Father, to know you approved . . . but things were in such a state here."

"Will you be going back to Boston?"

"Yes, in a few days."

But once again it was not to be. Nabby took a turn for the worse and lingered on death's threshold for days. On the twenty-fifth of

June, she passed quietly away in her sleep, once again plunging the household into the depths of grief and despair.

Caroline wrote another note to Jerome, hoping to rejoin him when he arrived for the funeral, but the day came and he did not appear. Now there was genuine concern, and Caroline knew she must return to Boston. The family would have to do without her.

The day after the funeral, she boarded the train. The clicking wheels, a sound she had always liked, had lost their charm for her. They seemed only to be marking off time—hours, minutes of her life, and she could not relax. Her mother was dead, and what awaited her in Boston? But Jerome would be there, would take her into his arms and lift her over the difficult days as he had before.

The horsecars that went directly past her house were late in getting there. It was a very warm day, and a feeling of nausea swept over her. When they turned into her street, she sensed the absence of people. Had they all closed their houses and gone to the ocean for the summer? Everywhere, blinds were closed.

Pulling her heavy trunk after her, she ascended the stairs. The stable doors across the street were open, and the carriage gone. Galvin must be out with Jerome. She fumbled in her purse for the key and fitted it in the lock. As she turned the knob, the door swung back with a whine.

"Kathleen, I'm home!" she called, her voice tremulous and uncertain.

No one answered. There on the floor she saw her own letters. They were still sealed.

In the long hall, her footsteps seemed to echo, the hollowness beginning to frighten her. In the parlor she was met with another disconcerting sight—the furniture was shrouded in white muslin. Caroline shivered and hurried up the stairway, then flung open the door to Jerome's room. There, too, all was silent—deathly cold and silent. The floor of the brick fireplace was swept and scrubbed cleaner than she had imagined a fireplace could be.

Across the hall, she opened the door to her own room—the vast, cavernous room Jerome had so lovingly prepared for her. The blinds were closed, making her feel shut off from all living. On her dressing table she saw a letter. Sobs swept over her as she tore at the envelope.

May 25, 1865

Dear Carrie,

I write this letter in the confidence that you will return for your belongings.

After you left, I visited the hospital to offer my help to your friend, only to learn that he, too, had left for home. At first I was angry enough to have killed you both, but I waited, hoping you would return and we could salvage something of our marriage. When you did not, I knew you had made your choice. I knew also that it was time to get on with my music, so I accepted several invitations in Europe. I have sent money to your bank in Newburyport, enough for you to take legal action when you see fit. I shall always love you, but I shall not stand in your way of happiness with the man you have chosen.

Dieu vous garde,

Jerome

The letter fell to the floor and Caroline, with her hands over her face, fell with it. She lay there for a long time, stunned and crushed. Then, descending the stairs, she walked through the house.

Stopping at the double French doors in the dining room, she looked out at the small patch of ground she had treasured so much. She could see tiny green leaves and pale sprouts coming up through the earth.

"Oh, Galvin, bless you! You knew I'd come back. Why didn't Jerome know?"

Entering the little garden, she knelt and sifted the dirt through her fingers, weeping as though she would never stop. Nabby's death, Jerome's mistrust and desertion, the empty house, the nausea, the utter confusion. . . . And all the while, the little plants stirring so gently in a wisp of a breeze, knowing nothing, never guessing that without care they would perish even before they bloomed. Was that to be her lot as well?

"My God, where is the strength I am supposed to have? Where?"

She did not know how long she sat there. Hours, perhaps, or maybe only minutes, but finally there were no more tears. She made her way to the dreary kitchen and found a small tin of green tea. There was no means of heating water, so she pumped cold water into the can and gleaned a scant cup of weak tea. At least it cooled her parched lips.

Then she returned to her room. She would have to select clothes to take home. There was no other place to go. She would return to her own city, her own family. There was no question that they needed her as much as she now needed them. She would forget she had ever been married.

32

THE RAILROAD CAR WAS STIFLING, and the thermometer bent on setting a record before the dews had vaporized. The travelers were conspicuously irritable and restless in the closed environment. Soldiers returning from their stations of service had taken possession of the stuffy car, and their ribaldry cut like sharpened steel into Caroline's tortured thoughts. Purposely she stacked her bundles in the vacant seat beside her and tolerated snide remarks from other passengers for her lack of consideration. That was better than the chance of getting a loquacious traveling companion.

How to tell her father . . . how to face the neighbors . . . and how to live without Jerome's patient, loving care? The sting of it, realizing too late that he was the only man she had ever loved or would ever love! And worse, the knowledge that for the first time in her life she had not been able to control the situation, that someone or something was in control of her destiny. A shame came with the new revelation. She was not as strong as she had always thought she was. In truth, she was weak, and the realization was tearing her pride to shreds.

She settled into her seat and leaned against the window, struggling to keep from vomiting. The smell of coal was doing drastic things to her stomach, and she prayed she would not become a spectacle. The long ride was tortuous, but every mile brought her closer to a place where she could hide from prying eyes and gain some composure.

The depot wagon was parked in its usual place, the driver kind and helpful with her luggage. What a relief to be out of the train's cumbrous atmosphere. The towering elms stood motionless, and the sun was so bright that every leaf took on a kaleidoscopic sharpness. The wagon rocked and jostled along in the familiar ruts and eventually turned down the lane that led to home. The odor of dusty fields hung suspended over the yard and the buildings. Even the shaggy hunting dogs declined to stir from their shaded retreat under the porch. Everywhere, life seemed to be at a standstill.

The driver helped Caroline to the door and left. The family must be in the fields. With much struggling, she managed to get her cumbersome valises in the side door. She walked into the kitchen, not expecting to find anyone there . . . but Clinton was waiting, facing her with questioning eyes and a deep furrowed brow.

She must not break, must not cry. That would be the height of humiliation. But what was there to say? She leaned against the pantry door and stared back at him. Then, with an impulsive gesture, she spoke.

"Well, you are looking at the world's most colossal failure, Father. What do you think of her?"

"Failure?" Clinton looked baffled.

"Yes! The strong, self-sufficient Caroline Haddon, who failed everyone and ruined everything! Jerome has left me. Does that surprise you?"

Clinton's silence now added to her misery. What was he thinking?

She floundered, grasping for the right words. "I'm not at all what you thought I was. I let my mother die from overwork, after promising you I would not let that happen. And now I have destroyed my marriage, and I've come to ask you if I may come home, which takes more courage than I thought I owned. You can see I've no pride left, or I would have remained in Boston. Imagine, me telling Matthew to have some self-esteem! Isn't that funny? But

I want you to know I really have tried . . . I did try to keep my promise to you."

Her struggle to keep from crying proved futile, and tears flooded down Caroline's pale face. Instantly Clinton moved across the room, reaching strong arms toward her, holding her, but still silent.

"Where are the others?" she asked at last.

"They went to the pond."

"The mercy of God. I couldn't face them."

"Carrie, sit down."

She obeyed.

"Of course you may come home. You are home in more ways than you realize." Clinton picked up her limp hand and held it.

"I knew someday you would come to this. Struggling to be a Christian without having been born into God's family. Like trying to live the life of a Laplander without being born a Lapp!"

"Father, what do you mean? I don't understand. I've tried to live as God has wanted me to, and now to be so unjustly accused. Where have I done wrong?"

"My girl, there is more to life than doing. There is knowing! Knowing the Lord Christ, and knowing some of the things He experienced. He was unjustly accused, too. Knowing how it feels to be alone. He was alone when He prayed and alone when He died. Knowing Him like that, like one knows his spouse, sharing an experience with Him, because you have been wed to Him. As the apostle said, 'from faith to faith,' until your marriage to Jesus Christ is perfected."

"But I have tried to be religious!"

"Religion isn't the answer, Carrie. Haven't you read the first chapter of John's Gospel, the twelfth and thirteenth verses?"

Caroline turned reproachful eyes upon her father. "I know those verses by heart!"

"Ah, but do you?"

"What are you saying?"

"You don't know them by heart. You know them by head! The words never got further than your head. Listen carefully, Carrie, to the twelfth verse. 'To as many as received him' . . . you do not receive Him because you have been born into a Christian family—not even into the Haddon family!"

"But I have tried, Father."

"Not of the will of the flesh! Not of blood! Nor of the will of man!"

"Merciful God! What is left?"

"Just that. A yielding, an agreeing with a merciful God that humanly speaking, we are fallible people. Sinners. Incomplete without Him. Come as you are to God, acknowledging your pride and your lack. Alone, we humans do not have the answers."

"Oh, Father, help me!"

"This is an individual thing, Carrie. Confess your pride and your failures to God and invite His Son into your heart—and I'll guarantee you a peace such as you have never known. Not as the world gives—transient, and only there when things go well—but peace in your darkest hour. Peace, now!"

Clinton's words cut deeply, like a surgeon's scalpel, and then he left. That was his way. He would guide to the portal, but his offspring must open the door.

The sun was coming in at the window, just as it always had, and sending its benevolent warmth upon Nabby's begonias. Caroline knelt, baring her soul to the Savior, sharing for the first time in her life a knowledge of the suffering, abandonment, and injustice He had known—seeking through her darkness for the light that could come only from Him.

Had he not said He was the light of the world? And had not John, the beloved apostle, said that Jesus was that true light? If ever she had needed that true light, it was now. She wanted more than human help.

At first the Son moved in much like the flickering mottled

sunlight on Nabby's plants. Then suddenly He burst upon her in His fullness, flooding her with a sweetness and a warmth she had never known, "not of blood, not of the will of man, but of God!" She saw the Christ as she had never seen Him; loving, caring, living, forgiving, and imparting to her soul His very being—new life, new strength, new hope!

Now she knew what lay behind her father's greatness, his strength and his wisdom, and knew the secret of her gentle mother. Now she was one with them. Caroline had indeed come home.

THE FAMILY WAS ECSTATIC to learn that Caroline had returned. If anyone wondered about Jerome's absence, they did not question her. She was certain her father had put up that buffer. Once Matthew brought news of Jerome's success in Europe. The article made no mention of his return to the States. Caroline found herself moving through the days with a serenity she had never experienced and a trust that God was working out His purposes in her life.

The summer wore on with a promise of bumper crops, just as Clinton had predicted. Rains came when they were needed, the corn was earing and healthy, and barley heads waved top-heavy in the fields. Root vegetables were swelling to profitable size, and it was evident that God was adding His benediction to the labors of the Haddon clan.

The neighbors had not forgotten their promise to help Allen rebuild his stables. The cost of lumber had so deflated that he opted to buy a shipment from Maine, rather than cut his own. It came in on the river barge, and one bright September day a group of men gathered to raise the new stables.

A letter came about the same time from Lindy, asking Caroline if she might visit.

We could do with some of her sparkle, thought Caroline.

The vivacious girl from Boston brought with her a splash of sunshine and spilled it freely on the Haddon family members. In her altruistic way, Lindy insisted on joining the workers in the fields.

Her eagerness to learn the daily routine proved a delight to all, and the evenings were even more to be treasured. She joined in the family's vespers, and even managed to bring forth smiles from the austere Matthew by giving him her undivided attention when he read his news items.

But most of all she seemed to gravitate toward Caroline, finding their time together to be soul satisfying as they discussed the things nearest a woman's heart.

"I don't want to go to New York," she announced one afternoon.

"That would take a bit of adjustment," said Caroline, not sure where the conversation was headed.

"I don't want to marry Timothy, either . . . and I'm sure he is expecting me to."

Caroline looked surprised. "I don't understand."

"No one does, and that makes it very difficult."

"I hope you haven't made any promises!" said Caroline, thinking of her own mistakes.

"No. Timothy is the one who does that, but I can see we are not at all compatible. We quarrel a great deal now. What would it be like if we were to marry?"

"We were all of the impression that you were smitten with one another."

"Oh, Carrie, I do love Timothy. Who wouldn't? He is so impulsive and funny and full of life. He's the kind who keeps the world laughing. We do need the Timothys, don't we?"

"Yes, Lindy, we do."

"He plans to leave for New York any day now, and he assumes I shall go with him—yet we haven't even discussed marriage."

"Then you had better not put this off. Tell him!"

Lindy hugged Caroline and thanked her for listening, then quite abruptly changed the subject.

"Is it too late to visit the new stable?"

"No, not too late. Hurry along and you'll be back in time for supper."

Lindy hurried out across the field, and Caroline watched her, remembering her conversation with Allen some weeks before.

"She is a precious girl, Lord. Do please guide her."

WEEKS TURNED INTO MONTHS, and in spite of the war's dreadful toll, men began putting together the shattered pieces. The South felt the devastation more than any part of the country, for already unscrupulous men from the North were moving in to control their politics. The Klan, hoping to keep the scalawags from succeeding, were fast evolving into a vigilante group, and Confederate soldiers were joining up with the imperialist Maximillian south of the border. Sheridan had been summoned and given much freedom to aid Juarez's cause, and the new president, bent on healing Dixie's wounds as Lincoln had wanted him to, was continually hampered by the ruling houses, both dominated by the vindictive Republicans. The rift would not heal quickly, and there were signs of serious Indian uprisings in the new West. Nevertheless, peace was restored, and life returned to what it was before the war.

Caroline followed her father to the front door stoop. It had been a warm day, and it was pleasant to rest awhile. They sat together in silence, watching the spread of pale pink clouds in the western sky.

"I want you to cut down on the work," said Clinton.

Caroline waited for an explanation, and he continued.

"When did you plan to tell me?" he asked.

"Tell you?"

"That there will be a child."

"I might have known you would guess."

"Will you tell your husband?"

"I don't know. I have learned not to hurry. He might come back because of the baby, and that would be wrong. I believe that God is dealing with him, too, and I must not get in the way."

"Are you certain of that?"

"Yes. I have a strange peace about it."

"Then that is good enough for me."

The bond between the two was stronger than ever. A heavenly peace had invaded their lives, and they both knew it was an eternal thing. They settled back to watch as eventide drew on.

33

THE SUMMER SEEMED LONG, and the hope of seeing Jerome had its moments of wavering. Still the promises of God burned on quietly, an undying flame in Caroline's heart.

In the meantime, there was a decision to be made; draw away from the public eye or take her place beside her father in the worship services of the old Federal Street Church. Already tongues were wagging, and she knew she would be an arena spectacle. But her new relationship and commitment to her Lord had brought with it a new strength, so with Clinton holding her hand, Caroline joined the family at church. There was good reason now for attending and worshiping the One who had given her new life. It was a rendezvous with the Creator Himself. She found she could close out the curious gazes, the searching glances, and bask only in the love of God.

One Sunday morning she noticed Eva Tuttle in their midst, looking in Caroline's direction. After the service, the two friends found one another.

"Gracious, Carrie, I have heard all kinds of tales! But I want you to know that I don't believe any of them, and furthermore, I don't want to hear any more—not even an explanation from you. You will always be my friend, I want you to know that. If you need me anytime, please know you can count on me."

The words touched Caroline deeply, and she hugged her old friend warmly.

"God bless you, Eva. Truly I have missed you. Come out to the farm and visit."

After that, Eva came often to the Haddon home, and the friendship blossomed on a deeper level than before.

It was into this time of waiting that little tokens of God's constant care seemed to fall.

One Sunday after church, and following a hearty dinner, the family had gone for an afternoon walk in the woods. Upon returning, they spied a carriage in their driveway and quickened their steps to see who was calling. Clinton called off the two dogs, who were advancing on the hapless visitor with menacing growls.

A man was getting out of the vehicle and paying the driver. He then walked uncertainly toward them, limping as he came.

Clinton's eyes narrowed, and he drew in a sharp breath. "It cannot be!"

The man with the crinkly lines around his eyes drew near.

"Drake?"

"Clint! Clint Haddon! Wa'al, swamp my birch!"

Then the two were embracing, laughing and slapping like two long lost brothers.

"What's the cane for?" asked Clinton. "You looked better with a rifle!"

The children stood quietly observing the stranger.

"Did you fight with my father?" asked Joshua.

"Your father saved my life—twice!"

"Come, let us go inside," said Clinton, anxious to avoid any citation for heroics.

Drake hobbled to keep up. "I see they got you in the snoot!" he observed.

"And a few other places."

It was the first time Caroline had heard her father talk freely about his wounds. She brought lemonade and cake from the kitchen and stood apart, watching the obvious joy of the two men.

Bethia, all the while, was observing the way Drake handled himself with the cane.

I could teach him to walk without that cane, she thought.

"I've waited a long time to meet this family," Drake was saying. Then he was introduced properly to each of Clinton's offspring. He looked at them questioningly. Where was the wife and mother about whom he'd heard so much?

"Nabby died a few weeks ago," Clinton explained, reading his friend's thoughts.

Drake looked down at his shoes, sorry to have stirred fresh sorrow.

"We miss her grievously, but we are adjusting," assured Clinton.

"You have one another," Drake replied. "My mother was ill when I was in prison, and she died before I got home. Now there is no one. You can thank God for these children!"

"I do!" declared Clinton. Then, changing the subject, he inquired, "How long can you stay?"

"Oh, I must return tonight."

"That's no way to renew an acquaintance. You must stay a week at least. I have so much to show you."

Long after the family had retired, they could hear Drake and Clinton reminiscing in the kitchen.

"He is like a tonic for Father," said Bethia. "I haven't heard him so talkative."

"Yes. You know, we have been very remiss, Bethia," Caroline replied. "So occupied with our own problems, while he has borne all of his so quietly."

Drake did stay for a week, his cheerful spirit bringing edelweiss to lonely hearts.

But after he had departed, Clinton announced, "He is planning to return. We shall build him a house in the eastern corner."

"But that is my corner," said Bethia, some resentment in her voice. No one seemed to hear her.

"You mean he'll live here forever, Father?" asked Joshua.

Clinton didn't answer his children. He was in another world, thinking with joy about the unexpected reunion.

"It's like—" and Bethia choked back tears.

"I know," said Caroline. "It's like having Uncle Hank back, except that Drake is young to be so handicapped. Otherwise, he is quite handsome."

But Bethia had already made that observation.

Drake returned after the leaves had fallen. There was still time to dig the cellar of his new house before the frost set in, and he had a mind to work. Bethia dogged his steps and extracted a promise from him that he would work with her and learn to get about without the cane.

One nippy day she sat on a log and watched him struggle with a shovel.

"I hope you aren't planning to stop there," she said.

"What do you mean, little girl?" asked Drake, smiling in his usual way.

"I mean, that is going to be a very little house!"

"But that is all I shall need."

"Really, Mr. Singleton, that is not the way to view things!"

"Oh?"

"There are people in this world to whom four walls would mean their very existence. I think one should always build at least one extra room for some homeless soul, someone God might send along!"

Drake studied Bethia. How could such insight come from such a slip of a girl? He rubbed his chin and looked away from the intelligent eyes.

"Perhaps you are right. I can return in the spring—but only if you promise to supervise."

That brought a new radiance to those blue Adkinson eyes.

THE SNOWS CAME IN NOVEMBER, and though the heavy farming ceased, there was still enough work to keep the Haddons busy. Ice cutting was resumed and the hay in the ice house replenished. Several new cows had been purchased, and fence-mending and wood cutting filled the days. Cutters had been dusted and painted early, for with the arrival of snow, there would be sleigh rides.

The holiday brought back memories to Clinton of his Thanksgiving in New Bern, where a little Jewish man had invited several homesick soldiers not only to go duck hunting, but to grace his table and share in the holiday meal. The man had prayed that day for the war to end, and now the prayer had been answered.

Lindy visited more often now, bringing letters from Timothy, who had gone on to New York and secured a position at a brokerage firm on Wall Street.

Added to Matthew's literary interests was the prospect of a position with a Washington, D.C. newspaper. Until that time came, however, he was satisfied to remain at the *Bugle*, and to open weekly classes in his home for aspiring young journalists.

More mills were going up along the river, and the country was gearing for an industrial revolution. There was still the great western advance and the Indian wars, but in general a spirit of peace was being initiated, and God was restoring the years the locusts had destroyed.

Jerome's daughter was born at Christmastime, her coming adding new joy to the Haddon household. Caroline held her close and wondered at the perfection of one so small. She was indeed a Haddon, with her mother's delicate features—until she opened her eyes and brought back the memory of the Grandmere's portrait. Those were definitely her father's eyes, black as midnight and with the sharpness characteristic of the Cavells.

"I shall call her Elise," declared Caroline, remembering the sweet melody and the way it had stirred her heart.

It seemed the longer her separation from Jerome, the more she longed for him, to share with him the miracle of their child as well as the wonders of her own spiritual birth. She wanted to see him, even if only from a distance. . . . Just to see those sharp features, the neat short-cropped hair, the magic expression. He was not easy to forget, but now, she consoled herself, she at least had a part of him. There was comfort in that!

IT WAS NEARING THE END OF APRIL, and already the pampered patricians were anticipating a return to the New England seashores for the summer months. On the island, windows and wrap-around porches were being stripped of their winter shorings, and paint was being applied.

The city social season was winding down, and Eva Tuttle sat one evening scanning the society column of a Boston evening paper. It seemed that the Hub City was gearing for the return of one of its favorite concert pianists. Buoyed by the accolades and acclaim of his native country, Jerome Cavell had returned to Boston. She mustn't say anything to Caroline . . . but Eva would attend the concert.

The coachman drove her to a large building, one that a Park Street organist had been instrumental in procuring for the event. She entered the spacious interior, impressed with the plush furniture and elaborate hangings. Jerome had certainly come into his own!

When the gaslights were turned down, he walked onto the stage and bowed. Taking his place at the piano, he began with a selection from Handel's "Rinaldo," proceeded to "The Harmonious Blacksmith," and then left the stage for a brief intermission. When he returned he received a thunderous ovation and settled into the melodies from his favorite Chopin, closing with Beethoven's "Fur Elise." Did Eva detect a sadness, a departure from his intimacy with the audience? When he bowed at the close, was he in a hurry to leave? The old Jerome would have remained to drink fully of his cup of success.

Eva herself left quickly and hurried to the side door. It was cold, but she would wait. Thirty minutes passed, and she was ready to leave when the door swung open and Jerome Cavell stepped out.

"Jerome! I just had to congratulate you! You were magnificent!"

Jerome appeared pale under the new gaslights. Otherwise, he looked the same; dark eyes in a strong, handsome face. A pleased expression came over his face as he recognized her.

"Eva! Eva Tuttle!"

"I wasn't sure you would remember me."

"I'd be an ingrate not to remember you, with the backing and encouragement you gave me! How are you, Eva?"

"Fine. Father has consented to give me my own place here in Boston—with a chaperone, of course."

"He spoils you!"

"Yes."

There the conversation died, making them both uncomfortable. Then, Jerome, always the gentleman, invited her to a late supper. He seemed quieter than she remembered, and away from the ghastly lights, she could see traces of dark shadows under the gemlike eyes.

"You are tired. I should not have accepted your invitation."

"Nonsense! I needed some pleasant company!"

They ordered and ate in silence, then Eva ventured into what she knew was forbidden territory.

"You have not seen Caroline?"

"No," he said tersely.

"What happened, Jerome? I was sure you loved her."

Jerome smiled a brief, sardonic smile.

Eva wasn't finished. "And I know she loved you!"

Still no answer, just a drawing back and a faint glimmer of doubt.

Then, "Are they happy?" he asked, a chill in his voice.

"I don't know if you would call it happy, under the circumstances, but for Caroline there seems to be a peace . . . something

379

undefinable. And Elise! I have never seen the darling unhappy!"

Jerome's face was blank. "Who is Elise?"

Eva dropped her fork and leaned toward him, looking as puzzled as he did.

"You do not know you have a child?"

"A child!"

"I cannot believe this. Caroline has changed, but she would most certainly have told you!"

Jerome's hands were trembling, and he was fighting for composure. He looked away from Eva, acrimonious lines around his mouth. At last he found his voice.

"Is he kind to her?"

"Clinton? Of course. She has always been his favorite. You must know that."

"I don't mean Haddon! I mean Paxton!"

Eva's genuine shock was displayed on her face. "Jerome! Where have you been? Thad Paxton left months ago. Went back to his old cavalry unit, I believe. Caroline sent him away right after Lincoln's death."

Jerome rose to his feet. It was clear that Eva was speaking the truth, and the truth was shaking him to his very foundation.

"She didn't send you here?"

"You must know her better than that!"

"God help me!" He summoned the waiter, paid him, and put on his cloak.

"You must excuse me, Eva. I am going to Newburyport."

"Wait—"

"I've waited long enough!" he said, and stormed out of the restaurant as though driven by a demon horde.

CAROLINE AND PHOEBE had filled the mitchin-box with enough food to last three days. They watched as the wagon pulled away carrying Clinton, Drake, Allen, and Joshua, who was grinning from ear to ear. It was the first time he had been included in the hunting party with a gun of his own—and that gun was the magnificent Henry.

The women watched until the wagon was out of sight, then Phoebe returned to her kitchen. The hired man, finished with the dairy work, took his leave. Bethia was in the sitting room cutting out baby clothes. Matthew was at his office, and Caroline had gone to the barn to check on the grain supply. This done, she stepped outside and pulled her shawl closer. A playful wind caught at her snood and blew loose strands of hair across her face.

In the distance she heard the sound of the train whistle. It was the morning train, leaving the station and heading north. She thought philosophically about the train. It wasn't unlike life itself. Its many stations, the changes in the scenery, sometimes bringing a hero back into new life, sometimes a coffin . . . and then it was gone and all was quiet. Only the sound of the cattle lowing and the hens clucking. She stood looking at the fields. Gone was the girl of just a year ago, and in her place was a new woman with eyes grave and full of wisdom, features soft, reflecting the inner self—calm, contemplative, not unlike her father.

It was good to be outside. Baby Elise was safe in the care of her doting Aunt Bethia, so Caroline walked casually toward the road. She heard the rumble of wheels in the distance, and as the depot wagon drew near she could see the shadow of a tall man inside. Someone would be welcoming a relative or a friend. Things were so much better with the war over.

The carriage drew on and stopped at her gate. It was then that curiosity became recognition, and she began to tremble, the sight of Jerome sending shock waves through her entire frame. He was quickly down from the carriage and walking toward her.

They stood for what seemed an eternity, each searching the other's face . . . then they were running and in each other's arms. No words . . . only loving arms and tears. His lips on her hair, on her cheeks, on her lips, releasing the words he had waited so long to hear.

"Oh, Jerome, I do love you. I always have. I knew you'd come someday!"

Together they walked toward the house and Bethia, seeing them coming, slipped out the side door to let the young family be alone. Jerome took his child in his arms, his eyes wide with wonder and pride. A flesh and blood Cavell for him, where before there had only been a wish.

Caroline thought her heart would burst. The words of the prophet Jeremiah came to her mind, "I will restore health unto thee . . . and I will heal thee of thy wounds, saith the Lord." A promise for the people and the nation whose God is the Lord! She would claim it for her own!

ABOUT THE AUTHOR

Promises Broken, Promises Kept is Janet Bedley's first book, into which she pours a lifetime of experience. The historic Massachusetts city of Newburyport, setting for the novel, was Janet's childhood home. Her love of history, and aptitude for accuracy and detail, are evident in her writing. The topic itself was a natural one for her to write about because her great grandfather was a Union soldier who left a diary recording his thoughts and experiences.

One entry from his journal reads:

> "My main object in giving my experience in this book is that my children may read it and hand it down to their posterity, that they may imitate the example of the father, to love their country, and if occasion requires, fight to keep it inviolate, and if need be, give their lives as a sacrifice for the blessings bestowed by our Heavenly Father upon this nation."

Janet reflects her great grandfather's sentiments when she says, "I hope to see this book in the hands of not only my grandchildren but the grandchildren of the nation so they might come to appreciate the moral fiber upon which this nation was founded—might realize the thanks they owe a past generation for their courage and their strength to stand up for their Christian beliefs."

In addition to her writing interests, Janet has been involved with Child Evangelism for more than 30 years. She is the mother of five adult children and now lives with her husband, Robert, in Twin Peaks, California.